PRAISE FOR DAN HANKS

"Twists aplenty, dastardly villains, and bombastic fight scenes combine to make this perfect popcorn entertainment. Fans of old-fashioned pulp adventure are sure to enjoy."
Publishers Weekly

"A big, fun, action-packed genre blender of pitfalls, monsters, damned Nazis, and good companions."
S. A. Sidor, author of *The Institute for Singular Antiquities* series

"Author Dan Hanks sets his war-weary protagonist on a pulp-paced adventure – cunning traps, ancient maps, and brutal scraps...semi-retired Nazis and aggressive corpses."
R.W.W. Greene, author of *The Light Years*

"Move over Indiana Jones. Captain Moxley has arrived and she won't ask you twice! A globetrotting adventure that fans of *The Mummy* and *Captain America* will love!"
Amanda Bridgeman, author of *The Subjugate*

Dan Hanks

Captain Moxley and the Embers of the Empire

ANGRY ROBOT
An imprint of Watkins Media Ltd

Unit 11, Shepperton House
89 Shepperton Road
London N1 3DF
UK

angryrobotbooks.com
twitter.com/angryrobotbooks
Ashes of the gods

An Angry Robot paperback original, 2020

Cover by Daniel Strange
Edited by Eleanor Teasdale and Andrew Hook
Set in Adobe Garamond

ISBN 978 0 85766 872 1
Ebook ISBN 978 0 85766 873 8

Printed and bound in the United Kingdom by TJ International.

9 8 7 6 5 4 3 2 1

To Mum and Dad for their unwavering love and support, but also for taking me to see whip-cracking adventurers punching bad guys, melting faces, and jumping out of planes in life rafts when I was at a young, impressionable age. This book is your fault.

PROLOGUE

Normandy, 1945

The troop of British soldiers sat around the fire, nestled safely in the grassy dunes of the beach. Their laughing was undercut by the lapping of waves against the nearby shore and the whip of a harsh wind overhead, threatening an extended winter.

In the distance, headlights split the darkness of the forest to the east. Twin sealed beams, the best that money could buy – or at least that's what Lieutenant Jeffries figured was still the case back in the real world.

He'd been over here in this wet, shitty place fighting the Nazis for over a year now. Who knew what kind of technologies were changing the car industry back home? Likely giving his grandfather even more reason to spit and curse as he sweat his days away in their family's East End London garage. *If* the bloody garage was still there, of course, and the Luftwaffe bastards hadn't wiped it from the face of the earth.

The car grew closer. It wasn't long before Jeffries could

make out the distinct shape of a Hudson Commodore, crouched low like a bullet skimming the ground.

Military, perhaps? That was his first thought. But it was one unsettled by a feeling he couldn't quite put his finger on.

The car pulled up close to the dunes and four figures emerged.

Suits, not uniforms. Two up front tall and thin, like bankers or businessmen. Two behind like Goliaths, so large they'd been veritably poured into their shirts until their buttons were ready to burst. Each appeared to be carrying at least one sidearm.

Not military, Jeffries decided. *Government.*

"So then I turn around and they're all dead. I mean all of them. Bits of Nazis everywhere, like bloody confetti after the world's worst wedding. I'd barely blinked, man, and she'd destroyed them all."

To his left, the stocky, balding Peterson shook his head, lost deep in the memories of the scene he was replaying for the boys. He blew out his cheeks and ran a hand through the remnants of his greasy hair.

Jeffries knew what his friend was picturing in his head. He hadn't been able to shake the images of those bullet-ridden bodies for weeks. But such was his life now. And the fact that he and his troops were able to tell these stories meant that they weren't one of the bodies lying in tatters on the floor. A definite plus.

Stocks Macgill cackled like a hyena into the night. "That's nothing, Peterson you pussy. You haven't been here since the beginning. You don't know what she did after she discovered her own bloody air force gave her up for dead. A compound of flesh confetti is nothing compared to the shit she pulled last year down at–"

His pale, pockmarked grin stopped short. He'd seen the stooges arrive.

"Government," Peterson muttered, instinctively reaching for his rifle propped against the log he'd been sitting on.

"Soiling their shoes on enemy turf?" Stocks hissed quietly. "I don't think so."

The inappropriately named Duke, all badly fitting clothes and as ugly as sin, got to his feet and gazed nervously between his best friend Stocks and the approaching men. "It's like I keep telling you. Haven't you heard the stories? Some kind of secret agency is over here hunting treasure or some shit. Racing the Germans for it. That's what they're saying…"

His ragged voice tailed off as the visitors reached the bonfire.

Jeffries watched as three suited figures spread out around them, before the fourth – chiselled face lurking behind horn-rimmed glasses – stepped forward to address them.

"Good evening, gentlemen." Clearly American, with a slight southern lilt. His voice quiet, but firm enough to mark him as the leader of his little band. The man took his grey fedora off, revealing neatly trimmed hair, and ran a careful hand through it. Definitely government. Nobody else in this bloody war gave a shit about how their hair looked.

Peterson and Jeffries glanced at each other. Then Peterson stepped forward, keeping the rifle handy at his side.

"Can we help you… sir?"

The government official seemed satisfied by the formality. He nodded and flashed a badge on the inside of his made-to-measure jacket.

"You can call me Agent Taylor, son. And, as it happens, I'm looking for someone."

Stocks laughed nervously and punched Duke in the arm. "We're all looking for someone, ain't that right Duke? Keep us warm on these cold French nights." He sniffed. "Ain't that easy to find round here though."

"Speak fer yourself," drawled Simpkins from where he was lying back against the giant log, digging his feet further into the sand beside his treasured cowboy boots. He pointed his cigarette in the air towards the distant hills inland, every bit the lazy cowboy he had idolised throughout his childhood in Manchester. "Why only last night I found myself a quaint ol' farmer's daughter in the town up there on the–"

"Stop." The smile had faded from Agent Taylor's face. "I'd rather not have the graphic details of what you boys get up to when you're not slaughtering the enemy, if you don't mind. The person I need was last reported working with a group of wayward soldiers such as yours." His hair hadn't moved a jot, despite the wind, yet he ran his fingers through it again before replacing his fedora. "Captain Sam Moxley is the pilot's name. Reported missing, presumed dead, by the RAF two years ago, but alleged to have been fighting on the continent with the French Resistance and other parties ever since. Causing some havoc for our Nazi friends too, from everything we've seen and heard." His eyes roamed the troop, looking for an in. "Did you know the enemy has taken a bounty out on the dear Captain, boys? Impressive sum of money too. All of which means that he's now become a person of significant interest for the American Government. It's imperative we speak with him quickly, if you please."

Jeffries knew Peterson had turned to look at him for guidance. But he kept his eyes on the agent. *Nazi friends?* The turn of phrase made him want to spit. Nobody who had been here fighting the bastards, who knew what they were capable of, would have used those two words together. Ever.

He glanced around, quickly weighing up the hierarchy of control on their little patch of beach. Did American government agencies have jurisdiction over them here? Exactly how much did they have to help these men? If it came to a fight, who would win?

Agent Taylor must have read his thoughts. His hand moved to his hip and pulled back his jacket just enough to show that he was armed too.

"Let's cut to the chase," he said. "I've got no issue with you and your men, and in fact I've enjoyed your work. Hell, we all have back home, boys! But right now I don't have time to argue the point, so I'm afraid I'm going to have to make this go a little quicker."

He raised his hand and the three other agents immediately reached into their jackets.

Jeffries stepped back, but realised he was too far from his rifle to get it in time. The others in the group were similarly blindsided. Only Peterson was able to lift his weapon and train it on Agent Taylor –

– at the exact moment they all realised the agents were not reaching for guns, but rather for cartons of cigarettes, packets of chocolate, and other luxury items the men hadn't seen in forever.

"Let's call it a reward for being such helpful chaps," Agent Taylor said, with a hint of a smile as he watched the soldiers react to the stack of goods being piled onto a log at the base of one of the dunes. There was instantly a flood of saliva filling Jeffries' mouth as he imagined tearing back the wax paper on one of those smooth, dark slabs of Fry's chocolate and taking a bite.

"Reward, bribe, whatever it's called, I'm up for it," Stocks said. He didn't even wait for the agents to finish stacking up the goods, he dove straight in, grabbed two tins of condensed milk, and pointed over his shoulder. "The Captain is over that dune, down by the water. Has been for the last two hours, in fact. Not one for company tonight. But I'm sure *he* would just love to have a chinwag with you Yank fellas."

Duke stifled a laugh. Even Peterson twitched. But neither of them said a word to correct Stocks.

Agent Taylor tipped his hat. "Then I shall go and speak with him."

Without further ado, he led his men towards the beach. Behind him, six of the eight soldiers started divvying up the goods they'd just been offered.

"Should we tell them?" Jeffries asked quietly, as Peterson joined him, watching the Americans in their fancy black shoes trudge through the sandy dunes.

"Nah," Peterson replied. "Not our fault their intel is shite. Let them discover Captain *Samantha* Moxley for themselves."

CHAPTER ONE

Lady Liberty

New York, 1952

Shards of moonlight cut through broken windows, bathing the hidden warehouse beneath the Statue of Liberty in an eerie glow.

Rows of wooden boxes marked "Authorised Personnel Only" filled the shadowy interior. Crates in their hundreds, stacked from the cold, tiled floor to the ceiling. All neatly arranged. All quietly waiting for their turn to be shipped off-site to destinations as yet unknown.

All except the crate that suddenly exploded into splinters of pine.

A man burst through it headfirst and fell to the floor in a bloody heap, his once immaculate grey suit in tatters.

His fedora rolled to a stop in front of him.

"I already told you–" he muttered, blindly searching the floor for something. His hat? A gun? Whatever it was, he didn't find it in time.

A dusty brown boot connected with his stomach. He doubled over again, coughing and wheezing like the last gasp of a Spitfire running out of fuel. He had to spit the final few words out, along with several globs of blood.

"–I don't know where she is."

The figure standing over him paused for the briefest of seconds. Head tilted, as though contemplating the merciful option.

Then Captain Samantha Moxley stepped into the light and kicked the man in the face.

I don't believe him.

He began to crawl his way back across the chipped black and white tiles, leaving a bloody smear in his wake.

Why would I?

She began to follow slowly, keeping a deliberate distance between them. Enough to make him expect another attack. Enough not to be caught by a trick up his sleeve.

I know what lies he's been trained to tell me. How to manoeuvre the conversation around until I'm not sure what's up and what's down. How to make me doubt what I know to be true. He and his friends are masters of spin and bullshit, twisting perceptions to suit their agenda.

Reaching a stack of crates, the man pulled himself until he was sat up. He looked tired and beaten. She knew how that felt.

I know, because I used to be just like him.

He coughed and more blood splattered his shirt. Yet a surprising sound issued forth from his broken mouth now. Filling the cavernous warehouse with an exhalation of pain and laughter. Had she broken him already? Cracked his facade?

Well, that hadn't taken long at all.

He smiled through shattered teeth, knowing his guise of innocence wasn't going to delay the inevitable any longer.

Sam put a boot on his shin bone and crouched down, taking care to dig her heel in just enough to make him realise she could break him further.

Her fingers reached out for his tie and straightened it. Then she slipped the knot right up to his windpipe and leaned in close.

"Last chance, Agent. Tell me where she is and I might just let you live."

He gave a whispered laugh.

"It no longer matters. You'll never reach your sister in time. The Nine are not to be refused, you know that. I guess you should have done what we wanted when you had the chance?"

Sam nodded and let the cheap, charcoal tie fall to his chest.

"So should you," she said.

She reached into her pocket for the silver disk she always carried in case of emergencies. An experimental piece of weaponry that she'd been given when she used to work alongside people like this. About the size of a dollar coin. Small and unthreatening.

Unless you knew what it did.

The man's eyes widened as he saw it. His lips started protesting weakly. But she didn't hear him now. Her boot held down his chest and she bent down to slam the gadget onto his exposed neck. There was a sharp THWACK as the hooks on the back fixed tightly to his skin.

She pressed the button in the centre.

5…

He grasped for the disk, but she punched him in the face. Hard enough to buy her time to rifle through his suit pockets.

4…

Her fingers found a folded piece of paper. She pulled it out quickly and glanced at what it said, as he groggily struggled beneath her.

3…

Yep, this was it. Exactly what she had come here to find.

2…

"Best of luck," she said. "I believe you'll need it."

1…

She lifted her boot. Just as a shimmer of purply black light silhouetted the man. And pulled him screaming into another dimension.

The heavy metal door to the warehouse slammed shut as Sam strode into the cool October night beneath Lady Liberty herself. The young pilot who had been waiting for her – no more than eighteen or so, with grease smudged across his white, freckled cheeks – was doing his best to appear casual as he leaned on the railing and stared out at the city lights beyond. He dropped his barely smoked cigarette, scuffed it underfoot in a scatter of autumn leaves, and raced over.

"What's with all that screaming in there?" Charlie asked. "Sounded like a fella. You okay, Miss?"

His boyish face, half-hidden beneath an oversized cap, showed genuine concern as he handed back her brown pilot's jacket and battered Smith and Wesson Victory. Sam holstered the revolver and slipped into the jacket, trying to hide her wry amusement as she discreetly pocketed the flyer she'd just retrieved.

"I'm fine, thank you, Charlie," she said. "And, don't worry, there won't be any more screaming from that gentleman for a while. I've just packed him off on a small trip. We all set?"

"Uh, yeah. Good to go whenever you are." His gaze wandered across the bloody smears on her ripped shirt and his head tilted. "You can tell me to get lost, because this *might* not be any of my business... but you know the war's over, right?"

"If only that were so," she sighed. The concept of there being peace in our time wasn't one that had borne much fruit in her life. She'd left the battlefields of Europe only to find herself in a war of a different kind. And now this? Wasn't this America? What happened to that quintessential American dream of finding a quiet part of the world to call her own, free from being knee-deep in other people's shit?

She started walking towards their transportation – a Grumman UF-2G seaplane, bobbing gently on the choppy waves of the bay as it clung to its mooring on one of the long timber docks.

Ex-coastguard and apparently ex-military, given its faded stars and stripes insignia on the fuselage. It had been '"liberated" for the night by Charlie from where it was usually locked up in his dad's Bronx marina. Not the sleekest or fastest bird in the sky, but Sam couldn't help but fall in love a little bit with its homely, no-nonsense design. A great way to get about New York City if you had some cash to part with and were in a hurry. Which tonight it turned out she was.

Charlie jogged to keep up. "Hey, whatever, Miss Moxley. I didn't mean nothing by it. It's like I always say, the customer's got reasons and nobody needs to know 'bout them but them. By my reckoning you've still got a few dollars left to burn tonight. You wanna take in a Broadway show? Or how about a flick? My sister said that new all-singing, all-dancing one with that fella Gene Kelly is pretty gangbusters. Although, she'd probably go watch him do anything, she's that mad in love with him." He looked up at her earnestly. "Seriously, I can take you any place you like. So where do you wanna go?"

Sam glanced to where the sprawl of city lights in Lower Manhattan twinkled and danced in the distance.

"Back, kid. By my reckoning, about ten thousand years."

His face was the picture of confusion, but she didn't have time to elaborate further. Because at that moment a shadowy break cut through the illuminations reflected in the bay.

A boat. Full of armed figures. Heading straight for them.

"And it seems I'm not the only one," she added, grabbing Charlie's arm. "Come on, best foot forward!"

They heard the yelling over the hum of the boat's engine before the gunfire started. Then a hail of bullets pinged off the granite walls and the ground around them. And even though she knew the men were too late and too far behind to be precise – no matter how many times in the past she'd tried to instil in them a sense of instinct – there was every chance their angry, scattergun approach could still take one or both of them down. A bullet in the shoulder. In the leg. A lucky ricochet.

That would end her rescue attempt real quick.

"Go! Go!" she yelled above the din, and thrust the young pilot towards the seaplane. She quickly untied the mooring and jumped in after him, slamming the door behind her.

"Who the hell are those guys?"

Charlie flinched as bullets started pinging off the metal shell and he attempted to strap himself into the pilot's seat. For a second, Sam considered letting him. But he was fumbling his belt, she could hear the shortness of breath in his words and despite the terror that had suddenly started to roil in the pit of her stomach, she knew there was no way he was going to get them out of this.

She grabbed his shoulder and yanked him out of his seat before he could buckle up.

"They're old friends," she said, ignoring his yelp of protest and collapsing into his place. She felt the thrum beneath her fingers, reaching deep into her bones as she started the engine.

Her hands fumbled over the controls, almost as awkward as Charlie had been, all sweaty and trembling. Was this the first time since the war? Since the crash that had put her on this path? She suddenly felt like she was once again in the ATA pool of trainee pilots in Hamble Airfield, back on the green, green grass of England. Just a rookie recruit, all fresh-eyed and eager to do her part for the war effort… before being confronted with the flying bus that was the twin-seater Magister and wondering if she was about to get herself killed.

More bullets bounced across the cockpit.

Life was a ridiculous circle, she decided.

"You're a pilot?" Charlie cried as she pushed them away from the dock.

"I am."

"But… but you're a woman!"

She gave him a death stare.

"I just mean, on the way over you were all fidgety and nervous and stuff, Miss Moxley. I thought you'd hired me by mistake, seeing as you seemed more scared of flying than anybody I ever knew. Figured the jacket was just for show, maybe the latest fashion on 5th Avenue or whatever?"

A glance out of the window and she saw the group of men gaining fast. Six or seven of them, all in suits. More bursts of light flashed from the muzzles of their guns.

Only a matter of time before they hit something useful.

"Miss?"

Her fingers gripped the throttle and lurched them forward.

"It's *Captain* Moxley, Charlie," she snapped, swallowing her fear as best she could. "And I don't mind flying, it's the crashing that upsets me." She fixed him with a look. "Now strap the hell in. We're leaving."

The small cargo ship bobbed uneasily as it made its way through the bay. The grandeur of New York City to its right. The Statue of Liberty lit up with gunfire to its left.

Standing quietly on the deck, a shadowy figure watched events unfold.

Agent Taylor's fedora dipped ever so slightly in resignation, as the seaplane they were trying to apprehend finally bounced off the waters and clung desperately to the sky. Away from the bullets. Into the safety of the night.

She's made this far harder than it needs to be, he thought with some irritation. *As usual.*

He raised his hand and beckoned the two hulking, fiercely unnatural figures nearby.

They stomped forward, each with a pair of guns in their clawed hands, while enormous leathery wings unfolded in readiness like bats preparing for their evening meal. As they reached him, their misted chrome and glass helmets inclined his way, revealing the spiderwebs of hoses connected to tanks at their backs – a potent mix of gases that kept them alive in this realm's atmosphere.

Looking up at them, he hesitated for a moment, wondering if using these... specialist tools... might be overkill, but his concern didn't last long.

Overkill was the only thing that had ever worked with Samantha Moxley.

"We can't allow the Captain to beat us to the prize tonight," he said loudly, once again feeling a deep sense of regret about setting foot on that beach in Normandy all those years ago. He pointed to the speeding light in the night sky. "Bring her down."

CHAPTER TWO

Sky Fight

Sam's fingers gripped the cold, shuddering metal of the yoke as they pulled away from the water – and the gunfire.

The plane bucked and fought, but she'd danced with worse partners in her life. That Spanish prince in Nantes for one, during a particularly traumatic undercover mission the year after the war ended.

And, of course, more recently there had been Taylor.

Is he down there now, orchestrating events from a safe distance?

As usual.

She watched the fine water spray streak across the cockpit window as they pushed through the skies above the bay. The idea that he was behind this made her shiver, but not as much as the terrifying thought of what his men would do to her sister if she didn't beat them to her. If there was one thing about Agent Jack Taylor that could be relied upon, it was that he always kept himself out of harm's way. Yet he had no qualms about instructing others to get their hands bloody – he had ordered her to enough times over the last few years, that was for damn sure.

A crack, like localised lightning, sounded just outside the window. A familiar noise, muffled by the engines, but loud enough to make both occupants jump and Sam's heart sink.

A bullet.

It shouldn't have been possible. They were too high, too far from the men they'd left behind. Yet it was what it was.

Sam immediately tensed in her seat, her eyes scanning the dark night outside, watching for whatever she could feel approaching. But it was Charlie who saw it first. The tight angles of his jawline immediately slackened as he stared out of his window in horror.

"Oh God."

She twisted around, but couldn't see past him. "What?"

"That's… that's not possible!"

Another gunshot, another crack against the plane. Then a whistling sound as air rushed out through a brand new hole in the fuselage behind them. Sam wrestled with the aircraft as it shuddered violently.

"Be more specific, please," she urged.

The young pilot's gaze slowly returned to the neon-lit cityscape before them. His face was as bone white as the moon rising above Lower Manhattan.

"I think we're in trouble, Miss Moxley."

Her knuckles tightened on the yoke as she glanced sideways.

"I told you, it's *Cap*–"

Then she saw the giant-winged figure behind him, careering through the sky towards the plane.

"Holy Christ," she gasped, yanking back hard on the stick, as whatever it was – a man? A dragon? – raised his guns and fired again.

The bullets screamed past as the plane groaned and fought against her reckless flying.

To her relief, it did what it was told. Just enough to get them out of trouble in that instant. Yet the flash of wings that suddenly shot past on the other side of the plane told her that she probably wasn't going to be able to keep this up. Not if there were two of those things out there.

She spun the plane left and right, as the creatures weaved around her, wings beating and folding, skimming the currents with ease. Cats toying with a cornered mouse.

Whatever they were, and whatever nightmare Agent Taylor might have recruited them from, didn't matter right now. The immediate problem was they were able to manoeuvre far more skilfully than this heavy bird. Even with her at the controls – and she'd been known to make broken Spitfires dance.

The Nine had truly outdone themselves this time. She'd been party to some of their tricks in the past, of course. The horrors that roamed the corridors beneath the city streets where they'd worked in secret over the years. The dimension disk that had sent that stooge at Liberty Island into godknowswhere. (Whether it actually was another dimension, she still wasn't sure. Some of her old colleagues had thought it might be. Regardless, wherever it sent people, they arrived back on Earth in a completely different location, and were almost always catatonic.)

But armed dragon…men? Well, they certainly weren't the strangest shit she'd witnessed in her time. Not by far. But right now they were enough to cause a small level of concern.

She turned to the boy shrinking into his jacket beside her. His fingers whitening from clutching his seat, trying to hold onto some kind of sanity. Part of her wanted to do the same. But she'd seen and done enough to be able to roll with the ridiculous now.

The dragonmen circled again, before one pulled away and fired. This time she felt rather than heard it. A shudder as bullets ripped into them again, somewhere at the back.

Somewhere important.

She pulled back on the stick but nothing happened. The city buildings directly ahead stayed at exactly the same height they had been in her eyeline. Growing closer with every second.

"Son of a bitch," she muttered.

For a moment she threw the stick back and forth, as though her sheer force of will would somehow fix whatever had been done to the elevators. But they didn't respond. The plane stayed level, unwilling to move up or down. Heading straight towards the Manhattan skyline.

Charlie twisted his head towards her. "You're going to climb above those buildings, right?"

"We lost the elevators, I'm afraid. Can't go up or down."

"Go around then!"

Sam opened her mouth, then closed it again. She licked her dry, cracked lips – tasting blood from the earlier fight. And considered the thought that just popped into her head.

Oh, what the hell. I need to get to the museum anyway.

"Don't worry, Charlie. I'm going to get you out of this mess, I promise." She shoved the throttle forward and the plane leapt towards the urban labyrinth.

"We can't fly into the city," he yelled. "Are you crazy?"

"Possibly," she admitted. "Hold onto your hat."

The Grumman UF-2G skimmed the tip of Battery Park and shot between the tall buildings.

The dragonmen dropped back momentarily. She didn't think it was owing to fear. Whatever these creatures were, it was unlikely they would be scared off by the neon lights of New York City, but she'd long ago found that the surprise of doing something unexpected had always caused others to hesitate. Buying you enough time to figure out how to get out of almost any ridiculous situation.

And this was one of the most ridiculous she'd faced in a while.

Over City Hall they flew. Then up Broadway. Tall stone buildings streaked past on either side. Flashes of incredulous faces pressed up against windows, watching the strange chase pass by.

Too soon came the thump of wings against her window, as one of the beasts pulled up and spun away again. *Shit.*

They hadn't been put off for long. And she still had no idea how to get out of this alive.

"I can't believe you're doing this," Charlie muttered beside her. Then, as more gunfire erupted from behind them, driving up the side towards the cockpit, added, "I can't believe *they're* doing this. What even are they? And what the hell did you do to piss them off?"

Sam shook her head as she suddenly tilted them a full ninety degrees to avoid a large American flag fluttering proudly outside the NYU campus.

"Long and painful story," she said, levelling them out again as the boy fell back into his seat with a gasp. "You'll be unhappy to discover there's a whole world of horrors out there that most people don't know about. And these appear to be some of the creatures who deal with them. Dangerous creatures for a dangerous job." She glanced over. "I know because I used to work with them."

"It sure looks like you left on bad terms, ma'am."

She let out a laugh, loud but humourless. "Don't ever do a deal with the government, Charlie. You'll be paying for it for years."

THWUNK.

Her eyes widened and she glanced over her shoulder.

That was heavier than a bullet impact.

She flinched as the rear door buckled, before a chunk of it came off completely and flew away into the night. A clawed hand swept in through the hole and pulled at the metal, fighting the air pressure to wrench it open inch by inch.

They were coming for her.

"Take over!" she yelled, leaping up and stumbling over the seat as she pushed the kid towards the stick, while keeping her eyes on the door at the back as it was finally torn off its hinges, allowing one of the dragonmen to squeeze himself in.

"Wha– what the hell am I supposed to do?" Charlie yelled in her wake.

"Keeping us alive would be great," she called back.

Framed in the doorway against the moonlit night, the dragonman's bulky figure seemed almost human. If you looked past the faceless helmet and the fact he was trying to fold his wings in behind him.

Sam leapt forward, meeting the creature with strength and fury. Still stuck in the doorway, buffeted by the winds outside, his gun barely had time to lift towards her. She kicked it flying out of his hand, then swept what she figured was his foot with hers. Off-balance, she grabbed his helmet and rammed his head against the doorframe with a sickening crash.

Noxious gases began to seep out of the glass, searing her eyes and throat. But the beast himself didn't go down. Claws slashed across her shoulder and shoved her away.

"It's ov-er, Cap-tain," his low, inhuman voice rasped in staccato fashion. It was, she realised, surprisingly loud against the screaming rush of wind filling the plane. An inbuilt speaker system, perhaps? Just another one of The Nine's little party tricks, designed to intimidate and terrify. As if the bloody claws and dragon wings weren't enough.

He gestured towards the cockpit. "Land the pl-ane now or–"

She took a swing. Hard, into the face mask again, cracking it further. Her knuckles exploded in agony, but it jolted him back for a moment.

Not today, you winged shit.

He slugged her back across the jaw and she fell against the opposite wall hard. Breath lost for a second, she couldn't move as he approached.

She snarled with what energy she had left. At him? At herself? She didn't know. Her sister would have found it amusing, if she were here.

Behind the dragonman, buildings whipped past in flashes of grey and neon, until finally they disappeared as his lumbering figure filled her vision.

A great big target.

Her foot shot out and caught him in the groin. There was a satisfyingly pained exhalation through the speaker as he doubled over, before she followed up to kick the back of his knee and dropped him half to the floor.

All those years of working for them. Working with them. And they still don't understand who I am.

She leapt up and grabbed his reptile-like shoulders. Kneed him in the stomach then followed up with an elbow.

There was a loud fizzing as the speaker gave up the ghost. More gases poured out. He tried to stand, but only succeeded in staggering back towards the door, coughing and wheezing.

She stalked towards him, balling her fist.

These lackeys they'd sent to do their dirty work probably didn't even have a clue. She had seen things... done things... that would make most men vomit into their precious fedoras.

CRACK. A punch to his throat. Not hard enough to crush his windpipe – if he even had one – but a nice little distraction.

It's over when I say it's over.

She reached for the tubes connecting his failing helmet to his tanks and yanked them out. Each came free in an eruption of whatever hellish gases he needed to stay alive.

"Give Taylor my regards," she said, and kicked him out of the plane door.

She watched him fall for a second or two. Just enough to make sure he didn't somehow survive and chase after them. Then, wiping a gloved hand across her lip and glaring at the crimson streak that came with it, she pushed herself back towards the cockpit.

Only to look up in horror as the young pilot cried out.

"Captaaaaaain!"

Beyond him, through the windshield, the other dragonman had appeared. Wings spread outward. Flying backwards before the plane.

Raising his gun towards the boy.

The windshield burst open in an explosion of bullets and wind. Sam could only throw her arm up against the deadly debris as she leapt forward. Catching a glimpse of the holes ripping through the back of the young pilot's seat.

He shuddered within it.

"No!" she screamed with fury as she raced forward, feeling the plane tilt beneath her feet.

This wasn't fair. This wasn't the boy's fight.

"Can't… control…" he groaned as she reached him. But not fast enough to prevent him collapsing against the yoke and pulling it hard left.

Their entire world of existence shifted to its side and dipped dangerously towards the ground. The boy fell against the cracked side window, his breath coming in ragged gasps. She couldn't hear it beneath the roar of the wind through the plane, but rather felt it under her fingers as one hand fought to keep them airborne and the other sought to see how badly he'd been hit.

"Hold on, Charlie," she yelled above the din, digging her knees into the back of the seat to stop herself falling onto him. "Stay with me, kid. Don't let g–"

The glass that held his weight cracked and shattered outwards.

And with a look of silent horror he fell through.

She clutched the seat as his shadow disappeared from view beneath the plane. Towards the line of police cars she could see snaking after them through the traffic below. His scream already lost beneath the steady roar of wind and the whine of the plane as it began to dip.

My fault.

She blinked, feeling her stomach churn. But it wasn't the dangerous descent. It was the thought that once again she was taking the burden of blame when it lay with others.

Wrestling the yoke, she slipped onto the torn fabric of the seat and brought the aircraft level again as it continued blasting through the streets, towards Midtown. Then she looked up, fixed her glare on the dragonman flying backwards in front of the plane.

A trick of the light, maybe. But she could almost see a devious smile flit through his otherwise intact and misty helmet.

And it made her angry as hell.

She reached for the handle of the harpoon gun she'd seen wedged down the side of the seat. The kid had told her he'd gone fishing with it in the Hudson once, pulled out half a shark. Didn't matter if it was true or not. She believed him.

No, not my fault at all.

The New York night raged through the shattered windscreen as she lifted the loaded weapon over the dashboard – and fired.

Yours.

The bolt burst through the dragonman's back and hit the gas tanks. His helmet lit up first, a beautiful ball of flame encased in glass – before the rest of him erupted in a giant orange explosion that blossomed out and out and out. Until he was just a flailing shadow of melting arms, legs and wings.

Without a thought, Sam jammed the gun under the seat. Wedging it firmly within the metal bars.

Just in time.

The rope went taught as the impaled body fell from the

sky. It was a pretty unorthodox way to bring them both down to earth. Her old wingman Jenkins would have scoffed in that affable manner of his, had he survived the war to witness this – but he would definitely have approved.

"Darned good idea, Sam," he would have said, "but let's hope he had a heavy last meal, eh?"

The rope strained against the frame of the shattered cockpit window. It groaned with the force of the corpse's weight outside. But the gun beneath the seat held tight.

The plane began to tilt down, bringing more of the city street into view.

And there it was ahead.

Central Park.

"Thank fuck," Sam gasped, as she held fast to the stick, unwilling to let them drop too fast if she could help it. The streets were full beneath them, but the park held enough green soft landing space to make surviving this night without killing anyone else a possibility at least. In fact, she could just about see the glint of moonlight on one of the lakes through the trees as they dipped further towards the ground. There was a shiver of memory. She held it at bay at they descended sharply, bursting from between the buildings, and she made one last course correction towards the water.

"At least it's not the English Channel this time, I guess," she said. Then closed her eyes and braced.

There was the barest sound of a crack below as the dragonman's body hit the ground, before the rope finally snapped – and the plane flipped over and splashed down into the lake on its roof.

This time she was ready. As much as you can ever be for a ridiculously close call with death, but ready nonetheless. She went limp with the impact, then sprang into life as the dark, chill swirled around her. Through the shattered window she went, ignoring the glass biting and scraping at her skin. Pushing away from the cold metal frame and up, up, up… until she exploded from the surface and gasped in a lungful of the oil and fume-tainted air.

A few weary strokes were all that was needed to reach the bank. But even then her sodden clothes grew heavier by the second – and she briefly wondered if it might be easier just to let go, slip beneath the water, and let the world move on without her.

It would have been a relief, certainly. And perhaps part of her felt she deserved it.

But then she thought of Jess and it was enough to keep her going. She could not leave her sister to the mercy of the government. Not to Agent Taylor and his sneering sidekick Smith and their insidious monsters.

Fingers found dirt and she pulled herself through weeds and moss, until she was on real land. Then she fell back onto her elbows and watched the still-burning dragonman scrape past her, as the plane sank into the lake and dragged him after it.

"The pleasure was all mine," she called over, as his charred wings disappeared beneath the water with a hiss of steam.

Reaching into her jacket, she drew out the leaflet she had pocketed earlier, pulled the hair away from where it had plastered itself to her face, and read the wet, blotted words again.

THE NEW YORK METROPOLITAN MUSEUM OF ART INVITES YOU TO THE VIP UNVEILING OF THIS CENTURY'S MOST IMPORTANT DISCOVERY...

Sam looked to her right. Beyond the lake, at the edge of the park, was the shadowy outline of a large, imposing building through the trees – the windows lit and figures gathered within. She could almost have cried with relief, had her lungs not been full of water and near-death.

"I owe you one, Charlie," she said, getting to her feet.

Feeling like a swamp creature from one of those monster movies her dad kept trying to take her to at the local picture house, Sam wearily climbed the steps of the New York Metropolitan Museum of Art. Bedraggled and unkempt, she left behind sodden, muddy footprints, along with a trail of moss and only-the-devil-knew-what from the lake.

A man in a tilted grey hat gaped and dropped his pipe. Two women in blue polka dot dresses, arms linked, rushed on past, as if whatever had happened to Sam might be catching. Their black heels clicked furiously, like a typing pool under deadline, as they headed for the safety of the subway.

More stares as she burst through the revolving door of the museum into a sweeping lobby full of the city's brightest up-and-comers, all dressed in dinner suits and ballgowns. Heads turned, following the trail of water she dripped through their midst as she searched for the exhibition hall. Slipping through their finery, she caught a glimpse, in the reflection of a silver platter, of a tall attendant in a black suit and tie, guarding a set of double doors.

The man's thin moustache twitched as Sam approached, pushing her way roughly through a small gathering of old white men who were leering over a waitress.

"Can I help you, miss?" The attendant asked, stepping in front of her.

She slapped the wet invitation to his chest and strode past him, through the double doors and into the exhibition hall.

Where she found her sister in the clutches of an ancient evil.

CHAPTER THREE

A Night at the Museum

The exhibition hall was a cavernous place, filled to its nineteenth-century rafters with all manner of terrifyingly weird and wonderful artefacts. Skulls and weapons. Death masks and figurines from the Yucatan. An imposing and fiercely detailed Aztec Calendar Stone. And three huge, snarling statues from Ancient Egypt waiting to scare someone's britches off.

But Sam's focus was on the blonde white woman in the red ballgown, her pale face – compliments of the Lancashire sun, their father had always joked – contorted in mock anguish as she pretended to have been captured by a demonic Neo-Assyrian statue.

A man laughed beside her, with slicked back hair like all the fashionable men these days. Tall, Asian American and slightly older than the woman – late twenties, perhaps – he wore a handsome smile and was dressed to kill in a white tuxedo.

Yet, unlike every other man Sam had come across

tonight, this Ivy Leaguer showed no signs of actually having killing on his mind. Rather, he was playing along with the woman's joke.

Nobody seemed in danger. He wasn't holding her hostage. The statue was just a statue and these two were just a couple at ease in their surroundings, playing about, while white-coated museum assistants busied themselves making last minute polishes to the centrepiece display next to them.

Sam bristled and shook, though through anger or hypothermia from standing here in her soaked clothes, she wasn't sure. It brought back the time she and Jess had been exploring an abandoned house in their little old English town on the outskirts of Manchester, when they'd been younger. Sam's idea, probably; it usually was. And to be fair it had all been fine until her little sister, who must have been about six, suddenly screamed her lungs off at the sight of a rat skeleton on the red and black tartan carpet. Of course, it was just a harmless little skeleton. But kids screams are contagious and before she knew it they were both scarpering down the stairs, trampling through the overgrown garden, and diving back out into the safety of the rain-soaked street – startling passers-by and falling about laughing and hugging in sheer relief at still being alive.

As her mind raced through the variety of scenarios she had been imagining these last few days searching for her sister, Sam knew that none of them had ended so innocently. She knew she should be relieved to find Jessica here, safe and sound, surrounded by far more harmless skeletons. But she was so bloody tired and confused.

And angry.

"Jessica J. Moxley!"

Her words thundered through the ancient collection, vibrating glass cases and causing every single head to turn her way. She shifted under their gaze, boots squelching loudly, but after the night she'd had did she really care about making a scene? They were lucky she hadn't cursed like a goddamn sailor until the skylights above them shattered and rained glass upon them all.

Her younger sister gaped in shock as the rest of the room grew silent. Then there was the barest flicker of the wide white grin Sam had once known so well.

"Samantha?" Jessica's American lilt was in direct contrast to Sam's weary British accent. It was something Sam had never really got used to, although she was still glad to hear it., because it meant that all her sacrifices had been for something and her sister had found a life away from the horror show of the war many others hadn't survived.

Jess threw a quizzical glance at the man by her side, as though he might have had something to do with this, then turned fully to face the visitor in their midst. Her dress swished elegantly around her legs, drawing the gaze of most of the men in the room.

Sam felt a pulling sensation in her gut. Even when taken by surprise, Jess held more grace and poise than she'd ever been able to muster.

The two walked slowly towards each other. Sam, half-drowned, increasingly feeling her age and exhaustion, looked her glowing, younger sister up and down. Jess did the same, seemingly torn between concern and horror as she noted Sam's blood-stained shirt and the puddles forming around her boots.

Finally they stopped about a metre apart and pointed an accusing finger at one another.

"What the hell happened to you?" they said in unison.

Sam opened and closed her mouth several times, trying to find the words, but they wouldn't come. Jessica simply laughed at the absurdity of what she saw and reached over to kiss her sister's cheek.

"You look like utter shit, sis, but it is so great to see you!"

Jessica's friend now appeared at her shoulder, a hint of alarm at Sam's bedraggled appearance hidden behind his warm smile, but he maintained it nonetheless. His hand stretched out. "Am I to presume that we have standing before us Jessica's infamous sister, Samantha? Honoured to finally meet you, Miss, and happy beyond measure you could be here tonight to share in our glory. I'm Doctor William Sandford, curator at the museum, and acquirer of ancient antiquities, lost or otherwise."

He wriggled his fingers, as if Sam might have missed the offer of a handshake. She ignored it as the water continued to pool at her feet. "You know, Dr Sandford, only my mother really ever called me Samantha. And the troublesome Jesse James here, when she's trying to *act* like my mother."

His handsome face crinkled in a delightfully puzzled way. "Jesse James?"

Jessica rubbed the back of her neck. "I was a bit of an outlaw at school."

"I'll say," Sam teased.

She was rewarded with a hint of mischief in her sister's eyes. But Dr Sandford was oblivious to the sisterly dynamics and simply turned back to Sam, hand still outstretched. "Jesse James it is then. But, please, no need for professionalism here. We're almost family after all! You may call me Will."

Sam straightened, trying not to shiver as her sodden shirt stuck to her back. She did, however, finally take Will's hand and give it a strong, wet shake.

"And you may call me Captain," she said with a wry smile. "I happen to enjoy a bit of professionalism."

Jessica harrumphed good-naturedly under her breath. "Last time I checked, *Captain Professional*, most normal people take cabs when they go out for the night." She gently ushered Will back to her side as the lake seeping out of Sam's clothes spread across the floor. "Did you swim here?"

"I had an unavoidable detour through a lake."

"Figures. Like that time when we went cycling around the Dark Peak and you ended up freewheeling down that hill? Oh, gosh, I still laugh at that one."

Sam's smile grew, remembering the terror and the excitement and the inevitability of knowing her fate, once she'd realised her brakes had failed. Yet all too soon the smile faded and she cleared her throat.

"There will be plenty of time to talk about my travel habits and reminisce over silly things I've done in the past," she said. "But I'm afraid we need to go, Jess."

"Go?" Jess replied, her perfect nose wrinkled in that way it always did when someone said something quite ridiculous.

"Go?" Will repeated, just as incredulous. "You can't go! Take a look around you, Captain. We only returned from our expedition earlier today and have been flat out trying to finish getting this display ready for the city. We have our mighty fine guests outside, some refreshments on standby, and of course we now have our prized artefact."

He stepped aside with a flourish to reveal the centrepiece pillar behind him. Atop it sat a stunning gold crescent moon of an artefact, subtly decorated with obsidian and lapis lazuli stars.

"The Isis Amulet!" his voice boomed theatrically. He may have been a museum curator, but Sam could tell he had a knack for the dramatic. "It's what they refer to in the ancient Mayan scripts as the Amulet of Life. And Jessica here helped me recover it, after years of searching. So what makes you think I'd let you steal her away from me tonight, just as we're about to unveil it?"

Jess tilted her head as she stared up at her sister. "He's not wrong, you know. Do you understand what I had to do to bring that piece home? Sailing down the Amazon, running from natives, basically risking my life on a daily basis. Surely you of all people can appreciate that I can't let that all be for nothing?"

"Did you ever think that maybe the 'natives' you speak of didn't want you stealing their culture?" Sam replied. "That perhaps you've pulled the old colonial trick of discovering what wasn't lost in the first place and then claiming ownership of it for the good of all mankind?"

"Oh don't start that again. You might never have liked what I studied, but archaeology–"

"Archaeology is wonderful, yes, I know and I don't disagree. I love the study of what makes us tick and I love the feel of history in your hands and the knowledge that the last time someone held that artefact was hundreds or thousands of years ago." Sam found her gaze drifting to the amulet, unable to help the quiver of excitement – or was it something else? – as she wondered just where the thing had come from. She frowned and continued, "Trust me, Jessica, I know that feeling more than you could possibly understand. But there are ways and means to these things. You can't just be wandering around, trespassing in people's lives. There is a matter of consent."

Her sister waited with folded arms.

"Have you quite finished?"

Sam hadn't, but she felt the heat of everyone's gaze on her again. She shrugged and said, "Sorry, but you know how I feel about such things."

Jess sighed patiently and walked over to tug at Sam's arm, pulling her closer to the display. "Ours is a noble pursuit, Sam. A cause of enlightenment, even if we may accidentally tread on some toes along the way. But–"

Jessica held up her hand before Sam could argue, "–in this case you'll be pleased to note that the locals were only custodians of the piece, not the owners, and most of them were willing to part with it in the end because they knew it wasn't originally theirs. I mean, look at the markings. It's not like any artefact ever found in the Americas, or many other places, to be fair. Without a shadow of a doubt this thing originated elsewhere. Although how and why it ended up in the Amazon is a mystery that we intend to find out."

Sam said nothing. They really didn't have any time to get into it further. And, besides, up close, looking beyond the dazzle and the finery, there was something about this piece that spoke to her… and she didn't particularly like what it was saying.

She'd come across enough of these ancient artefacts to relish the energy they brought just by being in their presence. That feeling of history. Of distant lands and long-dead people. Sometimes of magic (those were usually the more dangerous occasions).

Yet, right now, this amulet was also causing the pit of Sam's stomach to churn like it did whenever things were about to get nasty. Not, she decided, because of any dark curses or hellish energies at play (which made for a pleasant change). But because she now had a sickly feeling of familiarity.

She'd seen this piece before, she was sure of it.

"We really need to go," she whispered.

Jessica blew out her cheeks. "Oh come on, Sam. You

can't just turn up here with the jitters and expect me to run off with you. Give me one good reason why I should leave?"

Sam glanced at Will, then gestured for her sister to join her to one side.

Jess didn't move.

Sam gestured harder.

Jess slipped an arm around Will's waist. "Whatever you need to tell me, you can tell him too. Or did you miss that this was *our* exhibition?"

Sam looked from one to the other and back again, before it dawned on her there was more energy at work here than she'd realised.

"Good grief, I've no time to worry about your personal attachments," she lied, definitely feeling some worry there in the back of her mind and not a little envy. How come everyone else got to live their lives like normal people while she had to fight deadly creatures and shadowy governments? "I'm here because I was led to believe you'd been kidnapped."

"Kidnapped? By whom, exactly?"

"The... Nine."

"You think your old boyfriend stole me away?" Jess said laughing. She gestured in no uncertain terms to Sam's appearance. "Why on earth would he do that? My clothes are all in one piece, they're not stained with other people's blood, and I'm not wet through. I very much doubt I'm his type!"

Sam felt a flush creep across her cheeks, even as she

clenched and unclenched her fists. The pain burning through her body told her it wasn't all other people's blood.

Spotting a blue evening gown hung carefully on a hook at the back of the room, she went to fetch it and slipped behind a large Egyptian bust of Nefertiti.

One of the white-coated assistants – a tall lady, with fashionable black glasses and a sweep of white-blonde hair brushed across her forehead – looked aghast at what was presumably her gown being taken. She opened her mouth to protest, but Will shook his head.

"Not now, Audra," he urged which sent her striding off into a side room, muttering what were probably some very uncomplimentary things.

"Sorry!" Sam shouted after her, then nodded her thanks to Will as she began to change. His forehead furrowed in response. The showmanship had ceased. He knew something wasn't right about any of this, including the fact that one of his ancient artefacts was now being used as a clothes horse.

"Explain, please, Sam," Jessica persisted. "Why is it that you think your old flame and his friends kidnapped me? What exactly are you involved in?"

"*Ex* old flame. And unfortunately, despite Taylor's charming facade, I have discovered there is a long list of things of which that man will do to fulfil his twisted sense of duty. As for what I'm involved in, that's the problem. It's not just me now. I get the impression you might play a bigger part in this than I had initially considered."

Sam paused to grab folds of the green velvet display

drape hanging like a gaudy skirt beneath the 3,000 year old Egyptian bust, dried herself off as best she could, then slipped the blue gown over her head. It wasn't quite perfect, a little tight at the hips, but it wasn't wet and quite honestly that would do right now. She stepped out from the exhibit, leaving her wet clothes in a heap behind it.

"You see, The Nine didn't take kindly to me leaving their little government agency. I have a feeling they've been keeping tabs on me ever since, but until now they've kept their distance. Then about a month ago Taylor turned up again and tried to recruit me for one last job involving some psychic. When I told him I wasn't interested, he suggested he might find a way to change my mind. So when I couldn't get in touch with you…"

Jess shut her eyes and pinched the bridge of her nose. "What if he was just talking about getting you flowers or something?"

"You honestly think I'd have done what I have tonight if I wasn't sure?"

"Well I don't know what you've done tonight other than have a dip in what appears to be a not very clean body of water and, besides, you're not my mother, Samantha. When will you learn that only I control my destiny? I don't need rescuing every damn time you have a case of paranoia."

"You don't know these men like I do."

"So?"

Sam drew her gaze back to the amulet, twinkling beneath the lights. "So, they're on their way right now.

And we don't want to be here when they arrive. I honestly don't think you two realise what you've brought to bear by digging that thing up, but I'm beginning to have an idea."

Will looked concerned. His eyes flashed to Jess, but Sam already could see her sister wasn't in the mood to give in.

"This is our exhibition and we deserve our moment, Sam. The only people coming are the rich and famous of New York and we are ready to bathe in their awe."

"Bloody hell," Sam muttered. She glanced at the clock in the corner, then dropped her voice. "If we don't get out of here there isn't going to be much of an exhibition left. You have no idea what these people are capable of."

"And you've never had any idea what *I'm* capable of," Jess replied, crossing her arms.

Sam sighed in defeat, then grabbed her sister's shoulder and dragged her along towards the next room.

"Fine, we'll do it my way then. Thanks, Dr Sandford, that was a real gas, but we'll be going now if you don't mind. Quick word of advice: lock that amulet back up in the vault and call the police. You're going to have company."

But they barely got two steps towards the door when a loud, piercing alarm blasted through the room.

It was followed by gunfire and screaming.

Sam let out a long-held cry of anguish.

"*Son of a–*"

CHAPTER FOUR

Fortune and Glory

Will and Jess stared in horror as Sam threw her arms up and raged at the universe.

"Goddamn shitsville on a stick! Couldn't the people who want to kill me just once – *just this once* – have got held up in traffic or something? *Just this once* it would have been nice for the goddamn cards to fall my way. New York is always full of cars and buses and horses and people whenever *I* need to get anywhere! But, oh no, as soon as I need just a few minutes to do the right thing, everyone disappears off the streets and Taylor's goons apparently get a free ride through the city. How is *that* fair, I ask you? How in the name of all that's *fucking holy*?"

She spun around furiously, looking for another way out.

The doorway to the collections stood ajar, beckoning them away from the gunfire. In her experience this didn't necessarily mean it would offer escape. It might just as easily lead to a dead end. But they had no choice. It would have to do.

"I'm still not leaving," Jess said, eyes flashing defiantly

in the face of logic. "You've never given me much choice in the past, dearest sister. But I'm all grown up and I make my own decisions now, got it?"

Sam barked a slightly hysterical laugh. "Good for you! And yet in about thirty seconds you're going to have big bad men with guns bursting in here and demanding that amulet. What are you gonna do then, Jess? Dolly yourself up, throw your hair over your shoulder and try to charm your way out of it? Believe me, that shit doesn't work. Ever."

Will looked on the verge of a full blown panic. All mouth, no trousers, Sam thought, although he wouldn't be the first. She'd known plenty of other showmen who got stage fright when things deteriorated. Imminent danger could do that.

"D-demanding the amulet?" he stuttered. "But you came in here tonight thinking that Jessica was the one in danger."

"She still is, but it's the amulet they're after."

"Why?"

There were more gunshots. Getting closer.

"What are you, writing a book? You just have to trust me, Will. I have a feeling I know what that piece connects to and I've already seen what they're willing to do for it. We need to split. Now!"

Thankfully he didn't ask for more clarification. "Captain, we went through a lot to get this piece and if it is as important as you seem to think, we simply cannot let it go. Can you help us get it out of here?"

"Oh no, no, no!" Sam said, wagging her finger at him and laughing nervously. "I just came here for my sister. This isn't my fight."

"You made it your fight the day you joined The Nine," Jess snapped. "If they're here, it's surely because you played your part."

Sam glanced longingly towards the open collections door at the back of the room.

"I made a mistake. On many levels, admittedly."

"Well, if you want me to come with you, help fix it!"

Her sister's stare – as fierce as their mother's had ever been, indicating that there was responsibility to be accepted here without fuss or murmur – was unbearable.

Sam squeezed her eyes shut, trying to figure out her options.

She'd been in worse spots, hadn't she? Fighting her way across occupied France, working behind enemy lines, all in a race against Hitler's men in the search for Europe's paranormal secrets. Every damn time it looked from the outset like the odds couldn't be less in her favour and she still beat them.

Except… this didn't feel right. For the first time in years, she could conjure up no immediate way out of the mess that didn't put everyone in danger.

Why couldn't she think straight?

Because the consequences of failure no longer affect just you, she told herself. *Jess is in this now. You actually care what happens next.*

And that changed everything.

She gave them a reluctant nod. Will immediately rushed to remove the amulet from behind the glass display case, then pulled a face, aggrieved, as Sam snatched it off him and slipped it in her jacket.

"If I'm going to do this then *I'm* going to do this," she said. "The priceless artefact that might kill us all stays with me at all times. Any problem with that?"

He shook his head quickly.

"Super! Come on then."

They moved quickly through the door into the collections room.

Sam didn't bother to shut it behind her. She knew it offered no real protection, in the same way she had never felt the need as a child to shrink inside her blankets at night for fear of ghosts. It's not that she didn't believe in them (she'd witnessed far stranger phenomena since), rather that she understood when instinct wasn't thinking straight.

Blankets didn't protect you from the horrors of the night. Closing doors behind you didn't stop the enemy coming through. Accepting these things took the edge off the terror somewhat.

"So what's so damn important about the Isis Amulet that it is worth so much to these men of yours?" Jess asked tersely as they hurried through the collection. "I mean, Will and I know its archaeological importance is beyond measure. But what's the value to these bozos?"

Sam kept her eyes ahead, trying to ignore the exquisite

artefacts they were passing. Rows of painted stone sarcophagi and stelae. An amber-coloured sword and silver helmet. A five thousand year-old wooden ship with a prow carved in the shape of a mermaid. This exhibition was shaping up to be quite something.

"Their trouble is mainly one of obsession," she replied, spotting a single door in the back marked "Staff Only" and shifting direction towards it. "The Nine believe in what they call 'the greater good', no matter what the cost."

"And what's the greater good this time? Mysterious lights in the sky? Creatures from the deep?"

"Creatures?" Will asked, panicking.

Jess waved a dismissive hand. "You don't know the half of what she's told me about her job."

"And that's the way it'll stay, for your own sanity," Sam insisted. "However, in this case, it's something you'll both be interested in. Because, if I'm right, the amulet concerns a mythical lost repository of knowledge so extensive it would make the great Library of Alexandria look like a bookshelf."

"You're talking about the Hall of Records?"

Sam glanced at Will, impressed.

"I thought academics like you were told to stay away from the fringe elements of history?"

Will shrugged uncomfortably. "Jessica has, er, clued me in quite substantially on such things as they've cropped up in her studies. It appears the field of archaeology is getting a little more hip these days. There are some interesting theories."

"A good friend once told me archaeology is about fact," Sam said, pausing briefly at a carving on a tall, stone stele of three bearded figures looking to the sky. She traced her fingers up their line of sight to a mysterious oblong object above them. "Science, Dr Sandford. Not science fiction."

"And yet, as Jess keeps telling me," he replied, "even science needs to be flexible. We don't know everything about our world yet, after all."

Sam nodded at that. If only he knew how right he was.

More gunfire erupted in the background. The rat-a-tat firecrackers increasing in volume. Jess quickly led them through the staff door and locked it behind her.

They were now in a large conservation room. Ancient chaos lay before them. Desks piled high with all kinds of artefacts. Sarcophagi stood upright, awaiting their turn to have the dust of history brushed from their inscriptions. A thick black tomb – obsidian, perhaps – twice the size of the others, lay to one side, its lid leaning against it.

But it was the open window at the back that drew her attention.

"What could possibly be in the Hall that these men would want?" Will mused, as she herded them towards their escape route. "They seem like the type who want weapons. Yet this would be a library. A repository of history."

"Knowledge is power, Will. You of all people should know that. There's no telling what secrets lie buried in that place. And what these men would do with them."

"Well," Jess began, and Sam's heart sank immediately,

she knew what was coming, "if it's *that* important, maybe our work here lies beyond simply rescuing the amulet from their clutches? What if we use it to find the Hall ourselves? That way we can open it up to the world before these men have a chance to steal it for themselves!"

Sam slowed at her sister's words and the look of determination she saw creeping into her expression. Even Will's face had gained a little more colour and enthusiasm.

The window behind her suddenly seemed that much further away.

"What you're suggesting is a very bad idea," she warned. "And I don't think now is the time–"

She stopped and jerked her head around, hearing raised voices and heavy footsteps on the other side of the door.

Shit.

Clasping Jess's shoulders, she shoved her sister into an upstanding Egyptian coffin and kicked the lid closed. It wasn't ideal, but she could trust her sister to stay quiet and not to panic. But Will?

She pulled him over the edge of the obsidian tomb next to them, clamping her hand over his mouth, as the lock on the door to the room was shot out and agents stormed in.

Unfortunately, she heard someone being dragged with them. Whether it was a guest or an assistant, there was definite sobbing beneath the crescendo of footsteps.

"Window!" someone barked.

Footsteps passed the tomb. Will stopped struggling and stared fearfully at Sam beneath the thick curtain of her damp, chestnut hair falling onto his face. She lifted her hand away from his mouth and put a finger to her lips. He blinked and nodded.

"Go, find them," said another voice, right next to the tomb. One she recognised.

The odds of them making it out of here alive suddenly dropped.

"They've left the building," Agent Smith said on his walkie talkie. He still had that slight German accent they'd tried to bury beneath layers of vocal training – because it wouldn't do for the American Government to been seen working with the goons of the Third Reich, would it? "East wing. Pick up the amulet and kill whoever has it."

There was a muffled response.

"Yes, especially *her.*"

The sobbing inside the room intensified. The images of what might be happening outside the tomb flashed through Sam's mind. Her heartbeat raced, so loud she half expected Smith to be able to hear it.

It was one of the assistants crying. A man.

"Sir, what about this one?"

The immediate gunshot made both Sam and Will jump. She felt his fingers dig into her thighs hard, saw the tears pooling in the whites of his eyes. She clamped her hand back over his mouth and shook her head, even though she too felt like screaming out.

That was a fast kill, even for Smith.

Goddamnit, she thought, her head spinning. *God-fucking-dammit, you Nazi bastard.*

Yet as quickly as the fear overwhelmed her, she wrestled

back control. Tried to reshape it, like a potter with clay on a wheel. Trying to reveal the far more useful feeling hidden within. Something far stronger, responsible for her survival when times were at their worst.

Anger.

She continued holding Will down, even as the men left the room and the footsteps faded down the hall. Until she was confident nobody was left behind and that it wasn't a ruse to draw her out.

"I told you they were serious," she said, taking her hand away from Will's mouth.

A shadow appeared overhead and for a long, terrifying moment Sam thought she'd missed something. That Agent Smith was now preparing to pull his trigger and put a bullet in her head, as he'd wanted to do ever since they'd met.

"What the bloody hell was *that*?" Jess hissed.

Sam looked up to see her sister's red, oxygen-starved face move quickly from fury to incandescent rage.

"What?" Sam protested innocently.

"Next time you get the coffin and *I* get to sit on..." Jess paused as she looked at Will and her cheeks reddened further. "I mean, I go with Will, okay?"

Sam got off her sister's boyfriend, climbed out of their hiding place and feigned a shrug. "I panicked."

Jess shoved her out the way as Will emerged from the tomb looking like a ghost, his already gaunt face draining further when he saw the body of his assistant near the door.

His mouth opened and closed several times, unsure of

what to say.

Jessica pulled him close and clutched his hand in hers as she turned to her sister. “I think it’s clear we need to find the Hall of Records before them, Sam.” She gestured to the assistant, blood seeping from the back of his head onto the white, marble floor. “If they’re willing to do that, who knows what they’ll do with what they find in there. All those secrets. All that knowledge. All that power. You said it yourself only a few minutes ago.”

“I didn’t mean...”

But Sam let her voice trail off, as she realised Jess had a point.

She looked at the woman her sister had become, then to the dead man, feeling all hope of simply getting them out of harm’s way fading quickly. The weariness grew heavy on her shoulders in that moment, even as her sister’s eyes lit up knowing that she was about to cave.

“I… have an old friend who knew something of the legend,” she sighed at last. “He will know more about this amulet. I can’t promise anything, OK? But at the very least he can hide us until we decide what to do with it.”

Will jumped as he heard another gunshot in the distance. His eyes darted between Sam, the window, and the still open door. “And where is this friend? Where can we possibly hide from a government who would do something like that to one of its own citizens?”

Sam looked through the window. In the distance she could see the fading beams of torchlight as the agents made their way outside to search the park.

"*Un lieu d'amour et de choses perdues, Docteur Sandford,*" she replied, beckoning the pair to follow her back into the main museum.

A place of love and lost things.

CHAPTER FIVE

A Place of Love and Lost Things

In any other city it might have been considered late.

Not Paris.

As the four figures stood outside the tall townhouse in the centre of the city, soft light permeating though its wisteria-framed shutters, Sam remembered just what she loved about this place.

Time here stood still. There was no concept of late or early. There was only light and dark, each of which imbued the ancient streets and its beautiful inhabitants with a kaleidoscope of moods. Romance blossomed in the bricks and cobbles. Adventure called from the bars and clubs. And that fierce French pride could still be heard, untarnished by recent horrors, as a drunken rendition of *La Marseillaise* drifted from a nearby café.

If ever there were a place to come calling on an old friend at one o'clock in the morning, this was it. So when Sam knocked on the old, oak door, she was not surprised to see it open almost instantly, revealing a short, middle-aged man with olive skin, a greying beard, and a glass of scotch clutched gently in his fingers.

"Samantha Moxley, sweet girl!" Professor Teddy Ascher exclaimed in his quirky, stilted German accent, beaming warmly. "I'd say it has been far too long, but that much is obvious, is it not?" He stood back, looking her up and down, before raising his drink to her. "I take it back. Sweet girl no longer – you've grown up! Oh how time has surely flown, as we once did. How can that *be?*"

Sam found herself briefly enveloped in a small but very powerful hug.

"It's good to see you too, Teddy," she replied, before he excitedly cast her aside to get to Jess.

"And, oh boy, do I see the family resemblance here! This must be the sister I used to hear so much about. Miss Jessica Moxley herself, it is such a great honour to finally meet you. *And* a fellow archaeologist too, I believe?"

He grabbed the shocked Jess by her arms, kissed each cheek with vigour, then gave her an even bigger hug. She offered a muffled greeting into his shoulder as her wide blue eyes sought out her sister with a modicum of alarm.

Sam gave her a grin. It was rather fun to see her all-grown-up-and-confident sister a little out of her comfort zone. Although it was even more entertaining to see Will try to bury himself in the shadows of the Parisian night to avoid being next in line for a warm greeting.

"Everyone," she said proudly, putting her arm around her old acquaintance. "This is my good friend, Professor Edward Ascher. Although he prefers Teddy and he will make you call him that, whether you like it or not. Teddy, yes this is my sister Jess. And, behind her, is young Willy. You'll like him, he's a bit of an archaeologist too."

Will quickly stuck his hand out to prevent the hug, but was pulled into the Professor's embrace anyway and received two loud, wet kisses on each cheek for his trouble.

"It's Dr William Sandford of the New York Metropolitan Museum, actually," Will mumbled, as Teddy released him, only to pump his hand enthusiastically. "Er, charmed to make your acquaintance?"

"Splendid," Teddy replied, paying little attention as he went back to gather Jess up and usher them all inside the house. "Come, come. My home is your home this wonderful night."

Will frowned at Sam, but – ever the gentleman – gestured for her to go first. She playfully pinched his cheek as she followed the others down the long corridor.

"So, why'd you haul out of Cairo," she asked Teddy. "You always told me it was your dream to live in the land of your mother's family. I thought you were settled for life."

"Oh, Samantha. We had seven children, my friend. Seven! You cannot believe how my wife Aya and I have aged. Now they are all grown and flown far, far away and we decided to go into hiding so they can't come back!" He patted Jess's arm and laughed. "I am joking, of course. My children are my life." He turned over his other shoulder and whispered to Sam. "I think of this as my afterlife. As soon as the youngest moved out, we came to Paris."

"And there was me thinking you were a family man."

"Ah yes," he replied, his good mood faltering momentarily. "Speaking of which… Harry is already here. He arrived a few days ago by plane. He is not very happy."

Sam sighed. "Dad never is."

The kitchen they entered was traditional and cosy, with a checkered red and white tiled floor, and curtains for cupboards. In the centre of the room was a round country dining table, resplendent with bread, cheeses, stew, and mismatched wine glasses.

Two people sat eating.

Aya, Teddy's wife, smiled widely as she saw Sam and rushed over to greet them even more enthusiastically than her husband had. "Visitors!" she cried, kissing and hugging each one in turn. "Such a lovely surprise. Come! Sit! Eat!"

The other person at the table had their back to them. His shoulders seemed to slump as he heard them enter, though Sam wasn't sure if it was with relief or dread of the fight they were about to have.

Harry Moxley gently put down his knife and fork, pushed himself back from the table in his wheelchair, and regarded his daughters over his glasses. His eyes were pale. His cheeks unshaven for at least a couple of days. He looked beat.

"Hi, Dad," Sam said, kissing him on his forehead. "Sorry we're late."

"There's a good chance you will be, Sammy. Unless a bloody good explanation is forthcoming."

The venom in his voice took her by surprise.

"You know I don't like you calling me that…"

"You're worried about *names*?" he interrupted. "You disappeared from the house for a week, then called me up out of the blue and told me to buy a ticket to meet you on the other side of the world. That's the second time you've done that and, honestly, that's two times too many in one old man's life if you ask me. You can't keep packing me up and sending me around the globe you know. I'm not a bloody suitcase."

Will smirked from behind the relative safety of Aya.

"Dad–"

"No. No excuses this time, Sammy. What in God's name is going on? Why are we here?"

"You… always told me you wanted to see Paris?" she fumbled.

"Well, yes, I might have, maybe once upon a time," he tripped over his words angrily, "but not like this. Fourteen hours alone on an aeroplane and you don't even have the courtesy to be in the country when I arrive."

He pulled himself back to the table again and took a huge gulp of wine. Thinking it best to keep him happy, Aya quickly topped it up again before the empty glass hit the table.

"It was a difficult few days, Dad. You wouldn't believe what I've been through."

"No excuses, I said."

"But there was a whole thing in New York with a seaplane."

"I said–"

"–and a couple of dragon…"

Her eyes dropped quickly to the table.

"A couple of *what*?"

No. There was no point in finishing that sentence. He'd never understand.

"Nothing, Dad, forget I said anything. You're right, no excuses. I'm sorry."

Teddy shot her a sympathetic look, even as he quietly beckoned Aya and Will to follow him out of the kitchen into the reception room.

Jess began to shuffle after them, but Harry raised his hand.

"And where do you think you're going, young lady? Sit down and eat. Your sister probably hasn't even fed you, has she?"

"I'm… twenty-two?"

But he wasn't prepared to listen. He grabbed a ladle of stew from the cooking pot in the centre of the table and lashed it down onto one of the waiting plates like a splodge of a full stop to their argument.

They hadn't done this for such a long time, but it was strangely comforting to Sam – and a little irritating – how quickly they slipped back into these familiar roles like actors on a well-worn stage. So when Jess looked to her, Sam could only offer an apologetic shrug back. No way was she going to argue against Dad like this. She might be capable of fighting her way across the world, but family dinners were a whole other battle.

Jess sat down to eat with a huff.

"So go on, Sammy," Harry continued. "What's going

on? Why are we here? And why are you so late in arriving?"

Sam broke off a piece of crusty baguette and dipped it in the central bowl. It broke the surface of the cooling stew, releasing a thick waft of salted potatoes, carrots and gravy that made her mouth water. "We got held up and had to come by boat to avoid some old friends. You need to give out too much information to fly these days, so we would have been marked as soon as we collected our tickets." She shoved the stew-soaked bread into her mouth, even as she continued talking. "The illusion… of freedom… isn't what it used to be."

"So *you* had to take precautions, but you left *me* to fly?"

Jess blew on her food, hiding a smirk. "You're too old for them to worry about, Dad."

"Old?" His lips thinned beneath his salt and pepper stubble. "Right, well that explains the tardiness, but not why we're sitting in this admittedly lovely kitchen in the middle of Paris. Which brings us to the big question. Who have you two annoyed this time?"

"The United States Government," Sam admitted.

The look of weariness that crossed her father's face in that moment would have been amusing, had it not also been heartbreaking. Sam knew what the old man had gone through in recent years. And that she'd had a big part to play in that. "Wasn't the war enough for you, Sammy? I thought by letting you go off and fight you'd at least get it out of your system. Why are you still determined to seek out trouble?"

She bit her tongue at that. As if he'd *let* her go off to fight. She'd had to sneak out of the house just to sign up to the bloody ATA. The fighting part had come later and he hadn't known about it for months.

"If you must know, it's because I had to go looking for Jess. I thought they'd kidnapped her. Which I still maintain they might have done, but I beat them to it."

His face crinkled in confusion. "So you kidnapped her instead?"

"Wait, no–"

He waved away her protest. "If you thought she was in trouble, why didn't you tell me first?"

"I didn't want you to worry."

Her father pushed his half-eaten dinner away and picked up his wine. "You'll be relieved to know that I wouldn't have. Jessica called me on the telephone from New York just after you left, told me she was staying with a friend for a while."

Sam blinked and switched her attention to Jess, who was very intently pretending to be focused on her stew. "And you didn't tell *me*?"

"I... didn't want you to worry?" her sister said, quickly shoving a spoonful of stew into her mouth so she couldn't be questioned further.

Sam pinched the bridge of her nose for a moment, feeling the storm clouds of a headache forming behind her eyes. The image of Charlie falling from the plane replayed over in her mind. Could she have done things differently? No, perhaps not. The Nine would still have reached Jessica and Will before her. But none of this was helping set aside the guilt that was churning her up.

"Fine," she said, too exhausted to argue anymore. "But did Jess tell you that her 'friend' is a handsome, charming doctor of archaeology who whisked her off to South America to recover some relic? That she was in over her head. Is *still* in over her head… and we have to get her out of it?"

"Just like you got me and Dad out of England?" Jess said, waving her spoon in Sam's direction. "When you made your deal with the Americans to pull me away from my friends, leaving them all at home to fight for our country while you hid us halfway around the world. Like cowards."

"You were fifteen for Christ's sake! What did you want me to do? Leave you for the bombs?"

"We were in the Peak District, Sam! They weren't bombing us so much there. Manchester, sure, we saw the smoke from time to time. But never where we were – you know full well there was nothing but sheep and hills and reservoirs. We were doing just fine before you went and played your mothering card. Right, Dad?"

Harry looked uncomfortable at that. He rolled his chair back a moment as if trying to get a bit more distance between himself and the question.

"The country was suffering, Jessica. The cities were getting hit pretty hard and there was always the risk of invasion. None of us knew how it was going to play out and Sammy just wanted us to be safe."

"Just as I want you to be safe now," Sam said, relieved that at least someone had noted what she'd done. "Seriously,

Jess, you have to learn to be more careful. You can't just up and disappear adventuring to dangerous places like that. Anything could have happened out there and we'd never have known. Why would you put us through that?"

"Says the woman who spent the past few years with her agent pals off chasing long lost things that go bump in the night."

Harry nodded firmly at that. "You think *we* didn't worry all those years you were doing exactly the same thing for the people you're now running from? That's what family does, Sammy, we look after each other when we can, and we worry when we can't." He gave a long, weary sigh and took another gulp of wine. "Which, I'm afraid, is pretty much all the time with you two. I've seen off two world wars, yet still can't seem to settle down and bloody well enjoy life. Your mother would be incandescent with rage. Because, seriously, what the hell kind of family did I raise here? I had less trouble in the trenches and that's what dumped me in this thing!"

He slammed his glass down and wheeled himself around the table, pausing only to give Jessica's shoulder a gentle, paternal, squeeze.

"Just face it, Sammy," he said. "Jessica's only problem right now is that she's becoming you."

He left the room, leaving the two women alone to frown at each other.

"He says that like it's a bad thing?" Sam said.

CHAPTER SIX

A Plan

By two in the morning, Sam had drowned most of her family resentment in half a bottle of whiskey. She sat with Teddy at a table in the drawing room, the crackle of his wireless and the music of Nat King Cole, Glenn Miller and Ella Fitzgerald drifting in the background. Behind them, Jess and Will had cosied up on the couch. Aya sat by the fire, knitting, and Harry seemed to be asleep in his wheelchair, a shiny new book – with a dapper gentleman in a bow tie on the back of the dust jacket and something about Martians written on the front – resting open on his lap.

Teddy necked his third shot of the warm liquid and placed the glass upside down on the table top. His eyes gleamed. "So now that pleasantries are out of the way, and our bellies are fuelled with flames, shall we get down to business?"

She smiled and refilled her glass. Her mind was pleasantly foggy, but there was always room for improvement.

"Perhaps just a little more fire?"

He laughed, low and hearty. "It has been such a long time since we last saw one another my flighty young friend. But I admit I am intrigued as to the nature of your visit. What exactly has brought you here tonight?"

Sam glanced over her shoulder towards Jess and Will, then downed the whiskey.

Teddy nodded sympathetically. "I can never tell whether family is a blessing or a curse."

"I'll be honest, Teddy, I've known less troublesome curses."

His laugh slowly subsided as he realised she wasn't joking.

"Oh."

"Uh-huh." She swirled around the dregs of her drink, staring into the bottom of her glass. "Those two aren't entirely responsible though. Some people I used to work for wanted to bring me back. Approached me a few weeks ago. Government agency. Not official. Only barely on the periphery of official, if I'm honest. They told me they had someone they wanted me to talk to – a psychic."

"Was talking to people who communicate with supernatural beings a part of your job description?"

She gave a wry smile. "Occasionally."

"Interesting. And what happened?"

"I told them no. But they didn't take the hint, and now they are following us because of something these two dug up that I believe is connected with whoever or whatever is talking to the psychic. And it involves a myth I seem to remember is your particular area of expertise."

He raised a bushy eyebrow. "Yes?"

"The Hall of Records, Teddy."

He blinked, looking both excited and troubled at the same time. It was enough for his fingers to shakily retrieve his glass, turn it the right way round, and fill it to the brim.

"Samantha, you know what the Hall of Records means to me. My mother was Egyptian and the blood of that land runs deep in my veins and in my heart through the stories she used to tell. Stories such as that of the great Hall. Even as a child I would dream of unlocking its secrets."

"Well," she said, raising her glass in a salute, "now you're not alone. Exactly how close have you come?"

He drank in reply. Then got unsteadily to his feet, as if trying to remember how to stand upright, walked over to the dresser, pulled out the drawer, and extracted a brown, dog-eared notebook. He lay it open on the table for Sam to see.

She flicked through, feeling a strange hit of nostalgia she couldn't quite place. Notes and diagrams spilled across every page. Scribbles in English, German, Ancient Greek and Arabic filled every white space. Teddy sat down beside her and together they poured over it, before pulling up on a particular page with a drawing of a large, human-headed monument she recognised. He tapped his finger gently on it.

"Here," he said. "All the clues I have studied – those that hold the weight of truth, anyway – they all suggest that the great Hall was located lying hidden beneath the paws of this fine feline."

"The Sphinx?"

"Uh-huh."

"The Sphinx in Giza?"

Teddy smiled. "If you have come across another great cat during your travels, then please tell me so you and I can officially claim it and get rich! Until then, yes, the Sphinx that guards those magnificent pyramids is where I believe the Hall should be located."

Sam stared in wonder at the hastily drawn image in the book before her. Beside it sat another cruder drawing of a different head, far more cat-like than the one the Sphinx currently wore. The words *Pre-dating by 10,000 years,* had been scribbled underneath, along with a large question mark.

"You say *should be located,*" she asked him. "It's not there?"

His beard twisted into a disappointed grimace. "We have done extensive surveys, both manual and using the latest technology. Magnetic surveys using proton precession magnetometers." He waved his hand to ward off having to explain it, not that Sam had any inclination to ask. "Suffice it to say, we have scoured the area directly underneath and in the surrounds of the plateau. And still we found nothing. Which is strange, because in some texts the Hall is described as a fortress, with walls of stone as thick as houses. If it is down there, our surveys would have picked it up."

She scratched her head, feeling fuzzy. "I've seen some

strange things in my life, Teddy, but creating the most important centre of human knowledge ever known and then burying it in a fortified desert hideout for all eternity, with no way of getting in, would be one of the craziest schemes I've yet heard."

"Oh, the texts describe a gateway too. Glowing gold, in some cases. But, as with the Hall itself, I have not yet found that either." He let out a long sigh. "And even if we *did* know where it was, it is supposedly protected by a lock with two keys." He flicked through his notebook again until he reached another drawing and Sam immediately sat up straighter. It was a sketch she must not have seen in some ten years or so, since Teddy had showed it to her at an airfield in England while they'd been waiting for the next air raid. He tapped the page. "You see? One an amulet. The other a calendar stone. Isis and Osiris, the mother and father of Ancient Egypt. Only when these two are brought together can you unlock the entrance. But... you would have to find them first. And, as yet, nobody knows where they are."

Sam reached into her jacket and pulled out the heavy gold artefact she'd been carrying, carefully wrapped in her old RAF scarf. "I knew I'd seen it before, but until you just showed me that sketch I couldn't remember exactly where." She unravelled it in front of him. "Teddy, meet Isis."

Her friend's old brown eyes widened as he saw the amulet. His mouth gaped open and closed as if he was gasping for air. His fingers twitched. His gaze flickered up to Sam's, pleading like a puppy wanting a treat.

She handed it to him.

"Oh," he gasped, cradling the piece in his hands as gently as he might a newborn baby. "Oh my, Samantha. Praise all the gods of the pantheon. I should have known you would be the one to go where I could not. Where did you find it? Was it in the rivers of Tiutota, near the city of Xcheuchan?" She opened her mouth, but he didn't wait for her to answer. "Yes, yes, I knew it must be. How I had dreamed of travelling there and finding the amulet myself, but... well, you know me. I was never one for fieldwork and the war was enough action to last any man or woman a lifetime. Once you have made it out of the darkness of such times you owe it to those who did not to live a fruitful life, eh? I had family to consider. A quiet life to live. I was not allowed to go jaunting around the world on a whim."

His sudden rambling caused Aya to look up from her knitting with a frown. Teddy saw and spluttered a nervous laugh.

"Of course, I do not mean that Aya here forbade me from such things!" he added quickly. "Quite the contrary, I forbade myself. For that is how is should be. Putting family first, as you well know, Samantha."

Sam looked first to Jess chatting with Will, then to her father by the fireplace. He was snoring gently, his glasses slowly slipping down his nose. The waves of anxiety that usually frothed beneath the surface of her facade subsided at least for a moment, as she smiled with genuine contentment for the first time in a long while. A peaceful family scene. One of the few she could remember.

But it only lasted a moment.

Teddy peered with fierce intensity at the amulet, feeling its edges and running his fingers over the tiny inlaid gems. "Of course, out of what we shall refer to as academic curiosity, pure and simple... where exactly *did* you find this piece?"

The conversation between Will and Jess stopped behind her. Sam could almost feel the heat from her sister's glare burning into the back of her head like the midday sun through a shadeless Spitfire cockpit.

"*I* didn't find it," she admitted. "It's a story those two will have to tell you one day. But right now we have more pressing matters. Like where do we find the other piece?"

"The Osiris Stone?" Teddy's eyes glazed over and he suddenly seemed unsure about where exactly this conversation was leading, now that half the puzzle he had spent most of his life figuring out had been solved. His gaze flickered guiltily to his wife. "It has been said that searching for lost and dangerous antiquities is the business of a fool and always has been. For a long time I may have been such a fool, but I have since found there is no harm in a more peaceful life – and after everything you have been through, Samantha, I am quite certain you and your family deserve it too. Do not get me wrong. The fact the amulet is here, in my hands, gladdens my heart. Truly it does. But perhaps this is best suited to finding a home in a museum, where we can enjoy it without risk?"

"A lovely idea, but I have a feeling *someone* would go after it without me," Sam replied, not needing to turn to know that her sister was nodding vigorously. She gazed into her now empty glass, not liking what she saw in her mind's eye. "And, honestly, after everything I've seen recently, I don't think we have a choice. We don't get to go home now, because there are men after what we have. Men who have killed, and will kill again, and will not stop killing until they get what they want."

"A theme of our time," he concurred.

Sam topped up her drink and necked it in one go, pausing only to wince and gasp afterwards as the fire burned its way down her throat. "And yet in this case I have a bad feeling there's more to it than even that. It's not just about this priceless artefact for these men. They want what it can give them."

"The Hall?"

She nodded. "Tell me, Teddy. Why would the US Government want to open the Hall of Records, if it even exists? The knowledge, I can understand. But I can't shake the idea that there is something else down there they know about. Something powerful."

He frowned and his voice dropped low. The words carried softly around the room, punctuated only by the crackle of the logs on the fire.

"There are far greater secrets hidden in the Hall than you could ever imagine, Samantha. Some say the secrets of the Gods themselves are hidden there. Of an Empire long since lost, that gave rise to the glorious cities of Egypt and Mesopotamia. An ancient civilisation advanced beyond anything we know today." He paused. "Until it disappeared."

Sam could feel a strange sensation in the pit of her stomach.

"You mean the city of Atlantis, don't you?"

"I do," Teddy replied in all seriousness. "But not just the city of Atlantis. We are talking about a veritable *Empire* of Atlantis. A vast network of cities and outposts around the world. All connected to the one lost continent. A continent that destroyed itself in a cataclysm of unprecedented historical proportions."

Sam nodded warily. She had heard this story from him before. She had never really bought into it, figuring that it simply stood as a scholarly bedtime story, a warning from history not to let your society get too cocky. But Teddy had always been keen to talk her into believing and sometimes, only sometimes, she wondered if there might be more to it.

"You think proof of its existence is in the Hall?"

Teddy gave her a grim smile. "As you know, Atlantology was always my passion, even while I was teaching the more mundane principles and processes of archaeology and ancient history. I was not alone either. In Berlin, I was fortunate enough to work alongside a fellow scholar of Atlantis – one of the best, although later I discovered he was of dubious ideological leanings – by the name of Schultz. He thought me an amateur. Can you believe that? But he did at least humour my calls at his office to discuss the finer details of the philosopher Plato's texts, where the continent is first mentioned. We had many a heated argument into the night over the Hall and its connection to the lost civilisation. But, in the end, we at least agreed that the Hall of Records did not just contain proof of the existence of Atlantis…"

"…but also of the power that destroyed it," Sam finished with a sigh.

She now knew what this all meant. It didn't matter whether she believed in it or not. If Taylor and The Nine thought that there was even a hint of a clue to that kind of weapon lying forgotten in the Egyptian sands, they weren't going to stop chasing her for the artefact that could lead them to it. And, once they had that, they would use every ounce of their inhumanity to force her to help them.

Which meant it wasn't just her trapped on this dangerous path now.

Her family was too.

Teddy must have seen the look of fear in her eyes. He leaned across the table and put a comforting hand on hers.

"The Americans are not the first to be taken with the tale of Atlantis and the enormous power it could offer. The story was also beginning to interest those in power back in Germany at the time of my leaving. It is one of the reasons for my departure, in fact. Are you sure you want to do this?"

"I don't–"

But she didn't get to finish.

On the other side of the room Will suddenly got to his feet, his face like thunder.

"You're German?" he repeated.

Not a statement. An accusation.

"Half Egyptian, half German. Did not the accent give

away my secret sooner, Mister Sandford?"

Will's face flushed. "*Dr* Sandford. And I had hoped, being as we are in France, that your European accent might have been local."

Teddy nodded in that calm manner of his. "I am sorry to disappoint you."

Will's fist crashed down on the table making the others jump. "My father died during the war, you lousy bum. Don't you dare take that tone with me."

Sam watched her old friend's reaction carefully. She was unsurprised – albeit relieved – to see his pleasant demeanour unwavering, even as his eyes began to water. Teddy had been expecting this turn of events. As had she. Human nature could be ever so predictable.

"I am sad to say mine did too," Teddy replied. "Most of my family, in fact."

With that Sam stood, poured another whiskey and handed it to Will – while carefully putting herself between the two men. Will was good and handsome, but she would still break his nose if the occasion called for it.

"He flew with us, Will," she said firmly. "He flew with me."

Jess appeared beside him. Her hand on his shoulder. "It's true. Sam told me Teddy was one of the few Germans who escaped the country just before war broke out. He fought for the RAF. Saved Sam's life a couple of times too."

Teddy continued swirling the remnants of his whiskey. "Not a popular position I can tell you, being the enemy alien. The odd one out."

"About as popular as being a female pilot in a man's war, in fact," Sam said, raising an eyebrow at Will.

Will grew flush again, but this time it wasn't anger. His gaze flicked down just for a moment.

"I didn't mean–"

"Of course you didn't. But we're all friends here, do you understand? Meanwhile, the world has been balanced on the edge of madness lately and the men who want what we have might well push us over the edge. So do you mind taking a seat? We need to crack on with staying alive while we still can."

She sat back down and poured herself another drink, leaving Will to stand there, awkwardly, not really knowing what to do with himself. Jess dug him in the ribs and made him retreat to the couch, away from harm.

"Right," Sam continued wearily, pushing her fingers across her face and suppressing a yawn, "we're in a bit of a pickle here, if I'm honest. And unfortunately I can only see one way out. Where did you say this Osiris Stone was again, Teddy?"

"I have had a theory about where it rests for many years now. But, even if I am right, it will be protected too well. There are puzzles and traps and other things that would kill an old man like me."

"Luckily I'm an old woman, so I should be fine." She waved away his immediate protest of innocence. "It's OK, I know what you meant. But you can let me worry about the risks now, Teddy. Because I'm going after it."

"Now just wait a minute," Jess started.

Sam quickly held up both hands in a gesture of surrender.

"*We're* going after it, I meant."

Despite the black hole forming inside her, quickly consuming any thought of finally living her life without death lurking around every corner, she faced up to the fact there was no getting out of this now. Once again, adventure had found her when she'd least expected it and was handing her a baton to take up the challenge, and, while she didn't have to damn well like it, she had to admit there was a tiny part of her that was growing curious about what these particular puzzle pieces might end up showing them all.

Besides, her sister had waded too far into this mess already, too caught up in her dreams of fortune and glory. And regardless of what Sam might have believed existed – or didn't exist – at the end of this treasure hunt, she couldn't let Jess go on alone.

She knew what Taylor and his goons were capable of. If they caught even a whiff of their scent they would inevitably track her sister down and there would be no telling what they'd do to her to reach the Hall and get their increasingly bloodied hands on whatever civilisation-destroying weapon they thought might be there.

Fuzzy from the whiskey, wanting nothing more than a good sleep, but knowing that it would be impossible now – perhaps until this was all done, or she was good and dead – she asked a final time.

"Teddy, just tell me... where do we find the damned Stone?"

This time he didn't try to evade the question. But he did glance awkwardly at his wife, the colour in his cheeks reddening.

"I may have been bending the truth a little when I told you why we moved to France," he said.

Sam almost laughed. "The piece is in Paris, isn't it? You came here to try and find it, didn't you?"

He nodded, trying to ignore the look of daggers his wife was currently throwing him, the knitting needles twitching dangerously in her fingers as though she might soon be using them for non-knitting purposes.

"I may have."

Jess whooped in delight, leaping on the still embarrassed Will in a bear hug. Aya cursed in Arabic under her breath.

Only Harry stayed quiet and perfectly still. Sam looked over to her father to see that he was now awake... and apparently had been following the conversation long enough to know what was happening.

But she could see now the worry in his eyes was tinged with understanding.

The moment hung in the air between them of sadness and inevitability and letting go, until finally he nodded. Not approval, but acceptance.

Sam turned to Teddy.

"Let's go get it then."

CHAPTER SEVEN

In the Shadow of the Skulls

They stood in the shadow of the great Notre-Dame, as Paris slept around them.

The cathedral towers loomed large in the clear night sky, dark and powerful, while the central rose window watched on like a wary, unblinking eye, waiting for someone to unlock its secrets.

Now Sam was here, she wasn't sure how easy that was going to be. It was close to three in the morning. The tall wooden doors were closed and bolted. And although the city streets were mostly devoid of life – with only the occasional drunk tugging his hat at them, before staggering happily down the banks of the Seine – there was a presence here that meant breaking in could be tough.

A guard, keeping watch.

"Did you know, those doors are believed to be the work of the devil?" Teddy said, far too amiably for such an hour. Sam figured him nervous. Or possibly over-excited. The whiskey had played its part, certainly. "See that fourteenth-century ironmongery twisting and weaving across the wood. It was made by a man called Biscornet. They say he sold his soul for the talent to create such beauty, but that the doors refused to lock until holy water was sprinkled on them."

"Let's just hope the devil has the night off," Sam replied, still waiting for the effects of the coffee she'd had to kick in. Her head was beginning to throb, which was probably a good sign.

The small guard's hut stood to the side. Smoke slipped from a tin-pot chimney and the burliest white woman Sam had ever seen was sitting inside reading '*C'est Paris*'… what looked to be an erotic magazine.

"Now that's a job I've always aspired to," Jess said, nudging Will. He quickly pretended he hadn't been staring.

Teddy, on the other hand, was quite blatant with his gushing gaze, except that his was reserved entirely for the cathedral, admiring it like a lovestruck schoolboy.

"You really think the Osiris Stone is in there?" Sam asked.

"Not exactly *in* there. Rather it is buried deep in *l'Ossuaire Municipal*… the Catacombs beneath Paris herself. This is only the way in."

Jess looked between the guard's hut and the locked cathedral doors. "There isn't a less obvious way?"

"Of course."

"Then why are we here?"

"Because I did not think you would want to travel through the sewer."

Jess considered that for a moment, tugging on her blue neckscarf and glancing down at her pristinely pressed red blouse and skirt. "Cathedral's fine with me."

"Seconded," Will said, fiddling with the stiffly-starched white collar of his shirt. Even out of his tuxedo he was dashingly dressed.

Sam meanwhile couldn't help but feel a touch smug in her scuffed pilot's jacket, scuffed khaki trousers and, well, scuffed boots. She hadn't thought to bring any good clothes for this little trip to Paris and now that she considered it she wasn't even sure she owned any good clothes, but at least she was prepared for what lay ahead. The others might be dressed up perfectly for a night out on the town, but were they really ready for a night under it?

She grinned to herself at the thought of Will's face when he realised just how ruined his shirt was going to get. That might be worth the adventure alone.

"I'm assuming you've been here a few times," she said to Teddy. "Do you know the guard? Can you get us in at such a late hour?"

Surprisingly, he shook his head. "In the few times Aya has let me slip away here to investigate, I have had little success finding anything during the day. And the last time they let me stay after closing hours… well, I had a small accident. They asked me not to return."

"You had an accident?"

"I broke a few skulls."

"How many's a few?"

"About three hundred."

Sam sighed. "I guess I'll do the talking then."

Without waiting for the others, she strode over to the hut and knocked on the window. The guard inside looked up, but made no effort to move or hide the magazine. A defiant exhalation of cigarette smoke drifted from behind the pages.

"Please don't make me do this the hard way," Sam muttered.

She knocked again, louder.

The woman inside gave a low rumbling sigh that rattled the entire hut. But this time she folded her magazine, stubbed out her deteriorating cigarette in an ashtray, and got to her feet. She was so tall that her head disappeared up past the window and all Sam could see now were her thick, powerful limbs moving towards the door.

It opened in another puff of smoke, blown right into Sam's face.

"*Oui?*"

Sam tried not to cough.

"*Bonsoir*," she began. It had been a while since she'd had to survive on the Continent, back with her group of soldiers, but she could recall enough. They'd fought across most of the country, working with the Resistance, so she'd had to learn to speak local pretty fast. And now it came back in bits and pieces. Each remembered word striking a long-forgotten memory, like bullets ricocheting off a wall. She continued, in the best French she could muster, "I'm Professor Moxley from the University of Chicago. I'm here to undertake some important research, although I'm afraid we're a little late as my plane was delayed. However, the

Bishop who invited me and my team told us to come at any time."

The guard looked Sam up and down distrustfully. "Bishop De Sully?"

Sam nodded. "Yes, De Sully! That's the one. Anyway our visit shouldn't take long. Would it be possible to let us in just briefly?"

The tall woman smiled. Feeling victorious, Sam smiled back. And when the woman spoke next, it was in excellent English.

"*Professor* Moxley, you say?"

"Yes, that's right."

"You're a woman."

Sam's smile hardened. "That's right."

"And Bishop De Sully invited you?"

"Uh-huh."

The guard's smile disappeared.

"Bishop De Sully doesn't exist, I made him up." She pointed a meaty hand towards the rusty plaque on the side of the hut. "Visiting hours for the cathedral are between nine and five. Come back tomorrow."

Unfortunately, the guard then noticed Teddy skulking in the background. "You?" she shouted. "I thought I told *you* never to bother me again with these requests! The cathedral is not your personal playground, Monsieur. Take your ridiculous theories and friends and leave this place before I call the police!"

The hut door slammed shut, before they all heard a loud "*merde!*" from behind it.

Sam strode back to her group, a little annoyed. One of the few times she had taken the non-violent route and look where it had got her.

"Any other ideas?" she asked.

"I say we go around the back," Jess replied. "Should be a window or something we can break to get in there."

Teddy stared at her with disgust. "It's an eight hundred-year old cathedral! These stained glass windows have seen more history than you or I can imagine. Are you really an archaeologist?"

"Yeah, Jess," Sam added. "I'm no expert, but isn't the first rule of archaeology don't break the priceless artefacts?"

"Okay, well what do *you* want to do, Captain Wonderful?" Jess snapped. "Because I don't see you coming up with any answers yourself. I don't know exactly what you and that guard spoke about, but clearly you don't have the charm or charisma for this kind of work. Why are you even here?"

"To stop you all accidentally burying yourselves alive under Notre-Dame for all eternity in your haste to find ancient treasure."

"I am not being hasty! Teddy, Will and I are scientists and simply approaching this scientifically by ruling out the various options."

Sam narrowed her eyes, as the throbbing in her skull seemed to increase. "It's three o'clock in the morning in Paris, and two of us are half-drunk as we try to break into one of the most historic places on the planet. None of this is scientific."

Teddy put a tentative hand on both their shoulders as they squared up. "Perhaps we should go home and come back in the morning for the regular visiting time? I do not wish to cause any hassle for anyone."

Sam and Jess both ignored him.

"Look, I don't like it," Sam continued, judging the increasingly fierce look in her sister's eyes as something that could be used to their advantage. "But we might have to knock the guard out and steal her keys. We can leave her tied up in the hut."

"Brilliant," Jess replied. "You brought some rope, of course?"

"You're the scientist. Aren't you supposed to think of stuff like that?"

"I already found the first piece of the puzzle, Sam. If you're tagging along then you need to step up."

Sam clenched her fists. "Fine. Forget the rope. I'll just knock her out harder than I normally would. How's that?"

"Now you're talking."

Teddy stood rubbing his arms and looking around, as though he'd rather be anywhere else.

"You in, Teddy?" Sam asked.

"Oh… well… I do not know if I can sanction actual violence…"

But Sam had already turned away, heading towards the hut.

Only to see it was now empty.

At the entrance to the cathedral, Will was leaning up to give the guard a kiss on both her cheeks, before she returned the gesture with gusto. She then turned and swaggered past the group back to her hut.

When they reached Will he was rocking back and forth on his heels, whistling jovially beside the now open door.

"Oh, you are a clever man, Dr Sandford!" Teddy said, walking past with a shaky, relieved laugh.

"One no woman can resist, clearly," Jess added, giving his bottom a playful pinch.

Sam could only scowl as Will's lipstick-smudged grin grew more smug by the second.

"Only in France," she muttered.

They entered the cathedral and stood for a moment, taking in their surroundings. The high vaulted ceiling, the soft moonlight now filtering in through the intricate, stained-glass windows in the apse.

Sam breathed in the splendour of one of the finest examples of gothic architecture in the world, seen at an hour very few people would have the chance to admire it. She wished for more time to linger. To softly tread the stone floor as millions had done before her. To enjoy the calm and the serenity this space offered and let it fill her up in the hope it might carry her through the inevitable storm ahead.

But she couldn't. Time was never on her side these days and she could only imagine how fast The Nine were closing in on them. It wouldn't take the bastards long to figure out she'd left the country and track her to Paris. Sadly, she'd have to leave the sightseeing until another day.

Although, she considered, if Teddy was right there might be far more impressive sights ahead.

They followed him to an alcove at the rear of the cathedral, where he pulled a wrought iron key from his pocket and unlocked the door in front of them. Inside, he flicked a switch and the lights buzzed on. Sam could see stone steps, spiralling downwards.

It was a good two storeys below the cathedral when they reached an arch and stepped through into a magnificently ornate crypt. Or at least Sam *assumed* it must be magnificently ornate. Right now it lay underneath a flood of half-opened boxes of religious paraphernalia and scattered items balanced precariously around the room.

Jess peered curiously into a tin of white, octagonal sweets. Sam recognised them immediately from her time on the Continent. *Pastilles de Vichy* was written on the lid. She scowled and scooped it up, sweeping it all into the nearest bin.

"There is a lot of rubbish here," she said.

"Some people have no respect for the past," Teddy agreed solemnly, moving to the rear wall to stand next to a delicate-looking statue of a weeping widow carved into a hollow. At which point he put his hand on the statue's head and tried to snap it off.

"No!" Jess and Will yelled in unison.

Teddy looked at them in surprise, before they all heard a loud click. A stone door in the back wall began to open. He pushed the perfectly fine statue head – a secret lever – back into place.

"Do you really think I'm here to run roughshod over history? You lack faith, my friends!"

Sam grinned as she inched past him and peered into the darkness beyond the door.

"Faith is one thing. Unfortunately, we also lack torches. I don't suppose you happen to have any lying about, do you Teddy?"

He gestured back towards a table, where Will opened one of the boxes and grabbed a couple of large hand torches for her and Jess. American army issue, as far as Sam could tell. Relics from the war, but still in good nick.

They flicked them on and the two sisters crouched before the secret door, pouring light into the darkness. Sam couldn't see much down the tunnel. But right in front of them, Jessica's light passed over a sign hung from the ceiling. The old words were daubed with what looked like blood, and etched with crude skulls.

"What does it say?" Will whispered, his hand clutching Jessica's shoulder as though she might be sucked through the doorway at any moment.

"*Bienvenue… dans l'empire de la… mort,*" Jess replied, reading aloud in hesitant French.

"Welcome to the Empire of Death," Sam translated. Then, under her breath, "Oh, boy."

CHAPTER EIGHT

The Empire of Death

It was eerily quiet. Only the constant drip, drip, drip of water from the ceiling, like a clock counting down to some indeterminate fate, and the wet echoes of the group's footsteps as they trod the path towards it.

Two streams of torchlight revealed what appeared to be your usual dank, depressing tunnel beneath a city. Just enough room to walk two abreast, in between walls that at first glance were built of neatly stacked white cobbles.

Will ran his fingers along them.

"Careful of the ancient human remains there, Will," Sam said absently. She directed her torchlight up to show that the cobbles were actually hundreds of skulls arranged in rows interspersed with other bones.

He yanked his hand back as if he'd been bitten, causing Jess to stifle a laugh. "You really aren't much of a field archaeologist are you?"

"I just prefer my bones in well-lit museums, that's all," he replied.

Jess reached out to nudge a loose femur back into its hole so she could scrape past. Sam noted she wasn't perturbed by what she was seeing. Or, if she was, she was certainly covering it up well.

"So who are all these people?" Sam asked, shivering as a cold drop of water fell into the back of her shirt and rolled down her spine. "They must have done something pretty terrible to have ended up here like this?"

"It's not quite as macabre as you think, if I remember my Parisian history correctly," her sister replied. "Their bodies simply got in the way of progress, right, Teddy? These were all citizens of Paris, moved here in the eighteenth century when the government decided to reclaim the cemeteries for the expansion of the city."

"Yes, yes, that is correct. The good, the corrupt, wealthy and poor… they all ended up here. The product of capitalism and growth!"

"It's a little creepy," Will said.

"It's *archaeology*, Dr Sandford," Teddy replied brightly, shooting the younger man a beard-splitting grin. "As you would know if you got out of your museum once in a while! We are but material remains in the end and this is the proof of it. Whoever you are, whatever you did in life, this is where you end up. It is actually quite fascinating if you think about it like that. There is a paper to be written on human equality right here, if you are interested?"

Will laughed nervously. "We'll have our hands full with the Hall of Records, thanks."

"Speaking of which," Jess said, "how exactly did the

millennia-old artefact we're searching for end up in an eighteenth century French crypt like this? I know the French were the first western country to truly discover Egypt – was it a find from one of Napoleon's many expeditions there?"

"Nobody discovered Egypt because it wasn't lost, my girl. The people were already there, as they had been for thousands of years, and as they still are today. To think otherwise is to take the perspective of empire and colonisation, neither of which do the study of archaeology any favours at all. Archaeology is about objectivity."

"That's fine, Teddy, but like it or not, we are here because of empire and colonisation. We have made incredible advances in our thinking because of such discoveries and the artefacts brought back to our museums over the last hundred years. You can't dispute that?"

"I don't dispute that."

Jess waved her torch at Sam, casting her eerie shadow across the rows of bones. "You've gone quiet all of a sudden, sis. I thought all this stuff was your soapbox to clamber upon? You who used to take me to Manchester Museum and who once told me the British Museum was your favourite place in the world."

"It still is," Sam called back, kicking aside a bone on the path and hearing it splash in the shallow water running beside them. "I mean, I'm no expert, but I figure ancient things need to be preserved for everyone to enjoy. And, if that can't be done in the precise spot where the artefacts are found, then, as a good friend once told me, they belong in a museum. But I think there's a question that needs to follow that. Whose museum? Ask yourself, how would you feel if ships sailed into New York Bay and took the Statue of Liberty with them back to Moscow? Which, by the way, could happen one day. Or what about Stonehenge? What if we woke up to the news that the stones had been moved and were now proudly on display in a museum on another continent under the banner of 'discovery'? That wouldn't be right, would it?"

"When did you get so passionate about this?" Will's voice piped up, his words echoing through the splashes of water as the path grew a little more flooded in places. Sam didn't need to look back to know he was desperately hopping between the puddles, trying not to get his fancy brogues wet. "I thought you were a pilot, not a philosopher?"

"Sometimes pilots get shot down and find themselves in the midst of war," she snapped back. "And what I saw on the ground, in person, were invaders running roughshod over a whole bunch of different countries and cultures, stealing people and artefacts as if they were theirs to take. Once you see that, once you understand how that feels in person, you begin to recognise it in other less obvious areas."

"I respectfully disagree with your implications, Captain," Will replied darkly. "This is not the same thing as what happened during the war. Ours is a noble pursuit of science, not domination!"

"Very true," Teddy interjected, drawing up for a moment,

cold sweat and dripping water having plastered his hair to his forehead. He wiped it away as best he could with the back of his tweed jacket sleeve. "And I know Sam would agree with you, Dr Sandford. That isn't what she was saying. Only that maybe we need to make sure we tread carefully in our noble pursuits, because sometimes even good intentions might not seem that way to those on the receiving end of our actions. Our gaze into history should always be humble and respectful and undertaken with a light touch. And, to return to the question Jessica here asked moments ago, while it is true some of those men on Napoleon's expeditions went to Egypt for noble reasons, to study and learn more about the world – and our part in it – we must remember that in the end a great deal of history was stolen from those lands. Taken in great warships and sent back to France."

Sam stepped over what she hoped was only an animal skeleton lying broken across the crumbling pathway. "Except most never made it," she added.

"Because the British intercepted them?" Jess asked, and Sam nodded.

"It turns out our own empire has been pretty good at taking things that didn't belong to us. And, let's face it, we haven't always been the best of friends with France. So after Napoleon's adventures in Egypt, it just so happens that the British navy was lurking in the Mediterranean in wait. They attacked his ships and what wasn't sunk was captured. Of course, if you want a bright side, you can argue that they at least put everything on display in the British Museum, to be studied, enjoyed, and protected for generations to come."

"Everything except what they had originally sought in those encounters," Teddy added.

He recoiled as Sam stopped abruptly and directed her torch light at him.

"You think the British attacks on the French were designed to retrieve the keys to the Hall of Records?"

He shielded his face and waved away the light until she moved it, then rubbed his eyes as he answered. "Yes, I believe that's exactly what they were doing. The British and French were at the throats of each other at that time, of that there is no doubt. Yet I always had the impression these particular attacks were different. I have witnessed parchments that attest to the British looking for something in particular during these raids. However…"

"What?" she persisted.

"…however, it appears they left the scene of their crime without everything they came for. Yes, they took enough of the treasure the French had themselves taken from Egypt – certainly enough for the British to have crowed about their success. But what is less well known is that during the attacks a single French ship managed to escape and return to France. On board was the first true adventurer. One of those who had travelled to Egypt to seek knowledge, not fame or fortune or power. A world-wise traveller named Henri. Samantha Henri."

Jess gave her sister a sidelong glance. "Isn't that–"

Sam nodded. "That's who I was named after. Mum wanted a daring and fearless female role model for me to follow, apparently. "It'll keep life interesting", she said."

"And how'd that work out?"

"Not going to lie… some days I would have preferred a quieter namesake."

Teddy put a hand on her shoulder. "In fact, you have shared far more of her path to infamy than your mother would have liked. For the more I read about her, the more I believe she was working for her rulers. Her government. Just like you have been. Very much a gun-for-hire on their various quests and conquests around the world. Including in Egypt. After which I believe she was the one who snuck the Osiris Stone from the British and carried it with her to Paris."

"Gee, not much to live up to there, eh, Sam?" Jess said, the bare bones of a smile touching the corners of her lips.

"Not much at all," Sam agreed dryly. "Although at least *she* had some degree of choice with her adventures. She wasn't roped into it through her little sister and her boyfriend opening Pandora's Box and bringing it home to kill the family."

"I'm sorry, exactly whose old flame is trying to steal this thing to take over the world?"

"Old flame, Jess. *Old*. And I extinguished him for this exact bloody reason."

Will's lips thinned impatiently, and he held up his hand to stop either of them arguing further. "But if that's the case and Samantha Henri saved the Osiris Stone from the British… what is it doing down here in the dark and the damp of this wretched place? Why not hand it over to her government to protect? Put it in the Louvre, perhaps?"

Sam carried on along the path. "Because she knew the

British would come after it eventually. And likely she felt she could not trust her own government to do the right thing either. If there's one thing history has taught us, it's that governments can't be trusted with anything."

"True," Teddy agreed, following close behind. "Yet, in the end, Paris was perhaps the best place for your namesake to have brought the Osiris Stone for its own protection. It is said there are nearly two hundred miles of tunnels in these catacombs. These crypts were the perfect place to hide an artefact of such power. She knew all too well the danger of it falling into dastardly British hands." He added quickly, "No offence to you dear girls, of course."

Sam shrugged. "Dastardly is probably underselling it."

"So did anybody come after it in the end?" Will continued.

"Oh yes, of course," Teddy replied. "The British tried, as you can imagine. Other countries too. But, thankfully, not many of them knew where to start looking."

"So how do *you* happen to know what they couldn't figure out?"

Sam could hear the smile in her old friend's voice as he said, "Because I pride myself on being a patient man, Dr Sandford. Those who seek power can only ever see what's right in front of them. There is no patience in their makeup. They simply look for the gleam of the treasure they desire, without taking the time to follow the twists and turns of the trail that brought it there. My knowledge was earned through years of late nights in the place that keeps the answers to every problem – the library!"

"The *library*?" Jess repeated dubiously.

"Of course. Before the fieldwork and showing off your treasures at fancy museum exhibitions, you need to do your research. Being, as you might say, a *square.* I've always found that reading books allows you to stand on the shoulders of the giants who have come before, to better help you see your place in the world and where you need to go next."

Sam glanced over her shoulder to see Will's face twitch angrily at Teddy's inadvertent dig at his profession. But the museum curator didn't take the bait. His eyes were on the prize now.

"So it's definitely down here? The Osiris Stone is hidden in these catacombs?"

"Yes. I am convinced beyond reasonable doubt they are down here."

"Wait," Sam said. "What do you mean *they*?"

"Ah, well, that's the one part I have not yet mentioned, my young friends. It seems, Samantha, that your namesake disappeared from history after her return to Paris, which led me to believe that she is also buried here along with the Stone. All signs point to her last act in this life being to stay and protect the Stone. As a sacrifice to save those she loved. Her country. Perhaps even the world?"

A chill entirely unrelated to the cold catacombs ran through Sam's body.

It shouldn't have mattered. She knew it really shouldn't make any difference what had happened all those years ago. Millions of people had lived and died and loved and lost in that time. Wars had been fought. New ideas and technologies had twisted fate and driven destinies. The world had changed considerably.

And yet, as a child, this woman had been Sam's hero. She had shown the girl just what was possible for a woman to achieve, even in a world filled with power-hungry men. She too had worked for – and, now, seemingly against – her government. Always trying to do the right thing.

To consider, even for a moment, that she might have done this great and terrifying thing, burying herself alive in this dark, cold place all alone, knowing nobody would remember her great deed…

Jesus Christ.

She instantly pictured herself in the same situation, wondering if she would be capable of making the same choice.

Maybe. Back during the war. Back when she was younger and more naive and didn't feel as if she had anything to lose. There had certainly been times when she had let the bloodlust, the adventure, get the better of her as she rushed into the fight. When she had been willing to give up everything and nothing at all in the heat of the moment.

Yet as she looked at her sister, and remembered her Dad's sad nod of acknowledgement back at Teddy's place, Sam knew she would struggle to let go of her family now. They needed her – and she had come to realise just how much she needed them too.

"Are you okay, Samantha?" Teddy asked.

She nodded, turning quickly so he didn't have time to recognise the lie. She led them onwards, following the torchlight into the dark once more.

They moved in silence now. Every so often coming to a turn or a choice of paths. And Teddy would stare at them as he mentally charted their course, mutter to himself in German, and then nod in whatever direction they needed to go.

"Easy to get lost down here," Will said after a while.

"And many have, Doctor Sandford. You might not have noticed, but we have passed quite a few of our predecessors along the way."

"We have!?"

"Yes, although it is difficult to tell their bones from the others. After a while, all death looks the same." Teddy put a gentle hand on Sam's shoulder to slow her down and pointed ahead to where the path finally came to an abrupt end. "Let us hope this is not our time to join them, eh?"

CHAPTER NINE

Trapped

The path finished at a stone wall.

Real stones this time, not bones. Thick and heavy and cutting straight across the tunnel. Deliberate and impassable.

But while others might have figured it for a dead end, Sam could see why they would be mistaken. Because across it, barely visible in the flickering torchlight having been worn away by centuries of damp, were inscriptions of all kinds. And not just 200-year-old graffiti. There were older markings too, including faded Latin words and what looked like some stylised versions of Ancient Egyptian hieroglyphs.

She ran her light over the wall, at each marking, trying to get an idea for the story here. There was always a story to be found in archaeology – Teddy had taught her that much. Even if she hadn't gone on to study the subject like her sister, she had been fascinated with the science, engaging her old friend in long discussions on those nights in England while they waited for air raids and sirens and death.

"There is always a context to an artefact," he had said. "A beginning, middle and end as to where it is found, why it is there, and what shape it is in. Follow the signs and you will be able to piece its story together."

So what's this wall's story?

Her fingers traced the grooves, clearly discerning the sharper, more recent markings. Her instinct immediately removed these from her focus, letting her see everything that was left.

If Teddy was right, Samantha Henri had passed this way to seal her fate. Yet Sam knew she wouldn't have left a clue behind to alert anyone to the possibility the Osiris Stone might be down here too.

No, only the older carved symbols and words mattered. Telling the visitors what to do next.

Unfortunately they were badly worn away.

Her gaze drifted to the walls on either side. It was only now she realised that they were no longer bones, but were formed of the same impenetrable grey stone that blocked their way ahead. And, in each, several skull-shaped niches had been cut in rows and columns to form a giant square. Some had been filled with human skulls. Others lay empty.

Beside the holes on the right-hand wall, Jess was tracing her fingers across a pictogram which had been painted showing skulls in two different patterns.

"Well this looks easy enough," Will said as he joined her, trying to sound as though he knew what he was doing.

"See there, above the pictograms, it's very faint but you can just about make out the Egyptian symbol for 'mirror', can't you?"

Jess laughed. "So we just put the skulls into the wall in the patterns depicted in the nearest pattern? That's easy!"

"So I thought, but I have tried and nothing happens." Teddy sounded disconsolate as he gestured downwards, where the light revealed several cracked and broken skulls littering the floor.

"And you lot call yourself archaeologists," Sam said. She lifted her torchlight back up to the pictogram. "It's a mirror, yes?"

"So?"

"Mirrors *reflect*. It's not referring to copying the pattern next to it, but reflecting the pattern on the opposite wall."

Teddy looked between the pictogram and Sam, then spun to the wall opposite where another set of skull holes could be found. "I am a stupid, stupid old man. How could it have been so simple and yet I still missed it?"

But even as his face lit up in triumph, and Jess and Will squeezed each other's hands in premature celebration, Sam couldn't help the frown that crossed her face. It seemed too easy. Too simple an explanation. If this was a test of some kind, it wasn't nearly hard enough to prevent the wrong type of people from getting past, surely?

Jess wasn't prepared to stand around any longer. She was already fixated on solving the problem, directing Will to rearrange the patterns that Teddy had previously tried on the opposite wall.

Sam meanwhile kept her eyes moving, warily scoping their surroundings, trying to suppress the horrible feeling that she was missing something.

Until she saw her sister pick up the final skull.

"Wait!" Sam yelled.

Too late. Jess slotted it into place.

For a moment, nothing happened. There was only silence.

But only for a moment.

Then two stone panels slid from the walls behind them and smashed together in the middle to seal the group into the chamber, before two holes opened in the walls above the pictograms – and thousands of spiders started pouring out.

Will screamed as they tumbled over him, crawling through his hair and down his neck. Jess quickly pulled him out of the hideous waterfall and helped him shake them out again.

"I told you to wait!" Sam chastised loudly, over the sickening pitter-patter as the creatures now poured directly onto the floor and started clambering over each other. She started looking for the reset mechanism. There was always a reset mechanism.

"But it's the right pattern!" Jess cried, clearly panicking, though not as much as Will, who was now doing his best to climb up her to avoid the spiders trying to crawl back up his legs. Sam pulled a face. How *had* he survived South America?

They quickly huddled in the centre of the room,

stamping and kicking out as the army of spiders quickly filled the floor.

But as quickly as they appeared, the deluge stopped. And rather than attack the group in their midst, the spiders began escaping through each and every tiny crack in the chamber walls and floor as fast as they could.

Sam frowned and flicked off one particularly large arachnid she saw still clinging to Teddy's back. It scuttled off into a corner and disappeared.

Will removed himself from Jess and tried to straighten his jacket without it seeming like he had been anything but calm in the last few seconds. His face still a beacon of embarrassment.

"Is that it? H-honestly, I was expecting a little more danger on this trip," he stammered.

"How did they even rig that to pour spiders out hundreds of years later anyway?" Jess asked, peering into one of the holes. "That doesn't make sense."

Stretching up, Sam felt around inside the other hole. Then brightened as her fingers found what they were looking for.

"There's a lever in here. Which means I don't think the spiders were part of the plan. They just happened to be hiding back there. And if you look in the other hole, I reckon there'll be another one. This is the next step in the puzzle. We just need to solve it to get out."

Jess shook her head. "You were right before. Maybe we need to wait and rethink–"

But Teddy had already stepped up, reached into his hole

and grasped the other lever. At a nod from Sam they pulled at the same time.

The room immediately shook as another stone wall dropped down over the others that had blocked their retreat a minute ago. If there had been any hope of prising their way out of this place, it was now gone. The chamber was locked down. Water tight.

Which was unfortunate, because with a tremendous roar water suddenly began gushing out of the lever holes.

"And I told *you* to wait!" Jess yelled at Sam through the spray. "At least I only unleashed a few damn spiders. Why do you always have to go one better?"

Sam looked around wildly for a clue to get them out of this mess. There had to be one. This was a test, wasn't it? What was the point in a test if it didn't have any questions.

It was then she spotted the markings on the stone door that had dropped from the ceiling.

"Another riddle!" she cried above the echoes of panic and churning water. Then, less enthusiastically, "Although it's badly worn."

"Water damage," Teddy said mournfully, looking at the rising water as it passed his knees.

He was right, but there was no time to worry about it now. Sam waded over to the riddle as fast as she could, pulling Will and Teddy with her. They might not be able to see the markings properly any more. But the story was still carved there.

"It's only two words we need to figure out. You can't see them, so feel them."

She forced their hands to the wall, running them over the first word, then the second. The splashes of water seemed to darken the dry stone and lend a little more visibility to their form.

"Broken," Teddy said hesitantly. "Yes, I think this one says broken."

Will was less sure. Eyes wide, his normally immaculate black hair askew, and water rising to his chest, he looked a man on the edge of losing control. Sam wasn't going to be able to persuade him to do it, she knew that now. Her men in France had been ready to command no matter the chaos around them. But that was war. This was… archaeology.

Thankfully Jess saw what was happening and swam over to put her hands on Will's. It was enough to snap him back into action, as together they ran their fingers over the symbols.

"I think I've got it," he said, glancing over his shoulder back to the original pictogram. "It's the word 'mirror' again."

"Broken mirror?" Sam yelled. The water was now lifting her off the floor. "How the hell does that help us? Do we need to take the skulls out again?"

But even as she said it, she knew that didn't make sense at all. Nobody would go to the trouble of designing this trap only to have you completely undo everything.

"Oh dear Gods, I've killed us all," Teddy said, splashing around as he tried to keep his head above the waterline.

Sam wiped her sleeve against her face, pulling her sodden hair out of her eyes. Trying to stay afloat in front of the carvings which were about to go underwater themselves.

"Are you sure that's it, Will?" she pleaded.

He ran his fingers back over it, then fell away in surprise. "No, it's not! The symbol… it's backwards!"

"Reverse the skulls!" Sam yelled, swimming over to the right wall where the skull pattern was fast disappearing into the murky depths. There was only a couple of feet of air left in the chamber now. Not long. "The broken mirror symbol is reversed. It has to mean the skulls need to be reversed between walls too."

Will was spluttering as he and Jess held onto each other, trying to keep their heads and the torches above the water. He was eyeing the ceiling above them as they rose closer to it.

"But how do you know that's what it means?"

"This isn't the bloody time, Will. Just get moving!"

Everything was cold and slippery as they got to work. Sam's fingers desperately clung to the skulls as she prised them from the holes on the right wall and swam them over to the left. It was an ingenious trap after all. Making someone have to think under pressure was the ultimate test. Getting them to remain calm, use logic, and act fast, even as death closed in around them – while still having faith about what awaited, to keep them determined enough to see it through.

If she hadn't been so worried about getting Jess out of here alive, Sam might have admired whoever built this chamber of doom.

But the water was rising too fast.

Again and again she grabbed a skull and swam to

the other side to place it in exactly the same spot on the other wall. Around her, the others did the same. Yet now they were having to dive into the dark water to retrieve the skulls on the bottom few rows. Which ate up more precious seconds. More air. More risk of losing everything.

Teddy was the first to stop. He placed his left hand on the wall and let himself float on the surface, gasping for breath. Will soon joined him.

Then Jess's head burst through the water. "I'm done!"

"I've just one more to go," Sam replied. She dove under the water and swam to the final spot. Shoved the skull into the last hole. And waited.

Nothing happened.

She rose to the surface in a storm of bubbled expletives.

"Well?" Jess yelled, clutching to the others. All three craning their necks back to breathe in the last of the air.

"Something's… wrong," Sam gasped. "Maybe we made a mistake."

Nobody responded. They were out of time. There were only a few gasps of air left.

"Take a deep breath and hang on!" Sam said and took one final dive.

It was only luck that her torch had held on this far. It had clearly been built to withstand rain and being knocked around. But not being drowned in a subterranean Parisian deathtrap.

So when it began to flicker, Sam took a mental snapshot of both walls. It went out a second later, yet she still had the images in her head.

And they *had* made a mistake.

Feeling her way across to the left wall, she quickly counted the holes to move to the third row where she'd seen a hole that was filled and one that shouldn't have been empty. Her lungs were burning now, her muscles aching with all the swimming, but she managed to grab the skull out of the wrong place.

Then it slipped from her grasp.

Oh god.

For a split second, she knew this was it. And as she squeezed her eyes shut, her heartbeat thudding in her ears, a part of her accepted it was time to die. There was no fancy technological gadget to save her this time. No supernatural tricks she'd learned while working for The Nine. It was a perfectly human failure of her own making. There would be no way she'd be able to find the skull again in the darkness as it fell to the floor. A moment of carelessness would cost her life and that of her friends.

Her sister.

It was the thought of losing Jess that made her strike out blindly.

And she wedged the skull against the wall with her knee.

With the last of her strength, she grasped it with both hands. Shoved it into the right hole.

There was a loud, dull click through the water. Something in the stone chamber gave way. She wasn't sure which way was up or down now. Her balance was fuzzy and it was growing dark in her mind. But as she felt herself slipping away…

…she slipped away.

Literally.

Down.

Through an opening in the floor as the water rushed out.

Into a sloping tunnel of mud.

Over and over she spun, thrashing, kicking, flailing. Gasping for air through the churning mud and water. Smacking into walls, cracking her feet, knees, elbows on what felt like stones but could well have been bones and skulls. Hearing the cries of the others around her.

Until suddenly it was over.

Out into the open darkness they flew and landed with heavy splashes in a shallow pool. For a few seconds, Sam's ear swam with water and the muffled cacophony of moans, groans and not a little cursing from her friends.

Then there was a striking sound from somewhere nearby and each of them immediately shielded their eyes as hundreds of flaming torches ignited around them, enveloping everything in warm, flickering reds and oranges.

Sam gave a sharp intake of breath as her fingers dropped away.

And she took in a sight nobody had seen in living memory.

The car pulled up to the kerb outside Notre-Dame Cathedral and two men emerged.

Dressed immaculately in charcoal black suits and red ties, with fedoras worn straight and true, Agents Taylor and Smith strode across the cobbles.

Taylor stopped in the shadow of the magnificent French building and lit a cigarette, trying not to shiver in the brisk early morning air. He maintained a watchful gaze as Smith continued to the guard's hut – where two other agents were waiting – and walked inside with barely a nod in their direction.

That was good. No formalities. All about the job at hand. Considering Smith's past, it was really no surprise to see him continue to act in such a way. But it was one of the reasons Taylor had brought him through the ranks quicker than the others. He might not have been keen on the younger man's history, but he certainly could appreciate what it offered him now. If Taylor was honest, Smith's dedication to duty was not far short of his own.

Perhaps thirty seconds later, no more, Smith left along with a large bald agent and the pair walked over.

"Well?" Taylor asked.

He didn't really need to hear the answer. He could already tell what had happened. The tank-like Agent Roach was wiping blood from his knuckles onto a handkerchief as he followed Smith. Taylor knew instantly that if there *had* been a guard in that hut, he or she was now bloodied and unconscious. Possibly even dead, given that Roach was pretty committed to the job too.

Taylor shifted and stared up at the cathedral, sucking in a long-needed lungful of comforting smoke. Of course, death of collateral was always unfortunate and he tried his best to ensure such things were rare. But tonight, he wasn't going to let it worry him. He had far bigger issues to focus on.

"I'm afraid the targets have already gone through," Smith said, with his curious accent. American, if you did not know better. But the hint of German they had been trying to smooth out of him was still there, like a crease in an otherwise finely ironed uniform.

Agent Taylor sighed inwardly as he regarded his colleague. This would not do at all.

"The guard was supposed to stall them. You told me you had taken care of it."

"I had."

"Then why are Captain Moxley and her band of troublemakers already in the Cathedral?"

Smith stared impassively through his unnaturally blue eyes. "It seems the guard did not appreciate the severity of the consequences should she not follow my instructions."

"Does she appreciate it now?"

Agent Smith turned to Roach. The man-mountain scrunched up the bloodied handkerchief, slipped it into his pocket and nodded. For the first time that night, Smith offered what appeared to be a smile.

"What do you want us to do with her?"

Taylor took another drag on his cigarette as he stared up at the huge rose window. A relic of a time long since passed. Unable to do anything but watch as life passed it by.

He felt almost defiant in its gaze. Strong. Powerful.

And why not? He had carved a role for himself on this Earth that necessitated action. Had become a key player in everyone's destiny. While others studied themselves into becoming the perfect cogs in society, he worked in the shadows oiling the machine. They baked bread or drove cars or taught or acted or simply flitted through the day without offering any meaning at all.

Meanwhile, he and his men made sure the sun rose in the morning. Protected the arc of the moon at night. Kept the monsters under the bed where they belonged.

It was agency and action at work. Interference too, some would argue – Samantha Moxley for one. But regardless, it meant no sitting on the sidelines watching the game. He *was* the game.

His cigarette fell to the floor and was swiftly crushed beneath his properly polished black brogues.

Sometimes in games people got hurt. Especially those who didn't follow the playbook when instructed.

"We can't have the French jumping all over this," he said.

Nothing more needed to be said. Smith signalled to the two men still standing by the hut, who saluted and entered. Then he turned back to Taylor.

"I'm glad you are doing what needs to be done."

Agent Taylor kept his gaze level, but his eyes narrowed ever so slightly at his brash blond colleague. "It isn't your place to be glad or otherwise. I didn't bring you back from Germany for your opinion, Agent Smith, only your particular brand of efficiency. You know what's at stake and what your job is here. Have you scanned for them?"

Smith gave a curt nod.

"And?"

"They are deep underground now. Too deep for even me to see. I can identify their trail to a point, but, if you want them, we will have to go in."

Taylor didn't know how Smith did it. But the man's unusual abilities were certainly useful. It was almost a pity that those responsible for him had been eliminated in Berlin during the war. Taylor would have given good money to see what else they were working on that he could have taken for American gain.

He raised his hand to give the signal.

Behind him, two more cars pulled up and five other agents got out and hurried over. They included two tall, faceless, suited figures of a size that made Roach look like a child.

Agent Taylor gave them a wide berth as they passed, feeling the blood pump through his veins just a little bit faster, then handed the guard's keys to Smith, and followed his unusual team towards the cathedral doors.

CHAPTER TEN

X Never Marks the Spot

Soaked to their bones, Sam and the others sat in the underground reflecting pool and gaped at the sight unfolding before them.

What a reflecting pool was doing down here, Sam didn't know. There certainly wasn't any daylight to reflect. But as the ancient torches lit up around them, and she tried to catch the breath she had come close to losing forever, she knew instantly that's what it was. A Roman reflecting pool, very much like the one she'd pushed that overeager bureaucrat into during a party at Hadrian's Villa in Tivoli two years ago.

Except this one was underground. Buried beneath Paris. In a large cavern that could easily have fit Notre-Dame Cathedral itself in with room to spare.

And as above, so below. Because what she saw before them was an exquisite temple complex, filled with stone tombs, pillars, and statues of all manner of men, women and gods – a veritable web of ancient artefacts sprawled out beneath the imposing gaze of a primeval version of the cathedral carved into the wall at the rear of the cavern.

And it was all being brought to life by the torch flames now flickering through the darkness for the first time in a hundred and fifty years.

"This doesn't look very eighteenth century French to me," Sam said.

"Roman," Will replied. "It's some kind of Roman cathedral. But… what is it doing *here*?"

Teddy pushed himself to his feet and helped Will up. "Paris fell to the Romans under the reign of Caesar himself and it was said that the catacombs were built upon a much earlier religious ground. But this... I would never have believed such magnificent history could survive like this."

Jess glanced over at Sam. "Do you think Samantha Henri knew about this place?"

Sam tilted her head. "I'd say this is exactly the place she was looking to end her adventures. Buried deep underground, on the other side of a trap that clearly nobody else has been able to solve in all these years." The acknowledgement made her feel slightly queasy. "If I was going to choose to hide a valuable artefact anywhere, this might be it."

"And your own life with it?"

Sam saw the questions she was asking herself mirrored in her sister's eyes, but she was too scared to answer truthfully. Instead, she waded to the edge of the pool and stepped up onto the surrounding wall beneath the warmth of one of the flaming torches.

"I'm not sure I could have done it," the younger woman admitted quietly, joining her. "All alone down here? Not really the way I'd like to go."

"Samantha Henri probably wasn't happy about it either," Sam replied, feeling somewhat protective of her namesake. "But I guess she did what she thought needed to be done to stop the artefact being lost to men who would use it for the wrong reasons."

"That's a tad cynical, don't you think?"

"Maybe. But show me a time in our history when such power was ever used for good."

Her sister sniffed dismissively. "There's always a first time for everything, Sam. Not all governments are as bad as you make out. Maybe you've seen the worst of them, but I refuse to believe there haven't been decent people among their number, trying their best to make a difference in the world. Who can say what they might have done with the knowledge they found – maybe it would have been enough to prevent the wars that you and Dad fought in? It could have changed everything for the better?"

Sam frowned, but didn't say anything. The idea that the horror of what she'd experienced could have been prevented was a surprisingly tempting concept to explore. The possibilities of so many lives left to play out of their own accord, rather than at the whim of bullets and bombs and fascists. Who knows what quiet, delightful life she might have carved out for herself if she'd had the chance? Dad too.

The doubt was strong enough to burrow and crawl

under her skin like those carnivorous scarabs she'd heard about once upon a time. What if Jess was right – what if Samantha Henri had committed a brave and honourable sacrifice without needing to? What if the French woman had overplayed the threat of what might have been and made the wrong call, changing everyone's fate for the worse?

And what if Sam was doing the same now?

Her spiralling unease was interrupted as Will raised a sodden sleeve and pointed to a pagoda-style tomb near the centre of the cavern. "Do you think that's where she did it?"

This particular tomb was larger than the rest. But what really set it apart was the small rise of stone – like an island – it had been set upon, surrounded by a dry circular "moat" in the floor, all of which lay in the very middle of the courtyard before the cathedral, like a macabre centrepiece.

"Fitting," Teddy muttered thoughtfully, "for such a noble deed."

Satisfied with that, Jess and Will started towards it. Leaping off the pool wall and striding across the cobbles. Leaving Sam and Teddy to stand alone, dripping wet, and suddenly wary.

"I've got a bad feeling," she said to him.

"Too obvious?"

"Too obvious."

Instinct was a wonderful thing at times like these. It had kept her alive in the past. A gut feeling, a prickling at the back of her neck, a sense or paranoia that *danger lurked here.*

But the fact she had others to worry about was clouding the instinct right now. Making it difficult to concentrate on what it was trying to tell her.

She climbed down from the wall and moved slowly after her sister. Her gaze took in the tomb and its surrounds, working out methodically from the centre. If this was a trap, where was the trap? They had already managed to beat the catacomb puzzle. Would the architects of that little box of fun have rigged another down here? It seemed overkill… but then this whole damn place was overkill.

It was then she noticed the flames of the torches around the little island all flicker vigorously simultaneously. As though from a breath of wind.

And behind each one, built into the cavern rock itself, she could see large carved lion heads. Each jaw gaping wide. Each pointing towards the torch before it – and down towards the tomb.

Sam's eyes widened. "Jess, wait!"

She leapt towards her sister, just as she and Will reached the moat. Pushing Will out of harm's way, she managed to grab Jess's arm. But Jess had already placed a foot beyond it.

There was a howl that seemed to swirl through the cavern walls like a hurricane. Sam imagined what was coming next and quickly rolled her sister around, bringing her crashing down to the cobbled floor just as jets of gas poured out of the lion mouths, were ignited by the torches, and engulfed the stone tomb and the entire island in flames.

And now the moat made sense. Because it contained some kind of oil residue which ignited and sent a wall of flames rearing up before them, keeping whoever might have survived the initial blast of fire from getting off alive – as well as now protecting the tomb from further inspection.

"Well, shit," Sam said. "You OK, Jess?"

Her sister nodded and sat up on her elbows, cheeks flush with the heat.

"I absolutely knew that was going to happen."

Sam winced as she touched the back of her head, where it felt like she'd been slightly charred. "Don't you know the old rule about X never ever marking the spot?"

"I'm sorry, it just looked like the obvious place to start."

"Well take it from an old hand at this kind of crap… *obvious* usually means *death*. Whoever designed these traps did so to pick off those that aren't thinking or who might be too eager for what the tomb held. Which is pretty much everyone here. So please don't go off investigating by yourself, okay? Always check with me first."

"Old hand is right," Jess muttered, getting to her feet and offering assistance to Sam, who took it gratefully and pulled herself up too. "You've aged so much recently you've got a real mother complex going on."

"It's a not-wanting-you-to-die complex, Jess," Sam replied wearily, gesturing to the big wall of fire in front of them as if to make the point. Maybe she was getting carried away with her role as guardian here, but on the other hand she couldn't help feeling Jess was getting off easy. She remembered the fuss their mother had caused that time Jess barely scraped a knee going box carting with her friends, and Sam could only imagine what furious tirade she would have unleashed if she could see them now.

Of course, Jess did now what she had back then, by rolling her eyes and waving away any suggestion she didn't know what she was doing. She sidled up to Will – who was still brushing himself down and throwing his fearful gaze between the fire and Sam, as if unsure which might be the more dangerous at this point – and put an arm around his waist. Then, as if to prove a point, she pulled them closer to the flames to warm themselves.

Sam bit back another admonishment, but only because she was so bloody freezing in her soaking clothes. Suppressing a shiver she found herself joining them, drawn to the comforting heat along with Teddy, and soon the four of them were rubbing their hands together and watching the steam rise from their quickly drying clothes.

"So who is going to go across?" Will asked after a few minutes. "We can't come all this way for the Osiris Stone to be beaten back by a little fire. One of us will have to jump through, right?"

His gaze flickered hopefully to Sam. She returned it with daggers.

"First of all, Will, *no*, I am not jumping through fire for a bloody rock, no matter how magical it may be," she replied firmly. "Second of all, it isn't in there. Whatever this was designed to protect can stay behind that fire for all I care. Samantha Henri would have seen this island and used it to her advantage. She was smart, remember? There is no chance she would have picked such an obvious spot to hide the artefact, even if it was this well protected."

Will's cheeks went even redder and Sam was sure it wasn't simply the heat. He clearly didn't appreciate the implication about the state of his intelligence. But she didn't have time to coddle him. Suitably warm and dry now, she moved away from the island of death, surveying the numerous coffins and tombs around them, all brightly lit in the glow of the fireball.

"She'll be somewhere dark," she said to herself. "Inconspicuous. In the shadows."

"Just like the woman herself and the life she led," Teddy commented, giving Sam a strange, almost paternal look of worry.

Now who's got a mother complex, she thought.

They moved off, each taking a different part of the temple complex to investigate. It was a slow and painful process, and before too long Sam's mind began to wander.

Back when she was with The Nine, she had enjoyed access to all manner of weird and wonderful tools of the job.

The dimension disc she'd used on Liberty Island had been one of her favourites. A one-time fix to removing any troublesome being – human or otherwise – from their current location and sending them to a much less pleasant one, far, far away.

The sandblaster had been another. Unleashing a whirlwind of quick-drying sand that could encase any mythical nightmare and hold it for a considerable period, until the retrieval team could come in and take it back to the lab for investigation.

But perhaps the most useful had been a simple pair of glasses – the lenses of which allowed you to see through pretty much any building material known to man.

Except obsidian, apparently. They'd been working on fixing that when she'd left.

On reflection, it had been a shitty day indeed when Taylor had decided to sanction the use of that technology derived from Agent Smith. Not least because that Nazi shitheel deserved nothing other than the quick and painful death he had been heading towards before they brought him in. But also she reluctantly had to admit those glasses had ended up saving her life quite a few times.

And – she considered, as she drifted through the numerous stone and wooden tombs in the underground temple – they would be bloody useful right about now.

"Anything?" Jess called from the other side of the cavern.

"Not yet," Will replied.

"Still looking," Teddy added.

"Sam?"

Sam sighed, brushing her fingers across the rough, worn lid of the stone coffin next to her, tracing the outline of a dragon's head on what looked like a large sailing vessel. "Nothing," she called back, moving on to the next ornately decorated tomb. Then the next. And another after that.

In the corner of her eye she saw the others continue their fruitless search carefully, all a little hesitant after the fireball incident.

Teddy was pale and shaken, but relentless in his tenacity. He had dreamed of getting past that catacomb puzzle and Sam knew him well enough to know he wasn't about to stop in his quest now. Meanwhile, Jess and Will were exploring separately, but made sure to glance over at each other every now and then to check in. It was really quite sweet. Or at least Sam would have felt it sweet if their circumstances weren't balanced precariously on a knife edge.

She let her gaze drift.

Following the line of pillars around the complex. Resting momentarily on each finely carved tomb she had just wandered through. Then drifting again to the right, where more collections of coffins had been placed proudly beneath the watchful gaze of some limbless stone gods.

Until it came to focus on the shadows in between.

There.

It wasn't clear at first. But instinct held her focus on that spot until her eyes acclimatised. And she saw an indistinct shape in the gloom slowly take the form of a rather plain looking stone coffin, half-hidden by the majesty of the others.

"That's where I'd go," she muttered to herself. A cold shiver ran the entire length of her spine, the disturbing connotations twisting and intertwining in her mind like the rotting roots of trees two hundred years apart. She raised her voice before she could pretend she hadn't seen it, before she shied away from finding out for sure. "Over here," she said loudly.

Teddy approached the coffin first, tentatively reaching

out a hand to touch it, then sheepishly retracting it and looking to Sam.

Sam gave him a wry smile. She'd already run her eyes over the immediate area, looking for any signs of traps and imminent death.

"No fireballs that I can see," she confirmed. "This is it."

Together the group pushed the heavy coffin lid. It slid slowly, stone grating against stone. Before, eventually, the weight pulled it over the edge and it tumbled to the ground with a crash that echoed around the cavern.

"What was that you said before about not breaking the archaeology?" Jess chided gently.

But Sam wasn't paying attention to the living people beside her now.

She was too busy looking at her predecessor.

CHAPTER ELEVEN

The End of an Adventurer

Samantha Henri's skeleton was smaller than Sam had considered it might be. Her ribs were collapsed and sunken beneath ragged clothes. Her skull lolling slightly to one side.

Despite all Sam's childhood fantasies of this legendary adventurer who had travelled the world and faced down unthinkable foes, in the end she wasn't a superhero or a goddess after all. She was simply a bundle of bones like everyone else, unable to cheat death.

Yet the dark holes of her skull were defiant and there was still an almost tangible energy to her remains, thick with strength and courage and sheer stubborn will, as if her spirit refused to leave its tomb, holding watch here along with whatever dark feelings she must have felt in the last moments of her life.

Sam suddenly felt more than a little intimidated. Was this what it took to save the world? Was this the fate that awaited those who did the right thing when it needed to be done?

And was the baton about to pass to her?

It was all so unfair. That governments and people could lie and cheat and steal, yet be free to live out their lives regardless of their actions. That they survived to rewrite history in whatever way they saw fit while this small thorn in their side was left with no choice but to secretly sacrifice herself to ensure the world continued to spin for another hundred or so years at least.

Sam's skin was clammy. A cold panic threatened to seize her from within and turn her insides out.

What if she wasn't even the right person to save her sister, let alone the world? What if she too ended up like this, facing an unimaginably lonely death?

As she heard the murmurs of awe from the others around her, she dug her fingers into the side of the coffin as discreetly as she could, trying to soak some of her idol's strength back into her. Even as Teddy gently reached out to pull aside the skeleton's sleeve, revealing bony fingers clutching an object, Sam closed her eyes and sucked in as much air as she could, until her mind grew light, the panic momentarily subsided, and she could focus again.

"Oh, it's beautiful," Will whispered reverently.

Sam blinked and looked back to the coffin. Teddy had gently moved aside more of Samantha's deteriorating clothes to reveal her hands clutching the piece that had led to her end.

Even half hidden in the remains, they could all see that it was something special.

"The Osiris Stone," Teddy confirmed, almost choking

back tears as he said it. "After all this time of searching for it, here it is. Here it is, Sam!" His hand grasped her shoulder and gave it a firm squeeze. "How can I ever thank you?"

"I did very little," Sam replied, nodding to the skeleton. "*She* did this."

"That she did," Teddy said, reaching in towards the artefact.

That was when Sam saw it. A thin, black wire leading from the corpse's forefinger into a bundle of rags beside her that at first glance looked like part of her clothes.

"Wait!" she shouted, snapping her hand out to stop Teddy from moving any closer. Then she slowly moved his hand away from the coffin as he, Will and Jess all stared at her as though she'd lost her mind.

"It's just a skeleton, Sam," Jess said. "I don't think she can hurt us."

Sam glared at her sister and drew their attention to the wire, followed it to the rags, and carefully lifted them up to reveal a set of rusty iron spheres sitting in what looked like a spill of gunpowder.

Teddy's eyes grew wide. "Oh. Oh dear. Are those some kind of grenades?"

"Uh-huh."

Jess clicked her tongue impatiently. "Oh come on, it's been over a century since these things were live. They can't still be dangerous?"

Sam looked pointedly towards the still flaming tomb nearby. "You willing to bet all our body parts on that, Jess?

I don't seem to recall it working out so well last time."

"Okay, *fine*. What do you suggest we do then, genius? We didn't come all this way just to let two eighteenth century bombs stop us from getting the damn stone. You can bet your sweet behind that your government pals won't walk away."

"Nobody is talking about walking away," Sam sighed. "But can we at least be careful? You don't go blundering about your archaeological digs like this, do you?"

Jess looked to Will for support, but he shrugged. "You *have* been known to go a little crazy when you find something exciting."

"Oh, shut up," she snapped back.

Sam pointed to a crude handle that had been nailed to the inside of the broken lid at their feet. "Look, that's how she did it. Made sure she was able to pull the lid over herself."

"Dear God," Will muttered.

Unfortunately, Sam was sure God had nothing to do with any of this. It was solely the work of mankind. Of greed and corruption rising to power. Forcing good people to make desperate decisions. To climb into their own graves.

She reached in and slowly tried to disentangle the mummified hands from the Osiris Stone. Moving the fingers apart millimetre by millimetre. Sweat dripping down her forehead. Down her nose. Down her back. As she slowly… so slowly… manoeuvred the fingers connected to the wire away from the artefact underneath.

Until she gently slid the Osiris Stone from the dead woman's grasp.

There was a palpable intake of breath around her as she lifted the magnificent stone, turning it over slowly in her hands to see the light reflect off its blue-green surface, which – unusually for a stone – seemed to be coated with some kind of metallic sheen.

As artefacts worthy of dying for went, she had to admit it was pretty special. And the perfect companion piece for the Isis Amulet.

Beside her, Teddy coughed loudly. She muttered an apology and handed it over, before turning her attention back to the French heroine who had sacrificed so much to keep the stone safe.

"How I have waited for this moment," Teddy whispered like a lovestruck schoolboy. Will and Jess stared, similarly enchanted, over his shoulder. "Years of study and a dream I had given up on. Now I hold the final piece of the puzzle. The end is near."

"That's what I'm afraid of," Sam said quietly.

She watched as her old friend took the piece further towards the light of the torches, resting it on the flat surface of another tomb. Running his fingers over it, carefully examining the strange, otherworldly design and markings. Unable to help the smile take over his face, as he realised the last stumbling block had fallen in his lifelong search for the most important archaeological discovery of all time. He had what he needed to go to Giza and go down in history as the man who found the Hall of Records, eclipsing all of his peers and all those naysayers who had made a mockery of his work.

Meanwhile, Jess and Will pored over it with him, and Sam was unable to resist seeing the twinkle of fame and fortune in their eyes as they likely dreamed up another exhibition.

Yet all she felt was sick.

She looked down at the body in the coffin, seeming almost naked without the stone it had protected for so long. And in her imagination she thought she could see a faint look of disappointment in those dark recesses of the skull, as if Samantha Henri herself was trying to tell her something. To warn her not to do this.

Sam's fingers dug into the rim of the coffin again. She wanted to vomit.

"Are you okay, Samantha?" Teddy called over suddenly. "You look like you've seen a ghost."

Perhaps I have, she thought.

When she looked up from the corpse, she found herself on the verge of pleading with them. She tried to keep the emotion from her voice, but it was a struggle to do so. There was too much at stake here now. Too much riding on the decisions they were about to make.

"This isn't what she would've wanted," she said.

Teddy's shoulders dropped guiltily. He knew enough to understand the conflict facing Sam right now. But Jess and Will simply stared at her.

"What does it matter?" her sister said, pulling a face. "She's dead."

Sam bit back a cutting reply. Jess was still too young, with too much of her life ahead of her to understand what Sam and Teddy could see. And it seemed Will was the same.

"I'm sorry, Captain, but Jess is right. She's dead… and has been a long time, in fact. She's got no say anymore. Her work here is done. She protected the Osiris Stone when nobody else could and she kept it out of the wrong hands for long enough. But now it needs to be reunited with its mate. It deserves this ending."

Jess nodded enthusiastically. "Plus, if the Hall of Records is as powerful as Teddy says, it needs to be found by us, not your gun-happy friends in the government. Hell knows what they'll do with what they find if they uncover that place. We both know they don't really care about history, or archaeology or knowledge. *We* do. *We* can be the ones to take over the stone's guardianship now. *We* can be the ones to bring it to the people and make sure the whole world benefits, not just one little branch of political influence. A treasure like this… like the Hall… it belongs to everyone."

On any other day, in any other life, Sam could have seen herself submitting to such an impassioned plea. Her sister truly believed what she was saying, that much was clear. And there was a part of her that wanted to believe it too. It would be far easier to believe that there could be a happy ending to this.

But she could not.

"You don't understand, Jess, Will. Samantha Henri died to protect the Osiris Stone. To keep it safe. She gave her life to make sure it didn't fall into the hands of those who would use it for their own criminal gains. And here we are, about to take it from the one place it's been safe all this time, because we have the arrogance to think we can do better than those who came before." She straightened and looked to Teddy for support. "I think we're about to make a huge mistake, Teddy."

His face dropped. But not because he understood, she suddenly realised. Because he was too caught up in this now to let go of his dream.

"Mademoiselle Henri did what she needed to do, Samantha," he said gently. "I do believe your sister is right. It is time to play our part."

"Our part? No. This has to be the end of it. The stone should stay here." She put both hands on the edge of the coffin and leaned down over the corpse, trying to keep the emotion out of her voice and failing badly. "Look at the sacrifice she made. She gave up everything, from her family to her last breath. She could have thrown the bloody thing into the river and nobody would have found it for decades, if ever. But even then she didn't trust that one day it wouldn't be dredged up somehow. This was the only way she knew to keep it safe. Down here, with her, protected to the last. The woman climbed into her own tomb for God's sake. We can't undo this."

Teddy walked over to Sam. Placed a hand on her shoulder.

The look of understanding he gave her was everything. She was scared of continuing this story. Scared of where it might take her. Scared that she was not up to it – or, worse still, that she was.

He knew it all. But his decision had already been made.

"We have no choice, Samantha. Your sister and Dr Sandford are both right. This great woman died to protect the stone and guard the secrets of the Hall of Records. But I do not believe she did it to keep its knowledge secret for all eternity."

"Then for what? Why did she do it, Teddy?"

"To buy us all some time. Until another as worthy as her came along."

Sam opened her mouth, but whatever words she might have had ready to argue her point stuck fast to her tongue. She merely gaped, glancing back and forth between the skeleton and Teddy a couple of times as her fears came to fruition.

"*Me*?" she asked.

Teddy's beard twitched and his cheeks coloured. "I meant *me*," he said, removing his hand from her shoulder and wrapping it across the stone as if she might suddenly try to grab it off him.

"Oh." There wasn't much else she could say to that. She could feel the three of them staring at her now and her own cheeks threatened to burn brighter than any torch in this underground temple. "I mean, yes, of course it should be you. Sorry."

"What's *wrong* with you?" Jess asked. "Did you hit your head on the way down that mudslide?"

The way she was looking at Sam suggested she hadn't

seen this side of her older sister before. And, Sam realised with regret, perhaps she hadn't.

She'd gone to war when Jess wasn't even yet a teenager. Had come back hardened and protective. The fighter pilot turned surrogate mother. The government agent who kept her job – and her fears – well hidden.

Secretly, she knew it was why they hadn't spent that much time together in the last couple of years, even though they'd both been living at home together with Dad. How *could* Jess know the torment that drove Sam? Knowing how good people in conflict often ended up dying horrible deaths, cold and alone. That sometimes doing the heroic thing did not always end up as gloriously as the stories made out.

She returned to staring at the corpse whose path she had just chosen to follow, for better or worse. *I'm sorry,* Sam said in her mind to the dead woman, as she reached into her pocket and felt the amulet beneath her fingers. *I shouldn't have led them down here. But I will make sure we do the right thing now.*

"Sam?"

"I'm fine," she lied.

"Good. Then if you're quite finished, can we get out of here?"

They couldn't as it turned out.

Because at that moment explosive gunfire erupted through the cavern. Chips of stone flew in all directions around them as bullets peppered walls, pillars and tombs, and they all dove for cover – before the shooting stopped and a cold American voice with a hint of German spoke.

CHAPTER TWELVE

Bad Blood

"Apologies, Captain," Agent Smith called across the cavern. "Our trigger fingers must have slipped. I do hope we didn't startle you."

His words were clipped, but there was a trace of enjoyment in his tone. And why wouldn't there be, Sam thought sourly. He'd finally bested her.

She rested her head against the cold stone coffin she hid behind with Jess and chastised herself. She'd been so preoccupied with worrying about the final destination of this journey, it had escaped her notice there was a far greater chance of ending up dead much sooner.

Quietly, she unclipped her holster and eased out the revolver.

"You should know well enough by now that I'm not easily startled, Smith," she yelled back, disguising the lie as best she could. She checked the chamber to ensure it was fully loaded. What she wouldn't give to have a dimension disc or two on her right now. She'd love the chance to send that bastard to a place that would make him catatonic for the rest of his unnatural life.

"I didn't come prepared to fight," Jess whispered, staring at the gun.

"I know."

"Do you have enough bullets in that thing to take them all out?"

She snapped it shut. "No."

"What do we do then?"

Sam didn't have an answer for that yet. Instead she spun and peeked over the edge of the coffin. There were at least eight men in suits on the far side of the cavern. Smith and Roach stood out clearly. But even Roach was dwarfed by two other gigantic, sprawling figures that seemed out of place wearing finely tailored getups, their fedoras pulled too tightly over their foreheads, casting their faces in permanent shadow.

Her heart dropped like a stone into a pit of tar and any hope she was clinging to sank with it.

They brought the Shade Men.

At least, that's what the US Government called them. She didn't know exactly what they were. Had only heard rumours they were some kind of spirits… entities that weren't quite of this realm of existence. Which was ridiculous, but no less ridiculous than most of what she'd experienced in the past. Either way, she knew well enough that they were different. Made entirely of shadow, which made them almost impossible to kill.

"Samantha," another voice called.

Taylor. She hadn't seen him with the others, but she knew he must have been there. He wouldn't have let Smith out on his own to run things, not with Shade Men along for the ride. The devastation they could cause unguided was something even this dark, twisted part of the American Government couldn't live with – and for all Taylor's faults, of which he had many, he wasn't the type for that kind of bloody outcome.

Nevertheless, Sam's finger twitched over the trigger.

"I am sorry it had to come to this," Taylor continued. "You must understand that I have tried to avoid coming up against you in this matter. Given our past working relationship–" Someone laughed coldly. Sam didn't have to see to know it was Smith. "–I had hoped we could undertake such a journey of discovery together. But after the scene you caused in New York we couldn't let it go. As you can appreciate, my superiors were not happy."

"They're not happy about much these days, I seem to remember. As for our history–"

Before Sam could stop her, Jess risked a peek over the coffin to see what was going on. The stone exploded and they were showered in fragments as gunfire erupted again.

Sam immediately leaned out of the side and took out the gunman with a single shot to the forehead, before ducking back again and giving her sister a glare.

"Sorry," Jess breathed, brushing rubble out of her hair. "I didn't think they'd actually shoot. I mean, didn't you used to be on their side? You and Taylor were a thing, right?"

"I don't have many regrets, Jess, but he'd be one of them."

Even now, Sam could imagine Taylor was likely directing his men into a striking position ready to take them. But alive or dead?

"That was hardly sporting, Sam," Taylor called, his voice clearly only just holding onto whatever semblance of politeness he had left. The strain was getting to him. That was something, at least. "You know he was one of my best men."

"Fuck your best men," Sam taunted, looking around for a way not to die down here and seeing very little in the way of hope. She knocked the back of her head against the coffin, angry with herself for not scoping the place out for an exit sooner, and yelled, "It's not like you don't have plenty of so-called patriots lined up to take his place."

She mentally calculated the distance needed to get back to the reflection pool. But the results weren't promising. Even if they could somehow get past the agents, it would not be easy getting back up the mudslide tunnel that had brought them down here. Plus, she would have to kill most of the men – including Taylor – before they even attempted it, otherwise they would be easily pursued and most likely executed on the spot.

Then there were the Shade Men. They would be a problem.

"There are patriots and there are patriots," Taylor called back, as Sam continued scoping out their immediate surroundings. "But working for The Nine demands a high level of something else, as you well know."

"Stupidity?" Jess whispered beside her.

"Desperation," Sam corrected, with a wry smile. "Joining them was the price I paid to get you away from the war. The stupidity came later when I realised how much they were abusing their power and yet I still fell for Taylor's crap about duty and doing what's right."

"Well if it makes you feel better, from what I saw before his friend tried to blow my head off, he is pretty handsome. Don't feel too bad."

"Stow it, Jess. I need to think."

It was then Sam looked past Teddy and Will crouching behind a towering statue of Athena and caught a glimpse of something promising – what appeared to be a gateway underneath the main cathedral pillars. Sam wasn't sure that Mademoiselle Henri would have picked a location to hide the Osiris Stone that had two entrances. But the way she saw it they had little choice but to run into the darkness she saw there, head further underground, and just hope that in there, somewhere, was a way out.

"Let me just kill her now," she heard Smith hiss, his words echoing around them.

The fact Taylor didn't reply to his colleague immediately told her that she still might have some leeway with him. There might yet be a part of him that wasn't willing to commit to killing her just yet. But she wasn't sure if that goodwill would extend to her friends. He was a man used to getting what he wanted and the fact that he hadn't got the Amulet or the Stone yet meant that his patience would be wearing thin. It might not be that long before the talking stopped and the killing started.

"Come over here and say that to my face, you goose-stepping prick," Sam replied to Smith, only partly trying to buy them some time. She quickly whispered to Jess to start taking the others back, towards the gateway, where there were enough tombs littering the ground that she figured they could all crawl from cover to cover for most of the way. After that there would be a dash across fairly open ground and the hope of safety beyond.

"I see your British sense of humour is still very much intact," Taylor sighed loudly. "It was always my favourite of your qualities. Although that's not why we are all here today in this predicament, of course. Call it determination. Call it bravado. Perhaps even luck. We recognised all these qualities in your work during the war, which is why we collected you from that beach when we did and gave your sister and father a new life in the free states of America – at great cost to the American Government, I might add."

Sam barked a laugh as she watched Jess scrabble silently across the floor to the others and nudge them towards escape. "We both know I've repaid that debt in full, Taylor. And, besides, it's not like you weren't finding homes for far less deserving people, isn't that right, Smith? A high-ranking member of the German army and one of the finest Nazis in the homeland… now a true-blue American hero. The founding fathers might have a thing to say about that."

There was silence for a moment. Unnerving quiet.

Taylor had been quick-witted and charming ever since

they had first met. Words came to him easily, no matter how unusual their situation – and the pair of them *had* been in some particularly unusual situations over the years. So any time he went quiet, she knew it was time for someone to worry.

Another shot was fired as one of the agents caught sight of the others flitting between tombs. The bullet clipped the ground next to Teddy's leg, just as Jess pulled him into cover again.

This time when Taylor spoke, his voice had shifted position. And it kept moving now, keeping her off-balance. "We did what we did for the betterment of America and the world. Just as we are doing now. You don't have to like it, but you know we are in the right, Sam. Give up this fight and let us have the pieces we seek, and you have my word that we'll let you and your friends leave this wretched place alive."

Sam shifted against the coffin, gun raised.

I happen to love Paris, you bastard.

And she was about to tell him so, when she peeked around the corner to see Taylor standing where the two Shade Men had been, next to their crumpled – empty – suits.

Shit.

The son of a bitch had set them loose.

Fear rose, paralysing her, but she swallowed it back down again. Centring her mind as she ran through the senses.

It was a trick she'd learned in France in those early days

when luck was the only way you could survive, before you figured how to increase the odds yourself.

Picking five things you could see in that moment. Then four things you could hear. Then three things you could feel…

Her fingers closing around the clammy metal grip of the gun. The rough stone rubbing against the back of her jacket. The gritty feel of the dust she ground into the cobbles with the heel of her boot.

These feelings were enough to ensure she never made it to two.

Had never needed to, in fact.

Because by three the fear was always contained again. Compartmentalised and hidden away while she cracked on with whatever terrifying thing she had to do next. And, yes, she might still die, but at least right now she could move again – allowing her to look around for the Shades, knowing that she might not be able to see them directly, but would be able to spot movement in the periphery. That was always how they had been able to inflict damage in the field. They were only visible in the corners of your eye.

"We both know you can't let us leave," she replied, playing for time. Jess had stopped at the final tomb before the open ground. She, Will and Teddy were all staring back, urgently beckoning Sam to follow. She held a finger up to tell them to wait. "You'll have us killed before we even reach the catacombs. Just more bones collecting dust under the streets of Paris."

"Sam, you have always misunderstood my intentions,"

Taylor replied, and for a second she thought she could hear the sincerity in his voice. No, she chided herself. Don't fall for that crap again. Even if he's not lying, he unleashed the Shades. He's not playing about now. He continued, "I'm not in the habit of killing innocent citizens. Freedom for all, whatever the cost, remember? We are here to protect and safeguard the world, keeping the darkness at bay. But in doing so we must be able to access the knowledge that can help us achieve those goals. Information such as that residing in the Hall of Records."

"You'll never find it," Will shouted.

"I'm afraid you are sadly mistaken, Dr Sandford. You might hold the keys to opening its secrets, but from where I'm standing you do not have many options left. I do not wish to leave you down here to rot with the other corpses. You lost your exhibition in New York, but there can always be others, so why don't you leave the Hall to us and get on with your careers. There is an entire world of archaeology out there after all."

As the seconds of silence dragged on she wondered if Jess and Will were considering the offer. Did they seriously believe him? She could only hope Teddy was whispering some sense into them before they made a mistake, because–

There was a flash of shadow to her left.

A roar in her ear.

Then two meaty hands pulled Sam into the air and threw her backwards.

Someone screamed. Jess, perhaps. Maybe Will. She only barely heard it as she felt what seemed like every bone in her body crack when she hit a thick, round pillar and landed in a crumpled heap at its base. Her vision swam. All ancient stone, tombs and torchlight, now lit up in flashes of gunshots as the agents decided to close in.

"Run," she moaned to the others, tasting the salty, metallic tang of blood pooling under her tongue. She spat it into the dust. "Get out of here."

She went unheard in the din around her. Another flicker of darkness caught her attention and she kicked out hard, rolling away as the creature swiped for her. Not quick enough. It grabbed her boot and dragged her back.

"Sam?" a voice called.

Teddy, panicking.

"Go," she cried.

It took all her strength to be heard, but when she opened her eyes she caught a glimpse of the others finally making a break for it. The gunfire increased as they ran across the open ground. Yet as Sam was flung like a rag doll into another pillar, she saw that they had nearly made it.

There was a chance Jess and the others would get out. Then it would be just her, the agents, and the shadow creatures.

Even as she landed on the floor, she felt victorious… until she heard Smith chanting through the cacophony of gunfire and roaring, and a whole new sickening noise began to fill the cavern, somewhere between the tearing of flesh and bones breaking.

The dead, she realised with horror… breaking free of their tombs.

Oh come ON. When the hell had he learned to do that?

She watched, bleary eyed, as Roman soldiers, still clad in terrifying helmets and deteriorating armour, lifted lids and smashed their way out of what should have been their final resting places. Rusted swords were swiped this way and that, as they staggered to their feet in a blind fury.

Jess screamed as bony fingers struck out from the earth and clawed at her feet. Will stomped on the arm until it snapped from the body. Teddy then kicked it aside as he ran past.

"I warned you," Taylor said as he watched from a safe distance, a touch of regret in his voice. "Why do you never believe me when I say I will follow through on my threats? You and I both know how important this find could be for us. And what we must be willing to do to make it ours."

Sam got unsteadily to her feet, just as a tall soldier corpse with half a face lunged for her. She punched it in its one eye, thankful that at least this thing had some mass to it. Something to fight.

Yet as it stumbled back, she watched in horror as it fell into what must have been the Shade and was lifted into the air and suddenly torn apart by a flicker of darkness.

She staggered away from the explosion of bones, pushing through other grabbing arms and screaming skulls as they lunged for her, feeling them tear at her jacket, at her hair, scratching her face, fighting against the urge to use her gun on them, knowing it wouldn't make any difference…

…only to free herself and come face to face with the upright corpse of Samantha Henri.

Paralysis hit. She skidded to a halt, breath caught in her throat, feeling the stink of death envelop her like a moving smog. She was only able to stare, unblinking, as her dead hero blocked her way out.

It's not Samantha Henri, Sam thought, trying to convince her body to move. Her legs, weak and trembling, refused to cooperate. *It's just whatever dark magic that cold-blooded bastard Smith has used to reanimate her. She's not in there. It's not her.*

The corpse screamed and tried to lift her arms to grab Sam, but something stopped her.

The grenade wires, which were still tied to her fingers – which meant the grenades were still on her.

Sam dove forward, grabbed the woman who long ago had sacrificed everything to save them all, and spun her around.

"I'm so sorry," she gasped, as she pushed the squirming corpse face-first back into her coffin.

Then, as she saw the agents, corpses, and at least one Shade begin to surround her, she dove back towards the exit where the others had run and grabbed a torch off the wall.

"Good luck with your fortune and glory, boys," she cried, hurling the flame with as much accuracy as her agonised muscles could muster. It flew over the heads of the hordes of Roman mummies. The Shade flickered and recoiled, but it missed that too. Only to land harmlessly in Samantha Henri's coffin.

Smith laughed as he drew near. "You'll have to do better than that, Captain!"

At which point Samantha Henri stood, engulfed in flames.

And the grenades hidden in her clothes exploded.

CHAPTER THIRTEEN

Escape!

Sam ducked as the ball of fire ballooned outwards through the doorway, over her head, singeing her hair and the back of her legs. In the midst of the explosion and the crack of the coffin shattering, she could hear the cries of the nearby agents and howls of the corpses as they were flung away. But sweetest of all was the agonised roar of at least one of the Shades as it was extinguished from this world for good.

She got to her feet as fast as she could and ran down the darkened tunnel, feeling the cool, damp air give some relief to her scorched skin. Her hand torch had fallen in the cavern somewhere, but the others clearly still had one up ahead and she let the bobbing light lead her through the otherwise pitch-black tunnels.

"Samantha," Teddy called. "Oh, good grief, girl. Look at you!"

Jess spun and shone the torchlight directly into Sam's face, causing her to throw up her arms in protest.

"Jesus Christ, are you trying to finish me off?"

"Sorry, Sam, just making sure it was you. I don't know what the hell I just saw back there, but it's made me question pretty much everything I know about the world at this point. What the hell was all that? What just happened?"

Sam tried blinking away the glare temporarily burned into her retinas. "Spirits and dead men and a whole lot of fire," she replied curtly. "No time to get into it now. Have you still got the Osiris Stone?"

"I have it," Will said.

"Great, then let's get the hell out of this nightmare."

They pushed on, following Jess's torchlight as it bounced through the subterranean maze. Every now and then Sam caught a glimpse of their surroundings – cut-stone walls, reliefs in the ceiling. The Romans had certainly kept themselves busy down here all those years ago. It made her wonder just what else was hiding in this place.

No more coffins, she hoped.

It wasn't long before through the clatter of their fleeing footsteps she could hear shouting from behind them. A glance over her shoulder saw a couple more beams of light appear in the distance.

"Faster," Sam urged, feeling her lungs – and pretty much every other part of her – burning in agony from the fight with the Shade.

Jess stumbled over a crooked paving stone, then skidded to a halt to shine the torch up a side tunnel. It was lined on both sides by tall statues of Roman soldiers who either seemed ready for a parade or an execution. But it was the doorway at the end, with a soft light drifting down the steps beyond it, that had their full attention.

"What do you think?" Jess asked. Sam didn't have the energy to respond. She simply nodded and rounded the corner, hearing the others follow.

Yet as they sped up the corridor, someone stepped on something they shouldn't have and there was a soft scrape of stone and the click of mechanisms being activated in the walls. Sam only just reached out in time to pull Jess to a stop, as a huge curved blade swung from the ceiling across the corridor, close enough to lift their hair in its breeze.

Will let out a miserable groan as he joined them. "Why was everyone in the past so intent on killing everyone in the future?" he asked, watching more blades slice the tunnel ahead, before bursts of flame spewed across the path at regular intervals.

"Are you saying this *isn't* why you got into your line of work?" Sam replied, wiping her jacket sleeve across her bloodied face. "The study of long-lost civilisations. How they lived. How they died. Lots of death in archaeology I always thought?"

"Other people's deaths, Captain. Not ours."

Sam retreated to the beginning of the tunnel and peered around the corner, back the way they had come. Her revolver was up, waiting for the agents to appear.

"Everyone look around," she ordered. "There's got to be a switch to turn this all off. There's always a reset."

Jess pointed up the corridor. "Is that it, at the end of the hall? I can see a chain next to the final statue."

"That's it." Sam sighed and adjusted her position. Torch lights had finally appeared behind them, but they weren't moving very fast yet. Agent Taylor probably didn't want any more surprises. They still had time to do this. "Jess, take my gun. I'll go for the switch."

But when she looked back, she saw her sister was already standing on the edge of the traps.

"I found the amulet, Sam. I can do this too."

"No, Jess–"

"You have to trust me."

Sam took a breath, feeling the burn in her chest where she'd hit the pillars. She didn't like it, not one bit. But what choice did she have? If there was a chance of getting down this corridor to reset the traps, it meant someone going who wasn't clutching broken ribs.

"I'm so tired of this shit," she muttered. She leaned around the corner and angrily fired off a couple of shots at the torchlights. One immediately spun and fell to the floor – and she felt better for hearing the cry of anguish that accompanied it. "Okay, just go. But don't make me regret it, Jess. Dad will be furious if I have to take you back in pieces."

Jess glanced over her shoulder, seemingly surprised and slightly nervous. Maybe she'd been expecting Sam to refuse. Maybe it had all been for show and she really didn't want to do this after all.

But the decision had been made now. With only the slightest hesitation, she stepped forward into harm's way.

She jumped through the first test easily enough. And

after each test, she stopped and contemplated the next, quickly finding a rhythm for both the swords and the fire.

Duck, slide forward, wait for the flames, then slide forward again.

"Oh God," Will kept muttering.

But Sam had already calculated the way through the traps. Her brain couldn't help but instinctively analyse any given situation and map a way through it – no matter how ridiculous or deadly it might be. And she could tell that Jess had picked it up too.

She spun at more movement in the corridor behind them.

BLAM. BLAM.

The noise of the shots echoed around her. Neither found a target this time, but again the torch light paused and waited far enough away to be safe.

"You can't escape, Sam!" Taylor called from the darkness.

Trying to get a fix on her position, most likely. She ignored him, picked up a pebble from the floor and chucked it further down the main corridor, away from the agents.

It bounced. They fired in its direction. She popped out of cover and shot again, taking out another agent and earning her a choice set of curses in German.

That son of a bitch Smith was still alive then. She'd have to aim better next time.

She reached into the still damp insides of her jacket to check the ammo she always carried. Just a couple of rounds left. Clearly she hadn't foreseen just how much trouble they could get into in the city of love.

Teddy looked horrified as he watched her load the two pitiful bullets.

"Hurry, Jess!" he called over his shoulder.

"But be careful!" Will added.

Sam held her breath as she saw her sister instinctively turn to hear what they were saying… only to almost get hit by a rusty Roman blade swinging back towards her. She twisted at the last moment and dove forward, losing only a sliver of her sleeve – which drifted to the floor, to be neatly incinerated in a jet of fire a second later.

"Will you all shut the hell up?" Jess shouted back. "I'm trying to concentrate on not being sliced, diced and cooked alive here!"

But as she stepped forward to continue the final few yards, there was the very definitive click of another mechanism being activated, followed immediately by Jess yelling and sliding forward, as the floor opened up in front of her.

For a second – the longest second of Sam's life – she was sure that was it was all over. As more tattered, decomposing arms immediately writhed out of the darkness to reach for Jess, a whole slew of images ran through Sam's mind of her little sister growing up. Swaying on the worn red swing in the park behind their house. Riding Sam's old bike, with their father running behind, her arms aloft as he celebrated her staying upright – before she immediately crashed into a telegraph pole. The two of them throwing peas across the kitchen table at each other while their mother baked sweet-smelling cakes.

Sam felt her knees giving way, even as she watched as her sister leap.

It wasn't a thing of beauty, only an act of desperation, and Sam knew that if it had been her in that moment she wouldn't have had the strength and would have been swallowed whole by the darkness. But somehow Jess made it, avoiding the fingers of death and managing to grasp the edge of the opposite side, before pulling herself up quickly and rolling out of the way of a final burst of flames erupting out of the wall.

She paused only to catch her breath and pat down a small fire on her skirt. Then she reached for the thick chain at the end of the corridor and heaved it down.

Everything immediately stopped trying to kill them. The floor closed up again. The fire ceased and the swords swung back into the walls and ceilings.

"Ta-da!" Jess called back with a tired grin.

Teddy and Will ran. Sam fired off a couple more shots around the corner for good measure, then turned tail and followed them up the corridor, between the statues, and up the stairs at the end.

But not before she gave the chain a quick tug herself and heard the satisfying sounds of ancient murder start up again behind her, just as the government suits emerged from the darkness and began firing.

CHAPTER FOURTEEN

River of Bones

They hugged the wall of the staircase as it circled up through the cavernous heart of the underground lair. Whatever this place was, Sam knew it must have been something special. Her fingers skimmed mosaics and artworks adorning the blocks of stone around them. Scenes depicting ancient rituals. The early Parisian landscape. Villas and people and a whole lot of history that nobody had seen in some time.

Will began to slow down, though Sam knew it was not from tiredness. He might not have been too helpful in a fight, but she had already noted he kept himself in shape.

No, his academic mind just couldn't help himself.

"There's more archaeological treasure here than I've ever seen," he murmured, pausing to inspect a particularly grand mural of the Roman gods basking on the Seine. "All these undiscovered artworks. Can you imagine–"

"This stuff won't be any good to you dead, Will," Sam cut in, before he got too carried away. "Keep moving."

Where they were going, she had no idea. They were

going up, yes, but she had a bad feeling that it wasn't going to be quite so easy as reaching the surface, popping out of a manhole in the Parisian streets and hailing a cab home.

The roaring soon gave it away. Even over the group's heavy footfalls and gasps for breath, she could hear it now. Filling the tunnel they found themselves in. Echoing across the stones with such force that she wondered if they were about to be hit by a subway train.

"That can't be good," Jess said.

"It never is," Sam replied.

They entered a large chamber, through which ran a vast underground river. On the far shore the water thrashed and swirled past the feet of a tall, imposing statue of Neptune, while on this side a dozen life-size stone soldiers lined the walls either side of the doorway.

Except…

…they weren't statues.

They were moving, pinned to the floor by spears thrust straight through their bodies from tip to tail. Sam wasn't sure if they had been a singular sacrifice in honour of Neptune or a warning to any who ventured down here.

But either way, it appeared that whatever dark magic Agent Smith had invoked was strong enough to carry this far and awaken these dead men. And, even now, she could see that several of them weren't far off extracting themselves from their skewers.

"Don't look at them," she said to the others, gesturing to the large metal, coracle-shaped shield that each soldier still clutched. "Just grab a shield and let's go."

She could barely make herself heard over the deafening noise of the river. So she decided to lead by example, walking up to the nearest horror show and ripping the shield away from the struggling corpse. It screamed, but the thrashing arms were too slow to grab her.

It wasn't long before each of them had a shield. They stood lined up on the river's edge.

"Exit?" Jess shouted, pointing to where the churning water ran into the darkness.

Sam nodded with a grimace. Her lungs burned, her ears rang. Her entire being seemed on the verge of collapse.

"Exit!?" Teddy and Will said in unified horror.

Will waved his shield in her face. "This is two thousand years old, Captain! How in God's name do you know it won't fall apart when I get on it?"

She contemplated this for a moment, but in the end she knew there was nothing she could say that would convince him this was a good idea. Hell, even *she* didn't think this was a good idea.

Yet they had no choice. She dropped his shield in the water and pushed him into it. He barely had time to open his mouth to protest before he shot off into the dark.

She nodded to the others, then jumped in after him.

The noise of the river was everything. Sam couldn't even hear her own cries as it threw them around like ragdolls, the sense of death narrowly passing by unmistakable.

And then it got worse, as a bullet whizzed past and

exploded into the tunnel ceiling ahead – creating a burst of light that for a split second illuminated the jagged hell they had all thrown themselves into. Rocks shot past on all sides. Some cut through the water like shark fins. And above, horrifyingly, Sam caught a glimpse of the ceiling moving as even here corpses were coming to life. Reaching to pull themselves free from their rocky graves, before dropping into the river like a hailstorm from someone's worst nightmare.

If that wasn't bad enough, the next gunburst revealed a group of Taylor's men had followed them onto the river and were gaining fast.

With one hand she pulled back hard on the front of her shield, dropping the back end into the water to act like a brake. With the other she raised her revolver.

The first agent she came across hadn't paid attention in training. Not that you could really train for an underground river chase with two thousand year-old Roman shields, but you could at least prepare the mind for such rare occurrences.

Yet the man was too eager, with wild eyes and slicked back hair, clearly letting the adrenaline of the chase get the better of him. He wasn't ready for her to bring the fight to him.

She didn't even need to shoot. His momentary panic as she appeared out of nowhere caused him to lose control. A quick pistol whip across the jaw and he flew off the shield, never to be seen again.

Then the metal underneath her squealed and shuddered, as another agent slammed into her. She only just managed to stay afloat, but it came at a cost.

Her revolver slipped from her fingers.

It bounced inside the shield. But as she tried to retrieve it, the man's arm snaked around her neck, pulling her half across to his shield. The muzzle of his pistol pressed cold and wet and hard to the side of her head.

Shit shit shit.

For a split second, in the eerie darkness, she felt rather than heard the click vibrate against her skin, and she found herself wondering what the transition would be like between this world and the next. Would there be pain? Would it be seamless? Where was the tunnel of light she had often heard soldiers talk about on the battlefield, following miraculous recoveries from injuries they really had no right to survive.

Another, darker thought: would Smith's magic bring her back along with all the other dead people down here?

But when she opened her eyes, they were still skimming across the water together.

And the agent was now shaking his gun which had refused to fire.

Too wet.

She jammed her fingers underneath his arm and pulled it off her throat.

Lucky.

Twisting his arm, she forced him upwards. He cried out in anger, muttering several ways he was going to kill her… before a rotting hand reached down from the dark and pulled him up into the seething mass of death above, where his scream was suddenly cut short.

She gasped, feeling a spray of something splash over her back. She really hoped it was just the crest of a wave.

No more agents came. She thought she could still hear the rest further back, but for now, as she snatched up her gun, she realised she was alone again and even the dead people overhead began to thin and drop away.

Then, as the river began to slow, the end crept into sight.

Light. Up ahead.

CHAPTER FIFTEEN

Capture

"Sam!" Jess yelled.

She was standing on a raised platform cut back into the river tunnel. Beside her, Will helped Teddy crawl off his shield, before letting his temporary boat drift off again on the water.

Sam didn't bother to try to steer the thing over. The water was slow enough for her to swim and she was already wet through with sweat and blood. With a few agonised strokes she made it to the side.

Jess's arm reached over and hooked through hers, yanking her up to safety.

"I should throw you back in for what you just did to Will. Did you know he can't swim? Bloody lucky he managed to stay on his little boat."

"*Shield*," Will corrected, before launching into a coughing fit to bring up the rest of the river he'd swallowed.

"Well, we're alive, so you're all welcome," Sam snapped, crawling on her hands and knees along the worn stone cobbles. She couldn't quite believe they'd made it out in one piece, nor, quite frankly, that everyone was being so ungrateful about her methods. Yet it wasn't over. She pointed to the back of the platform, where she could see a set of steep stairs heading up. Hidden in the darkness at the top was a rusty gate. "Unfortunately, Taylor and his army of bones aren't far behind, so there's really no time for a chinwag. Up and at 'em, everyone."

She pushed her sister onwards. Jess in turn reached for Will, pulling him to his feet and dragging him along. On the way, Sam slipped an arm around a shell-shocked but grateful Teddy and helped him get some momentum up the first few steps.

Jess was first to reach the gate. She gave it a tug, then a shove, to no avail. It was stuck fast. Locked or maybe even rusted to its frame.

Will joined her and tried to force it, but had just as little impact. He seemed perturbed by this, as though his masculinity might be slighted. So when he spotted a switch on the wall, he strode over and threw it up before Sam could even offer an exhalation of protest.

It was such an obvious switch. Placed in plain sight, for any who had come this far and needed a way back from the depths of Paris.

Given the traps and challenges they had already faced, Sam knew it couldn't be that simple. It never was.

And she was right.

As soon as Will threw the switch the gate opened. But there was another noise and a shuddering beneath their feet.

And the stairs tilted until they formed a steep slope of rock.

Will was the first to go. Arms and legs flailing off balance, fingers desperately scraping at the wall to stop himself, he slid all the way back to the landing platform before tumbling to a crashing halt on the dock, the Osiris Stone rolling out of his jacket.

Jess cried out and half fell, half dived for him. But Sam's hand snapped out and grabbed her sister's belt before she was out of reach, just as her other hand held fast to Teddy – the only one smart enough to have made a grab for the frame of the now-open gate.

He yelled out as the two women came to a sudden halt and hung off him.

Jess wriggled furiously.

"Let me go, I have to save him."

"I can't. I have to get you out of here."

"This isn't your decision, Sam!"

Summoning her remaining strength, she pulled her sister up until they were face to face. "I haven't been through all this just to let you go again. People have *died* to get us this far. To make sure I could protect you."

Teddy cursed under his breath behind her, his strength almost spent.

"The Stone, Samantha. They will get the Stone too."

Will groaned below. "It's too late."

Over the sound of rushing water, Sam could hear voices drifting from upriver.

Jess turned back to Sam and placed her hand on her sister's. "I need to save him. Please?"

There was something in her voice that planted a seed of hesitation in Sam. Put a momentary pause on a decade of cynicism, where she almost… *almost* let go. Her sister was a grown and capable woman now. Not the little girl she had looked after in their adventures through the backstreets of their little northern town. Not the teenager she had made sure she kept safe during the war, selling herself to Taylor and his goons to do it.

Jess had retrieved the amulet and had saved them already tonight.

She could save Will too, couldn't she?

"Teddy," Sam said with resignation over her shoulder. For a second Jess looked hopeful. For a second Sam herself didn't know what she was going to do.

Until she hauled Jess up quickly enough for Teddy to grab her arm and said firmly, "Get her out of here."

"No!" Jess screamed, struggling. "You can't do this!"

But Sam had made her decision. She knew she would never be able to live with herself if anything happened to her sister. Jess was capable, sure. However she didn't know the agents like Sam did. And Sam hadn't lived through the past ten years only to give her family up to them. Not without a bloody fight.

"I'll save him, I promise," she said.

And let herself go.

Gravity did the rest as she slid inevitably towards her doom. Agents were now appearing from the tunnel, some on shields, some swimming, dragging themselves up onto the side like drowned rats.

They quickly surrounded Will. And as soon as Sam hit the bottom, she rolled to a heap in front of two burly men, who dragged her up and pinned her arms behind her back. She could only watch as more men rushed past, trying to run up the ramp to get the others.

But Teddy and Jess were already through the gate. And even as another Shade Man pushed the agents aside and leapt metres into the air, they managed to slam the gate shut just in time.

THWACK sounded the bolt from the other side, as Jess locked it, gave Sam one last look of fear and desperation – and a flash of rage – before the pair ran off.

The Shade slammed against it, rattling the bars, before its invisible mass scraped ineffectively back down to the platform.

Sam felt her wrists suddenly released as Agent Smith climbed up to join them. The agents holding her backed off, though kept their guns trained at her face, looking like they had every intention of putting a hole in her head if she gave them an excuse. The Shade growled as it lurked in the background somewhere.

Smith gave her a look of disgust as he passed and went to roughly search Will. The poor academic's face looked bruised and dazed in the low light and he didn't struggle as Smith pulled aside his jacket and roughly dug his hands around.

The agent pulled out the Osiris Stone without emotion and examined it methodically, before handing it over to Taylor, who ignored Sam as he took the artefact and turned it over in his hands with far more care than Smith had taken. He studied it with the intense gaze of someone who thought he might have just created a whole new future for himself. Sam didn't even want to begin thinking about what kind of future it might mean for the rest of them, but she knew it would be nothing good.

Now his bright eyes flicked up to hers. Whatever semblance of smile that had been forming grew wider – the contented look of a man who finally had what he wanted.

"Once again, Samantha, the US Government thanks you for your service." He tipped his finger to his forehead.

Smith stared at her blankly.

"What about the two who got away? They have the amulet."

"They won't get far. Take as many men as you need. Track them down and do what you must to retrieve the item. We are done playing games."

"No," Will moaned, only now finding the strength to struggle against his captors. He took a punch to the gut from Smith for his troubles, dropping him to one knee. They dragged him upright and Smith was about to go for him again when Taylor raised his hand.

"Enough," he said, then turned to Sam. "I'm afraid you haven't given us much choice in the matter, Sam. They have the amulet and we need it. If only you had decided to join us – or at the very least not stand in our way – this would have been a lot easier for all concerned. Did you know that you killed a Shade back in the temple room? The expedition to retrieve it took months of planning and half the military budget of the year to enact. You're lucky I don't let these men kill you right here, right now."

Sam balled her fists. "I really wish you'd let them try."

He seemed to think about it. Then shook his head and clicked his fingers.

The agents holding Will dragged him closer and Taylor's gun was at Will's head before Sam could even blink. An involuntary "No!" escaped her lips.

Taylor didn't smile, but he knew he had her. "Is there any particular reason why I shouldn't?"

She had tells, he had told her once. They'd been playing cards one night on shift and he had won every single time, cleaning her out of her pay packet for that week – rent and everything. Only afterwards had he let on he'd been reading her like a book. And right now he could see what she was trying to hide, in the hope she might be able to distract them momentarily and stash it somewhere down here to collect later.

"You win," she said, and with an apologetic glance at Will, she reached into her jacket and pulled out the Isis Amulet.

Taylor nodded as though this was what he was expecting, then lowered his gun and let Will go.

"We have what we came for," he said to his men, gently relieving Sam of the artefact. "Take them away."

An agent threw him a briefcase and he laid it on the floor, flicked it open, and slid the two artefacts into the padded interior.

Then Sam had her arms pinned behind her back again

by one of the agents, as Smith walked up and put his face against hers, close enough that she could feel his breath on her lips, hot and rancid.

"You're not going to resist, are you, Captain?"

There was hatred in the black pits of his eyes. Pure evil. But she refused to look away.

"I'm afraid I have a history of it," she said.

He grinned and smacked the butt of his gun into her face.

CHAPTER SIXTEEN

Old Friends

It was dark when she regained consciousness.

There wasn't much to it, at first. A twitch in her fingers. Subtle movements as they tapped against a cold surface. But when she went to adjust her wrists, they burned. There was something wrapped around them. Rope or cord, she couldn't tell, but it was enough that she had no freedom of movement.

It didn't matter. Her mind wasn't ready to surface just yet. She didn't know if the darkness was present because her eyes were still shut or whether she'd been left bound in the tunnels underneath Paris, or maybe even blindfolded and left in a shipping container somewhere – she was happy to embrace it for a while longer yet.

Her body ached. Her spirit more so. So it was almost a relief when she slipped back into the comforting nothingness, accompanied only by the images of long-dead corpses and the look of a sister she had saved and lost all at the same time.

When she awoke again it was lighter – almost painfully so.

And she knew she wasn't alone because of the gentle clink of metal, like someone had just clipped the edge of a cutlery drawer.

She opened her eyes and immediately regretted it. The light was overwhelming. A clinical, punishing white that enveloped everything around her. But she held them open, even as they began to water, waiting until she could make out some detail of where she was.

It took a few seconds before the horror became clear.

She lay strapped to a tilted surgical table. To one side, against the wall, sat a trolley with her brown pilot's jacket folded neatly, on top of which had been placed her gun. Probably to torment me, she thought sourly. It's always the hope that kills you. Meanwhile on the other side of her sat a much closer trolley containing rows of surgical instruments. She tensed against her bonds as she recognised tiny puddles of blood pooling beneath a couple of the blades and wondered for a terrifying moment if it was hers.

"Welcome back."

Taylor stepped from behind her and smiled warmly. There wasn't anything unkind about it, but it was certainly a smile Sam had long ago learned never to trust. She flinched as he put a hand on her forehead – his skin was warm against hers and it made her shiver – but she was too weary to shake him off.

The door to the room opened and Smith and Roach

entered. The former with that impenetrable, unnatural gaze of his, although there was a sickly touch of excitement there too, as though he was looking through her physical form into some dark and twisted future silhouette of what she might become if he had his way. Behind him, the larger man had to duck as he squeezed through, the few black hairs still clinging to the top of his balding head scraped against the doorframe.

Roach positioned himself by the door. Smith stood just behind the bloodied tray of implements, looking down at them with familiarity and eagerness.

"And here I was hoping you three were just a bad dream," she said. Her voice was broken. The words forced over cracked and bloody lips. But she made sure she was heard.

Taylor's handsome features tightened just for a second. "Appropriate analogy, I suppose," he considered. "You might not have liked it when you worked with us… with me… but as you well know there must be times when we are forced to fade away with the light, slip back into the shadows, and cease to be anything but a niggle in people's memories. An unfortunate but necessary part of our job, existing, as we do, on the periphery of society."

"Like germs."

Smith tensed behind the tray and he looked eagerly to Taylor, but the taller man shook his head and continued, "Sadly for you, Sam, we are very real indeed. As is the rather precarious situation you find yourself in today."

She tried to laugh, only to end up wincing at the pain in

her shoulders and ribs. The bruises from the battle under Paris were clearly still fresh.

"I've had worse."

"No, you haven't," he replied in all seriousness. "And in this case you've created trouble for us all. The United States Government wants you dead, Sam. They wanted you dead after you stole the Amulet from us in New York and they wanted you dead when they heard you gave us trouble again in Paris. It's only through personal courtesy that I've kept you alive until now."

"I guess I have a habit of making things difficult for people. Sorry about that."

"You will be," Smith said, picking up one of the scalpels.

This close, she could see where his masters had changed him. Taken the exemplary SS soldier and moulded him into their version of the perfect, invincible, almost supernatural human-machine hybrid. The scars around his eyes and neck, his bulging shoulders and knuckles, his far-too-blue pupils that hinted at repeated nano-injections over months... maybe even years. All to pursue some notion of harnessing the godlike abilities a couple of the bastards had accidentally stumbled across on their travels.

And, worse, she knew it had all been done at his request. That was truly the sick part: Smith had volunteered willingly to become this abomination.

Of course, his transformation hadn't helped the Nazi cause in the end. But as they had fallen, he had risen. Too valuable to destroy in the aftermath of the war, he had been put to work as part of the American dream, like so many other evil assets they had recovered from the smoking ruins of Europe. It boiled her blood to think that they'd saved so many of the enemy, while so many of the Allies – and her friends – remained where they had fallen.

"Go to hell," she muttered. "Both of you."

Smith's lips twitched in a half-smile, even as his fingers tightened around the scalpel. But Taylor's hand on his shoulder stopped any idea of a more vigorous response.

"One day, maybe," Taylor replied. "I recognise that we've done things you might not have liked in order to safeguard our country. Only time will tell how that sits with the maker when we meet him – and I have no doubt that we will. But today we want to go somewhere else entirely." He leaned closer. "What do you know about the gateway to the Hall?"

"You took the keys. You figure it out."

He suppressed a light sigh – the very same she remembered from every time they used to argue, which towards the end of their relationship had been daily.

"I am doing, but your friend Professor Edward Ascher is the world expert on such matters and, although he escaped us for the time being, we know your history together. I refuse to believe you haven't discussed it with him on this little adventure or even when you used to be pilots together during the war, shooting the shit as you waited to take to the skies for King and country."

She narrowed her eyes. "You have a strange understanding of what we went through back then, but I guess you weren't exactly on the frontlines were you, Taylor? Always keeping yourself just out of harm's way, working behind the scenes, while the rest of us did the right thing, isn't that right?"

"Sam–"

"Get stuffed. Teddy didn't tell me a damn thing about the gateway or where to find it. I doubt he even knows. You're barking up the wrong tree."

"Oh, we already know roughly where to find it," he replied calmly. "In fact, we are closing on a location as we speak. But it never hurts to learn more, and, given your relationship to this Teddy, I can't help but think you know more than you're letting on. We have known of him for a long time, of course, but he had given up his quest of late and we knew he would not be easily persuaded back to it. The SS tried before he left Germany. Their pursuit of him was one of the reasons behind him taking his family and leaving for England. But you, Sam... we knew if you were brought into the equation you could change his mind. Get him back into the quest. Kindred spirits and all that?"

"So you wanted me back just to get to him?"

"Partly. It certainly wasn't for your cheery British disposition."

Roach gave a gruff laugh near the door and Sam glared at him.

"Anyway," Taylor continued, "what he knows is neither here nor there now. Teddy has helped you and you have helped him and even if it took a while longer than I would have liked, you've both helped us. We hold the keys to unlocking the greatest treasure in the history of the world and we are near enough to setting out to do just that.

So there is really very little reason for withholding any information you might possess."

"Let Will go and I'll think about it," she said, feigning confidence, even as she twisted her wrists again to discover there was still no give in the ties holding her down. This was looking very bad indeed.

And it was about to get worse.

Before Taylor could reply, there was a knock on the door and Roach opened it to another agent, who poked his head in.

"He's found it."

There was a very slight relaxing of Taylor's shoulders as though a weight had been lifted. Then he picked up his hat from the cupboard in the corner, tugged it onto his head and stepped towards the door which Roach held open for him.

"I'm afraid you're in no position to demand anything, Sam," he said, sounding distinctly disappointed. He stopped only to give Smith a firm nod. "See what you can uncover from her, but remember your orders."

With that he was gone, along with Roach and any chance she felt she might have of getting out of this in one piece. "That's right, run away again!" she yelled after him, but knew it would do no good.

She was alone with Smith now.

"His orders were for me not to be harmed, right?" she joked, half-hoping it was true.

He wasn't listening. He gazed down at the scalpel in his hand, turning it this way and that to catch the light, entranced, only to let it clatter to the tray as he moved around the table to the trolley containing her belongings.

"You can drop the act now, Captain," he said. "We know you're overplaying your hand here, as the British are always so fond of doing. Your special brand of confidence is once again misplaced and not for the first time I might add, seeing as the entire time you worked with The Nine you still didn't grasp the truth before you. You were just a rat in a maze of our design – as you continue to be today."

"I always thought I was more of a dog person, actually."

His lips thinned and he picked up her gun, studying it with disdain. "Such an instant way to end a life is something to be admired, don't you think? I'll admit there was a time when they fascinated me with their power, but over time I realised I didn't like them. They are too powerful, I think. Too instant. Clumsy and cumbersome and they ruin the fun of the fight."

His fingers wrapped around the handle and slipped over the trigger. He moved around the table, caressing the barrel up her arm, then her shoulder, and her breath caught as he paused just behind her head…

…before he passed back to the other side of her, casually tossed the heavy gun directly onto her cracked ribs, and returned to the surgical instruments.

"I myself prefer a tool that gets straight to the point," he continued. "Solid. Sharp."

"Cold?"

He picked up the bone saw and smiled.

"Always."

She wanted to pretend that this was all fine. That maybe

Taylor was just playing with her and he was outside waiting for her to cave and spill what she knew. But she couldn't help the panic rising within her that maybe that wasn't the case and this was actually going to happen, even as she grit her teeth and held the man's gaze.

"If you're going to do it, just get on with it. I'm not one for small talk."

Smith's shark-like smile widened as he turned the blade over in his hands to reveal a bloody smear along the edge. "I wish I could say the same about Dr Sandford, but it turned out he was more than talkative when persuaded."

Sam suddenly strained against the bonds holding her down, arching her back with a cry as she tried to break free from sheer force of will. The anger and fear vied for control. The adrenaline surged through her. All in the hope that one might loosen just enough to let her free, grab whatever weapon she could lay her hands on, and end this shithead right now.

But all she could do was fall back defeated onto the table, her breaths ragged and her hope shot to pieces.

"Must have some guts to take a knife to a captured and probably bound museum curator. I guess the Nazi in you never left, eh?"

"It was just a bit of harmless fun, Captain. He is expendable, after all."

She snarled. "And what am I?"

He leaned in closer, eyes shining, holding the blade to her face.

"Let's find out, shall we?"

CHAPTER SEVENTEEN

Echoes from the Past

The door slammed behind her as she was unceremoniously tossed into a small stone cell. She tried to stay on her feet, to prevent them getting any kind of satisfaction at her weakened state. But they had really done a number on her today.

She fell to the floor, cheek pressed against the gritty stone, lying directly between the two wall-hung benches. Collapsed and unmoving, she stayed there for a few minutes, glad at least for the respite.

Every inch of her skin, bones, and muscles screamed in agony. The places she had been cut were still burning fiercely and bleeding out through her shirt and trousers. Not enough to kill her. Not yet, at least. Smith had been careful enough to see to that. Had just cut where it had hurt the most, without draining her of too much life, in case they needed her for whatever they had planned next.

She wondered if Will really had endured similar today. And what kind of state he might be in now.

With a groan, she rolled onto her back and stared around her, trying to figure out where the hell she was. The sandstone blocks in the wall were old and worn, so clearly somewhere pretty ancient. And now she was out of that sterile torture surgery, which must have enjoyed some kind of insulation or a fan, she could feel air that was thick with heat. Oppressively so, to the point that breathing was a struggle.

It reminded her of that mission she'd undergone in Cyprus. One of her first for The Nine.

Was this a Mediterranean heat? Or had they taken her further afield?

A polite cough startled her. Had she the energy left, she might have spun around and lamped whoever had snuck up. But she remained immobile on the ground. Only able to tilt her head back, to regard the small, thin, ghostly shell of a man sitting a little further along one of the benches.

He gave her a smile, as if he had been expecting her to drop in like this. Then bent down to offer her some help getting to her feet.

"Friendly, aren't they?" he said in a gentle American accent, gesturing to the cell door. She collapsed on the bench next to him. "I'm assuming that you must be the infamous Captain Moxley they've been talking about?"

"I used to be," she groaned, sitting down next to him.

"They have been toying with you."

She nodded once, then pressed her face into her hands, feeling the pressure of her palms on her eyes. It eased the encroaching headache a little.

"He never even asked me any questions. I guess he'd already got everything he needed out of poor Will. Shit, I hope he's all right."

At this, the man paused. When she turned her head, she noticed his pointed glance to the small barred window in the wall opposite, beyond which seemed to be another cell.

"He is unconscious, but alive I think. At least, he was the last time I checked."

She leapt to her feet faster than she should have. But even as her cellmate reached out to steady her, she swatted him gently away and climbed onto the bench under the window, before peering through.

There was a figure lying on a similar bench, barely covered with a tatty grey blanket. A man who at some point had definitely been Dr William Sandford, although right now he was dishevelled and out for the count.

"Will?" she hissed. Then, louder, "Will, you goof! For pity's sake, wake up!"

His chest continued to rise and fall in a rhythmic pattern, but there was no other movement and no indication he could hear her. She continued to clutch the bars, but for support rather than anything else. Her eyes closed. Her head hung in defeat.

"They have the keys now, don't they," the man asked behind her. The tone in his voice made it sound like a weary statement of fact, not a question. "The amulet and stone, Isis and Osiris, have been reunited at last. The keys to the underworld together, ready to lead whoever holds them through the gateway that has stood for thousands of years, protecting the secrets that lie beneath the sands of Egypt. My father warned me this day might come."

Her immediate question as to how he knew so much was overridden by the revelation of where they had been brought. Egypt – of course – where Teddy had suggested the Hall was located. And now those government goons finally had what they needed to steal the knowledge and power they so desired.

"I think I've made a huge mistake," she said, her fingers tightening in frustration on the bars. "I mean, hell, I've made loads of them. A huge convoy of mistakes, all winding their way through the barren wasteland of my life to bring me here. But, honestly, this last one might be the worst. A real nosebleed of a decision. Because now there is nothing in The Nine's way."

"Then why did you give them what they needed?"

She turned and frowned at him.

"Not that you'd understand, given we've never met, but I had no choice."

He stared at her so intently it suddenly made her doubt the validity of that sentence. Was it strictly true? Now she wasn't sure. And somehow he seemed to know it too.

"A woman like you always has a choice. The question is, why did you make yours?"

"I have a family to protect. I took a risk that I could deal with these men myself and get back to living my life. Not the ideal situation, but let's call it a compromise."

"Compromise?" he repeated, somewhat sympathetically. "If you compromise the good in you, you might as well have no life to live."

She let go of the bars and sat down on the bench, staring at him: this white wisp of a fellow, whose quiet and calm demeanour placed him as a strange occupant of any prison cell operated by Agent Taylor and his friends.

"Just who *are* you?" she asked. "Why do you know so much about what's going on? And what the hell did you do to The Nine to end up in this place?"

The man leaned over to shakily offer his hand.

"My name is Edward Cayce."

She raised an eyebrow. "The famous psychic?"

"*A* psychic," he replied, smiling. "I'm not sure about the famous part."

Sam gestured to the cell door. "I wouldn't say that, given why you're here. Taylor… *Agent* Taylor… wanted me to meet you not so long ago." She thought of Will lying unconscious in the next cell and of Jess and Teddy likely in hiding in Paris. "Maybe I should have taken them up on their offer?"

She was grateful he didn't seem to judge her. His bony shoulders limped skywards in a shrug. "You did what you thought was right. As they are doing."

"That's the bit that scares me, Mr Cayce. They really do think this is all for the greater good, don't they?" He started to shake. "Mr Cayce, are you all right?"

For a few seconds, she wasn't sure what was happening. His eyes were blinking furiously. The lank, dirty hair on his head seemed to rise of its own accord, as if it had been rubbed on a balloon full of static. His fingers twitched, although not in any random order, but as if conveying a secret code all of their own making.

He didn't seem to be having a fit or a breakdown or anything like that. Yet she had no other way to explain it. Maybe Smith had done a number on this poor fellow too.

Yet as quickly as it had started, it stopped.

He grew calm again. His breathing more measured.

He opened his eyes properly and was back in the room with her.

"They got to you too, huh?" she said.

"What do you mean?"

"They tortured you, didn't they? Agent Smith and his little tray of delights. He's been working on you, I assume?"

To her surprise, he laughed. "Oh, no. I almost wish that were the case. It would certainly be a change, but unfortunately my sufferance is of a... *different* kind. I would explain more, but I would imagine it's not something that you would understand."

Now it was her turn to laugh, though it burned her throat to do so. "Mr Cayce, you'd be surprised. I've seen an awful lot of strange things lately. One more surely can't hurt."

He smiled at that, but said no more.

"You have a connection to the Hall of Records, don't you," she said.

"Not me, exactly..." He grew pale again.

"Then who, Mr Cayce?"

The shaking came more violently this time. His body erupting in spasms, his knuckles white, his fingers gripping the bench as if he was suddenly cast adrift at sea and was fighting to keep his head above the water.

She reached out to grab his shoulders, try to help him regain control. Yet as his back arched, wisps of ethereal blue began to form around his body, streaking through him, causing him to glow brightly.

She fell back as he began to lift from the bench, his arms were outstretched, his legs too, as the blue around him grew brighter and brighter.

Until, with an unearthly scream, he disappeared in a blinding flash of light – the force of the explosion so hard that Sam was thrown back against the wall. She collapsed onto the bench, trying to shield her eyes from the form that appeared before her.

It was the body of Edward Cayce – still his physical form at least – hovering on the other side of the cell, but now the features of another being were overlapping his. A beautiful grey face whose amber eyes were open and staring straight into Sam's soul.

"You," its voice boomed. Not deep or threatening, but with such a power she could feel its words reverberate in her chest. She also knew its words were not in English… and yet she could understand them perfectly. "I have been waiting for you for a long time."

It was a voice of ages past.

Of time itself.

Of someone – or something – beyond anything she had known before. A god or goddess maybe. A being used to being worshipped, certainly. There was so much power pouring out into this tiny, insignificant cell that Sam couldn't help but feel a desperate need to get down on her knees and bow her head in reverence.

Which made it all the more important she not do that.

"And who the hell are you?" she said weakly.

The being flickered, perhaps contemplating snapping its fingers and erasing her from existence.

"I am of the Belial, one of the guardians of the great repository of knowledge. What you call the Hall of Records. I know who you are, Captain. You will help me retrieve what is rightfully mine."

Sam gave a small laugh, though there was little humour and a great amount of fear in it. "If you know who I am, then you'll know I don't take kindly to orders."

The spirit in Cayce's form leaned forward in the air, looming over her with a sneer. Then it sent a wave of blue energy knocking her across the room and slamming her into the cell door.

She dropped to the floor in a crumpled heap, with more bruises and most likely a few extra broken bones. In the back of her mind she could almost hear her sister saying, "*Great work, Sam. Just great. For future reference, the next time an ancient godlike being asks for help... JUST AGREE!*"

She spat out the blood pooling in the back of her throat as she rose to her feet.

"You're going to have to do a lot better than that," she wheezed.

The spirit drifted towards her, eyes ablaze with darkness.

Then its face contorted in pain. Flickered in and out of

existence, as the ethereal blue wisps surrounding it begin to fade and Cayce could clearly be seen in the centre, trying to wrestle back control of his body.

"You *will* help me, or pay the price!" the being roared, before the man finally won and he dropped from the air, all his energy sapped.

Sam grabbed him as best she could. They fell awkwardly, but she was able to get her hand under his head as he landed on the floor.

They lay there, gasping heavily, for a few minutes. She half wondered what the guards might think if they chose that moment to open up the cell. The thought made her laugh out loud.

"What's funny?" Cayce whispered. His normal voice.

"I think you need to explain what the hell just happened," she replied. "Because I've seen a few possessions in my time and that was something on a whole other level."

She rolled to her knees and pushed herself up, then helped Cayce to the bench. They both fell back against the wall exhausted.

"The Hall is proof of the existence of an ancient civilisation far more advanced than we are today. The Empire of Atlantis… now lost, wiped clean by its own ingenuity and carelessness. Can you imagine the power it would take to destroy an entire civilisation?"

"So there is a weapon," she muttered.

He inclined his head. "But not just any weapon. *The* weapon. The only one in the history of this planet – and probably any planet – that truly means the end of all things. The survivors of that great civilisation knew it as *The Destroyer of Worlds,* and it was this power that ended Atlantis, which is why your government wants it and why this thing inside me wants it." He pointed to his chest. "The being you just saw has lived with me for years now, possessing me as it had once possessed my father. It was one of those Atlanteans responsible for protecting such a secret."

"But if they were guardians of the Hall, surely that makes them the good guys? What the hell pissed in that one's teapot to get it so riled up?"

Cayce sighed. "Being kept in this state, in me, has driven it mad. Or at least that's what I have come to believe. This creature wants the Hall to be found now, against its primary directive, because it believes the Hall can grant it life again."

"That can't be a good thing."

"It wouldn't be, no. We must keep it trapped if we can, even if it costs me my own life." He fixed her with a determined look. "Captain Moxley, we can't let it or any of the men out there reach the Hall. If they do, we are all doomed to suffer the same fate as those who built it."

Sam frowned and leaned forward, elbows on her knees, face in her hands. Her fingers found each scrape and bruise across her face. The tears in her lips. The blood encrusted down her cheeks and neck.

But even as she could feel the pain inflicted upon her by The Nine, she knew it could all be much, much worse for those who were not used to such things.

She had been through hell. Figuratively and literally. But there had always been a home to come back to, no matter how battered and broken she could now see it was. The end of Atlantis would have meant the end of everything for its people. If the same thing happened today…

"And there occurred violent earthquakes and floods," she quoted quietly to herself, "and in a single day and night of misfortune, the island of Atlantis disappeared in the depths of the sea."

"You studied Plato?"

"Not studied exactly. I had a good friend during the war who knew the myths around the lost civilisation. It was his specialty. And, well, he liked to talk a lot. I mean, for hours. He said talking about his interests kept him calm, but really I think even the nightly threat of dying couldn't shake the teacher from him. 'We all have it in us to learn a little more,' he would say." She smiled. "To be honest, some nights I longed for the Luftwaffe to arrive early."

"Well, Captain, I would say you'll be hearing more before our time on this earth is done, unless we can stop your friends from opening the Hall and prevent this spirit from returning to our world to unleash the power contained within it."

Sam closed her eyes, seeing the quiet life she often fantasised about getting further away by the minute.

"Does anybody else know about your secret, Mr Cayce?"

"Not yet. They suspect I'm in contact with something… but they don't know the full extent of my possession."

"OK, well that's something we can take advantage of, I

guess. Can you control its power? As in, would you be able to use the creature to control their minds and throw them off the scent?"

"I would be afraid to give it the opportunity, if I'm honest."

"So how do you suggest I stop them finding the Hall?"

He shook his head. "I'm afraid it is too late for that. The artefacts they took from you aren't just keys to open the Hall; when combined they contain a map of where the entrance is – and not so long ago I sensed their resident experts bring this secret to light. We don't have long before they come and collect me, after which they will take me to the site and under the statue of the four wings we will begin the journey into the underworld… into the Hall. It is imperative you get there first. Do whatever you must. They cannot be the ones to unlock its secrets."

She sighed. "I'll try."

Cayce closed his eyes. His breathing was laboured now. He seemed on the edge of passing out.

"Captain?" he murmured.

"Those possessed by powerful gods can call me Sam."

He laughed weakly. "Sam, I took on my father's burden – this spirit – for a reason. He was not strong enough to go against its will, but I am. Or at least I have been until now. I have survived long enough to be able to warn you of what needs to be done. But you must realise there will be sacrifices ahead. If I am no longer able to keep it at bay for good, you will have to do the honourable thing for the good of us all. Kill me if you have to…" he opened his eyes then and peered firmly into hers "…and whoever else stands in your way."

There was something in the way he looked at her in that moment that she didn't like.

As if he had seen the future.

CHAPTER EIGHTEEN

A Place in History

The corridors of the Egyptian military base were dusty and claustrophobic. Neither of which were helping Agent Taylor's increasingly dour mood.

He sneezed twice, then swore loudly. None of the local soldiers in the prison block where he was waiting gave him a second glance. Trained well or just apathetic to his presence, he wasn't sure. But as he blew his nose on the pressed silk handkerchief he always kept in his pocket – a Christmas gift from Sam, he suddenly remembered, all the way from Savile Row in London no less – he decided he needed to keep a close eye on them. Allies they might be in this particular venture, but this was their country and they were proud and fierce, and if they truly came to understand what lay beneath their desert sands it could become problematic.

Right now, only he and The Nine truly knew what was at stake here. Which is why he had to ensure his team was the one left holding all the cards when this convenient little deal with Colonel Arif was done. History was his for the taking. He wouldn't let native pride stand in the way of what needed to be done to lead the world into a brighter, more stable future under America.

Freedom for all, whatever the cost, he told himself. The same mantra that had been ingrained in him early on – and the one he repeated whenever he needed reminding to hold his tongue and smile sweetly in order to get the work done.

"Agent Taylor," a surprisingly jovial voice boomed at him down the corridor. The Egyptian soldiers around him suddenly stood all the straighter. "Welcome to my humble fortress!"

A handsome, bearded military man with a false smile adorning his lips strutted down the corridor in his pristine uniform, a ridiculous number of probably fake medals pinned to his chest. It was a wonder he was able to stand upright, Taylor considered, offering a polite smile of his own. He knew the man had fought at the Suez against the British recently, but there was no way anybody could earn that many medals and not have been killed or at least seriously maimed.

Nevertheless, he had presence and respect, and the soldiers all saluted him as he passed. Taylor fought a degree of envy as he held out a hand. If only his team of men – and especially that woman – had been the same.

"Colonel Arif, thank you for hosting us. I trust you are well?"

The Colonel grasped his hand and shook it vigorously.

"The day has come, Agent. We stand on the precipice of one of the greatest discoveries mankind has ever known. A great day for Egypt. Can you feel the gaze of history upon us?"

Taylor nodded as he knew he must. Like it or not, Colonel Arif remained the key to reaching the Hall of Records safely and securely. Diplomacy was the order of the day… for now.

"A great day for us all," he replied carefully. "I am glad that our two nations could come together on this matter, in the noble spirit of cooperation. One giant of civilisation alongside another."

The Colonel laughed, but something underlying it immediately had Taylor on edge. There was a coldness to it, which felt distinctly out of place in this oppressive heat.

"Ah, good Agent," the man said. "Like all Americans you mask your true feelings well. But let us not stand here and speak nonsense. Bullshit, as you call it." His brow knotted over his powerful eyes ever so slightly. "There are no giants anymore, for the last war left the battlefield barren of such things, no matter that you and your friends claimed victory. All that's left now are agendas. And mine is to see the glory of Egypt rightly restored."

He motioned for Taylor to join him, as he began walking down the corridor. Towards the cells. The wave of salutes on either side followed them, rankling Taylor further.

"We do not dispute that. America wishes only–"

"Bah, I do not care for what America wishes. You are

lucky that I intervened on your behalf to allow this mission to take place at all. Our country, our people, are fed up of you Americans intervening in places you are not welcome, sliding yourself into cultures you do not understand, waving your flags of righteousness and entitlement." He raised his chin and added, "w ma btitkallam arabi, sah?" When Taylor simply held his gaze, unwilling to admit he didn't know what the man had said, the Colonel sneered. "You fought for your independence, yet you are just like the British and French masters you once served. They too came here to dig in our sands and steal away our treasures in their great ships. And then," he blustered, specks of spit flying onto Taylor's cheek, "they had the audacity to display our stolen culture in their museums as though they discovered us, when we are still right here! Well not this time, Agent Taylor. Not with the Hall of Records. You have keys we need to unlock the treasure, but this is our land. The Hall lies beneath our sands. You have no claim here. The finds will belong to the Egyptians."

Taylor wiped the spit off his face with the back of his sleeve. The gun he carried at his hip bounced against his trouser leg, as if reminding him it was there if he needed it.

"But will you give the people the treasure or will your government control the information as they did with what you found at the Pyramids?"

That stopped the Colonel in his tracks. "How did you–"

"We know everything, Colonel Arif. We know what you found and what you did with it and that you did not distribute any idea of its existence to the people you claim to represent. And do you know what? I am fine with that. Governments are there to protect those they represent, are they not? What you do with the Hall of Records is not our concern. We came for one thing and one thing only. An artefact of relative insignificance to you."

"Is that really why are you here, Agent Taylor?"

"As I said," Taylor replied, spreading his hands as if to show he had nothing to hide, "we come in the spirit of cooperation."

The Colonel looked him up and down, as if suddenly wary. As he should be, Taylor noted, as the man then continued apace down the corridor.

"Speaking of cooperation, she is down here and has so far refused to give us hers." Colonel Arif spat the word "she" with venom. Taylor held back a smile. Clearly the man had met Sam before. She had that effect on people. "I do not trust that she will not become a problem."

"We can handle her," Taylor lied.

The man sniffed haughtily. "I have never held much love for the British. You, being an American, must appreciate that. They are arrogant fools. Their insidious Empire lies at the root of every cultural weed around the world. But she…" the Colonel literally spat on the floor now, "…*she* is especially intolerable. Intolerable and dangerous. Your Captain Moxley has been a thorn in my side for many years now."

"Our Captain Moxley?" Taylor replied, though he didn't put much effort into the feigned surprise. "I don't know what you mean, Colonel."

"Of course you don't. And neither do your 'Nine' I'm

sure."

A sneer jerked up the edges of the Colonel's beard. Taylor ignored it for now, more concerned that Egyptian intelligence was more on the ball than the boys back home had given them credit for. He might have to rectify that with an "accident" or two at the Egyptian Ministry of Defence in the near future. America had enough trouble worrying about the Red Menace without any other countries causing problems for them.

"Colonel," he said tightly, "I am not at liberty to discuss the past, but please realise that this deal my employers have offered you will secure a bright future for American-Egyptian relations. And believe me when I say that you have the assurance of the highest levels of the United States Government that you can trust us in this matter. Let us be honest: the Soviets will not be as generous should they get wind of what we are doing."

"Perhaps. Perhaps not." The Colonel shrugged as he walked. The medals clanked together pitifully. "Trust is a funny thing, my friend, and I will tell you now that I do not trust the Moxley woman. She must stay here. I will not have her setting foot upon our sacred site. Is that understood?"

"She could be an asset to the team. Are you sure you want to risk leaving her behind?"

"Agent Taylor, if I'd had my way she would be dead already."

"So I have gathered. But your thoughts on the matter only demonstrate just how useful she can be. Her knack for being where she should not may yet help us all reach the great Hall."

The Colonel's shoes scuffed to a halt and he had the temerity to jab his fingers in Taylor's chest. "My decision stands and I will not be questioned further. Do with the troublesome woman as you wish after our business is concluded and we have the Hall. Uncovering the secrets of our ancestors is all that matters to us. It will finally allow Egypt to retake its place as a global power to be reckoned with once again."

Taylor looked down at the finger poking a crease into his silken red tie. There was a time when he might have reacted badly to such provocation. Broken the man's hand, maybe. But one did not pull the strings of modern government without learning the skill of feigning acceptance of another's will – while secretly devising ingenious ways to kill them.

"As long as we get what we need from the Hall," he replied coolly.

"If what you are seeking truly exists, then good luck to you, Agent. But I believe you are chasing ghosts. The existence of the Hall only proves how strong this great land of Egypt once was… and will be again. There was no mysterious lost civilisation that came before. There is no Atlantis to be found."

"You can let us worry about that."

"Indeed I will. All that matters to me now is gaining access to the Hall. Everything else is irrelevant. Thankfully you have secured the keys and I believe Professor Shultz has just used them to locate the gateway in an inconsequential village on the edge of the Giza plateau, has he not? I have already sent word out for the best diggers in Cairo to excavate the site tomorrow if we cannot reveal the entrance ourselves tonight. But if you are truly concerned about whatever challenges we may find once we are through the gateway then I suggest we take the other hostage, Dr Sandford? He was the one who recovered the Isis Amulet after all. He might prove a worthy, if less troublesome, substitute."

"Fair enough. And Cayce?"

The Colonel rubbed his nose. "Yes, I want the psychic taken as well. I am not yet convinced of the power he claims to hold access to, but he has spoken much truth so far. He may still be of some value."

They reached Samantha's cell door. The two guards outside it held their salute perfectly. Colonel Arif ignored them both, smoothing out his beard and adjusting his collar. It seemed he cared more about what the woman inside thought of him than he wished to admit. A laughable scenario… if Taylor could have found anything to laugh at in this whole damn mess.

He hated working with foreign powers. It was so much easier when his government gave him license to work freely across borders, while they diplomatically smoothed things over afterwards.

"We will do it your way then," Taylor said reluctantly. "We will take Dr Sandford and Mr Cayce with us, and leave Captain Moxley here. Although, I may set her to work for my research team in the meantime, if you have no objection?"

The Colonel was visibly sweating as he gestured to his guards to open the door. "Fine," he muttered. "But you and your men will be held responsible for any problems. If she even so much as puts a foot where it is not wanted on my base, I will see to it that her foot – and the rest of her – is incinerated and the ashes shipped to your President. Along with those of you and your men."

Taylor narrowed his eyes, but he didn't have a chance to respond. The cell door swung open to reveal Samantha talking to a weary looking Edward Cayce. Both heads turned their way. Sam gave a pained grimace as she saw Taylor, but he was pleased to see it grow worse when she clapped eyes on Colonel Arif.

"Ah, our gracious hosts," she said, as the Colonel strode into the room to inspect Cayce. Even though she remained sitting on the bench, Taylor knew she was tensed, poised and ready to strike out if she even got a whiff of opportunity to do something stupid.

"Sam," he said from the doorway.

Half acknowledgement. Half warning.

She gave him one of her best smiles, despite the pain it seemed to inflict upon her to do so. Had they beaten her? She certainly looked like she'd been put through the mill since he'd seen her last, despite his orders that she wasn't to be touched. He would have to talk to Smith about that later.

"I didn't realise losing me would make you this

desperate, Taylor. Jumping into bed with a mass murderer. You know all about those civilians that went missing, don't you?"

Without hesitating, the Colonel backhanded her across the face. Taylor watched, uncomfortable, but silent.

"And that's not forgetting the journalists too…" Sam continued.

The Colonel raised his hand to strike her again, but Taylor stepped into the room fully now and cleared his throat. "Colonel, we have work to do."

For a second, it seemed as though the man might actually turn on him. His shoulders tensed and his eyes blazed as he glanced over his shoulder. Taylor's fingers twitched, ready to go for his gun despite knowing how that would turn out. Kill the Colonel here and the entire base would turn on him and his men. The mission would be over and any evidence of his team would be buried along with the Hall.

Thankfully, the Colonel saw sense. He whistled and used his hand to beckon his guards into the room.

"Bring him," he said, gesturing to Cayce.

The psychic's head turned towards Samantha. And although he kept his voice low, Taylor heard every word before he was dragged to his feet.

"Don't forget what I said, Captain."

With that he was dragged away. At the same time, there was a commotion in the next cell and Taylor knew that Dr Sandford was also being hauled up and taken away.

Sam leapt to the bars and called his name, but he was

already gone. And the worried look that crossed her face in that moment was priceless. They'd finally cracked her, it seemed. Perhaps the Colonel had been right to suggest she stay here, if only to let that crack widen and fester.

"Where are you taking them?" she demanded.

"To secure our place in the history books," Taylor replied. "To locate and reveal the secrets of the great Hall of Records. To retrieve the power hidden within. And although it pains me to say it, I'm afraid you won't be joining us at this time, Sam." He motioned for two more guards outside the room to enter the cell. "Instead, we hope to make you at home here for the time being. We have some work that you might find stimulating. Research to keep your mind where it should be."

"And if I refuse?"

He held her gaze. "Then Dr Sandford dies. And we will make sure your family soon follow."

One of the guards, a short, squat fellow, stepped up to Sam and grabbed her wrists. The handcuffs he slapped down were old and rusted, but they bit into her skin enough for her to know she wouldn't be breaking them anytime soon. She eyeballed the man as he gestured for her to walk out of the cell ahead of him, following the other guard.

Yet she made sure she came face to face with Taylor as she passed.

"I'm really beginning to dislike you," she said. Then, pausing to stare up into the impassive face of Agent Roach, who had just appeared at the door, she added, "And I always disliked *you*."

Taylor left the dingy cell and stood beside Roach in the corridor as they watched Sam being half pushed, half dragged in the opposite direction to Dr Sandford and Edward Cayce.

"The feeling is fast becoming mutual, Captain," Taylor replied under his breath. Then, to Roach, he said, "I don't trust that she won't become a problem and I know for certain the locals won't be able to deal with her. So I'm changing the plan. You stay here. Keep an ear out for any trouble. Make sure she doesn't try anything… dangerous."

"That's all she ever does," Roach muttered. "Maybe the Colonel is right. Maybe we should just tie up this particular loose end for good?"

Taylor contemplated this for only a second longer than he had meant to.

"Captain Samantha Moxley may yet have a part to play in this operation," he said quietly, making sure there were no soldiers around to overhear. "If things turn sour with the Egyptians, we could need her special brand of trouble. Keep her alive for now."

Freedom for all, whatever the cost, he recited in his head.

But as Roach strode off after her, he wondered just what the cost might be. Could he really give the order to finish Sam once and for all?

He had a bad feeling they were closing in on the moment he would have to find out.

CHAPTER NINETEEN

Amateur Hour

The base was a labyrinth of far-too-small corridors and troops in a hurry to get somewhere. Most ignored Sam as she was pushed along by her two captors – one tall and young, the other short and wide and rough as guts. Unfortunately, there were still enough leers from passing soldiers to make her wish she had her jacket on.

Of course, there was nothing to be done but keep her head held high and walk as straight as she could, despite the aches in her joints, the bruises across most of her body, and the shoving the stocky guard was currently giving her – his fingers prodding her along, always a little too low for comfort.

They passed through a set of double doors and here the chaos subsided. Cells and torture chambers now became libraries and laboratories, and the occasional person rushing past was dressed in a white coat instead of fatigues.

The base wasn't entirely military then. Some kind of research station too?

It didn't really matter. She wasn't planning on staying very long.

They soon reached a room she recognised. Passing it quickly, she could still see her jacket and gun on the interrogation room trolley where she had last spotted them. But on they pressed, until finally she was herded into a large area filled with shelves of books and maps. Photographs and drawings were plastered all over the walls, some with scribbled notes, some maps with pins.

One in particular caught her eye. It showed the pyramids and the Sphinx, and a nearby village labelled *Wadi Sais* located just beyond the southwest edge of the great city of Cairo.

There was a big red X marked over the northern edge of the town.

She knew instantly what that meant.

They must have found the way in. Somehow uncovered the location of the gateway to the underworld beneath the Egyptian sands. The entrance to the Hall of Records itself.

X marks the spot after all.

But to her surprise there was more. Because from here strings spread outwards to other maps, charting various courses around the world, creating links between cities new and old, and connecting to places she knew to be archaeological sites. And it didn't take much for her to see the subtle clues to what they were looking for in their tangled web, centred around the Mediterranean and stretching out beyond Plato's infamous Pillars of Hercules.

The Empire of Atlantis.

Stocky prodded again, his long fingernail jabbing into the small of her back as he motioned for her to sit in a rickety chair next to a long, empty table.

"Stay here," he said in English. "No trouble, OK?"

"Can't promise anything," she muttered, but gave him a subservient nod, while continuing to scope out the room for opportunities. Opportunities for what, she wasn't sure yet. Only that she'd know it when she saw it. "What is it exactly that you want me to do?"

"You'll be helping with our work, doing research, checking maps and photographs." He gave her a creepy leer. "And whatever else the Professor might want you to do."

She raised an eyebrow, but declined to take the bait, instead gripped by a very deep panic. There was a Professor here? Had they already captured Teddy and forced him to endure Smith's torture too? Oh god, what had she got him into?

"The Professor?" she asked carefully.

As the guard gestured behind her, she turned and expected to see her old friend being dragged into the room in a beaten and captive state. Yet, to her relief, a completely different fifty-something bespectacled man in a lab coat walked in and took a seat.

He ignored the group at first, poring over the books that lay open on the desk. But then the young Egyptian guard was himself prodded by his stocky superior.

"Naguib," the older man growled.

Visibly sweating, the boy, Naguib, hurried over to have

a quiet word in the Professor's ear, who then peered over his glasses at Sam with a look approaching disgust.

"Must I?" he groaned.

And that's when she heard the sliver of accent and attitude she'd heard so many times before, and felt the cold dread deep in her bones as she understood she was now at the mercy of another of Agent Smith's kind.

She had figured the war was over when the Allies had won. That the warped fascist ideology would bleed away into the gutters, never to be seen again. Yet it seemed its followers had simply scarpered like rats from torchlight, finding new dark corners in which to continue breeding their hatred of everything good.

The Professor stood, but made no effort to come over. Instead Sam was pushed in front of him, to be inspected like an animal awaiting its fate at a farmer's market. The stocky guard meanwhile yelled at Naguib again to fetch him a drink, punched him hard in the shoulder to spur him into action and made a very uncomplimentary remark about him before he'd even scurried out of earshot.

Sam watched dispassionately as Stocky laughed at his own joke, taking care not to give away that she'd understood every word he'd said. Let the scoundrel believe she was the usual brand of western woman who was unable or unwilling to speak another tongue, content only to yell louder when she needed to be understood. It had played in her favour before and it might yet again before the day was out.

The three stood in silence some more, Sam unwilling

to give either man – but especially the Nazi scientist – the satisfaction of her having to speak first. To ask why she was here or what he had planned for her or, even better, to beg him to go easy on her.

Nope. Fuck him and his friends. She could wait them out forever if she had to.

The Professor finished dissecting her appearance and nodded as though he might have been reading her mind using one of those remote viewing techniques she'd been hearing about at The Nine before she'd quit.

"I told them I didn't need an assistant," he said. His words were short and clipped, just like Smith's. His tone superior, as though speaking to a child. "But I have been advised that you have experience with matters of the... unusual?"

He waited. Sam still didn't talk.

"Well, then, here we are. I am Professor Schultz. And I believe, you and I have a mutual acquaintance, Edward Ascher, who has most likely told you a little of his research, otherwise you would not be here. Is that correct?"

Now that surprised her. "You know Teddy?"

Professor Schultz smiled as though she had just walked straight into his trap. There wasn't anything human about it.

"Good. I see that I was properly informed. And, yes, I had the displeasure of spending time with that irritating little man before the war. Now, to you. Miss Moxley, isn't it?"

"*Captain* Moxley."

"Ah, yes, a female pilot! I remember your story now. How your countrymen decided to throw caution to the wind – and women too, apparently. My, my… the English were desperate weren't they?"

Her frown deepened. Yet she could feel the handcuffs bite further into her skin as she curled her fingers into a fist – a painful reminder that she had no power here. It might be satisfying to headbutt this vile little man into a coma, but she would have no chance of escape. The stocky guard would take the opportunity to punish her in any way he saw fit… and unfortunately she saw in his eyes the many ways they might likely be. Execution on the spot was a given, but there would be unpleasantness preceding that no matter what orders to safeguard her general wellbeing Agent Taylor might have left them with.

No, she had to wait.

Luckily, the Professor didn't press the matter. He gestured for the guard to take her to another desk far away from his, where she was forced into a chair in front of a scattering of aerial photographs.

"Pilot or clay pigeon does not matter. It is clear you are a woman who might be of some use in certain situations, and with your time in the air you will surely know how to read the terrain, am I right? Study these photographs, if you please. There is a lost temple said to be buried beneath the ground on the island of Thera. Nothing physical remains above, so we are looking for patterns in topography, an entrance in the cliff face, basic geometric patterns in the dry soil. Even an amateur like you should be able to spot them for me. Understand?"

Amateur?

She took a moment to compose herself, trying to at least seem agreeable to this utter travesty of affairs.

"I understand."

Even so, Professor Schultz looked unsure as to whether Sam was intelligent enough to grasp the concept he was putting in front of her. "We can but hope that is true," he replied, then pointed to the guard. "You. Pass her the aerial shots from batch 191. Quickly now."

The gruff man rolled his eyes, but must have understood who he was dealing with. He nodded curtly and went to retrieve an armful of rolled-up maps from a nearby shelf, only to throw them down on the table in front of Sam.

She smiled her thanks, then carefully fumbled them off the table and sent them rolling across the floor. The guard said something even more unpleasant than he had before, but reluctantly bent down to retrieve them. Sam, meanwhile, glanced over at the scientist and held up her handcuffed hands.

"This has already been a long day and it's going to be even longer if you insist on keeping me in these, don't you think?"

Schultz scratched his nose below his glasses, clearly impatient to get on with his work. "Take the handcuffs off," he barked at the guard, who threw the maps back on the table.

"But Colonel Arif said–"

"Colonel Arif says a lot of things, but he is not here and I am. She is a woman! Are you not a man? If she tries anything, simply prevent her as you have been taught: with force."

Schultz returned to his desk and began to pore over his research again, once more oblivious to the world. Sam and the guard looked at each other for a moment. His eyes narrow and wary. Hers wide and innocent.

She held up her wrists and waited.

With another choice insult in Arabic, the man pulled a key from his pocket, roughly grasped both of her hands in his, and unlocked the cuffs.

She nodded gratefully and rubbed her wrists, then sat back down again and set to work unrolling the maps and looking over the photographs as she had been asked. With each one, she would carefully shuffle down the elastic band preventing it from unfurling, then smooth the paper down over the table and crane her neck over the entirety of the image – every now and then offering a murmur of interest.

After a few minutes, she popped her head up and asked the guard – standing at the door nearby, watching her carefully – to retrieve more maps for her.

He laughed as though she was joking. But then the Professor lifted an arm and waved it in her direction. And so the guard wandered over reluctantly, his attention and anger now diverted towards his superior. Which suited Sam just fine. Because she was ready to leave.

As he dropped the next batch of photographs onto the table, she grabbed the first one, pretended to inspect the number, then called him back.

"Sorry, but can you make out this catalogue number

for me? It's been printed in the corner here, but it's a bit small and unfortunately I didn't think to bring my glasses on this little trip."

The guard's face hardened. "That is not my job."

Sam nodded. "Of course, in which case Professor are you able to come over here and help me with this?"

The Professor glared at the other man. "How many times do I have to tell you, do whatever she needs. I am not here to serve. You are."

With a curt nod, the guard leaned closer, while distractedly mumbling about how much he hated babysitting prisoners.

Perfect Sam decided.

She didn't wait for him to lean over the desk this time. She gripped the top of the map in her left hand and held it up.

"It's the number in the top right-hand corner," she said.

"203.222 Ez07," he read back to her, from where he stood.

"That doesn't sound right, are you sure?"

She pushed the map closer to his face.

With the barest of groans, he started reading the numbers out extremely slowly, as she knew he would.

At which point she punched him clean through the map.

Only now did Schultz look up from his work, as the guard collapsed like a ragdoll to the floor. The Professor's face was a mask of disbelief as Sam stepped over the unconscious body and towards him. He was so shocked, in fact, that he didn't even try to get out of his chair and run. Just sat there with his mouth open, until his head snapped back as her fist met his chin, and he toppled over backwards.

"Now who's the amateur?" she quipped.

It would have been a good moment. But it was instantly spoiled when she realised with horror it's me, I'm still the amateur, as she looked over and saw the young guard had returned. He stood in the doorway, the steaming drink he had been sent to fetch cupped tightly in his hands.

They looked at one another.

Then Naguib dropped the mug and reached around for his rifle, flinging it up in her direction as the drink spilled around his feet. And although he was nervous and slow and had clearly not had much experience with such situations, there was too much ground to cover between them for Sam to do anything but wearily watch him gain the upper hand.

"Well, shit," she said, giving him a faint smile. Then, realising that she hadn't yet heard him speak any English to her, she decided to chance showing the ace up her sleeve. She switched to Arabic. "You're fast. I was almost out of here. Want to let me go anyway?"

He blinked and the rifle wavered. "They did not tell me you spoke our language."

"I'm not surprised. What exactly did they tell you about me?"

"That you… you are here to steal our treasures. Our history." The words came slow at first, but then Sam could feel the rage overcome the nervousness and they began to spill out of him in a torrent as his lips moved faster and faster underneath the wisp of a post-adolescent moustache – the kind she had seen on so many soldiers forced to grow up far too fast during the war. "Our land is not yours to rape and pillage, and our people are not yours to rule over, to get to do your dirty work. We do not exist here for others to come and take away the gifts that our ancestors left us, like you and your friends always do. No more. I will not let you steal from us again."

Sam felt the heat in her cheeks rise unbidden. But whatever plans she had been concocting to disarm the boy with violence now subsided. She could not argue the point. She would not argue the point. It was the same she had raised with Teddy many times before.

She lifted her hands in a gesture of surrender.

"For what it's worth, I'm sorry. But I'm not here to steal. Those people you call my friends? I don't think they should have what they came for either. The Hall of Records is a..." she struggled to find the right word, "...tremendous? It is a tremendous treasure. And if it exists here in Egypt, then here it should stay."

Naguib looked confused. The barrel of the gun wafted over the two unconscious bodies behind her. "But here you are, trying to escape. You want to chase after them. To beat them to the Hall?"

"Only to protect it."

"You lie. Colonel Arif himself is there. You say you do not want your friends to have the treasure and yet you don't think he, an Egyptian, should have it?"

"Those treasures belong to the people, Naguib. Not a government. Not the military. The people. Even if Colonel Arif allows that, my American friends will not. They will betray him and steal what they want anyway. But I can stop them. Why do you think they left me here?"

Sam risked a tentative step forward. The boy frowned and wiped the sweat from his top lip. But the gun wavered some more and she could see she almost had him. The doubt in his eyes was enough to tell her he probably wasn't going to shoot.

Probably.

"It might not seem like it right now," she said calmly, "but you and I might just be on the same side. Unfortunately, if I don't leave now, the others will find the Hall of Records first. Its treasures will be stolen out from under you, and the American men and their Nazi accomplices," she gestured to Professor Schultz, sprawled backwards on his chair, "will get what they want. Which, let me tell you, friend, will not be good for anybody."

Now the gun lowered. Naguib stared between her and the unconscious scientist. "He was a Nazi?"

"Still is. That's the problem with their kind, kid. They shed their skin from time to time, but they never stop being Nazis. And I don't know about you, but any time I see them pick a side, I'm going to pick the opposite."

She didn't know if it would work. She hoped it might. The war had spread far enough beyond the bounds of Europe to devastate places like Egypt too in recent years.

But how much of the Third Reich's evil had this young man seen?

Enough, it turned out.

Naguib stood straighter, his face hardened, but his eyes were now full of understanding. The gun dropped to his side and he stepped away from the center of the door.

"I did not know," he said, almost apologetically. "These men who are not men are not welcome here. They do not just steal, they destroy. Please, go, save what you can."

Stifling her sigh of relief, Sam put her hand gently on his shoulder as she stepped past. "For a long time I worked with one and I did not know either. But what matters is how you react when you find out." She paused as she slipped out of the room. "If it helps, Naguib, today I plan to react with a lot of violence."

He seemed to accept that.

"Shukran," she added, touching her heart.

"Taht amrik," he replied.

And with that she went to find her gun.

CHAPTER TWENTY

Roach

Dressed and armed – although she wasn't surprised to find the revolver had been emptied – Sam ran through the tight labyrinth of corridors looking for a way out. There was no point going back towards the cells. There were still too many soldiers wandering about. So she went the other direction, towards what looked like the sleeping quarters.

She had no idea what the time was, but it felt like afternoon. It had to be something like that if they had already dragged Will and Cayce out for a trip into the desert.

They'd try and reach the entrance towards evening, when it began to cool. Giving them more time, and less pressure in the heat, to use the keys and find the way in.

Which meant that she had to get out of here quickly or risk having to chase them down in the dark of night, facing all manner of extra challenges.

As if she needed more.

Hiding momentarily behind a series of lockers as a lone

soldier bustled past, she dove into the next open door and found herself in a sunlit room full of bunks. At the back of this was what looked like an emergency fire door, in front of which sat a trolley full of dirty clothes.

She frowned, then ran to the nearby window, just in time to see a decrepit military truck pull up on the road below, at the end of a sloping path that led down from the barracks.

"Laundry day," she mused, looking back to the trolley and figuring whether she could fit inside. A wry smile crept over her face. "*Too* easy?"

There was a rasping cough behind her and Agent Roach stood up from his bunk, running a freshly oiled bullwhip between his fingers. He put down the tub of oil and began to curl the weapon around his hands.

"Too easy," he agreed.

The wide, cheap window shattered into a thousand pieces as Sam flew through it.

He'd been so fast. Faster than she remembered. Or maybe she was older and wearier and still woozy from what Smith had done to her earlier.

She fell onto a corrugated roof below, the metal grazing her hands as she tried to cling on. It wasn't enough. She tumbled off it and dropped a storey onto the hot, dusty street.

It hurt. Everything was on fire. More pain than she could remember for a good long while.

Yet still she somehow pulled herself to her feet and staggered towards the truck, before collapsing in the shade of the vehicle and launching into a coughing fit, eyes filling with water. How many hits could one woman take? Her body felt like one big bruise and it was difficult to tell where in particular she was suffering the most.

Pressing her fingers into the road, she tried to get to her feet. Staggered a little and fell back to her knees.

A man with a mass of dusty black hair, dressed in old fatigues of about the lowest rank possible, popped his head around the side of the truck. Seeing Sam wavering on the edge of death, he frowned and pushed his trolley filled with bags of clean laundry in her direction.

He spoke in fast, worried Arabic. The words flew at her like panicked birds, scattered and senseless, and she couldn't make them out. It seemed to be a question. Probably wondering why she had just been thrown through a window and, maybe, if she was okay.

But just as he moved to help her up, a meaty growl bade him to stop.

"Leave her," Roach barked, standing in the doorway of the barracks, curled bullwhip in hand. "She's mine."

The laundry man looked from him to Sam. He clearly didn't understand English and tried to move towards her again. She shook her head, warning him off. There was no point in two of them getting killed today.

Roach strode down the path to the truck. Sam was too dizzy, too shaky to watch him approach. But she could hear the thud of his footsteps as they grew nearer, before there was a tug at the shoulders of her jacket and she was yanked to her feet.

Like a child being picked up and dusted off after a fall.

And dust her down he did. Brushing her shoulders and straightening her jacket, all with a huge smile on his face.

Before smacking her with the back of his bullwhip-carrying hand.

She spun in circles. Round and round, legs like jelly, arms thrown feebly up to protect her from whatever came next. She would have gone down again, if not for the truck.

She bounced onto the bonnet and it bought her the stability she needed to keep herself upright.

Just.

"Is that all you've got?" she slurred through broken lips. She had a fix on him now, even as she backed away around the side of the truck, fists raised. "I've had stronger drinks put me on the floor."

He pursued her slowly, a wide grin splitting his face all the way across between his disproportionally tiny ears. Clearly he was enjoying this.

A fist flew out. Huge. Like a bloody meteor.

She just about managed to duck it. Swung upwards with a weak one of her own. Her knuckles bounced off his chin like pebbles against a cliff.

The smile widened, if that was possible. In fact, he began to laugh. And it was enough of a distraction to get in the shot she really wanted.

She kicked him hard in the nuts.

All his good humour trickled out of him in a grunt as

he staggered backwards, knock-kneed, using the truck to keep him upright.

"Bitch," he hissed through clenched teeth.

"And proud," she spat.

She went in again, throwing punch after punch. Cracking them against the side of his face, as he remained prone to attacks. And while they didn't do anything other than bruise her fists, it was enough to provoke the man-mountain into fending her off.

He tried to swat her away with the whip. She grabbed it, ripped it from his grasp, and backed away.

"Unlucky," she said.

Scuffing her boots through the dirt, she moved slowly past the rear of the truck. One of the large double doors had been left open. The other, nearest her, was closed but looked unlocked. Its long handle was twisted downwards.

Agent Roach staggered upright and lumbered towards her again. She waited as long as she could, until he was in the clear past the doors.

Then she struck out with the whip.

It had been a bloody long time since she'd used one, but her muscle memory didn't fail her. The action was smooth. The strike hard.

He didn't even flinch as she missed him by a good couple of feet. The end of the whip wrapped itself around the truck's rear door handle.

He glanced at it, then grinned.

"Luck never has anything to do with it, my girl. Did you never listen to any of my lessons when we worked together?

When we fought together?" He cracked his knuckles, then raised his fists and loosened his shoulders as he readied himself to finish her. "Using such a weapon like that takes practise. You might be talented in other areas, but this isn't something you can just pick up and wield." He took a step forward, now behind the truck. "You should have taken me up on my offer when I said I'd teach you."

He took another step closer.

Close enough.

She pulled back on the whip with every ounce of strength that remained. It tugged the truck door open with such speed and ferocity it smacked into Roach hard enough to send him crashing sideways to the floor in a cloud of dust, like an ugly, demolished chimney.

It was enough to buy her only seconds. But she'd used less to her advantage in the past. Seeing a collection of older weapons and ammunition in the back of the truck, she grabbed a box of bullets, tossed away the whip and glanced around. Then saw the abandoned laundry trolley at the top of the sloped road. That'll have to do, she thought as she rushed over and gave it an almighty push down the hill.

Down it went, past the truck, picking up speed as it shot towards the main street at the bottom.

Roach struggled to his feet and ran around the other side of the truck after it…missing Sam moving quietly in the other direction.

"Stop!" he yelled, stumbling as he tried to manoeuvre his big frame down the slope after the trolley. "Stop her!"

His shouting brought another guard running out of the

building further down the road. Right into the path of the trolley, and the two collided with a crash. Yet only as Roach finally skidded to a halt in front of the lone sprawled figure did he realise the trolley was empty.

Sam saw him turn back up the hill and grab the guard's machine gun as she scrambled over the wall to the barracks. Bullets sprayed behind her, sending chunks of rock cartwheeling into the air, followed by his howl of rage as she dropped down the steep slope into the heart of the village surrounding the military base.

Then she ran. Taking one small street, then another. Running through houses, surprising villagers in their homes, knocking over the odd market stall seller. Moving with no way of knowing where to go from here. Only that she was running out of time.

The sun was lowering in the sky. She needed a vehicle, and quickly.

Which is when she saw a group of elderly passengers waiting to board a ramshackle local bus.

There was a queue.

In the middle of this small Egyptian town. A goddamn queue to get on the bus.

Mostly the elderly, hobbling slowly up the steps. Although there were a couple of women with young children too.

Through the windscreen the driver looked almost catatonic with boredom, keeping the bus idling while barking at each and every passenger to hurry. One child burst into tears at his admonishment. His mother scowled and swore back at the driver, who sneered and ignored her.

Sam staggered over and joined the back of the queue, reloading her gun as she waited behind a heavyset man who would have given Roach a run for his money. The driver must have thought twice about insulting him, because he simply waved him on board.

He was about to absently wave Sam on too, when he did a double take.

"Who the hell are you?" he demanded in English.

"I'm–"

He held up his hand. "I don't care. *You* pay double!"

She sighed. Then grabbed him, wrenched him out of his chair and tossed him down the steps. He landed in a heap in the dusty street.

Sam turned to the passengers as they applauded her. Her frown deepened and she thumbed towards the door and said in Arabic, "Sorry, need the bus. Please can you get off?"

The applause stopped and the passengers looked at Sam, then each other.

"Everyone off!" Sam said more urgently.

She slid into the old, battered driver's seat as the women and children quickly got up and hurried past her to safety. But in the rear-view mirror she could see that some of the more cantankerous elderly passengers were staying seated, as though they either didn't hear what Sam was saying or simply didn't care.

One of the old men saw her looking and gestured to her rudely.

"We haven't got all day!" he snapped.

"No we haven't," she agreed, hearing yelling from down the street and seeing the bus driver running towards her with five soldiers in tow.

She reached for what she thought might be the lever to shut the door and the windscreen wipers started instead. Dusting off her hands on her trousers, she tried not to panic. OK, so she'd never driven a bus before. In truth, she only had a passing knowledge of driving a car. The war meant petrol shortages had taken hold in England before she'd had a chance to learn properly. She'd become a pilot before anything else.

Which would make this escape tricky.

"Sod it." She left the door open and wrestled the stick into gear. "Sorry everyone, but this is about to get a little dicey."

With only seconds to spare, the bus leapt forward and scattered the soldiers, as the passengers behind her began to scream.

CHAPTER TWENTY-ONE

Bus Trip

Agent Roach regarded the tiny, out-of-breath Egyptian soldier cowering before him.

"She's been spotted, sir," the man barely whispered. He licked his dry lips. "The main street. On a bus."

"A bus?"

The soldier handed him a walkie-talkie. "And your superiors want an update."

Roach put a hand on the man's small, bony shoulder. Squeezed hard enough to make him realise just how important it was that he pay attention to what came next.

"There is only one road in or out of this little shithole," he said in a low, threatening voice. "I want you and your men to get there immediately and make sure – by *any* means necessary – that she does not pass beyond the town walls into the desert. Do you understand?"

"Yes, sir."

The trembling beneath his fingers made Roach want to crush the man's bones even more. Snap his shoulder blades in half. Watch him drop like a wounded deer and writhe around, waiting to be put out of his misery.

But there was no time for that now.

So he scowled and released the soldier, who scuttled off with his colleagues, making every effort to ensure they looked like they were taking this more seriously than anything that idiot Colonel Arif had ever asked them to do.

They leapt into a jeep and shot off, towards the gate.

Roach followed slowly after them, lifting the walkie-talkie to his lips, as he watched another soldier ready a second jeep for him.

"Agent Roach," he said, thumbing the transmit switch.

It crackled into life at the other end.

Agent Taylor sat in the back of the car speeding through the Egyptian desert, his mind on the man beside him.

Colonel Arif sat perfectly still, eyes front and centre, staring at the back of the head of their driver. His hands were clasped together tightly, clearly trying to hold onto his emotions. He must be excited. And impatient. How long had he been waiting for this moment? Since he was a young man? A child?

That the Egyptians were proud of their heritage was no surprise, given their rich culture and the scatters of astonishing historical artefacts and architecture that still glittered across their land today. Like nuggets of gold in an old mining pan, Taylor thought. Who knew what gleam of knowledge had lit the patriotic fervour that swept through the military man now, eagerly awaiting the moment he would bring his country back to its former glories.

At least, that's what Colonel Arif thought was going to happen.

Taylor looked out of the window, scanning the vastness of the shimmering afternoon sands.

Restoring Egyptian pride and standing in the world wasn't high on America's agenda. The locals were useful, and this was their country after all. So, of course, there was decorum and procedure to follow. But it was a means to an end. A way to get things done without too much bloodshed or international bullet-pissing contests, that only served to waste men and ammunition and created tensions that made future operations difficult.

Taylor would go along with it until he didn't need to anymore. There was only one thing that The Nine needed out of this mission and until that artefact or information or whatever the hell it would turn out to be was in his possession, he wasn't going to allow himself the reward of feeling complacent or even excited.

They still had some way to go before reaching Wadi Sais, and the Agents of The Nine had long been trained not to count their inter-dimensional eggs before they'd hatched into a grotesque and dangerous life force.

So he sat quietly, scanning the desert and watching for anything that might get in his way. Any delay or anything that might slip a rock under their wheels or a blade between their ribs.

The knowledge that Sam was alive and he couldn't see what she was up to rankled him. He should be content, knowing she was back at the base under armed guard by hundreds of soldiers, with Agent Roach on watch. But just her being in the same time zone kept her a threat. He would much rather she have travelled with them, not least so he could keep an eye on her – or put a bullet in her, if needed.

But, no, Arif had refused. And right now Taylor was feeling more and more inclined to make sure his frustration was reciprocated. The Colonel's search for what the Hall represented to Egypt was – at least to him – a noble cause. But it would be a futile one. Because what the Hall meant to him paled in significance compared to what it contained – and what that could mean for America's already great standing in the world order and its ability to fight the battles ahead.

He may well let Arif and his soldiers see the Hall. They deserved that much.

But he was still undecided if any of them would leave it alive.

"Taylor?" The walkie-talkie in his hand suddenly buzzed and a gruff voice came through. Colonel Arif twitched in irritation as the interruption broke his contemplative mood. He muttered something in Arabic under his breath, then closed his eyes. "Taylor, come in. It's Roach."

Taylor lifted the device to his lips. There was something in his agent's tone that he immediately didn't like. And he hated that he might know why.

"I asked for an update five minutes ago, Agent Roach. Is there a reason you've kept me waiting?"

There was no immediate reply.

Taylor watched a tumbleweed blow across the desert road ahead, careering helplessly into the sands at the whim of the wind. He pushed down the jolt of helplessness that threatened to erupt in a cascade of fury out of his mouth, and kept his lips tightly shut. He was not a tumbleweed. He was in control here. Whatever was about to be said was bad news for him, but it would be worse for Roach when this whole mess was over. The Nine always rewarded those who served them well. But they were also masters of making sure you were punished for not doing your job.

"Roach?" he repeated.

The handset crackled again. "She got out."

"I knew it," the Colonel whispered to himself.

Taylor kept his face straight, making sure not to let the man see the anger now bubbling beneath the surface. It was difficult though. He wanted to snap Arif's neck and put a bullet in the back of his driver's head for making him leave Sam back at the base to pull the kind of crap he had once trained her to pull.

But he couldn't. Not yet.

"How did she get out, Roach?"

He listened to the man's stilted explanation. Of course, his agent said nothing about whether or not he'd had a chance to stop Sam escaping, but Taylor could hear the truth wriggling beneath the excuses like an eel trapped in a rapidly evaporating swamp.

"She cannot be allowed to leave the base," Taylor said, then kept the button held down while trying to decide how severe his next order should be. No, not yet, he decided. "Find her quickly, take her back to the cell, and leave her in there until we return – however long that takes. OK?"

To his surprise, Arif reached over and grabbed the walkie-talkie from him. The fear in his eyes was now very apparent indeed.

"Scratch that order, Agent Roach. Captain Moxley cannot be allowed to interfere with our plans. On behalf of the Egyptian government, I am instructing you to find her and kill her. Is that clear?"

Taylor looked to Agent Smith, who until now had been staring out of the other window. Now his cold blue eyes regarded the uniformed Egyptian impassively, as though one might regard a bug on your shoe... before you casually flicked it off.

Or crushed it.

"You have little faith in your men," he said. "Agent Taylor has given an order to be followed. Rest assured, our man will ensure he recaptures her."

The Colonel bristled. "And you fellows have little respect for that insufferable woman. *We* have a history and I know full well what she is capable of – as do you, I'm sure. Now, I grow tired of tolerating you gambling with such important matters. Kill her."

"No," Taylor said.

"Very well," the Colonel replied. He turned to his driver. "Sergeant?"

Without even taking his eyes off the road, the driver pulled a gun and pointed it directly at the head of Smith.

"Now, Colonel–" Smith began, a cold hint of humour at the corner of his lips. He hadn't even flinched.

"–I will not argue with you again. Give the order to kill the woman. Now."

Smith looked to Taylor. His question was clear.

Should I kill them both here and now?

Taylor thought about it for a second as his finger tapped the knee of his trousers. It would be easy to do, but it would lead to complications later and there was a way to go before they reached the Hall. Perhaps it was best to cede power for the moment and let his hosts think they were in charge of this little trip.

"As you wish, Colonel," he said, taking back the walkie-talkie.

He hated to admit it. But there was a lot at stake today. And even though he too had a history with Sam, one that at the time had certainly kept him entertained more than maybe he should have let it, perhaps it was finally time to scratch the itch that had been bugging him recently.

With a sigh and a silent apology to the woman who continued to drive him to distraction, he confirmed the instruction for her termination.

His agent's response came back immediately.

"About fucking time, sir."

Roach tossed the walkie-talkie to the nearest soldier, unable to help the grin that was fighting for control of his face.

After all this time, he was finally going to get to end that bloody woman for good.

He had no idea what must have changed Taylor's mind. His usually uncompromising boss had only ever let one thing get in the way of his decisions in the past. Samantha Moxley. Former pilot. Former agent. Massive pain in the ass.

But it seemed her luck had finally come to an end. And what a sticky, painful end he would make it.

"Orders, sir?" a waiting soldier asked him.

Roach slapped him on the back. "Oh we have them, boy. We finally have them."

He lifted his head and addressed all those who had been assigned to him. They waited obediently to be told what to do. He liked that about these foreign armies. When dealing with America, they had seen what his beloved country could do. They had witnessed America's absolute power at the end of the war. They knew their place now.

"Today is going to be a good day," he continued, addressing everyone who could hear him. "The escaped prisoner is to be apprehended at all costs. Spread out, search the village for the bus she has stolen. Get to the gate and ensure she cannot leave. Do you understand me?"

To a man, they nodded.

"Shoot to kill?" one asked in his broken English.

Roach pulled out his gun.

"Only if you can beat me to her."

* * *

The people in the bus wouldn't stop screaming.

Sam's Arabic was solid, but the cacophony of different voices, pierced every now and then by the squeals of the bus as she spun it around another corner, made it difficult to understand exactly what she was being told.

She knew it wasn't nice. That much was clear.

The noise intensified as the jeep full of soldiers behind them tried to overtake again. It rammed the side of the bus once, twice… then she slammed on the brake. It shot past, just as she nudged the wheel to the right and gently clipped the back.

It spun at speed. Blew a tire. And came to a shuddering halt against a wall.

Sam gave them a small salute as she drove past. Not entirely ironic either. She had noted the lack of bullets sent their way – despite being armed, not one of the soldiers had raised their guns in the direction of the bus.

Not just being friendly. She knew it was because she had hostages and the soldiers didn't want to harm them to get to her. She could respect that. Especially because there was no way the Americans would have been so careful.

It made her smile to think of Roach, catatonic with rage, later discovering nobody had fired a damn bullet at the bus.

The smile faded as another jeep appeared from a side-alley and slammed into them.

"No!" she muttered, as the bus tilted dangerously. "No, no, no!"

She only just wrestled back control this time. But then the street began to narrow. If the jeep got ahead of them there would be no need for bullets. They'd just slow her down and she'd have nowhere to go.

Goddamnit.

The driver of the jeep had seen it too. He stuck his foot on the gas, pushing them faster.

She tried to do the same, but the bus was already threatening to fall apart as it was. There was a clanking underneath. The suspension was wrecked, so she could feel every bloody stone on the road.

Sam did the only thing she could.

Pulled her gun and took a shot at the other vehicle.

Her aim wasn't true. She'd gone for the wheels and hit the windscreen, which wasn't ideal.

But it had the desired effect.

Hitting a jolt in the road, the jeep leapt up and down hard. The windscreen shattered. The driver covered his face and took his foot off the pedal momentarily.

Sam pushed ahead and swerved in front, just as the street narrowed to a single track.

"Next stop... *the hell out of here*!" she called brightly.

But as they pulled through the shadow of the leaning buildings and the view opened up into the distance, she finally saw the gateway to the complex she had been heading for.

And noted the giant armoured truck blocking their way.

A truck with a gun turret on the back, swivelling in their direction.

* * *

Roach had been on his way to the gate anyway. He could have chased her around the streets, but he knew Moxley well enough to understand she wasn't going to be stopped easily like that. Better to cut her escape off at the one and only place she could leave the town with the biggest goddamn gun he could find.

The M37 Dodge that carried it was a beautiful bitch too. He'd seen her earlier in the week. All sturdy chassis, thick tyres and desert camouflage. But it was in the modified cargo bed at the back where the real power was – a pair of Browning machine guns stripped from an old Lancaster bomber topping a swivel turret.

He'd ordered the Dodge up to the gate earlier, just in case, and got them to position it just to the side of the gateway. It wouldn't be nearly enough to block the bus, should she be stupid enough to try to drive right past, but that wasn't the point. It might tempt her into trying and that would give him an excuse to open up the gun and erase her from the face of the fucking planet.

Screw the hostages. He wanted her dead by any means possible.

The jeep he was in bounced along the road, heading west to the gate. They'd taken a higher road, so he had the perfect view when the rusted bus burst into sight along the main north road heading towards the Dodge.

He picked up his walkie-talkie.

"Tear her apart," he ordered.

There was a crackle at the other end.

"U–understood, sir."

Yet, as he watched the truck intently, waiting to see the bright yellow fire burst from those big bloody Lancaster barrels, he knew something wasn't right.

"What the hell are you waiting for?" he yelled into the device, seeing the bus speeding up as it headed for the gate. "I said fire!"

"I..." There was a waver in the soldier's voice now. "I can't. There are people on there with her. Passengers."

"Are you shitting me? Fuck the passengers! Shoot the fucking bus!"

"My grandfather takes that bus, sir."

"Fuck your grandfather!"

There was no response to that.

Roach could feel the veins trying to tear free of his face as he unleashed a ferocious howl into the air. He pulled his own gun and stood up in the jeep as they neared, firing repeatedly at the bus as though his anger might push the bullets to find their target. But he was too far away and that son-of-a-bitch vehicle wasn't slowing down.

It shot past the Dodge and ploughed through the gateway onto the desert road beyond, leaving those fine Lancaster guns swivelling harmlessly as they followed its escape.

Moxley was free.

Roach kept standing as his jeep skidded to a halt beside the gun truck. He stepped out casually, aware that all the soldiers around him were staring, especially the man at the turret. The perspiration on his face gave him away, even though he had his chest out and his chin held firm.

"I'm sorry, sir, but I–"

Roach shot him in the head and jumped into the cargo bed. He threw his body off the truck, and took his place at the turret.

Then he swivelled it around to target the driver, whose eyes widened to the point of almost popping out of his head.

"Get in the fucking truck and drive," Roach said.

CHAPTER TWENTY-TWO

Desert Chase

The day was bright and beautiful.

Fayah and her husband stood at the bus stop in their sleepy village, waiting for their transport to the market in the next town.

The children played around them. Some silly game with a rope and marbles which Fayah didn't pretend to understand. Things had certainly changed in the years since their own children had grown and flown, when she and her sisters had spent most of their days working. But it was nice to see life as it should be, the beauty of an innocent childhood, after their country had seen so much war.

She rested her head on her husband's arm and closed her eyes, smiling at the peace and warmth of it all.

In the distance, the rumble of wheels on dirt sounded. She waited for it to grow nearer, before opening her eyes again and standing up straight, waiting to board.

But it grew nearer far too quickly. And in an instant her husband pulled her backwards to safety as the bus halted with a screech before them, the doors already open.

They watched in horror as a flood of crying, screaming and cursing passengers spilled out into the street, leaving behind a bloody and battered white woman at the driver's wheel.

To Fayah, she looked half dead. A corpse in waiting. Yet, as she smiled wearily through the door, she spoke with a strength that Fayah had known before. The strength of someone who does not know when to give up.

"Wadi Sais?" the woman asked.

Fayah lifted her hand shakily to point to a road off the main street.

The woman nodded her thanks. And the bus sped off again, taking the corner far too roughly as it sped in the direction Fayah had indicated.

If that wasn't enough, not even one minute later, the wailing group all had to jump out of the way again as a military truck whizzed past and skidded around the corner after the bus.

Fayah looked up to her husband, whose lips were parted in horror at what he was seeing.

"Bike?" she said.

He took his hat off and wiped a big forearm across his brow, before looking down at her and nodding.

"Bike," he agreed.

The bus shot through the wide expanse of desert like a rusty bullet, with the enemy in fast pursuit.

Sam swerved from left to right across the narrow strip of road, as heavy gunfire splattered the back of her vehicle. She caught glimpses of the gun truck behind her. The fearsome turret spewing bullets in a frenzy.

Roach.

She knew it must be him. The Egyptian soldiers would be far more accurate and careful with their aim. Military training taught you to be precise and deadly.

Roach was another matter entirely. If he'd had professional training before joining The Nine, it didn't show. He was simply a thug, dressed up in an expensive suit. Which, she figured, was how the governments usually liked them. Someone to instil fear in the enemy, yet lacking enough sense to question what it was they were being asked to do.

Of course, his unpredictable actions also made him a liability. And although his superiors could turn a blind eye to that when it suited them, it meant he was far more dangerous to his opponents and anyone else in the immediate vicinity.

Gritting her teeth, she glanced over her shoulder to see splinters of evening light poking their way through the bullet holes in the rear of the bus.

Time was slipping away. She needed to get a move on.

She floored the accelerator pedal, but it only had a little more give in it. They were already moving about as fast as they could – and even then she wasn't sure the bus was going to last much longer. One way or another, this wasn't going to end well. Either the bullets would stop them… or old age would.

The road was busier than she had expected. Apparently the route east towards Wadi Sais from wherever she had been held was a main thoroughfare. Cars shimmered into existence in the distant haze, then honked like angry camels as they had to swerve off the road to dodge Sam's evasion tactics.

All except one car. She didn't know what it was, only that it looked too fancy to be out in the desert. Jeffries would have known, she thought suddenly. He knew them all. Could have told her what make and model it was, how fast it went, even how strong the bloody headlights might be. He loved shit like that.

All she knew was that it looked fancy and right now it didn't seem to care much for anybody else on the road. She smacked her vehicle's horn and it blared long and loud, but the driver did nothing other than stick a pale arm out of the window and lift a pudgy middle digit at her.

Bloody tourists.

In the wing mirror, she realised the truck was now trying to pull alongside. Boxing her in. Giving her nowhere to go as the car headed their way at speed.

She rammed into the truck, forcing it back, just as the car approached. It was tight, but she made it, swerving around – although she couldn't help giving the steering wheel a little jolt and sending the sweaty, red-faced driver and his jewellery laden female passenger crashing off the road to be deposited in a large sand dune.

It felt good. And, for just a moment, she enjoyed it. A split-second of justice in an otherwise cruel world.

Then Roach took advantage.

The gun truck pushed up the other side while she was distracted. A barrage of bullets started spraying up the entire side of the bus from back to front, sending shards of glass and metal flying into the aisle and ripping the seats to shreds.

The bus began to disintegrate around her.

Still the bullets holes continued inching forwards.

Closer.

Closer.

Until finally she had to duck forward as the bullets ripped apart the back of her seat.

The noise was deafening, all wind and fury and imminent death.

Before, all of a sudden, it stopped.

Still clutching the steering wheel, Sam popped up to see Roach reloading. Then, through a ripped hole in the bus, she glimpsed the terrified face of the soldier driver who was now alongside her.

She snarled as she twisted the steering wheel suddenly, slamming into the truck once, twice, three times.

"My… turn… mother…fuckers," she yelled over the roar of the wind, the growl of the competing engines, and the squeal of metal tearing against metal.

Again and again she hit the truck. Shaking the driver off the wheel more than once. And sending Roach flying in the bed of his truck.

She could have sworn she heard him yell in anger through the din.

But as satisfying as that was, he was up again as quick as anything and he managed to finish reloading. The barrage of bullets began again.

The turret swung in the cargo bed, out over the side of the truck, its heavy barrels ablaze with firing. Were they aircraft guns? Shit, they just might be.

The side of the bus was almost all gone now. Twisted and unrecognisable.

Again the bullets came spraying up the aisle.

Tearing straight through the holes and into the other side now.

One by one, from the back to the front, the windows on that side were blasted outwards.

He was decapitating the bus.

"Sod this," she yelled into the wind.

She spun the wheel so hard this time that she almost expected the two vehicles to become one. The collision was horrendous and brought back memories of the wrench and scream of metal doing things it was never meant to do when she'd ditched her plane in the Channel all those years ago.

But it worked.

The barrels of the guns were now wedged hard in the mangled side of the bus.

She couldn't see Roach, but she could sure hear him, screaming obscenities as he tried to free his weapons without success.

He gave up quickly and started firing again.

Sam didn't care. She was busy grinning as she saw the

road begin to narrow ahead. The desert giving way to jagged, rocky hills, through which they would have to drive.

Only wide enough for a single vehicle.

The gun truck driver must have seen it too, because he desperately started trying to wrench his truck away.

Big mistake.

If he had tried to force the bus the other way, he might have stood a chance. Sam wasn't sure the bus carried much weight anymore, not with half of it shot away. The truck may well have forced her off the road into the upcoming rock.

But his instinct was to run, to escape.

So she gently began steering in the direction he was trying to go, nudging him off the road on the other side.

The driver realised his mistake, even as Roach began yelling at him.

But it was too late. Sam had the momentum.

Out of the corner of her eye she watched the driver raise his hands in horror. Before Sam shot into the narrow cutting and the truck hit the rocks head-on.

The explosion was huge, searing the side of her face as the force of the blast knocked her sideways. All she could do in that moment was grimly hang onto the steering wheel and hope that it held.

It did.

Soon all that was left of the truck was the turret dangling momentarily from the bus, before its weight peeled away half the side of the vehicle and it all fell clattering into the road.

At that moment the bus doors finally decided to close.

Sam laughed, then coughed through the dissipating cloud of smoke in the cabin.

Until it cleared and she saw a pair of boots briefly dangling beyond the smashed window at the back of the bus, before they were pulled up out of sight.

Agent Roach had leapt to the roof.

She started swerving, as much as the road allowed, banging the bus on the rocks just enough to try and shake him off. But she could hear his boot steps above as he kept on coming for her.

THUMP.

THUMP.

Until there was a moment of silence. And he appeared, climbing in upside-down, through one of the shattered windows only a few rows behind her.

She pulled out her gun. Lifted it behind her and began firing blindly, while still trying not to crash.

In the distance ahead, the back of Taylor's military convoy came into view.

The vibration told Agent Taylor all he needed to know.

A thump that he could feel deep in his chest. A shockwave with no sound, but hard enough to jolt the car and silence the argument that was in full flight.

The three passengers turned their heads to witness the fireball ballooning into the air above the canyon pass.

"Moxley," Smith hissed through gritted teeth.

Arif could barely contain his rage. "You see?" he seethed.

"*This* is why I wanted her dead. Had we acted when I said so she would already be nothing but an unpleasant memory. I thought we could trust your men to do the job?"

Taylor ignored him, keeping his face neutral, unwilling to give anything away. Especially the fact that Arif was right.

As they shot out of the rocks back into the open terrain of the desert, he caught a glimpse of a mangled bus trailing behind the convoy. One side almost entirely gone, as though it had been shot through. While behind the cracked windscreen he saw a figure in a brown pilot's jacket.

The bus began to gain on them.

Taylor reached for the walkie-talkie. Not to speak to Roach, but his man in the jeep at the rear of the convoy. If Roach was still alive, Taylor would make sure they had *that* particular conversation in person later – and it would not go well for the hulking agent.

He thumbed the transmit button.

"Agent Bannerston," he said.

"What do you want me to do, sir?" came the immediate reply from his man.

Taylor glanced back at the steadily approaching threat.

"I'd very much like you to remove that goddamn bus from existence – and the same goes for whoever you find in it. Do you copy?"

"Loud and clear."

The jeep peeled off from the others. The soldiers all trained their weapons on the chasing vehicle. And they began to fire.

CHAPTER TWENTY-THREE

Showdown

What was left of the bus windscreen disappeared as it was blasted with gunfire.

Sam had already ducked. She now swerved the bus from side to side, just enough to make her a harder target without coming off the road – because if she hit the sand the game was over.

Fortunately it worked.

The bullets strayed from the vehicle long enough for her to pop her head up and see the attacking jeep now crossing her path to come around for another shot.

It was off balance. An easy target.

Taylor really hadn't drilled these guys very well.

She drove into it right in the sweet spot, just at the back right corner.

The gunfire stuttered across the bonnet, but it wasn't close enough. The enemy vehicle tilted for the longest of seconds, then furiously barrel-rolled into the desert.

Behind her she heard Roach curse her out as he

She threw him a sidelong glance. "Some relationships just don't work out, Will. Haven't you ever experienced that?"

"If I'm honest, my break ups never involved this much throwing people from moving vehicles!"

She grinned as she gunned the jeep after the others.

"So what's your plan, Captain?"

"We need those artefacts. Do you know who has them?"

"A man named Cayce. He told them he needed to charge the Amulet and Stone before we reached the gate or they wouldn't work."

Sam gripped the wheel tightly. "I figure that might just be a lie. He wanted to stall Taylor and the others and stop them taking control. The artefacts don't need to be charged – he's holding onto them because he knew I was coming."

"How is that even possible?"

"He's a psychic."

"That's not even a real thing!"

"Who's to say what's real and what's not any more, Will. Do you know where they're keeping him?"

Will lifted a finger to point to the truck ahead. She peered after it, trying to make out the figures through the dust as they neared. There were two guards, by the looks of things. And Cayce was quickly obvious. The sickly figure in their midst, clutching a bag to his chest as though his life depended on it.

As they saw the jeep approach, both guards moved to crouch at the rear of the truck bed and raised their guns.

Will ducked behind the dashboard, but Sam held her

position. Because she could see they weren't going to get a shot off.

Cayce had sensed she was close. And he clearly still had some fight left in him.

He threw himself at the soldiers.

One immediately fell off the truck, bouncing nastily in front of the jeep. But the other managed to grasp the back of the truck as he tumbled off.

His feet dragged from side to side through the sand and grit as he lifted his gun towards Cayce.

Sam looked around, spied a pistol that one of the soldiers must have dropped, grabbed it and leaned around the windshield.

Through the roar of wind and engines, she could only feel the gun fire, rather than hear it. A powerful recoil. A shockwave up her arm. But the end result was the same.

The soldier went limp and dropped out of sight.

Only for a *third* soldier to appear from the darkness of the truck to leap on the psychic.

Sam's boot was already jammed on the accelerator. All she could do now was will the jeep faster. It was clear Cayce was still weak. He wasn't going to last long against a fully trained military man.

"I didn't realise he had it in him," Will yelled across.

"It's what's in him that's the problem!"

She raised the gun again and tried to train it on the soldier, but they were struggling back and forth too much.

"Get me closer," Will urged, grabbing the frame of the windshield and standing up on his seat.

She glanced at him as if he was joking. He wasn't. Dr William Sandford was getting ready to jump.

There was a part of her that resisted. The part that knew what Jess might think.

But right now she knew Cayce was going to lose the fight. And if the human in him was beaten into submission, there was every chance that the spirit buried underneath would take over and claim the artefacts for itself.

And that couldn't be a good thing.

"Go get him, Will," she cried, and rammed the jeep into the back of the truck.

The soldier had been standing over Cayce, poised to bring the butt of his rifle down. The jolt shook him off balance and he slipped sideways, just as Will vaulted over the jeep windscreen and leapt off the bonnet into the back of the truck – before punching the soldier back into the shadows from where he'd appeared.

Sam could have cheered. Will, of all people, had just saved the day!

And yet the relief was short lived, because just as he reached down to help the psychic up, she saw that Cayce was shaking uncontrollably, his face contorting in pain as he pushed Will away and shoved the bag of artefacts at him instead.

Sam couldn't hear what he was saying, but whatever it was caused the academic to frown and not even attempt to argue. He simply took the bag and threw it to Sam, who caught it with her driving hand and tossed it in the passenger seat.

Yet just as she beckoned Will back, Cayce's back arched.

"Will! Back in the jeep, now!" Sam yelled, as ethereal blue strands began shooting from the psychic's body.

But it was too late. An explosion of blue energy enveloped the back of the truck and everyone in it, bright enough to momentarily blind Sam, who swung the jeep one way, while the truck driver panicked and veered the other way, off the road, smashing through the dunes.

The last thing she saw was Will raising his hands and crying out, and then they were gone, over the crest of a small hill and down the other side… before a fireball rose into the sky with a thunderous roar as supernatural energy, man-made truck and sand were blown in every direction.

"Oh God," Sam gasped, as she slowed and began to turn the wheel, before more gunfire sprayed the road next to her as the remaining cars ahead doubled back. She grimaced and swerved around them, catching a glimpse of Taylor's furious glare as she passed them and shot her jeep down the road, while in the cracked rearview mirror, she saw them turn towards what remained of the truck, obviously unaware that she now had the pieces.

Alone on the road, she knew she should feel relief. Once again she'd beaten the odds to make it out alive and she'd done it with the artefacts she needed to prevent a corrupt and evil organisation from increasing their control over the known world – artefacts that Taylor would now spend hours trying to sift through the truck wreckage to find, only to come up short.

But the reality was that this particular jaunt had

been far too close to home for comfort. She was used to escapades around the world but she'd never had to worry about anybody else before.

She caught a glimpse of herself in the wing mirror, revealing someone she hadn't seen in a while.

A face bruised and bloodied and possibly on the edge of death.

She was alive. But two innocent people were not.

One of whom she had promised her sister she would keep safe.

My fault.

As her fingers flexed painfully and gripped the wheel, keeping the jeep heading towards the setting sun and a showdown with her sister, she wondered if perhaps The Nine had already won.

CHAPTER TWENTY-FOUR

Sisters

An hour later, Sam brought the smoking, bullet-riddled jeep to a juddering halt next to a clean, white house.

A family were sitting outside, eating a magnificent spread of food beneath the dazzling purple evening skies. They looked up as one, with a mix of consternation and confusion at the carnage the white woman had parked on their doorstep.

She gave them a polite nod – and promptly fell out of the vehicle.

One of the teenage children, a tall girl who looked more curious than fearful, stood immediately to come to her aid, but the mother snapped out an arm and held her back to whisper something in her ear.

In her exhaustion, Sam couldn't make it out. But, if it had been a warning, she couldn't blame the woman. Her own father probably would have done the same if someone had turned up looking like she'd been through the entirety of a war in only a few hours.

She held up her hand. "I'm fine, I'm fine," she said as she got to her feet, trying to smile through her exhaustion. It faded quickly as she stood to her full height and switched her brain into Arabic to address the wide-eyed parents. It wasn't easy, but the words were still somehow there in the chaos of her mind. Enough to get her message across, at least. "There will be people following me later. Bad men. Please keep your children inside until they are gone."

The father looked warily at Sam, as though this might be another trick by another foreigner in their country, and quite frankly she couldn't begrudge him his doubt. The violence that often rippled in her wake and that of most western interlopers on foreign shores was always significant. The Suez crisis most recently. What was happening in Korea right now. It felt like those in the west had a talent for skipping straight out of one war and into another, as though they had a lust for it, while the locals would be left to clean it up when they had gone. More and more, the glorious ideals of "Empire" were revealed to be nothing more than fancy dressing when you saw the realities of those who came to suffer beneath its polished boots, blinkered ambition, and secret agendas.

But while the father hesitated at the paleness of her face and the trouble in her eyes, the mother saw through it all and understood. A mother's instinct right there, Sam's father used to say once upon a time, usually after he had failed to keep the two sisters from some kind of trouble (because, as he liked to joke, his own instinct had been blown out of him in the Great War).

With a quick nod to her husband, the family were soon gathering their food to take it back inside.

Relieved they had heeded her warning, and that they might be a little safer off the streets, Sam slung the bag of artefacts across her shoulder and shuffled off across the road. Only to feel a tap on her shoulder.

The mother stood there, large brown eyes offering kindness and support. She reached out and offered one of their apples.

"Inti kwayissa ya sitt?" she said. *Are you OK, girl?*

Sam blinked, unsure of what to say. Unsure if she *could* even try to say anything, given she felt like collapsing in fits of sobs at that moment. After all she had been through in the past few days – the past ten or so years, in fact – this act of kindness in the midst of constant violence was too much.

"It has been a long time since I was a girl," she joked, using all her reserves of stiff-upper lip to not break down. They shared a smile and Sam gratefully took the apple and inclined her head. "Shukran."

Eyes stinging, she turned and headed off as fast as she could, not willing to linger and risk the family's lives any more than she already might have done. It occurred to her that she must be a strange sight in this town, all pale and bloodied face, her mass of chestnut hair matted to her cheeks and ears, her beloved pilot's jacket all scraped and cut, and a bag of ancient Atlantean artefacts slung over her shoulder. Certainly not your typical tourist.

Almost certainly trouble.

The night was close now, the light disappearing behind the distant dunes, the cold beginning to cause her to shiver. She needed to find the entrance to the blasted Hall and quickly. She had the drop on Taylor and the others, but it wouldn't last long. She needed to be already under the Egyptian sands, heading for the past, before they got here.

What was it that Cayce had said?

...under the statue of the four wings we will begin the journey into the underworld. The way that leads to the Hall.

Fortunately, she'd seen that map in Professor Schultz's research library. The one with the big red X at the northern edge of the town. If it meant what she thought it meant, she just needed to head north and hope she made it before anyone caught up with her.

Stopping to shelter in the deepening shadows of a small shop, she pulled out the artefacts from what was now a worn and bloodied bag. It wouldn't do to come all this way, find the entrance, and then realise the keys were broken. So she held them up to the light, turned them over time and again to ensure they weren't damaged. There wasn't a scratch on either of them. The Atlanteans – whoever they might have been – clearly had a skill in making artefacts to survive the test of time and the rigours of humans fighting over them.

A sudden movement from up the street caught her eye: two figures in white robes leaning over a balcony, both seeming a bit *too* interested in what she was doing. They quickly disappeared back into their building just as she looked up.

She was about to have company.

She quickly returned the artefacts to the bag and hurried up the street, before taking the next turn-off towards the north of the town.

Did Taylor have people here already? Cayce said they'd only just discovered the location of the entrance, but she wouldn't have put it past The Nine to be one step ahead. With their resources and reach, they were like an organisational Cthulhu, with their tentacles in every city, town and village that had a whiff of being useful to them.

Her fingers slipped down to her thigh, touching the revolver in the holster at her side. Hearing soft footsteps behind her. Waiting for the moment she knew must be coming any… second… now…

A finger tapped her on the shoulder.

She turned warily to face the two figures in white and immediately her fingers curled away from her gun. One was stooped, gasping, as though out of breath. But a fierce and familiar pair of eyes stared out from the folds of the other headscarf.

Jess pulled away the covering to reveal flushed and tear-stained cheeks and even as she leaned in to grab her older sister by both shoulders, it felt to Sam, just for a moment, as though it was all going to be OK. She was no longer alone to have to fight the hordes. Her sister was pulling her into an embrace she so badly needed and maybe they were going to survive this together after all and–

"Where's Will?" Jess's voice seethed with barely contained despair as she stopped short of any kind of sisterly hug and instead dug her fingers into Sam as though she might try and shake the information out. Water began to collect in the corners of those deep blue eyes as they flashed dangerously, levelling all kinds of silent accusations. "We saw the state of the jeep you arrived in. We heard what sounded like an explosion in the distance. Where is he, Sam? Where's Will?"

Despite the lingering heat in the air, the horror of knowing that her sister's first thought was for Will – and not her – created a cold burn that froze Sam from the inside out. Even as Jess began to shake her viciously, the tears now streaming down her face and soaking into her scarf as pent up worry and anger spilled out, Sam could only stare, gobsmacked, as a rush of feelings poured back into the empty void inside her.

Anger. Helplessness. Grief.

But most of all she felt utterly alone, as she had done that night her plane had been shot down over the English Channel all those years ago – the wreckage of her Spitfire the only comfort in the bone-chilling cold of the black depths, clutching to it with every wet ounce of energy she had left, despite knowing nobody out there in the darkness was coming to save her and if she let go and slipped below the waves the world wouldn't care.

Now she was lost and drifting all over again, and although she felt ashamed by it, figuring a stronger person would try and understand her sister's pain, she couldn't find it in herself. But neither could she rage against Jess as she so badly wanted to and in explicit detail reveal all the goddamn shit she had been through to save the artefacts that had led them on this godforsaken journey in the first place.

No. Even as she glanced from the heat rising in her sister's face, to the horrified look on Teddy's, as his sand-bitten fingers pulled back his own scarf and reached over to intervene, Sam knew deep down it was almost fitting that, once again, this was all on her and her alone.

She had tried and failed to get Will back and now he was dead, and it was her responsibility to explain that to an eternally ungrateful sister who would never understand, because she had never really grasped how much Sam had done for her all these years. Failing to realise that Sam joining the RAF to serve her country was really about protecting her family. How she had only let Taylor convince her into joining The Nine to get Jess and Dad away from the war, even as she continued by herself to fight it on some level.

And now this mess. Tagging along to try and rescue the Hall of Records from falling into the wrong hands, just to make sure her sister stayed safe.

All for nothing, with no thanks to show for it, just like every damn mission I was ever sent on. Except, this time, the only person I have to blame is myself.

She steeled herself for what needed to happen next. Her mouth opened in the hope she could squeeze some words out to excuse what she'd done. To offer comfort, little good though it would do.

All she could manage was, "It's nice to see you too, Jess."

Teddy finally got between them long enough to pull Jess away. Without her sister holding her, Sam suddenly felt spent, shaking against the stiff warm breeze as though she might be just one breath from collapsing for good. He looked her up and down, horrified at what he saw.

"Give her some space, Jess. Look at what the poor woman has been through. I'm sure it is all fine and Will is OK. Give her a chance to explain, at least?"

But Sam could see Jess reading her reactions. She had always been smart, that one. Teddy couldn't see it, but her sister already understood that what was coming wouldn't be good news.

"The only explanation I want is how *poor* Sam here managed to get the artefacts back, but not Will," she snapped. "Because that wasn't the deal. You promised you'd bring him back too, Sam. You promised!"

"Jess, I'm so sorry."

"No! You recovered the artefacts. They would have been carefully guarded and yet you somehow got them out. How did you manage to do that and not bring back Will? Did you leave him behind to rot under the thumb of your old friends? Do you honestly care more for what lies in the Hall than for the rest of us?"

That was enough to ignite the fire, lighting Sam up even as she threatened to collapse into herself. She jabbed a pointed finger in the air. "Don't you dare start with that rubbish. *You* dragged me into this godforsaken mess. *You* were the one who begged me to help save the artefacts. *You* were the one I came along to protect, as you set out on your bloody quest for fortune and glory. This isn't on me."

"And yet here we are, with you holding the keys."

Sam thrust the bag towards her sister, shoving her in the chest. "Take them, if you think you can handle what comes next. Because I know what we're up against and you don't have a clue what it'll take to save this world because you can only see what's right in front of you: your own selfish needs that change on a whim, from moment to moment. I recovered these because it was right to do so. And poor Will gave his life to retrieve them, to make sure we would be the ones to reach the Hall of Records before The Nine."

Jess's face paled and she dropped the bag at her feet.

"He's... dead?"

Sam's anger drained as quickly as it had spilled over. "Wait–"

"You let them kill him?"

"No... *no!* He was helping me. He went to help Cayce. He–"

Jess wrenched herself out of Teddy's grasp and threw herself forward, fists raised. Despite her utter exhaustion Sam stepped into it, grasped Jess around the back of her neck and spun her, until she had her forearm locked against her sister's throat.

Jess gasped, struggling for breath. But Sam was done with messing around. She held her sister tightly, feeling sickly nostalgic, remembering those fights they'd had when they were children. Fights that only stopped when Jess would gurgle her surrender, slapping Sam on the arm.

Which she did right now.

"I'm sorry, Jess, but I can't undo what's happened," she said, pushing her sister into Teddy's arms.

She tried not to acknowledge the concern etching his already weary and worn features, even as he pulled Jess to him both in comfort and to make sure she didn't try anything else stupid. He'd never seen this side of Sam. Maybe he'd heard the stories of her time fighting across the continent, but had only ever seen her as a pilot, a fighter in the skies with her plane – all class, no fists.

Now he saw her for the survivor-at-all-costs she truly was and frankly she didn't care for his or anyone else's judgement. For better or for worse this was who she had become and she would not hide or make excuses for it. The fight for the greater good was still there to be won, and she had no intention of letting that slip through her fingers. Not considering what she now knew was at stake.

If The Nine got their hands on the Hall and everything in it, who knows what they could do. They already had access to supernatural forces she couldn't yet comprehend. With what lay in the Hall, they would be unstoppable.

Jess rubbed her throat, glaring at her sister with the same hate and fear Sam remembered seeing in her enemies over the years. It was exactly what she had been trying to avoid all this time. Yet here they were anyway and time was ticking. Sam drew strength from the knowledge that she had done her best and there were bigger problems to deal with now.

"Will bought us some time," she said. "We shouldn't waste it if we want to honour what he sacrificed, because if we don't beat Taylor and his men to the entrance to the Hall they will lock it down and we'll never get in. They will hunt us and these artefacts until they get what they need and it'll all be over. All of it. He'll have died for nothing. Do you want that?"

Jess glared through her tears, but she said nothing. Only shrugged Teddy off and stalked away down the street.

Sam sighed, though it was not all relief. "We have to move quickly," she said to Teddy. "The entrance is supposed to be close. Just on the edge of town, I think."

"We know, that is why we are here. After we escaped in Paris, we had little else to go on but what I had already researched. So Jess and I came to Cairo to meet up with some old friends and plug ourselves into, shall we say, the Egyptological grapevine."

"There's a grapevine for things like that?" Sam gingerly touched the bruises on her jaw from where Roach had repeatedly hit her earlier. "Let me guess… lots of old white men with beards and tweed suits, sitting about with shishas and talking about their mummies, right?"

"Not all old or white, and, as it happens, I like tweed suits," Teddy replied, feigning offence and doing a horrible job of hiding a thin smile. They both remembered all too well that he'd been the one to complain of such things as a younger man. "Regardless, our decision was a fortuitous one. Only an hour or two ago we heard news of a sudden rush of requests for diggers to ready themselves for a new excavation in this very town. A reopening of a long-abandoned dig site, starting tomorrow. We figured we might learn something more, so we came here ahead of everyone else… and that's when we saw you."

"The keys contained a map to the entrance," she said by way of explanation, bending down with a groan to pick up the bag of artefacts as her bruised and broken ribs complained with vigour. She passed the bag to Teddy. "Now we just need to open it. Are you ready?"

"I think so," he said quietly. He gave her a strange look. "Are you?"

"I look worse than I feel, I'm sure."

"That is not what I mean." He suddenly couldn't meet her gaze, pretending instead to inspect the contents of the bag. "The gateway we are seeking… it is supposed to be the entrance to the underworld. Entailing a journey from the ravages of our primitive world to the greater enlightenment left behind by the gods."

"Sounds peachy. And?"

"And only the worthy may pass."

She blinked in surprise.

"You're worried I might not be worthy?"

"I admit, I have never seen you act that way." He gestured vaguely to Jess, still unable to look up. His tan cheeks darkened further. "We may yet find judgement under these fine Egyptian sands, Samantha. Judgement wrought upon us by the spirits of the gods themselves. Are you sure *you* want to do this?"

She couldn't quite respond to that.

It made her feel sick to be laid bare like this. Her oldest friend, questioning her worth in such a way. But, in truth, it really didn't matter now. She had done what she had done in life. Now, she had no choice but to accept whatever fate lay ahead and whatever judgements her family, friends, and even the gods would make about her.

This had long moved past being about what she wanted.

She nodded with little enthusiasm, gave him what she hoped was a meaningful slap on the shoulder, and walked gingerly down the road after her sister.

CHAPTER TWENTY-FIVE

Temple of the Two-Headed God

The three companions reached the summit of the hill outside Wadi Sais just minutes later.

In the west, a thin strip of sunlight continued to cling to the land as the dusk fought to take over. In the north, a full blood moon rose beyond three large outlines on the horizon.

Giza.

Sam stared for a moment, breathing in the vision. Even from here they towered over everything, distinct markers of human creation. A statement of achievement... as well as a memorial to those other all-too-human traits, slavery and death.

"Quite a legacy to leave behind," she said.

Teddy came up quietly beside her, still trying to catch his breath. "One of the wonders of our world. Now and forever, I would imagine. It's hard to think that we will ever surpass such monuments. Or create more fitting declarations of mankind's ability to do such great and terrible things."

Jess sniffed unkindly, slipping down the slope into the dig site. "Leave the sightseeing for later. Let's get what we came for."

She gestured to the huge pillared temple structure below them, carved into the surrounding sandstone that was now half-buried beneath the dunes. In the centre of the open-air plaza stood a giant winged statue, easily eighteen foot high, with two snarling jackal heads side by side – each facing just off from centre.

Sam paused on a small, solid outcrop. "That thing there. Both of its heads are Anubis, right?"

"Yes," Teddy replied. "Or, to give him his Egyptian name, Inpu. *Anubis* was how the Greeks referred to him. Protector of the underworld."

"So all in all not a bad place to hide the entrance to the greatest treasure history has ever known? Under his watchful and fairly terrifying gaze?"

Teddy scratched his beard. "That would be my theory. Clearly it worked well enough to cause whoever started to dig here once upon a time to abandon the place – and from what I gleaned on our arrival earlier, even the locals suggest the place is haunted."

"I guess we'll find out soon enough," Sam said, sliding down the sand after her sister.

Soon all three of them stood at the base of the gigantic statue, gazing up to inspect the details high above them. Sam started to circle the monument. Reaching the back, she beckoned Teddy over.

"It appears as if the thing has only two wings, but if you

look closely you can see that they are carved with feathers on *both* sides. This is the four-winged statue that Cayce told me guarded the entrance. We're close."

"Edgar Cayce?" Teddy repeated in surprise. "The famous psychic who first told the world about the Hall of Records… you've met him?"

"That would be difficult, given his death," Sam replied, then thought for a minute and added, "Although perhaps not impossible with his talents. But, no, his son Edward was being held captive by Taylor, and me and him – and his friend – had a chat."

"And he told you to come here?"

"He told me the journey would begin under the gaze of the statue with the four wings. He was very clear on that part. Which means the entrance should be here, somewhere."

They split up, each of the three instinctively heading for a separate part of the temple. The light was almost gone now, the sky darkening beyond the high rim of the excavated hill around them. Sam knew they didn't have much time. They had very little light to work with, outside of the two small torches Teddy and Jess had brought along.

Yet, ten minutes later, they still hadn't found anything. Sam had covered most of the east side of the temple, looking for anything out of place – a subtle crack in the sandstone, a block that looked like it could be pushed – but nothing suggested itself.

When they gathered back at the statue, she figured Teddy must have been pulling at his hair in frustration, because it was now sticking up in all directions, and he looked absolutely flummoxed by their lack of success. Meanwhile, Jess's mood clearly hadn't improved. She slammed her foot against a loose rock and sent it shooting across what would have been the temple interior.

"All for nothing," she muttered, glancing darkly at Sam.

Sam tried not to let the sick feeling that her sister might be right overwhelm her. She needed to stay calm and focused, or else Will's sacrifice really would have been in vain.

She raised her torch skywards and began to study the statue again.

The body held no obvious clue. No markings, other than the decoration. The wings were large, but again nothing stood out. They had simply been marked in feathers or scales.

Then there were the heads. Their jackal noses pointing out, teeth bared. Eyes…

Sam stopped. Fixed the torchlight on the faces.

The eyes of the two heads weren't gazing in the same direction. Everything else had been carved to match, but their separate gazes were ever-so-slightly outward facing.

"They're trying to tell us something," she said, and followed the line of sight of the left one to a wall that had only barely been excavated out of the side of the hill. "Follow their gazes. Look where they're looking."

She ran over to the wall, let her fingers feel their way across it. Until she found an unmistakably clear niche. One that was a very familiar shape.

"Son of a bitch, there's a depression on the wall here. The statue is telling us where to put the keys! This for the Isis Amulet by the looks of it. I can't tell for sure, but it seems almost exactly the same size and shape. And there are little indentations in the centre where it could fit around the amulet's decoration."

Jess joined her at the same wall, running her torchlight over it until she was about ten yards distant. Then her eyes lit up and she reached out.

"I've got the one for the Osiris Stone," she said. She looked over at Sam, confused. "But why are they so far apart?"

"I was afraid of this," Teddy called from behind them, having not moved from the base of the statue. He looked concerned.

"Afraid of what, Teddy?" Sam asked, not really wanting to know.

Her walked over hesitantly, looking between the pair of them. His tone was such that he seemed almost reluctant to voice the words. As if he suddenly wanted to keep them at bay.

"I have read many things in my studies," he said. "And one of the recurring themes in the texts is that enlightenment only comes with balance. Of course, we have heard these things before. It is one of the great clichés of our archaeological search for truth, eh Jess!" He smiled nervously. "But even clichés have their place, and here we must remind ourselves that these were secrets of the gods they were talking about. The knowledge of a higher intelligence."

"What are you saying?"

Teddy sighed. "I am saying that it looks like the Hall of Records was protected so that one person could not find it alone. Where you have two, you must have teamwork, cooperation, balance. The strength, intelligence and wisdom of both must be flawless. As must their trust in each other." He looked pointedly between Sam and Jess. "At least, that was the thinking."

Sam closed her eyes for a second, hand resting on the wall. "These ancient civilisations never make it easy, do they?"

"I am afraid not."

"So we're talking two separate paths down to the Great Hall. Probably some dangerous tests to complete along the way, where each one can only be overcome by someone in the other path. Is that about the size of the task ahead?"

"That would be my guess, yes. I think they meant for us to be a team in order to make our way down through their version of the underworld. Alive, at least."

"And if one of us fails?" Jess asked.

"Then in my experience nobody comes back out," Sam replied. "It's all or nothing now."

There was silence as they considered the point of no return. The evening breeze grew harder and colder as it whipped over the hill and scattered the sand about their feet. Sam shivered, although it was only partly due to the dropping temperature.

She glanced at Jess, wondering if she should just get her out now. Get them all out. Leave this place to whoever came afterwards and let them walk towards their inevitable doom. She was too tired for this ancient death trap lark, especially when it involved keeping everyone else alive at the same time. By herself, she could have done it. Maybe. But the responsibility to ensure the others made it back to the surface in one piece was too much. They'd been on the run since New York and she was exhausted trying to worry about everyone. All she really wanted was a warm bed with clean sheets, a bath, and to nap for a century or two.

For a second she fantasised what that might be like. To just drop everything and walk away. Be like Teddy and settle down and actually enjoy living instead of constantly fighting to ensure others could do the same. A house would be nice. She'd never had her own house before. Wouldn't that be something? Her very own house and her own front door which she could happily shut to keep out the world, and, hell, maybe she could find a good honest dog (was there any other kind) that liked nothing more than to curl up on her lap and prevent her from having to go anywhere.

It didn't seem like much, but bloody hell it was a nice thought.

Unfortunately, the fantasy collapsed as soon as she recognised that familiar look of determination on her sister's face. Jess had already lost Will and quite clearly her faith in her sister. She had nothing else to lose now.

Sam knew how that felt. She also knew full well that if they left, those who came afterwards would be Taylor and Arif and a whole convoy of men-you-didn't-want-in-power, who wouldn't rest until they had the artefacts. And when they had them, they would be only too happy to open up the entrances, grab that beautiful family she'd met and whoever else they could find in town, and march them into whatever traps awaited them – until the bodies had piled up and statistically they passed whatever tests they needed to.

At which point the secrets of the Hall of Records and whatever ancient powers lay within would be theirs to use however they wanted.

The house and dog would have to wait. As nice as it was to dream of walking away, there was only one direction she was going now.

Down.

"OK then, choose your poison," she said to the others, pointing to the tunnels.

"Come on, Teddy," Jess said. "You might as well come with me seeing as you know how much Sam loves to work alone. Chuck us the Osiris Stone, Sam."

Reluctantly, Sam reached into her bag and handed it over. Jess took it without so much as meeting her gaze.

"Are you absolutely sure you want to do this?"

Jess ignored the question. But before she could turn away, Sam put a hand on her shoulder.

"Just be careful."

Her sister shook her off and beckoned Teddy to join her at the right-hand tunnel. He shuffled over to stand beside the younger woman, looking old and frail in the moonlight.

"Good luck, Samantha," he said.

"You too," she replied grimly.

She walked back to her niche on the wall. Took out the Isis Amulet, watched as Jess inserted the Stone into its slot. Then did the same with her artefact.

A nod between them and they turned the keys at the same time.

The ground trembled. A roaring, rippling vibration that Sam felt deep in her bones as she held onto the wall for support.

Then with a resounding BOOM, two separate sections of the stone wall beside each group shuddered and began to drop slowly into the floor, revealing a pair of gold portcullis style gates.

Sam grasped the bars and peered into the corridor beyond, hearing the trickle of ancient oil run along grooves either side of the sloping pathway into the earth. Before one, two, then three scrapes of stone against stone echoed from the darkness and suddenly there was flame.

It spread like the trail of a fairground sparkler along the walls, igniting the oil, and throwing everything in low, ominous light.

She looked over to see Jess prise the Osiris Stone from the wall again and hand it to Teddy. As she did so, her gold gate began to lift into the ceiling, opening the passageway.

Sam quickly did the same with the Isis Amulet and watched as her own gate pulled up, granting her access.

A very subtle clicking in the background suggested that there would only be seconds before it came down again.

She needed to move.

The gate dropped behind Sam, crashing into the ground with a heavy air of finality – the echoes ringing out all the way down the tunnel before her.

But beneath all that was a new sound now. A screech of tyres and the bark of men giving orders from outside. She spun to see two pairs of headlights appearing at the rim of the hill surrounding the temple. Several dark figures then broke the light as they streamed over the ridge and down the slope. They appeared to be pushing two hostages between them.

One of them cried out in pain.

Will?

Running back to the gold gate, Sam could just about see her sister through the gloom as she stepped away from her own passageway, leaving Teddy inside.

She looked panicked and hopeful as she took a stride towards the approaching figures.

"No, Jess!" Sam called urgently. "Get back in there."

Too late.

She saw the glint of gold as the gate dropped down behind Jess.

Teddy grabbed the bars, the fear in his face plain to see. "Jess, no, no, no… what are you doing!?"

The sandstone walls began to close again.

"He's alive," Jess said, finally turning to acknowledge Sam. Her face a mess of emotions, but chief among them, now, was hope.

She ran off into the shadows.

"Jess," Sam hissed, as the opening to the outside world grew smaller. "Jess!"

But there was no response.

"What do we do?" Teddy called over, panicking, as the stone wall began to cut him off too.

Sam didn't have a chance to respond.

The wall slammed shut over the gates, sealing them off from the world for what she feared might be the last time.

CHAPTER TWENTY-SIX

Into the Underworld

Sam moved reluctantly into her tunnel, following the light of the fire spreading down the wall.

Above her, old, gnarled roots hung from the ceiling. Below, the floor was rocky and treacherous. More than once she stumbled over an outcrop, as she made her way along carefully, keeping an eye out for anything that might indicate a trap.

Yet there was nothing. Just the light and the overwhelming silence.

Until she came to the first rectangular hole cut into the wall.

She approached it with caution. Pulling off a root and waving it in front of the gaping darkness, in case it triggered some kind of terrible ancient weaponry that would end in a cataclysmically painful death.

Then she saw the light emanating through it and began to hear the familiar mutterings and gasps of an old friend, as he edged into view on the other side.

"Teddy!"

He jumped with such a shock, she wondered if he might drop dead then and there.

"Of all that is holy and decent," he groaned. "Please never do that again."

She couldn't help giving him a smile, as she gestured to the window and looked further along where pinpricks of more light could now be seen. "It looks like there are a few more holes like this along the tunnel, so you're stuck with me I'm afraid."

"Are you serious?"

"It looks that way."

The relief on his face was palpable. He mopped his brow. "Then we will be able to talk each other through the challenges if need be. Perhaps this will be easier than I thought?"

She gestured for him to keep walking. "Don't get cocky," she called, hoping he could still hear her. "In my experience that's usually when the ground falls out from under your fe–"

She stopped talking as the floor in front of her simply disappeared.

The rest of the tunnel continued, but where the floor should have been was nothing but a deep, black chasm for at least ten yards.

Too dark to see the bottom. Too long to jump across.

"Samantha?" Teddy's voice rang out.

"I'm OK." She kicked a pebble into the darkness and waited, but there was no sound of it hitting anything. She added under her breath, "Although that's probably not a great sign."

Backtracking to the hole in the wall, she found a wide-eyed Teddy trying to peer through.

"We're at the first trap already," she said. "Nothing but a giant hole in the floor. And although I'll be honest and say I've had far worse to deal with in the past, I won't be going any further without help. This is all part of the theory, right? That two of us must work together to get to the Hall without dying?" He nodded, less enthusiastically than she would have liked. "So tell me what's on your side. Are there any switches or levers or puzzles? Anything that stands out from the usual stone?"

"I will have a look."

Sam could hear him in the background. Just low heavy breathing and the odd muttered German word drifting up the tunnel towards her. Before an exclamation of "Eureka!" and he quickly popped his head back into view.

"Got it. A curious mechanism on the opposite wall, a little further down the tunnel. Three small stone levers and a series of questions, I think."

"Don't think. Just solve them."

"Ah, well, yes they are in pictograph form. But the hieroglyphs are different somehow. A variation of ancient Egyptian. Quite beautiful, in fact. You should see them!"

She tried to keep her sigh from being too audible. "Teddy, we can't afford to be trapped here by The Nine and their goons if they manage to make it through the gateways. I need you to concentrate. Can you read them?"

"Of course, yes, sorry," he replied. He popped on a pair of spectacles he had been carrying inside his jacket and disappeared again.

She waited quietly, imagining him adjusting his glasses as he peered at the markings on the wall and tracing their outlines, moving his fingers to the first lever, perhaps flicking it across a notch.

There was a thud in the wall somewhere.

"That is the first solved!" he called out brightly.

Another thud, very soon after the first.

"And the second. Just one to go now."

"Look I didn't mean for you to rush," she shouted through the hole. "I just wanted you to concentrate. Take your time, you don't have to–"

"All done," he interrupted.

There was another loud thud. But this time it came from the ground, a vibration that shook Sam from her boots to her neck.

And then the floor beneath her feet dropped suddenly, tilting at a steep angle towards the chasm.

With a yell of horror she began sliding.

The walls sped past. She couldn't see any outcrops of stone. Nothing to grab. Nothing to hang onto at this speed.

There was only one option.

She leapt forwards, towards the gaping death trap, and grasped the low-hanging root dangling from the roof.

She only just caught it. Tightened her fingers around the thick bark.

And felt it slip freely from the rock above, dropping her

into the darkness.

Shiiiiiiii–

She didn't even have time to finish swearing in her head before the root snapped taut and she began to swing in an arc across the bottomless pit.

"Samantha!" Teddy's panicked voice called out. "Samantha, are you okay?"

The up-swing briefly brought her face-to-face with him at the hole.

"Fix…" she snapped.

The creaking tree root carried her through the darkness again, before returning to her friend.

"…it!"

Flustered, Teddy disappeared from the hole and hurried back to the lever.

Seconds later, there was another thud in the wall. A series of stone slabs slotted out from the wall, one by one, below her.

At which point the root finally snapped and she landed face first on the very last one.

"Are you still alive in there?" Teddy's words echoed around her.

Sam coughed out a lungful of millennia-old dust and gingerly picked herself up, wishing once again that Agent Taylor had never found her on that beach all those years ago.

"For now," she said.

She stumbled on wearily down the tunnel.

CHAPTER TWENTY-SEVEN

The Enemy Swarms

From behind a pillar, Jess hid and watched the explosions as Agent Taylor's men blew open the temple wall.

They had discovered the location of the hidden entrances far quicker than she had hoped they might, thanks to the scuffed footsteps in the dust in two distinct places at the wall. There had been too much commotion in the main plaza for them to have spotted her trail leading away to the shadows where she hid now. But even if they had seen them, she wondered if anyone would have cared. All their focus was now on the wall. And although without the artefacts they never would have found this site in the first place, the fact that the ancient keys were now in the tunnels with Sam and Teddy wasn't going to deter the agents. They had come prepared to use modern-day brute force if necessary.

So out came the dynamite, and while the first attempt didn't quite make enough of a dent, the second explosion brought down a whole section of the wall, revealing the glint of golden gates holding firm behind. Yet even as Jess dared to hope that this would somehow be an obstacle too far, she suddenly realised that the rest of the enemy had now poured over the crest of the hill into the plaza of the sunken temple and she was trapped.

Which was a real son of a bitch, because she could clearly see her beloved Will being held captive.

He looked like he'd been through hell. Was, even now, clinging to another man, a sickly looking chap who Jess figured must be the psychic that Sam had talked about. Will's face was bruised and battered and one side of his neck looked scorched, as though it had been in a fire.

She was caught between relief to know he was alive and sheer, unadulterated terror at what he must have been put through. Jess had no idea if these men were responsible or whether something else had happened – she had heard an explosion, and hadn't Sam mentioned something about a crash? – but it twisted her stomach in knots to even think about him suffering.

Will, who was so sweet and not nearly as slick as he wanted to appear, had been awkwardly charming ever since their first dig in the hills of Cyprus. And even on their recent sojourn to South America to recover the Isis Amulet, when it had become apparent that he might not be the adept and heroic Edgar Rice Burroughs character he thought himself, she couldn't help but keep falling for him. His curious mind, his passion for antiquities, his ability to instil that excitement for history in others.

Yet right now he was a broken man, barely able to

stay upright without the aid of the other hostage. This adventure they'd started together had taken its toll, and even though she now knew that Sam wasn't responsible for his death, the resentment still festered. Rightly or wrongly, Jess wasn't about to forgive her for not helping Will out of this mess sooner – just as she couldn't quite forgive herself for encouraging him to get into it in the first place.

A blond, cropped-haired agent – suited and booted and looking completely out of place in this ancient environment, just like his government comrades – stepped from the dust cloud up to the gates. She remembered seeing glimpses of him in the cavern under Paris. He was shorter than Taylor, but there was a presence to him that was hard to miss. Not an entirely human presence, with an unnatural movement and stance that set him apart from the others. Like an evil Howdy Doody, with a dead-eyed puppet stare.

Agent Smith, as she recalled.

"So which path do we take?" she heard him ask Agent Taylor, as the taller figure eventually joined him. Jess noticed he held back a little longer to let the cloud clear.

The superior agent gazed between the two gates, before reluctantly raising his hand and deferring to one of the Egyptian military men standing nearby. A man with a lot of medals.

"Colonel Arif?" Taylor asked.

The Colonel stayed where he was, his face locked in an expression of neutrality, but Jess could tell from the way his eyes shifted about that he was playing it safe. He didn't trust anything or anybody right now.

Clearing his throat, Colonel Arif gestured to two of his men, who immediately pulled Will away from Cayce and dragged him over to the gate. Only then did he speak.

"This journey might be mine," he said, "but this decision is not for me to make. My ancestors were skilled in all things and ensuring a painful death to any who happened upon their secrets was one of their particular passions. We should let the expert answer."

Behind the pillar, Jess tensed. Will was trying gamely to stand up and shake his captors off, but they were too strong.

"Dr Sandford," the Colonel began, "it is time to prove your worth. To show everyone that your archaeological escapades around the world, digging into cultures other than your own, do have a point to them. Your friends have beaten us here, but they are now trapped. Only you can save them, by cooperating and helping us down to the Great Hall."

"Drop dead," Will said weakly.

It was heartbreakingly admirable and pitiful all at once, and Jess loved him for it even more – while continuing to curse him out in her head for being so stubbornly reckless.

Her heart froze as Agent Smith grabbed him from the soldiers, held him by the collar and looked at him dispassionately, the way a butcher regarded the animal he was about to dismember.

"You have gained some of the Moxley girl's spirit, I see," he hissed. "How unfortunate."

Before anyone could do anything, he punched Will

hard in the stomach. The archaeologist's legs collapsed, leaving him to dangle at Agent Smith's mercy, and Jess had to dig her fingers into the pillar she was hiding behind to stop her rushing to save him.

Yet help did come – from an unexpected quarter.

"Stop," Agent Taylor said firmly, stepping in as Smith went for a second attack. He caught his subordinate's wrist and held fast. "Dr Sandford is a valuable asset and, let us remember, an American citizen. He will be treated as such."

Only now was there a flicker of emotion behind Smith's dead eyes. Humiliation, quickly followed by anger. He dropped Will to the floor and twisted to face his superior, not quite squaring up to him, but not exactly standing down either.

Well now, Jess thought, this just got interesting.

She'd been wondering exactly what Sam must have seen in Agent Taylor to have partnered up with him in the past, and maybe this was a glimpse of it. Regardless of the shit his men had put them through in the last few days, right here and now she could not help offering him a silent thank you for protecting Will just when he needed it most.

"Dr Sandford," Agent Taylor said loudly, keeping his eyes on Smith until the agent finally, reluctantly, stood down. Taylor's shoulders seemed to sag just a little in relief. "Will, we both know what must happen now. There is a choice facing us and you must help us make it. We have your friends cornered. Even if they reach the Hall before us, we will simply capture them when they return to the surface and Captain Moxley, the Professor, and your girlfriend will spend the rest of their lives in a military prison under Colonel Arif's particular brand of justice." Will's eyes grew wide as Taylor bent down to help the archaeologist to his feet and dust him off. "Yes, we know all about you and Jessica Moxley. Who do you think funded your trip to retrieve the amulet in the first place? The US Government is not in the habit of handing out a research grant without keeping a good eye on where it is going and who will be spending it. So I'm going to ask you nicely in the hope we can help each other out now. Please tell us which path to take and you have my word you can return home to enjoy a largely peaceful and settled life..." he offered a small grin of solidarity "...as much as one can with a Moxley girl, anyway."

Will's head dropped. He was clearly terrified, but doing his best to look the government man in the eye as he admitted what Jess already comprehended. He didn't know. This wasn't his speciality area. He loved archaeology, but he was an academic at heart, a museum man, more at home in the collections and archives than in the field.

He couldn't help them.

She readied herself, knowing that as soon as he admitted it even Taylor might not be able to prevent the others taking the matter into their own hands. Will would be outed as expendable. A dead weight. She couldn't allow that to happen.

Thankfully neither could Cayce.

"It doesn't matter which gate you pick," he called over,

shaking as he spoke as though having difficulty getting the words out. "It's not about making the right choice, Agent Taylor. It's about *not* making a choice. They had smarts, our ancient brothers and sisters. They made it so the path on the left clears the traps on the right and vice versa. Two people must make the journey at the same time, which your friends down there have obviously already done. Now we must wait to see if they can solve what must be solved."

"And if they can't?" Agent Smith asked.

Colonel Arif laughed humourlessly. He gestured to the gathered soldiers in the temple complex.

"Agent Smith, I started this day with twice as many men. You have also lost comrades, including that big bear of a man you called Roach. If you continue to underestimate Captain Moxley you will compromise our entire operation. She will make it down through the traps and to the Hall – of that you can be assured. Our problem is that we need to ensure she does not reach it without us. The gods alone know what destruction she might cause simply to spite us all."

"She wouldn't–" Agent Taylor began, but the Colonel held up his hand, unwilling to hear it.

"Do you honestly think it is in our best interests to stand here and discuss it further? Time is of the essence, Agent Taylor. We need to move quickly to ensure the glory of Egypt is not stolen out from under our noses by these foreign interlopers. Now, please instruct your men to get these gates open before I reconsider your involvement in this operation and alter the terms of our political alliance."

It took a moment before Agent Taylor relented. But even from her hiding spot, Jess could see something in the stare he gave the Colonel that told her the American was now doing some reconsidering of his own.

Teddy watched as the light from Samantha's side of their underground journey suddenly darkened. Her face, grazed on one side and with blood smears intermingled with dust, filled the hole in the sandstone wall.

"Did I get it?" she asked.

He continued to crouch in the middle of the sealed chamber, nervously looking up at the collapsing ceiling.

It was now less than a metre above his head. And dropping fast.

"Keep going if you please, Samantha. Faster now, if possible. I do not wish to end up a permanent relic down here!"

He was trying to be funny, but the wavering in his voice was clear even to him. Indeed, he wondered if the dead that must surely be buried down here could hear it too. The remains of those who had worked on this ingenious and terrible pathway into hell, who had fallen by the wayside and been swept up into the walls and floor – as they had with the pyramids and probably at many other now-sacred places.

Buildings and temples and palaces, all built from the blood of others, with his to follow imminently unless his friend could figure out the puzzle on the other side of the wall.

He could hear Samantha cursing in that very British

way of hers. Running back and forth across the light, as she tried desperately to stop him being flattened.

If he had to put his life in the hands of anyone, he was glad it was her. The thought had crossed his mind several times since those gates had closed, that if he had somehow managed to find this entrance to the Great Hall with Schultz, he would absolutely be lost now.

There was no way his megalomaniacal, if brilliant, former colleague would have been able to put aside his own ego in order to work together down here in these dark tunnels. He would have had his eye on the prize. Yes, he would surely have tried to do whatever it took to pass the challenges and reach the Hall intact. But he would have been acting out of a sense of selfishness. And, quite frankly, Teddy preferred knowing that Samantha was trying to save *him,* not just trying to get another step closer to the reward.

Still, he considered – as the ceiling touched his head and he ducked another few inches lower, squeezing his eyes closed and pressing himself close to the floor – right now he would be happy to have anyone who was able to solve the damn puzzle.

"I do not mean to rush you, but are you close yet?" he called out.

"Nearly there."

"How nearly is nearly?"

"I'm almost done. Keep your socks on."

"Keeping my socks on is not going to be a problem if you don't solve the puzzle soon. They will be on permanently. Forever."

He offered up a silent prayer. To whose god, he wasn't sure. Maybe all of them. But just as he wondered if his faith – in his friend *and* in this whole ill-advised obsession with finding the Hall of Records – was about to finally kill him, he heard the echoes of a triumphant laugh.

There was a grinding of ancient mechanisms. The ceiling stopped. Began to retract. And the stone slabs blocking the way in and out of the chamber now pulled back into the floor.

Sam's face appeared at the hole again.

"See? I told you not to worry. It was just a simple hieroglyphic puzzle based on the Book of the Dead. Took me a little while to remember all the beats, but it turns out I *was* paying attention all those nights you used to talk my ears off. Let's hope the rest are all this easy, eh?"

Teddy could feel the sweat lying thick in the backs of his knees as he crawled to his feet and wiped a sleeve across his brow.

"Easy?" he repeated.

Jess rubbed her calves to stop them cramping up, as she continued to crouch behind the pillar, watching Agent Taylor direct his men to open up the gateways they had just revealed by blowing the front of the wall off with dynamite.

She knew she should be worried. Surrounded by the enemy. Unable to help Will. Unable to reach her sister and Teddy who had no idea they were about to be caught. She should be feeling alone and frustrated and despairing of the fact there were few legitimately safe options available to her now that ended up with her and everyone she loved still alive.

But she couldn't help feeling somewhat awed as, in a shower of sparks, she watched the government men cut open the left gate – leading to Sam's tunnel – with what looked like some kind of raygun from the Flash Gordon serial her dad had taken her to see when she was about six years-old.

They were cheating, plain and simple. Whoever had created this elaborate pathway to the Hall of Records had done it to filter out those not worthy, but Agent Taylor had a job to do and he was getting on with it, worthiness be damned. First explosives, now rayguns. Was there something to be appreciated, if not admired, in the practicality of that approach? The understanding that mankind had evolved and maybe we needed to let go of the morals and ethics of what had come before and refuse to jump through all the hoops left behind to prove ourselves to people long since dead?

It was one of the few things to make sense to her recently.

As the thick gold bars were sliced through one by one, and swiftly removed by the soldiers under Colonel Arif's watchful eye, Jess watched the party gathering around the gateway, readying themselves to go in.

She noted Will and Cayce in their midst and weighed up the odds.

Six military, two agents, and a small tunnel. Will and the psychic won't be any help, but it'll be pretty gloomy down there. If I can get in behind them, I might be able to pick them off?

It seemed as good a plan to get herself killed as any other, but as Sam might say: "screw the odds". She wasn't about to wait up here to let her sister and Teddy get caught unawares. Whatever had passed between them, she still loved Sam fiercely. She was family, even if she spent most of her time acting like their mother and doing a piss-poor job of it.

As the raygun began cutting through the penultimate bar, Agent Smith got impatient. He kicked aside the soldier doing the cutting and the weapon fizzled out. But it turned out he didn't need it. He simply leaned down, grabbed the remaining piece of gold, and with a loud screech of metal wrenched it off and tossed it to the side.

Jess stared in horror, feeling the last vestiges of hope desert her.

"I'll leave him until last," she whispered to herself.

The group stepped through the mutilated gate into the tunnel beyond. Agent Taylor led the way, while behind him, Agent Smith forced Will and the psychic through the gap. Colonel Arif and his soldiers brought up the rear.

Only one was left at the entrance.

Which made the first part of her plan easier, at least.

Waiting for a moment, until the guard's gaze peered off in another direction, she quickly left her hiding spot and dashed from pillar to pillar around the other side of the plaza, getting as close to the gate as she dared.

Then she crouched again, her fingers skirting around the floor until they hit upon a small rock, which she tossed over the guard, hitting the wall on the other side with a such a smash that it tore small chunks off the ancient sandstone.

No time for archaeological guilt. The guard immediately lifted his gun and strode away from the entrance to investigate, which felt instantly like a complete cliché, like something from a movie, but Jess didn't care. She ran across the remaining ground as quietly as she could and dived into the tunnel before he could turn back.

Whatever works, she remembered her father saying. *If it gets the job done, that's the only thing you need to worry about.*

Jess had always loved that quote. But she couldn't help wondering if old Harry Moxley would still say the same thing if he knew what his little girl needed to do next.

CHAPTER TWENTY-EIGHT

Who Do You Trust?

Down in the dark, Sam was taking her time... even though she knew it was running out.

The explosion behind her had been distant, but distinct. *Dynamite.* She knew the sound well by now.

To the credit of the ancient architects the tunnel held firm. Only minor shaking. Waves of dust falling from the roof. But nary a stone shifted around her.

This place had been built to endure. Sam didn't know if they were beneath the Sphinx yet, but they'd certainly walked far enough to make it possible. And she remembered what Teddy had originally told her about the Hall. That its fortifications would be immense and solid.

Which meant they could be close.

The Hall of Records. All that knowledge from history. Surpassing even the records and books and maps and artefacts once held at the Library at Alexandria.

She hadn't been a true scholar like Teddy, Will or even Jess. Academia simply wasn't for Sam and never had been.

But it didn't mean that the subjects didn't fascinate her. And though she'd seen some sights that would boggle even the greatest, most open minds of her generation, she was keen to see how all that stuff she had experienced fit together with what had come before.

Had the ancient civilisations of Egypt and Atlantis known about the unseen forces that still lurked in the shadows, like the Dragonmen and Shades? What might they have discovered that even The Nine didn't yet know about?

It was a thought to keep her moving deeper underground, albeit with great care, one foot at a time with an eye on her surroundings, knowing that the closer you got to the prize, the more dangerous things became.

She peered into the gloom ahead. The fire along the wall was still lit, but the air was dank and oppressive here and didn't carry the light as it should.

Another hole soon presented itself, giving her the chance to talk with her companion.

"Still with me, Teddy?"

"Despite the best attempts of those vines," he replied, absently touching the bloodied bruises and burn marks on his neck, from where he had been lifted to the ceiling in the last trap. "I have never witnessed... not even in my worst nightmares..."

He didn't need to finish. Sam nodded, recalling the squirming ceiling, wondering if he realised just how close he'd come to death after she'd *almost* made a mistake in the puzzle she'd had to solve. A mistake which would have left him hanging there for good.

"You were never in any danger," she lied. "I had you covered."

He peered at her over the top of his bent and cracked glasses and gave her a wry smile. "I never had any doubt," he lied in return.

She gestured to the window between them. "Have you noticed? The wall isn't as thick here. The tunnels are converging."

"Oh, thank God. Do you think we are close?"

"Only one way to find out."

One step after another. Who knew where it would lead. Adventure, knowledge, death… or all three.

She reached through the hole to give his shoulder a squeeze. His fingers clamped down over hers momentarily. A second of human contact in a dark, dangerous place.

"Onwards then," Teddy said. He straightened. Took a breath.

They left each other behind again, possibly for the last time. Five yards. Ten yards. Walking slowly. Sam treating each block beneath her foot as a potential trigger. Each shadow in the wall the hiding place of something that wanted to rip her open or eat her or crush her to death.

At fifteen yards a stone slab crashed down behind her.

She didn't bother checking to see if she could move it. There was no way it would budge.

Onwards.

The light began to grow ahead. Then the tunnel came to an end. A chamber lay beyond a small door.

Putting her hand on the stone frame, she hesitated only for a second or two, held her breath and ducked through.

Teddy stepped into his last chamber at the same time as Samantha entered hers.

A stone column rose from the floor. Split into three segments, he could see that each was engraved with a rich variety of hieroglyphic symbols. It looked like the segments could be twisted and spun. To what end he was not yet sure.

He gazed around at the walls for clues on what to do. There was an area about the size of a small coffee table that appeared at first glance to be lighter in colour than the rest, but then again he wasn't sure if the low, flickering flames were playing tricks on his eyes. There wasn't anything inscribed or painted on that part of the wall anyway, or anywhere else, in fact. A sense of unease crept though him as he realised it was just him and the stone column – and the heat drifting through the hole in the wall from Samantha's chamber next door.

He pressed his face up to the square cut to see his friend standing in the centre of her own chamber, bathed in an ominous orange glow. There was a shimmer of heat in the air. But although he could see her sweating and pushing her hair from sticking to her face, she made no effort to remove her jacket. Even he had tied his around his waist.

"Why are you so insistent on wearing that battered old thing down here in this heat?" he asked.

"It's nice to have pockets," she replied, looking around her chamber with growing concern as she reached into one of them and pulled out a band to tie her hair up.

Her space was about the same size as a good-sized country kitchen. All stone. No conceivable exit. Yet around the perimeter wound a thick obsidian gutter that sloped down from the corner ceiling and around the walls, before running from the far wall straight into the centre of the room.

It led right into the head-end of a black, Inpu-headed sarcophagus.

At first glance it looked like every other exquisitely carved jackal figure sarcophagus or image that Teddy had ever seen, but as he squinted into the haze he realised there was one very clear exception.

This version was screaming.

Samantha was staring at it too. "This isn't good, is it, Teddy?"

What could he say? This was about as far from good as he could remember in many years, which was saying something considering everything he had witnessed in the last few days.

"I am sure it is better than it looks," he offered.

"Teddy."

His shoulders sagged. "Okay, no, it is bad. It is very, very bad! Inpu was the Protector of the Underworld, the overseer of embalming and–"

"*Nobody* is embalming me," she interrupted fiercely, hand going immediately to her revolver, looking around as though a host of Ancient Egyptians might suddenly pull themselves out of history to start preparing her for the afterlife. "I like my organs kept internal and my brain unstirred, thank you very much."

Teddy didn't blame her for being wary. It was a ridiculous notion to be sure, but after everything he'd seen on this ill-advised adventure who could tell what harm might befall them next. He replied as calmly as he could, trying not to fixate on the highly concerning sarcophagus. "I cannot think that would be part of the test. Like all the other challenges, this must be solvable without sacrifice and death."

Her gun hand relaxed a little. "Now there's the pragmatic Professor I needed. So do you know what *this* is exactly?"

He took a moment to answer, thinking it through as best he could.

"If this truly is the final test, then it will be in keeping with the journey so far. Consistent with the theme of trust."

"Which means?"

"You will have to climb inside."

Samantha's lips thinned. She looked back at the sarcophagus. Then at him. Then at the sarcophagus again. From where Teddy watched, the agonised face seemed very much alive in the torch light.

"Honestly, Teddy, I've survived two plane crashes, a war against a whole host of awful people, supernatural monsters, and a rogue government who made me America's most wanted. But I'm beginning to wonder if my luck might have finally run out. Want to swap?"

"If only I could fit through this window," he replied, torn between guilt and relief that he could do no such thing. "I'm sorry."

"Uh-huh, me too."

She walked around the sarcophagus, stopping only to bend down and examine something in the side of the large coffin. "Air holes," she said, just loud enough for him to hear. Her fingers then dropped to the floor next to it and brushed across the stone back and forth. "And scorch marks."

Teddy gulped. "I'm sure it is fine?"

"From this side of the wall, Teddy, I can honestly hold my hand on my heart and say it doesn't feel fine at all. Are you sure I can't just stay outside this thing while you solve the trap?"

"I'm afraid not. If I am right, the point of the challenge is to trust the person you are with. You must get inside the sarcophagus and I must solve the puzzle."

"Right… right. And how does the puzzle look over there then?"

Teddy looked back into his far-too-sparse chamber, hoping something had revealed itself while he'd been talking.

It hadn't.

"I think there might be clues behind a secret panel on the wall in here that I cannot yet see. Some kind of weight-activated mechanism will reveal them, once you are inside. Of that I am almost sure."

"You want me to climb into my coffin for *almost*?"

"I am 95% sure."

Her eyes narrowed.

"OK, 90%," he said quickly. "But definitely no less than that. Remember, I have been studying for this test my entire life. I am ready if you are."

"The things I do for other people," she sighed, standing and placing her hands on her hips. "So how do I get inside this thing anyway?"

Teddy held up a finger to get her to wait, then looked around his chamber again. He walked along each wall, running his hands into the shadows, feeling around for some kind of lever.

Then he saw a discoloured stone slab next to the column and stood on it.

The floor shook and something immediately began grinding in the walls. A low, ancient groan of gears or levers or goodness knows what else they had built into this place.

The gasp he heard from Samantha told him it had worked.

He rushed back to the window to see the lid of the sarcophagus opening slowly. Only to realise that wasn't what she was looking at.

He followed her horrified gaze to the segment of the ceiling above the gutter in the corner.

It had slid open.

And steaming lava was pouring through.

Hissing and spitting, it fell directly into the highest point of the gutter and began to bubble slowly down and around the room.

On its way into the sarcophagus.

"Oh come *on,*" she cried out, looking to him for help.

But he couldn't offer it.

"No time. Get in. Get in now!"

With a few choice British curses he didn't fully understand, she climbed in and lay down.

"Now I know how French Samantha felt," she said, before she was immediately cut off as the lid slammed shut.

The noise echoed with an air of finality about it that sent shivers down Teddy's spine, despite the heat now permeating both chambers.

"OK, *now* what?" her muffled words sounded through the air holes in the sarcophagus.

Teddy spun around, expecting to see the puzzle suddenly revealed. The discoloured part of the wall dropping away to reveal clues, maybe. Or the column lighting up whatever glyphs he needed to decipher and match up. He would even have taken the disembodied voice of an Atlantean spirit – perhaps a friend of the one Samantha said had taken hold of Edward Cayce – to suddenly start asking him riddles in his head, presenting him with a plethora of choices upon which he would be judged, Inpu style.

He would have taken anything, literally anything at all.

Instead, what he got was nothing.

Samantha was now trapped in a sarcophagus about to be filled with lava, waiting for him to solve a puzzle.

And he had no puzzle to solve.

CHAPTER TWENTY-NINE

Navigators of Death

Jess quickly discovered that following in someone else's wake made walking into a labyrinth of death much easier than normal. Especially when that someone was her sister.

The enemy still moved slowly ahead of her. But they had shifted gears after the first trap, transitioning from inching down the tunnel to careful walking, content that Sam had overcome all the challenges so far and hadn't reset anything – probably to ensure she and Teddy could get back out again if they survived their trip. It wasn't like the multi-tunnelled catacombs beneath Paris, Jess considered, as she followed from a wary distance. This was likely the only way down or up, and Sam wouldn't have wanted to undertake the challenges twice. Even she wasn't that much of a masochist.

Either way, the ease of their passage down was lulling Agent Taylor and his men into a sense of security and Jess was getting ready to exploit it.

She'd pegged her target a few minutes ago. One of the

soldiers near the rear who she recognised had helped drag Will to get punched by Agent Smith. This guy was getting a little fidgety and it was a sign she recognised, having spent plenty of time in New York.

He was itching to have a smoke.

All too soon, the moment came. The others pushed on past yet another chamber of horrors – a pit full of spikes, crossed only by a narrow bridge that wove this way and that above it – while the soldier pulled to one side, unable to continue.

He waited for the others to slip ahead without him, then lit up a cigarette.

It took him a moment. There was no wind this far under the desert, of course. Yet there was an eerie, underground breeze circling down here and it made the man's desperate fumbling to ignite his smokes that much harder.

Distracting him.

Distancing the others as they continued pushing on.

And buying Jess just enough time to see what Sam had done in here to pass by unscathed.

There was a wall of levers just behind the man. She spotted the one she needed, then snuck towards it, keeping an eye on him.

So much so, that she didn't see the stone until she'd kicked it and sent it tumbling past the man's boots, over the edge of the pit, clanking loudly as it fell between the spikes.

The soldier spun, cigarette dangling from his bottom lip, and tried to get his gun up, but Jess knew she had the momentum. She leapt the last few yards, yanked down on the lever with one hand and reached for his weapon with the other… just as the section of bridge he was standing on gave way.

He dropped out of sight without even being able to scream, simply gasping his last breath like a quickly deflating balloon and leaving behind the glowing cigarette perched neatly on the edge of the chasm.

Jess held her nerve as she gazed down at his unmoving corpse as it slid further onto one of the spikes, even as she felt the vestiges of her last meal try to punch its way out of her throat. But she held it down. She would not give into guilt-infused nausea – not for this man who was complicit in Will's suffering. Her sister wouldn't have. Sam had fought her way across Europe and killed and killed and killed and it had not only helped save countless lives, it had given her the skills she needed to survive in this world.

A terrible thing, maybe, but Jess gritted her teeth and accepted the idea that it might also be a necessary thing too.

So she made herself look at the man's limp body until she could feel the thick wall of pity and guilt inside her begin to peel away. At which point she kicked the smouldering cigarette into his grave and strode over the bridge to continue the hunt.

Sam couldn't move.

The sarcophagus was far smaller than she had anticipated. Which seemed logical, considering that they were usually used to house the dead, not a tired, ex-pilot who had been dragged on some fool quest for lost archaeological treasure.

You weren't meant to be able to move. Just lie there and be dead.

She tilted her head as far back as it would go, rolling her eyes up to see the opening through which lava would soon be pouring. There was nothing yet. Which meant there was still time to get out of this alive, but plenty of time for her to continue panicking.

"Teddy?" she urged again.

"I cannot comprehend this." His voice wavered in and out of earshot as he ran around his chamber. "The puzzle… I do not know what this means…. it should be here."

Heart thudding against her chest, she shifted uncomfortably within the hard granite tomb, unable to wipe the growing sweat from her eyes or blow away the loose strands of hair that had escaped her tie and were still sticking to her cheeks. Her arms and hands could move around ever so slightly, but not enough to reach her face.

"Ninety per cent sure, you said, Teddy! Ninety per cent!"

"It seemed a logical number!" he yelled through the window. Then, "I am sorry, Samantha. The clues are not here."

She tried shoving her shoulder against the lid, but it didn't budge. "So I'm in here for nothing?!" She pushed her hands and knees against the stone. Trying everything she could to manoeuvre her way out. "I thought this was about trusting the other person? There must be something over there. Because if

I got in this ancient cooking pot ready to flambé myself alive, you sure as shit better have something to do too."

There was no response.

That's when the panic really started to set in.

What if he'd passed out? Or he'd set off another trap and killed himself?

She was going to die, wasn't she?

Then his words broke the silence. Slowly and deliberately spoken, as if he was thinking this through.

"Yes, yes… you are right, of course. They would not change the rules. But perhaps they decided to toss in an added challenge, just to be sure of our worth? Something to throw off all but the most committed seekers of truth. A twist in the tale…" His voice trailed off for a moment, then he cried out, "Look around you, there may be something in there to help you help me."

She laughed, feeling the hysteria set in. "It's a goddamn coffin, Teddy! I can't look around. It's smaller than a budget New York apartment in here."

"No time for jokes, Samantha. Time is against us."

"What the hell do you mean by *us*?" she muttered, looking up again. The glow of the lava outside was growing stronger. Blinking away the sweat, she twisted her head around anyway to see if there were any clues. Symbols, paintings, whatever. But there was nothing.

"There's nothing in here but me, Teddy," she said, feeling the heat begin to suffocate her. "And if we don't figure this out in about two minutes then not even that."

"Do not look then. Feel. It could be carved or etched.

Maybe it is hidden by your hands. A switch of some kind?"

Trying to stifle a coughing fit on the smoky air, Sam closed her eyes and felt around the inside of the sarcophagus by her sides.

At which point she located a subtle button just near enough her hand to activate. A hidden mechanism she realised she would have found much earlier if only she'd held her nerve and searched properly.

You sneaky ancient bastards, she thought, and pressed it.

Immediately another hole slid open in the side of the stone coffin next to her head. A beam of lava light entered and illuminated a hidden array of crystals embedded in the lid above her face.

She blinked away the sweat as best she could and squinted up. "All right, there's some kind of pattern now. The light from the lava is bringing it to life. I don't know what it is though. It's almost like writing, but if it's a language, it's unlike anything I've ever seen."

"It must look like something? Perhaps Egyptian, Greek, Roman?"

Sam coughed again, banging her head on the lid. But as the heat increased with the encroaching lava outside, so did the light pouring in. The crystal patterns dazzled, even through the steam.

It didn't matter though. She realised she could still not understand them.

"I'm not the archaeologist, Teddy. You are."

"But I am not in there!"

She let out a moan and lifted her head to see the lava

edge into view around the corner of the volcanic gutter, into the straight that would bring it into her final resting place. "Tell me something I don't know."

The next words she heard took her back to the airfields in England. Those long nights, sitting out under the stars with Teddy. No longer pilots waiting for their turn to save the country or die trying. But master and student.

It wasn't what he said, but the tone he used. Calm and patient.

"Samantha," he began, "you were the best accidental student I ever had. More than anyone else I ever bored to death about my work, I *know* you were listening while you waited for the next dogfight in the skies. I know you read those books I loaned you. So take a breath *and tell me what you see.*"

Ignoring the acrid stink and blistering heat from the encroaching lava, she stared at the images again.

And something popped into her head.

Sitting under the stars with Teddy.

The stars.

"Oh," she said, her watery eyes widening. "Oh!"

"What? What!?"

"It's not a language… I used to navigate by these. They're stars. They're all stars!"

His whoops of delight grew muffled. He must have retreated into his chamber. "Of course! And that is what I have here. Not hieroglyphs, but star charts. Which ones do you see?"

"Gods, Teddy," she replied, almost laughing through

the tears. "I see gods. It's Orion and Sirius."

"But that's…"

"Osiris and Isis! Yes, the amulet and the stone!"

She heard him let out another whoop. "How could we be so stupid? The answer was in front of us the whole time! We will laugh about this one day, I am sure. Now, wait there, let me assemble these segments on the column."

Sam waited. The stone around her was growing hotter by the second, while the light from the lava blazed as the molten rock finally inched around the bend and started towards her head.

It didn't matter though. Any second now, Teddy was going to solve the puzzle and release her from this trap.

Any.

Second.

Now.

"What the bloody hell are you doing out there?" she yelled.

"I'm so sorry, but we need a third pattern!" he called back. "We only have two, but I have three segments to align. Is there another star map you've missed? Another one of the Gods?"

"Oh for fuck's sake," she whined softly, barely able to open her eyes now. She could almost smell her hair burning. "No, there's nothing else. Just align those two, damnit."

He disappeared again.

"Okay, that opened up my wall! But I cannot see anything yet… no patterns… no…" He paused. "Wait!"

"This isn't the time to keep me waiting, Teddy! I hate

waiting!"

"I know, but the light from your chamber is coming through now. It is.... showing me something!"

Sam couldn't even bring herself to look up. The heat was unbearable. Molten death was only inches away.

"Hurry," she gasped.

"Wait... wait..."

Her hair begin to smoulder.

"Teddy!"

She closed her eyes.

Heard something in the distance. A voice, perhaps. The sound of her own screaming as she died, maybe.

Or a cry of delight.

There was a rumble and the heat and light disappeared from behind her. She squinted through watery, stinging eyes to see the gutter had shifted away from the sarcophagus.

Another rumble shook her as the lid finally lifted and relatively cool air poured in.

It was a blessed relief. But she wasn't about to take any chances and get stuck again.

Fingers gripping the sides of the granite, she pulled herself up like a traumatised vampire from its coffin. Strands of loose hair were either sizzling or stuck with sweat to her face. Her eyes burned. Her lungs were trying to wrench themselves free from her body as she coughed through the steam.

Until it cleared and revealed Teddy's pale face framed by the hole in the wall.

"Are... are you okay?" he asked.

She climbed shakily out of the sarcophagus and stared at the scorch marks around the newly opened hole in the floor where the lava was currently pouring. "I'm not going to lie, Teddy. I've witnessed the birth of monsters. Fought creatures from hell. Seen men in war tearing each other apart by bullet, grenade and tank with only the barest notion of why. But *that...?*" She stepped back as the last of the lava disappeared, the hole in the ground closed, and the gutter shifted back to the sarcophagus. "That was really unpleasant."

With another rumble, the room shook as she finished speaking. Had she the energy, she might have panicked again. But all she could manage was a look of drained resignation as another secret revealed itself.

Thankfully it turned out to be the door out of there.

Death was just going to have to wait a few more minutes to take her.

"So what was the third constellation?" she called to Teddy. "The third map that almost got me killed?"

He laughed though whether with nerves or excitement she couldn't tell. "Taurus," he replied.

"The bull?"

"And the figurehead of a certain lost civilisation."

Sam patted down the smoking collar of her jacket as she strode for the door.

"I guess this is it then."

CHAPTER THIRTY

The Cavern of Legends

They stepped through their doorways into the cavern at the same time.

It stretched out ahead and to the sides, its red rock walls smoothed and covered with colourful murals of stunning settlements, impossible technologies and people of all descriptions engaged in ancient life.

"Holy Gods," Teddy whispered beside her, as his gaze fixed on the central image on the far wall – a gigantic fresco, two or maybe three storeys high. It depicted a magnificent city, with silver towers spiralling upwards in the centre, an expansive outer wall gleaming like a moonbeam, and glorious canals circling inside, with many a varied vessel sailing them – from small barges and sail boats to what looked like a black and red pirate's ship.

And above it, like the sun, hung the golden image of a bull's head.

Sam could almost feel the excitement pour off Teddy. Whatever trials they had just encountered, the weariness and fear was easily shaken off and forgotten now. They were here. In the presence of an ancient world that hadn't been seen by human eyes in thousands of years.

"Atlantis," Teddy breathed. His single word of validation echoed softly through the cavern as he removed his scratched and dirty glasses and cleaned them with his shirt, while still squinting at the marvel around them. "All this time I was right to believe. Right to pursue this dream of dreams. Oh, Sam, isn't it beautiful?"

Sam nodded absently, her eyes fixing on the outline of a door in the rock underneath the grand painting.

"Now where do you go?" she mused.

Teddy put his glasses back on and gave her a broad smile. "Why, to the Hall of course. Which makes this the infamous Cavern of Legends, Samantha. A place few know about. I think its origins were, in fact, derived from readings given by the father of your psychic friend. It serves as the antechamber to the Hall. We are very close."

"And yet, not close enough, I'm afraid," Agent Taylor said behind them.

They spun to see him step into the chamber, followed closely by Smith, Colonel Arif and three Egyptian soldiers – with Will and Cayce pushed between them at gunpoint.

"Son of a bitch," Sam sighed as she and Teddy raised their hands.

Will lifted his head as he saw them, looking like he'd been through shit, but he was still alive after all and that gave her a little jolt of hope. "I'm sorry, Captain," he said, his voice shaky and seemingly on the edge of giving out.

She dismissed his apology with a shake of the head, while scanning for Jess – whom she was suddenly concerned she didn't see. "Nothing to apologise for, Will. It's good to see you." Smith strode towards her with a wicked glint in his eyes. She stood unflinching as he moved in close. "These guys, on the other hand…"

The agent smiled, cold white teeth to go with his cold white skin, and ripped her gun from its holster. He put the barrel to her forehead. "I say we kill them now," he said. Not quite asking permission, just scoping out whether he could get away with it. He'd always been the kind of agent who asked for forgiveness from his superiors rather than permission for doing unspeakable acts. He had found he'd been able to get away with a lot more that way.

To her surprise, it was Colonel Arif who disagreed. He had been staring around the cavern, eyes bright with pride as he drank in the ancient paintings, and as he spoke he barely turned to regard the stand-off. Yet his words carried such a calm air of authority that even Smith seemed to hesitate.

"Put down your weapon, Agent. As much as I would like to see Captain Moxley dispensed with, this is not the place for murder. We can kill her later or not at all, it is really beside the point now. We have control of this sacred place at last. The history of my country."

"Of all our countries, Colonel," Taylor corrected tightly. Sam noticed he didn't look as chipper as she figured he might, standing on the edge of getting everything he wanted. In fact, he was regarding the Colonel with a degree of suspicion.

Suspicion that turned out to be justified.

The Colonel smiled patronisingly and raised his gun at Taylor. At once, his three soldiers immediately followed suit to target Smith, Sam and Teddy.

"You westerners, always casting yourself in the central role of other people's stories. I'm afraid you'll find you are mistaken here. This history belongs to me and my brothers and sisters, Agent Taylor. The rock beneath your feet, the walls around you, the ink that tells these stories... it is all Egyptian." The Colonel raised a hand towards the doorway in the far wall. The path to the Hall of Records itself. "Beyond lies the greatest discovery mankind has ever known. The key to Egypt's rise, to once again being a force unmatched in the world. To making us truly invincible. No longer will we sit idle on the main stage while American and Russian clowns contest their so-called intelligences against one another. Egypt's day has come again. Once we unlock our Hall of Records, its secrets – the wisdom and knowledge and power of the gods – will be ours once more. As they were before. As they should have always been."

Agent Taylor held his gaze at the man's back. "Killing us isn't an option, Colonel, I hope you realise that. You know who we work for. The Nine don't take betrayal lightly."

"Betrayal?" The Colonel let loose a booming laugh. "What betrayal? Come now, Agent Taylor. Nobody will ever know what happened down here. Perhaps the mission was a failure? Perhaps your former agent, the troublesome Captain Moxley here, killed you and your men? Maybe it was us who intervened and managed to stop her. Leaving only a few of our number to unearth the Great Hall and reveal its secrets to the world?" He waved his gun in the air like a conductor. "History will then become what we make it. We will be able to orchestrate the hymn sheet from which the world will sing in future. And, honestly, who would ever know any diff–"

Gunfire thundered through the cavern. To Sam's surprise and horror, the three Egyptian soldiers standing near Will and Cayce dropped like puppets whose strings had been cut, while Colonel Arif screamed in agony as he was shot in the hand and his gun spun away across the cavern floor.

Smith, who hadn't flinched, immediately switched his aim from Sam towards the lone Egyptian and for a moment she wondered if this was her moment to tackle him.

She edged closer.

Then stopped short as a figure stepped out of the darkness.

CHAPTER THIRTY-ONE

Jesse James

"Jess?" Sam cried.

Smith realised immediately she was too close to him and stepped out of her reach. But Sam didn't care about that now. Her little sister was alive and well and had done what Sam had failed to do by gaining the upper hand in this catastrophe of a situation.

And yet…?

Now she saw that Jess looked a little different. As if the shadow of a lone cloud had passed over her usually sunlit uplands. Sam couldn't quite put her finger on it. But her sister stood a little straighter, more confident.

A real-life gunslinger.

"Sorry I'm late," she said, smiling at the group, but there was no life in it. It was cold and distant and Sam was suddenly wary as she watched her little sister barely give the bodies of the soldiers she had gunned down (none of them much older than Naguib back at the base) a cursory glance. There was no nauseous lingering on their torn wounds or faces. No consideration about the ramifications of the unnatural action she'd just taken. Sam had witnessed many men kill for the first time on the battlefield – and sometimes off it – but there was always a look of regret after they'd done it. Always.

Which meant these weren't the first men Jess had killed.

And from the look in her eyes, they were not going to be her last.

Sam felt icy fingers of guilt squeeze her insides. She'd tried so hard to keep Jess safe, away from the death and destruction and violence. Away from the aftermath that filled even the good people up with hurt and hate for years to come. She'd put her own life on the line to give her sister everything she hadn't had herself… but in this moment she knew she'd failed.

Jess gave her a cursory nod as she passed, yet strode straight to Agent Taylor, who stood calmly in the centre of the group despite the gun now levelled at his chest.

"Young lady, you are a credit to your country," he said, tipping a finger to his forehead in salute.

Sam saw the growing confidence in his eyes. She recognised what he was going to try and do and started to protest, but Jess held up a hand to shush her. "I've got this, sis."

Unfortunately, she hadn't at all.

Taylor stepped forward, pressing the barrel of Jess's gun against his tie. "I'm afraid that despite your commendable efforts, Jess, that you haven't quite got this. But I have a good feeling about you. I always did have, to be honest, which is why I'm willing to make you an offer."

"And what could you possibly offer me, Agent Taylor?"

"The name's Jack," he said, with a tired smile. His finger loosened his tie and undid the top button of his collar. "Sam might not have ever told you, but that is my name. And as for what I can offer you, it would be the most important thing anyone can possess: a purpose."

Her eyes narrowed, but she motioned for him to continue.

"We have been on opposite sides of this journey so far, but that doesn't have to be the case going forward. Our methods are… unusual, I grant you that. But it is all with the highest purpose. And it is that purpose I can offer you now by giving you the chance to come and work for us. For your country."

"Are you kidding me?"

"On the contrary, my offer is deadly serious. We could use someone with your talents and determination, who did what even your sister could not by rescuing us from the Colonel's betrayal. Trust me, Jessica, the world needs you. It balances on a knife edge right now. The Soviet Union is growing in power and there are other, darker foes out there that you can only imagine in your worst nightmares. The United States of America is all that stands between these forces and the freedom of every living person on this planet and, quite frankly, we need all the help we can get." He wiped his forearm across his brow. "You have shown your worth here. Come and show it on a larger quest."

"Sounds great and all," Jess admitted. "But I think

you've failed to grasp that I'm the one in control here?"

The click of a machine gun being readied echoed around them as another suited agent stepped silently from the shadows behind her and motioned for her to lower her gun.

Taylor smiled apologetically. "I'm afraid we are still in control and always have been. We knew there was a chance someone would be following us, so I advised Agent Dillon here to hold back, ready to clean up any detritus."

Jess's lips curled with barely restrained frustration as the agent stepped forward and she dropped her weapon into his free hand. He took it, then forced the two sisters back together.

"Guess I screwed up again," Jess sighed.

"Absolutely not," Taylor said, with an air of sincerity Sam hadn't witnessed in him for a long time. He stepped closer. "It's not your fault, Jess. You did remarkably well considering your lack of training and I am impressed to see that the apple of your family's particular brand of courage and, dare I say it, recklessness hasn't fallen far from the tree. You are a resourceful young woman, just like your sister, but what I've just seen makes me wonder if you might be more equipped to succeed with us where she could not? You recovered the Isis Amulet after all. This journey to Egypt, to one of the greatest treasures in human history, could be but the beginning of your adventures. No longer kept on the sidelines offered to you by your sister, but leading the charge to better this world of ours. Honestly, who better to do it, given it was your courage and tenacity that made this whole remarkable discovery possible?"

Teddy caught Sam's eye and pulled an indignant face. *Didn't we solve all the puzzles,* he mouthed. She ignored him, feeling the prickle of worry inch across her skin as she saw her sister begin to believe in what she was being told.

"Come with us and take your sister's place," Taylor continued in his charming southern drawl, placing a hand lightly on Jess's shoulder. A gesture of understanding. Of comradeship. "Join our team and do what Sam could not. Protect your people, help your country, and make your mark on history. Today it is the Hall, but tomorrow it will be Atlantis!"

Jess shook her head, but it was a feeble gesture. Taylor's bullshit was clearly cutting through and setting down roots.

"Sorry, Jack. It's a nice offer. But I was hoping my sister and I would see this through."

Jess turned to her with a look of hope that Sam really wasn't ready for on any level. Atlantis? The idea would have made her laugh if it wasn't so terrifying. If they made it out of here – and that 'if' was doing a lot of work, given how Agent Smith was looking at her right now – there was no way she was going to go off on another fool's errand. She had already been nearly drowned, torn apart by the undead, beaten to a pulp by a god, and melted by lava to get here. What the hell would a journey to Atlantis involve?

"Maybe?" she replied a little too weakly. "Can we talk about it later?"

It wasn't nearly enough, and in that moment she knew

she should have been far more convincing, lied through her teeth to keep her sister onside. But it was too late.

"What do you mean, *maybe*?" Jess said. "After all this, you want to give up? Atlantis is the endgame, Sam! It's the pinnacle of archaeology, the truth behind everything that exists today. Its discovery would reshape everything we know about the past."

"I'm not an archaeologist, Jess."

"But you *do* want to change the world for the better, don't you?" Jess persisted, growing angrier by the second. "Isn't that why you left me to fight your stupid war in the first place? Isn't that why you took me away from England to keep me hidden in America with Dad? And yet after all these assholes have put us through, you're not even going to put up a fight?"

"You ungrateful little shit! Since you dragged me into this mess, fighting is *all* I've been doing."

Jess looked at the guns trained on them both. "Clearly not well enough."

"You think you being caught unawares by that rent-a-spook is *my* fault?" Sam pointed a finger in the direction of the blank-faced Agent Dillon. "Check the bloody shadows next time!"

Smith chuckled, low and humourless. The sound drifted through the cavern like someone had disturbed a nest of snakes. Taylor fixed him with a glare, before continuing his charm offensive.

"Your sister has a point, Jess, but that will come with experience. And the fact of the matter is that Sam isn't who she once was. You can see for yourself how she has changed. The prize of Atlantis awaits and only the strongest, only the most determined will survive to see it. Sam clearly wants no part of it. But we can provide you with resources and opportunity and the might of the most powerful government in history, with everything you can imagine at your disposal. I can see we have underestimated both you and Dr Sandford over the course of this unfortunate misadventure… and for that I am truly sorry. But we had a job to do and now perhaps we can help each other find Atlantis together? For the good of all."

"Good?" Sam snapped. She'd had enough. But she was also damn sure she was going to use this moment to her advantage too, because the longer this dragged on, the less chance it was going to turn out well. She stepped towards her sister, while edging closer to Smith at the same time. "Look at what they've done so far, Jess. And now they want the weapon that took down an entire civilisation. There is no *good* to be found there."

"Like it or not," Taylor replied sharply, "America is the new Rome. The world needs us to lead and so lead we must, however we can. While it may not be pretty at times, patriotism is our only sin."

"You're confusing patriotism for nationalism. No country is worth what you've done to people. And, let me remind you, the Nazis also thought torturing people for information was patriotic too."

Taylor frowned at that and she saw a glimpse of genuine confusion flash behind his eyes, before he composed himself. He gestured to Will and Cayce holding each other up. “We treated Edward Cayce with respect while he was in our charge, and if you’re referring to Dr Sandford’s unfortunate presentation, I can assure you his injuries are largely the result of your reckless driving across the desert. For most of the time he was with us we had him under sedation to keep him calm, for his own safety.”

“You tortured Will back at the base,” Sam replied, gesturing to Smith, even as she stepped towards him again. “He told me.”

“He was clearly baiting you, Sam. Rest assured, I was there the entire time Dr Sandford was conscious. We asked our questions of him, but at no point was he harmed. I made sure of it.”

Sam looked to Will, hoping for some kind of confirmation from him that Taylor was lying, but he simply stood there and looked embarrassed. Goddamit, they hadn’t touched him after all. And Smith had got a rise out of her again. She bristled and tensed.

“Well it’s a pity you didn’t stay for me then,” she muttered.

Taylor’s frown deepened and he shot his agent a look of distrust, to which Smith responded by finally taking his eyes off Sam and holding up his hands in a rigid and false gesture of innocence, even as his smile gave his lies away.

“I work for the American Government,” the Nazi said. “We do not torture our own citizens. What do you think I am, a criminal?”

He started laughing.

Sam smiled back.

Then punched him in the jaw as hard as she could.

Smith was a monster.

Whatever he'd been turned into during the war was staggeringly hard. Yet as her knuckles cracked against his genetically altered face, and the agonising white fire of more bones breaking shot up her arm, she knew it had been enough.

He staggered momentarily and dropped her gun, buying them all a second to act.

Jess must have been waiting for Sam to do something, because she reacted almost instantly, spinning and kneeing Agent Dillon in the crotch. The impact dropped him to his knees and she didn't hesitate in diving on him to wrestle away his guns.

Sam only barely saw the blur of Teddy rushing off to intercept the Colonel as he raced, clutching his injured hand, for one of his dead soldier's weapons. She was far more concerned with Taylor raising his own gun – although at who, she wasn't sure – only to be leapt on simultaneously by Will and Cayce.

Which just left her and Smith.

He grinned as they squared off. "I've waited too long for this, *Captain*."

"Not as long as I have, you evil fuck," she replied, clenching her damaged fist, ready to damage it some more.

He stormed forward in an explosion of punches. She did her best to parry some and sidestep others. Threw a fist or two of her own.

But it was all to little effect.

The man wasn't human. Not entirely. His masters had created an abomination of sheer strength and unnatural desire to kill. His attacks were incessant and violent, pushing her slowly away from the others, across the cavern, towards the mural.

Until the final hit.

Caught in the stomach, her energy depleted instantly. She staggered, head down, unable to anticipate the next attack, then feeling the man's rough hands clamp down on her shoulders and lift her off her feet to face him.

She was flung backwards into the wall beneath the picture of Atlantis, where she dropped into a heap on the ground.

And triggered something.

Instantly the cavern woke from its millennia-long slumber. Dust shook free from the walls and flecks of paint, disturbed for the first time after thousands of years, rained down as the doorway behind her opened.

Smith didn't care about such things. His blood was up and he was ready to finish the job.

He pulled her to her feet again.

Clocked her across the jaw.

It was as bone-jarring as the impact she knew all too well of a plane hitting water. An unnatural collision between machine and the natural world.

She stumbled back through the doorway, beyond the wall, leaving the others behind. Only barely conscious.

Trying to stay on her feet and failing miserably.

She collapsed in the middle of the small dark space.

Smith stepped in with her, a grin on his face.

The doors shut behind them.

CHAPTER THIRTY-TWO

A Battle Between Worlds

Sam's head swam.

There was blood trickling down her nose, but she couldn't wipe it away. Her hands were the only thing holding her up.

Yet, in the haze, she could feel something wrong. The touch beneath her fingers wasn't stone or rock or any kind of material that should be found under the Egyptian sands.

It was cold and smooth and metallic.

Smith had seen it too. He could have killed her then and there and she wouldn't have been able to stop him. But he had hesitated to take in their surroundings. It was enough to let her gather her wits for one last round.

She managed to scramble backwards, stagger to her knees, then push herself to her feet and face him groggily in the low, strange light.

"Come on then, you piece of shit," she slurred. "Let's be having you."

Where they were didn't matter right now. Her brain was

still trying to figure it out, but she kept shutting down the theories it threw at her. The fact that they were in a completely circular room constructed of hundreds of strange black blocks with stained holes didn't matter to her as much as the fact she was trapped in here with *him*. The glowing amber seal in the centre of the floor next to her boots, with its strange, possibly Atlantean writing in cold, harsh strokes – obviously a warning – was inconsequential compared to the machine of a man who was trying to kill her.

"Can you feel it?" Smith said with a smile, his perfect white teeth like so many picket fences in small-town America. The kind behind which monsters could often be found. "We're so close to the end. It will be a pleasure to kill you here. To wipe the light from your eyes within touching distance of the prize. To finally silence that stupid British accent of y–"

She leapt and punched him square in the nose with every ounce of energy she had left.

The bone shattered beneath the skin. The fragments grinding against her knuckles. The blood exploding over his cheeks.

It was goddamn satisfying.

A feeling which only lasted for the single second it took him to recover, before he came at her with a throat-bursting scream, fists flying, and the unhinged look of a creature who wasn't going to quit until he'd feasted.

* * *

It was chaos in the cavern.

Teddy found himself up against Colonel Arif, desperately wrestling to reach one of the dropped rifles. It was a mismatch from the start, even with the man's shot hand bleeding everywhere, but there was too much at stake now for Teddy to give up. So he clung tight to any part of the man he could get his hands on.

"We don't have to do this," he repeated again in Arabic, his teeth bared as he tried to pull the Colonel's arm back from the gun. "We both want the Hall for Egypt. The Americans will betray you and steal whatever they can. Let us at least prevent them doing that?"

He hated having to try to negotiate with this awful man, but right now he didn't feel like he had a choice. An elbow found his face and he blinked away the tears, clinging on even tighter.

"The English have stolen their fair share from us too and yet you came here with one of them," the Colonel spat back. "Captain Moxley has taken artefacts from this land on their behalf before. You think I would trust that woman with our most precious treasure now?"

He turned suddenly and punched Teddy in the stomach. Teddy doubled over, only barely holding on. He might have fought in the war, but there was a difference between putting your body into an aircraft and fighting in the clear blue skies, and going toe to toe with a trained killer in person. On reflection, he had not appreciated that enough.

"She is not like that anymore, trust me," he wheezed.

"Sam wants to make up for what she's done in the past. Why do you think she stands against the Americans now? We both want what's best here. To protect the Hall. To safeguard our heritage!"

"Do not presume to talk to me about heritage. Your blood is impure. You are only half Egyptian. You could not possibly know the true value of what lies beyond those walls."

"And you are a military man who only sees things in black and white. Our culture is so much more than that. It shouldn't be left up to us. Why not let the people decide?"

"Because, you old fool, the people must only ever see what we allow them to see."

Teddy lashed out and kicked him in the shin. A manoeuvre he hadn't used since the school playground, but it still worked a treat and bought him enough time to get back to his feet and square off against the taller, stronger man.

"Governments," he groaned. *"Always controlling the people, never working* for *the people."*

Then the Colonel roared and Teddy found that he had a roar of his own as the two came together again.

As Teddy's yell echoed around the cavern, Jess found herself still struggling with Agent Dillon, although the kick in the crotch she'd managed to get in was hampering his efforts.

The old ways, still effective, she considered humourlessly, as she forced his weakened gun arm up and up, letting him fire the weapon into the roof, before she spun him under the big chunks of rock that rained down.

He collapsed under the rubble and his gun skittered across the floor. But no sooner had she retrieved it when she heard an unearthly cry.

She turned to see Will still wrestling with Agent Taylor – Jack – while Cayce had fallen to the ground clutching his head. He was screaming.

And it sounded like something else was in there screaming with him.

Jack had heard it too. He looked all at once furious and terrified, as though something he had been worrying about was finally happening. It was enough to get him to finally shove Will away, although with as much care as he could, almost as though he didn't want to hurt the man. Like a parent, Jess thought as she ran towards them. Firm but fair.

She wondered again if he had been telling the truth before. That this was all about a bigger cause she didn't yet understand and maybe that's why he had to work alongside some awful people, because didn't every workplace have one or two people you simply hated, but had to work with in order to get the job done? She'd known enough herself.

Perhaps Jack was just doing this for his country? And perhaps if Sam hadn't blustered into the museum that night in New York, Jack and his men wouldn't have rushed in guns blazing? Was it possible that her sister created this mess in the first place and in another world this could have all been handled in a better, more professional way, with the two parties working together?

And wasn't it only fitting and right that the majesty of Atlantis be found in a similar spirit of cooperation?

Cayce screamed again and this time the noise blew all other thoughts from her mind. He was shaking uncontrollably now. His mouth stretched open wider than should have been possible and quickly the scream became a roar and a strange light began to pour out of his throat, spilling from his eyes and nose, like the glow of a too-bright lightbulb.

Before she could reach any of them, Jack levelled his gun against the prone man and stepped immediately into what Jess instinctively knew was harm's way.

"I'm sorry, Edward," she heard him call out, and could hear that he meant it, too.

But as the light grew fiercer, Jess now saw another figure materialise around Cayce… growing out of him like a genie from a human lamp… swallowing him whole. A being of such immensity that it caused the cavern around them to rumble and for stalactites to crash down as it saw what Jack was about to do and cried, "Nooooo!"

From out of nowhere, a bloody and dusty Agent Dillon appeared and grabbed the gun from Jess to take aim at the thing, but the beautiful, terrifying figure raised a hand and in a flash of light the agent was sent spiralling across the chamber, twisted beyond all recognition.

Mouth agape, Jess could only stay where she was as what had been Cayce, now shrivelling within the power of the spirit, looked up at Jack and begged for his end.

The agent's suit and hair began to flutter in the supernatural gusts swirling around them as he grit his teeth and fired, and the last thing she saw on Cayce's face was gratitude, before his head snapped backwards and he collapsed to the ground.

The whirlwind of light intensified instantly. The roar almost burst Jess's eardrums.

But just before it seemed like it might explode and kill them all, another figure leapt into the centre of it.

Will… rushing to Cayce's aid.

"Dr Sandford, no!" Jack yelled, lowering his gun and reaching out to stop Will from getting close to the psychic.

But it was too late.

Will touched the corpse. And an explosion of ethereal blue light enveloped the pair of them.

As Sam fell to the floor, Smith kicked her hard in the stomach.

She felt another rib crack as the momentum carried her sliding across the smooth floor… straight across the central seal.

The room began to shake.

Fucking hell, give me a break, she moaned silently.

It shouldn't have surprised her when the metal blocks began moving. She should have known that there would be a final test. One last chance for the ancient architects to have a little fun with whoever was foolish enough to embark on this adventure.

But surprise her it did. And piss her the hell off too, as one by one the blocks slid towards the centre, closing in on them both.

If that wasn't enough, short, sharp spikes began thrusting in and out of the blocks in waves.

As if the chamber wanted to eat them.

Sam got to her feet. Bloodied and battered, she looked from the encroaching walls of death to Smith.

"Truce?"

He spat out a mouthful of blood to the side. If there had been any level of sanity in his eyes before, it was now completely gone.

"We die together!" he said, grinning.

Their violent dance continued. Punch after punch. Some barely dodged. Some landing like bricks dropped from a great height.

Sam had been in precarious situations before. Sometimes facing off against more than one person. But her skills and survival instinct and sheer dumb luck had always carried her through. There had always been a way out. A way through. A way not to die.

She couldn't see it here. She was losing because she was old, tired, beaten up and terrified that Smith's unnatural machine-like endurance was going to see him through to the end.

Too slow to react, she felt his hands grab her arm and spin her into an encroaching block.

There was a scraping sound. She moved her head as quickly as possible, only just turning away as a spike knifed out from the thing, grazing her cheek. But there was no relief to be found. Smith was on her again, throwing her to the other side of the increasingly small antechamber.

She bounced off the wall and collapsed. She hung

her head and spat out more of her own blood onto the increasingly slippery floor.

There she held. Doing her best to look spent, barely needing to act the part. She figured she must be pretty convincing by now.

Smith approached with the kind of confidence that all mediocre men unfairly lifted beyond their station, and given every advantage possible, have at the moment of their triumph.

Which made it all the more satisfying when she twisted at the last moment and connected with the back of his leg, just behind the knee.

Not enough to drop him. She didn't have the strength for that.

But sufficient to catch him off-balance. And allow her to leap up and ram him backwards into the wall.

He landed just as another set of spikes shot out, pinning him through the side of his chest and his left hand.

This was it. The last push.

She threw everything she had at him, trying to take advantage of her sudden fortune. Trying to beat him into submission, even as the walls continued to close around them, with the scream of hundreds of spikes jutting in and out of their blocks becoming increasingly unbearable.

Until the one in him retracted and he was free again.

He thundered forwards, fists raised, the left one spraying blood in a wide arc as he threw it at her.

It missed. Yet as he prepared to throw the right, there was a new noise in the room.

A panel in the floor had swooshed open, just in front of one of the walls.

Sam half expected something nightmarish to swoop out of it and devour them both.

Yet it held quiet and empty and alluring in the surrounding madness.

An escape hatch.

They both hesitated as they saw it. Sam instantly regretted not using that moment to hit him. To shove him out of the way and take the hatch. But she had nothing left now. She could only stand there, wobbling on her feet as he grabbed her jacket and slammed something into her shoulder, before diving into the hiding hole.

She winced and looked down at the dimension disc he'd just clamped to the top of her right arm.

"Goodbye, Captain," he said, his laugh quickly muffled as the wall passed safely over his head.

Sam spun around in a panic, looking between the walls and the disc that was beginning to burn through her jacket as it started to activate itself.

The blast was so intense, Jess couldn't see for a good few seconds afterwards.

She could still feel the heat in the cavern and could still hear Will's name echoing from wall to wall, taunting her with her own instinctive cry as she had watched him swallowed whole by the light.

She almost didn't want to be able to see again, knowing

that once she saw what was left of him, it would be real. An event horizon crossed. No going back.

So when she blinked and saw him simply standing there, unnervingly tall and straight, looking like he hadn't a care in the world, her heart leapt. It didn't matter what had happened. She didn't care what kind of ridiculous supernatural miracle had just taken place. Or why he suddenly looked so strong and vibrant, his bruises faded, the blood wiped clean.

Somehow, he was still alive.

Jack was still standing there too, his gun half raised at Will as though unsure of whether he should be targeting him or not. He blinked in confusion as his gaze swept from the scorch marks on the ground around Cayce, back up to Will.

Yet just as she reached out to ask him to put the gun down, she heard someone scuff through the dirt behind her. And for the second time in this damned place, something cold and metallic was pressed into the back of her neck.

She turned just enough to see Teddy lying beaten on the floor nearby, before Colonel Arif leaned in and snarled in her ear.

"This is for my men."

Any moment.

Any moment now, Sam was going to be transported to hell knows where, already beaten to within an inch of her life. Others who'd been at the mercy of the disc had come back. She knew that. But she'd also seen them afterwards. Catatonic with fear.

There was no way she had it in her to survive whatever they had gone through.

I will not go like this.

It was just a single thought. A voice from the crypt of her mind where she had buried all those unpleasant memories over the years. Yet it was loud and focussed, and it gave her something to cling to, even as the disc continued to vibrate, its heat incinerating a hole in her jacket and its barbs stuck fast in her skin underneath.

"They're all relying on me," she muttered, spinning around one last time for an answer to her problem, as the walls continued to close in. "I can't let go."

She reached up with her left hand and tugged at the thing, but already knew there was no ripping it off. These discs were designed by top minds – smart, awful minds – to stay on for as long as possible.

Unless it was destroyed.

Sam's eyes went wide as she watched the spikes continue to knife in and out of the encroaching blocks. She quickly threw herself against the nearest one, jamming her shoulder – and the disc – against the hole. And just as the purple light began to spread out around her, the metal spike shot out and pierced the disc – popping it with an explosion of heat and flame that would have been agony in itself, had the spike not also gone straight through her shoulder.

She couldn't help the cry of despair as she found herself saved, but impaled. Any relief from knowing the disc would not take her now dissipated along with the smoke and the pain.

Then the spike retracted again and she fell free to face another death.

For the walls continued closing in.

And there were plenty more spikes looking for a taste of blood.

"Think," she mumbled. "Who did they want to reach the Hall? Who did they want to survive these tests?"

She could hear Teddy's words in the back of her mind.

Only the worthy.

Sam stopped in the centre, clutching her shoulder, but no longer feeling the pain. She looked around. Then up.

"They wouldn't have devised this room for the strongest to win."

Above her, hidden from all but those who knew where to look, she could see what appeared to be a counter-mechanism chain.

She grinned. "Not the strongest. The smartest."

As waves of spikes lashed out angrily, she made her move, jumping onto the lowest set and running up them as they appeared from the walls. Going higher and higher. Until she was able to leap.

She reached for the chain and stretched with every sinew and fibre of her being.

And caught it.

Anything could have happened next. It could have snapped or disintegrated with age, dropping her to be crushed below. It might have been rusted in place, leaving her dangling like a pinata ready to be punctured full of holes.

But for once her luck held.

It dropped and locked in place, causing the walls to shudder to a halt, before retracting again.

Sam dropped heavily to the floor. Swaying, but upright. Feet planted wide to keep from falling over.

She waited near the escape hole as the wall pulled back and exposed it again.

The man inside blinked and shielded his eyes against the sudden light, then stared in surprise as he saw Sam, still alive and standing over him.

"Goodbye, Agent Smith," she said.

His angered cry was cut short as the trap was finally reset. The walls and floor of the hole he was in suddenly disappeared. And to both their surprise, he began to drift away into a dark, thick fog. A mist that pulled the man away into its clutches, muffling his thrashing screams until finally the panel in the floor closed off the view and he was lost forever.

Then she understood where she truly was.

"A bridge," she found herself saying, as she looked around in shock. "The metal… this room… it's a bridge across a divide. From this world to–"

She didn't get to finish her thought.

Because, in the background, back in the Cavern of Legends, she heard the distinct sound of her sister screaming.

Before a gunshot cut it short.

CHAPTER THIRTY-THREE

A Choice

The Colonel stopped talking.

Fell to his knees.

And collapsed at Jess's feet.

She tried to stay calm as she stared at Jack's smoking gun. It was difficult with her heart trying to crawl out of her chest. She could still feel the flash of heat on her cheek from where his bullet had brushed past, before plunging straight into the face of Colonel Arif.

The American agent regarded her carefully, then lowered his weapon. Whatever reason he'd had for training it on Will a minute ago was now forgotten. Or at least reprioritised. He seemed like a man who just been forced to make a decision and was now committing to it.

"Are you OK?" she whispered as Will wandered over, moving in an awkward, stumbling way, as though he had only recently remembered how to walk.

He gave her an odd look, but said nothing.

"It seems we are at an impasse," Jack said to the pair

of them. He glanced at the Colonel and then the dead soldiers behind him, before eyeing Teddy as he groaned and pulled himself to a sitting position from the floor nearby. "It may sound contrived, Jess, considering our conflicting journeys to this place, but I am truly sorry for everything you have been put through. It was not my intention to bring you into this. We only ever wanted the amulet."

Jess was unsure what to make of this man before them now. A man who was outnumbered, but the only one armed… and yet showed no signs of trying to use the gun to his advantage. Was this an act? Or was he finally being sincere now they'd stripped him of his companions.

"Sam maintained you wanted the Hall of Records for the power it could give you," she said, glancing around for her sister. "Is that true?"

Jack gave her a thin smile, as if reading her mind. "These things are never for me, but those we work for. The American people first and foremost, but the wider population too. We do these things to ensure our freedom and safety, in ways only a few would understand. Your sister certainly didn't appreciate the nature of the work. I live in hope that you still might."

Worryingly, Jess couldn't see Sam anywhere. Nor Agent Smith. Yet even as she played out anxiety inducing scenarios in her mind about what that meant, Jack's statement and his next act kept her attention in the here and now.

He spun the gun around in his palm and offered her the grip.

"I meant what I said earlier, Jess. You have shown great courage and skill, but more importantly you have demonstrated what you will do for the greater good. So let us move on from this mess stronger together. Join us, join our cause, and together we can forge a peaceful world with America at its head. We can take back control of society from those who would seek to destroy it. Not to mention…" he paused "…well, let's just say that there is a bigger picture that would blow your mind. Your sister had but only a glimpse of what we know, but she was not a good fit. You could help us where she could not."

Jess stared at the gun for what seemed like centuries. Every instinct was telling her it was a trick. That he was trying to trap her into making a mistake. And she was sure as shit that if Sam was here she'd be saying the exact same thing, warning her against joining up with this man of many offers.

Where the hell are you, sis?

She looked around again, the concern for her sister growing.

Or was it concern for herself?

Jack was offering her control, something Sam had never done without a fight. He was giving her a chance to lead. But the very idea of making this choice herself felt terrifying and on some level wrong. Like a betrayal. After everything that had happened, could she simply believe Jack and take the gun and maybe even accept his offer?

Sam would have a fit.

And yet it was so tempting. To leave here alive was a

start, but to do so knowing that she and Will would have the legitimate backing of the American Government behind them – no more running, hiding or fighting – as they pursued Atlantis together and used whatever secrets lay there to create a better world? Well, that was a once in a lifetime type offer.

Besides, hadn't Sam done exactly the same once upon a time, joining with this man and his people in an attempt to do good? If it was good enough for her…

She looked to Will for help. Again he stayed silent. But this time he gave her a very definitive nod.

Take it, as your sister would. Atlantis awaits.

The words popped into her head unbidden and Jess wasn't even sure if it was her voice or Will's she heard. Yet it didn't matter. They were enough to push her over the edge of the decision and commit to a path.

She took the gun.

Then, as her fingers curled around the handle – and as if by some quirk of coincidence and a sign of destiny, the door beneath the mural of Atlantis behind her began to open – Sam appeared, battle worn, but alive.

"Oh thank God," she uttered as she saw Jess, the agonised relief in her words plain for them all to hear as they echoed around the cavern.

For her part, Jess offered up a silent 'thank you' to whatever gods were listening, as she went to meet her sister.

"You're alive," they said simultaneously as they grew closer, grinning at each other, but stopping frustratingly short of a hug as Sam suddenly saw her gun, bent down to pick it up, and slide it back into her holster.

"You still look like shit though," Jess noted, looking from Sam's bruised face to the shoulder of her battered brown jacket which was torn and thick with blood. "Where the hell did you go?"

"Had to give Agent Smith a good send off."

Sam's smile faded as she sized up the scene, taking in the various bodies around the cavern, including Cayce's unmoving corpse. Until finally her gaze rested on the gun Jess held loosely at her side.

Jack's gun.

Jess shifted it guiltily in her sweaty palm.

"As you can see, I've got everything under control here," she said quickly.

Sam nodded, her eyes narrowing ever so slightly in Jack's direction. And just when it seemed as though she might finally envelop Jess in the hug she so badly needed, she instead stepped past and all Jess felt was a quick pat on the back as her older sister moved on to help Teddy to his feet.

"You're welcome," Jess muttered, annoyed at herself for expecting anything different. But annoyed more by feeling her cheeks redden as she tried to ignore Jack's sad, pitying look.

When she turned back, Sam was leading Teddy gently towards the doorway she'd just appeared from.

"Where you off to now?" she called.

"You still all want to see the Hall, I take it?"

Jess turned again to Will, but he had already started

following her sister without so much as a look in Jess's direction. Still clutching the gun, Jess gestured for Jack to walk with her… although who was in control of whom in that moment she wasn't entirely sure.

"Just don't stand on the seal," Sam added, as they entered the strange little metallic room beyond the door and passed into the passageway that had opened up on the other side.

Jess saw it and had half a mind to stand on the blasted thing anyway, but stepped over at the last minute. She'd had enough trouble for one day.

As had Jack, it seemed, who walked through beside her with a puzzled expression at seeing no trace of Agent Smith, but decided to keep his mouth shut.

The small, thin passageway out the other side of the metal chamber of death wasn't a long one. Only ten yards, by Sam's count. Maybe twelve.

It was a little difficult to gauge, because it was pitch black. With only a small white glow at the end leading the way.

After what she'd seen happen to Smith, she had been wary about setting foot in here. Quite honestly, she just wanted to go home and have a cup of tea and forget this entire adventure had happened. She didn't want to accidentally end up being sucked into some otherworldly fog.

But they were here now. All the bad guys, except Taylor,

were dead. And although she would have felt far safer with dear old Jack tied up so he couldn't cause any more trouble, Jess currently had his gun. It seemed safe enough for them to at least take a gander at the destination they had fought so hard to reach.

"What is this place?" Teddy asked. "That room we just passed through was all metal. And now this… it doesn't feel right. It is not rock or stone or anything else that should be down here."

"It's a bridge," Agent Taylor replied, before Sam had the chance.

The two shared a glance.

"What the hell does that mean?" Jess snapped, walking behind Will who had seemingly forgotten she existed and was being remarkably calm and quiet for once, considering they were on the verge of one of the biggest discoveries in archaeology. "A bridge to where?"

"I'm not sure yet," Sam said, honestly.

"But we are still beneath Giza, are we not?" Teddy asked, now walking gingerly by himself. "The direction of the tunnels from the temple on the surface took us towards the pyramids. Towards the plateau. We should be underneath the Sphinx now."

Sam shook her head. "And yet I don't think we are, Teddy. We're somewhere else entirely."

The dark path ended in light.

They went to meet it.

CHAPTER THIRTY-FOUR

The Hall of Records

It was a space larger than Sam could have ever imagined. A hall the size of a small city, illuminated by glowing strands of light that rippled above them like the Aurora Borealis on the surface of an invisible lake.

The colours cast everything in a dreamlike pall. Beyond the lights, tall, vaulted ceilings swept overhead, with rich, gleaming amber beams criss-crossing between them. Far into the distance ahead and on both sides, the walls – what Sam could see of them anyway – were pure white, dazzling like the finest Mediterranean villas beneath a blazing sun.

And, high up, strokes of glass like ancient Celtic runes hinted at the existence of windows, although the colours and shapes and swirls of stars Sam could see in the skies through them were beyond her comprehension.

We are somewhere else.

The words repeated over and over in her mind. She had rarely stopped to think about the truth of "other" places whispered about in the dark halls of government. She had worked with (and against) creatures that should not have existed in our realm, without really considering exactly where they might have come from.

Despite everything, she had never questioned the reality she had been presented with.

Now she was full of questions. The idea of there being a somewhere else made so much sense in the context of her past experiences, but it also opened up a whole new universe of understanding and hope and foreboding to explore – and, despite feeling small and naïve in its presence, she was thankful not to be alone.

She was here, in this other place, with Jess and Teddy and Will – and Taylor too, whose usual brand of calm she could see cracking under the immense weight of the sight before him, even though he must surely have known the possibilities of where they might end up.

The way he gazed around silently, soaking up the entirety of what he saw, told her that whatever he had seen before on his preternatural escapades for The Nine, it paled in comparison to the discovery of this palatial repository of wonder. Just like the rest of them, his horizons were being stretched beyond all measure right now. There were no differences between them here. They were simply a group of beings standing on the shores of their own existence, with historical knowledge and treasures beyond anything any of them had dreamed possible laid out before them.

And Sam knew in her bones that this here… this *somewhere else*… was not on Earth.

Which was why Teddy never found anything with his

surveys, she suddenly realised. They didn't reveal anything under the Sphinx, because the tunnels that started in Egypt did not finish in Egypt. They disappeared into an altogether different world.

"Bloody hell," she breathed.

"That's just the opposite of what I was thinking," Jess replied beside her, unable to take her eyes off the rows and rows of shelves and tables and displays that stretched out before them, containing all manner of magic. Old parchments, rolled up like maps. Sheets of silver and gold, as thin as butterfly wings, scribbled with script. And stacks of mysterious objects that would not have been out of place in a Jules Verne novel, including what appeared to be an elaborate tabletop game depicting a series of islands that Jess was currently ogling, except from here Sam could see the illustrations of the seas between them actually crashing and churning and sending spray into the air, while a variety of unusually realistic figurines were shuffling themselves across the board in their own eternal game.

"We made it," she heard Teddy whisper to nobody in particular, unable to help his beard parting in a childish grin. He laughed with glee at a clockwork owl that must have woken at their presence and was now chattering away to itself, then gasped and pointed to a series of steps winding their way up to a balcony of sorts that ran the entire perimeter of the Hall, where, squinting, Sam could see enough books to likely rival the combined might of every library on Earth. Teddy jiggled on the spot. "The Hall of Records is real and we are seeing it with our own eyes, Samantha! Can you believe it? So much knowledge and history in one place."

"Yes, but whose?" Jess remarked. She shared a look of understanding with Taylor, who inclined his head encouragingly.

They spread out now. Eyes wide, mouths agog at every little discovery they made.

Jess picked up a device that started playing a strange, otherworldly music in her hand.

Sam drew up in front of a painting of some kind of sailing vessel in space, only to see it move and disappear beyond the frame.

While Teddy reached for a scroll on a suspended shelf, sliding it out from the pyramid of others it had sat with for goodness knows how many years, and unrolled it carefully over the top of a nearby chest.

"Ancient Egyptian, Greek, Sumerian, all the languages of the ancient world in one place. And look," he cried, pointing to an image on the side. "A map of the land mass of Antarctica!"

Jess and Taylor joined him and pored over it.

"Beneath the ice?" she asked. "How old must this be?"

It was Will who replied, even though he was standing too far behind them to be able to see the thing. Yet he answered with the confidence of someone who somehow already knew.

"Older than you can imagine," he said.

Jess's face lit up at the thought and she spun to grab his arm, while gesturing with her gun to everything around them. "This is it, Will. The greatest exhibition mankind has ever known. A whole new world of discovery, of truth, that will change our understanding of who we are and where we're heading, altering the course of human history for the better – and we get to be the ones to set it all in motion! Can you imagine the headlines in New York when this thing opens? Everyone is going to be blown away!"

"Why New York?" Teddy asked suddenly.

"Why not?" Jess replied brightly. "Our museums are the best in the world. We can make sure these artefacts are properly investigated and conserved for the entire planet."

"Once again setting yourselves up as curators of a history that is not entirely yours, Jess. I thought we had been over this?"

She harrumphed. "Look around you, Teddy. This isn't Egyptian history, this is human history! It deserves the widest audience possible, surely?"

"Some would argue it deserves to stay where we found it. In Egypt."

"If this is Egypt, still," Taylor interjected quietly, and now it was Jess's turn to nod.

The argument at an impasse, they all turned to Sam as though she might be about to offer a penny's worth of her own thinking, given her previous rants on the subject. Wanting her to referee the debate and pick a side.

But she had no answers anymore. She was tired and hungry and half dead and her shoulder was bleeding and quite honestly she was still coming to terms with where this adventure had led them. Right now, the only thing she could offer was a pained shrug and an exhausted wince.

"You're digging in the wrong place if you're looking to me," she said. "Given where we are and what we're seeing, this is clearly a discussion for wiser minds than mine. I did my part nearly killing myself to get us here. How about you academics battle it out? What do you say, Will?"

Will had been looking at a thick, dusty tome, which he shut with a snap at the mention of his name. He tried to smile, but for some reason couldn't quite manage it. It was stuck on his face, like a scratched gramophone record, trying to move on and failing, and although it was a little disturbing, it didn't occur to Sam that it was anything other than him being distracted.

"This is only the first marker," he replied, gazing through her as though looking for something else. "Words. Trinkets. Trivialities of civilisation. In the end, it will be rendered meaningless by what it can lead us to."

"Still fixated on Atlantis, huh?" Sam sighed.

He didn't respond. Simply wandered off, still muttering to himself.

Teddy did likewise, leaving the scroll with Jess and moving on to new objects, a collection of which looked like jetpacks from a comic strip Sam had seen once. Teddy ran his finger along them, truly in his own little world now.

"Wonder of wonders, it is more beautiful than I could ever have imagined."

Sam had to agree with him. This place was like finding gold at the end of a very dangerous rainbow, a worthy reward for their trouble getting here. But as stunning as the treasure trove of knowledge and artefacts was – and it was admittedly the most astonishing sight she had ever seen – she couldn't help the niggling feeling that something wasn't quite right.

In fact, she was certain that things were about to go very badly wrong.

There was a sudden sound. A siren, but not unpleasant. Less a warning and more a guide. But it still gave Sam the shivers.

Here we go, she thought.

She watched as Will immediately dropped whatever he had been inspecting and turned his head like a dog who had seen a squirrel. His gaze fixed on the centre of the hall, where a new, more powerful glimmer of light appeared rippling in the air, drawing their attention.

"Will?" Jess said, as he started walking towards it. "Sweetheart?"

Without a moment's hesitation, she hurried after him. Teddy too followed in her wake, intrigued enough by the new revelation not to worry about what it might mean.

Sam looked to Taylor.

"You first," she said, gesturing him onwards. She waited until he was a couple of yards ahead of her, before adding, "As usual."

It broke his stride just enough to make being stuck here with him worth it.

They all moved towards the light, drawn in, until finally they skirted a collection of drawings and came upon a round clear dome rising from the floor. One that even to Sam's untrained eye seemed to be made entirely of pristinely clear diamond – except for a small hole about the size of a fist in the top. Shards of light bounced off the surface, thrown by the glowing waves now circling overhead.

Everybody shielded their eyes.

Except Will, who stepped up to it.

That the waves above them were concentrated here told Sam that this was the focus of the collection. Which in a collection of this magnitude meant it must be pretty special.

Or dangerous.

"At last," Will breathed, sounding not at all like himself.

It's the latter, Sam thought, shifting her jacket to free up the gun at her side.

She had no idea what he did next. But as his hands flew over the diamond dome like he was conducting an orchestra, flashes of red could now be seen flowing *through* the stone itself.

Forming patterns. Then what appeared to be script.

Then a map of the world.

It wasn't the one any of them knew in the traditional sense. But Sam had navigated her way across both the skies and the land with only patchwork pieces of maps before. So she recognised the countries and continents before the others. Saw how they fit together.

The red colours seemed to pulse specifically around several areas on the map. One of which was in Egypt. Another in the Eastern Mediterranean. Yet another off the coast of England.

"There are nine markings altogether," she said, counting quickly. "Nine locations around the world."

It was just a thought, spoken aloud. Yet as soon as the words had passed her lips, she knew what it meant.

The Nine.

She glanced at Agent Taylor, sure he had cottoned on to her line of thinking. If he had, he gave no clue. He was too busy watching Will – if he was still Will – run his hands over the dome again. They all were. All except for Teddy, who had been distracted by something in one of the aisles nearby and wandered off.

"Will, what are you doing?" Jess asked.

"What I have waited so long to do," he replied.

Suddenly the map disappeared, leaving the red markings behind. They slowly began to drift towards each other, forming a ball in the centre. Before the red sphere took form, lifted up and rose out of the hole in the surface of the dome.

Will gently removed the artefact.

"Now do you believe, Captain?" he said, holding the apple-red orb before her, as if offering her the chance to uncover its secrets for herself. "Now do you see why we had to journey here. And what lies ahead?"

Shivers ran up and down her spine as she met the gaze that peered out from behind Will's eyes.

The piece began to glow.

"Atlantis," he whispered.

Sam glanced around the group, seeking help. Jess was

too busy staring at Will, captivated by what she saw, but Taylor understood exactly what Sam was thinking – and the subtle shake of his head was the only thing that stayed her tongue from asking the question.

Will-who-was-not-Will continued, his glazed-over eyes drifting back to Sam, "You have proven your worth to get us this far, as I knew you would. Will you help us with what comes next?"

"Please, Sam?" Jess asked again.

Sam looked between the pair of them, panic setting in. She didn't answer. She couldn't. Her exhausted mind was spinning in circles trying to understand what had happened and what she was being asked to do.

"Maybe we should put the apple back on the tree for now?" she said carefully. "How about we take stock of what we have in the rest of this magnificent place before we rush into making rash decisions. What do you think?"

She went to take the artefact from him, but he quickly caged his fingers around it and his face darkened. "I'm afraid this map will be leaving with me," he said, then turned to Jess. "Your sister has had her chance, now we have ours. I have what I came for. Let them have the Hall. You will come to understand in time that we have something far more valuable ahead of us now."

Jess hesitated as she glanced around at what she was being asked to give up.

Enough of a hesitation for Sam to make a spectacular mistake.

With one hand she reached out to stop Will as he

moved off. The other moved to her gun again. Whatever the hell was going on with him, she wasn't about to let him leave just like that, not after all they'd been through. She couldn't risk it. Not until she'd figured out what this all meant.

"I don't think so," she began.

But even as Will's face turned, his eyes burning with defiance, his teeth bared and his free hand twitching as if he might strike Sam down with lightning or whatever godlike powers he now possessed, something held him back.

Or, rather, someone.

There was no hesitation in Jess's demeanour now. Sam's little sister stood straighter and taller than she ever had before, her fingers firmly resting on Will's arm as she put herself in harm's way and stepped between them.

"I admit, it's been an experience catching up with you this past week, sis," she said softly, patiently even, straightening Sam's jacket in a motherly fashion and brushing her hair out from her eyes. Jess even tried to smile as she did it, although the trouble in her gaze betrayed her. "You've even taught me to accept some stuff. Like sometimes people need saving, and sometimes the whole world needs saving, and maybe you can do both or maybe it's one or the other. But I can see you're over that now… that you don't really care what comes next for anyone but us… and I get that! Honestly, I do. But you've said it yourself in the past, the world can't cope with these cycles of violence for much longer. Wars will keep happening and people will keep dying, only with different antagonists pulling the strings. Wouldn't it be something if we could stop that?"

She gestured around to the Hall. "Perhaps I wasn't thinking big enough with this place. How it might change things. You said that knowledge is power, but maybe in this case there is something even more powerful out there, something we can use to ensure America can keep the peace for the good of all humankind?" She sighed, as though having just made a decision. "Whatever. You don't need to worry about it now. Please just know that I'm grateful for everything you've tried to do for me, Sam. I love you, I really do." There were tears in Jess's eyes as she leaned in as if to give her sister a hug… only for her fingers to slip to Sam's holster instead. "But I have to step from your shadow now."

Sam stared in abject horror as Jess raised her own revolver against her.

"I believe this is yours," Jess said, handing Agent Taylor back his own pistol. She grasped Will's arm with her free hand and gave Sam what appeared to be a look of pity. As if her sister failed to understand what she and Will were trying to do. As if this moment of betrayal was really for Sam's benefit. Maybe to give her back the quiet life she longed for, while Jess went where she could no longer go.

"Jess, you can't," Sam pleaded.

But Jess shook her head. "Of course I can. You once joined up with The Nine to save the world, remember? Who's to say why I shouldn't now?"

Teddy suddenly blundered out of nowhere carrying

stacks of parchment, only to drop them as he saw Jess pointing the gun at Sam.

"Oh, no," he cried. "No, no, no! Jess, what are you doing?!"

"That's Agent Jessica Moxley, Professor," Taylor said, standing at Jess's shoulder.

"No," Jess said thoughtfully. "Let's go with Agent Jesse James."

Taylor tipped the barrel of his gun to his forehead. "As you wish."

Sam felt physically sick. This moment, a moment that was going to change everything, was getting away from her. She was so tired, so done with everything, yet she couldn't accept it, she just couldn't. After everything she had done for her sister, everything she had put herself through, and now this?

"Jess, please," she said, stepping forward to grab Jess's arm, not caring if her sister fired the gun deliberately or by accident. It would probably be a mercy either way. "I came on this journey for you. For family. And together we did it – we found the Hall of Records when nobody else could. Now we have all this treasure to take back to the world. We'll get back and see Dad and show him what we've done, and you and Will can have all the exhibitions you could ever want. Isn't that enough?"

Jess blinked away her tears and dug the gun into Sam's chest.

"This is bigger than family now, Sam."

With that she pulled away from her sister and walked

back through the vast collections of the greatest repository of knowledge known to humankind. Ignoring the maps, the books, the artefacts, the evidence of life beyond our own, the answers to every question that had ever been asked… she passed by it all as she trailed Will and his orb towards the exit.

"Don't follow us too quickly, Samantha," she called back.

Shadowing his new agent, Taylor glanced briefly at Sam with something resembling regret.

He shrugged an apology.

Then they were gone.

It was another hour before Sam and Teddy reached the surface.

The climb back up, through the tunnels, had been far smoother than the journey down, but no less torturous.

Thankfully, Teddy hadn't said a word. He had simply carried all the artefacts he could fit in his arms and stuff in his pockets, huffing and gasping the entire way. His face red, his beard scruffy and matted with blood and ancient Egyptian dust.

Sam was grateful for his silence. She had enough problems with the voices in her head.

Voices cursing her out for all the mistakes she had made to lead them to this moment.

Eventually, cool night air swept down the tunnels and hit them like a freight train. It was enough to shake Sam out of her head and back to reality as they passed through the shattered gates into the night.

The temple complex was empty. The only sign of Jess, Will, Taylor and whatever soldiers had been left on guard were the scuff marks that led away from the exploded tunnel entrance, which Sam and Teddy followed to the summit of the dunes surrounding them. There they saw the tyre marks leading away from the site. Tracks that were already being swept clean by the low desert breeze.

"What have I done, Teddy?" she asked.

"Nothing that was not already going to happen, I'm afraid. Jessica is her own woman. Like the older sister that you are, you have been watching her like a hawk this entire time, but you did not see what was right in front of you – that she is grown up. She is smart and capable and, well, she is *your* sister after all." He smiled, trying to be helpful. "Doing what you think is right when all others run the other way clearly runs thick in the blood of your family. As does survival when all seems lost. She will be fine, trust me."

Sam nodded, knowing that it wasn't so much The Nine that was the problem for Jess now. She was thinking of Will.

Or, rather, what she feared had made a home inside him.

"So I guess it's just us two now?" she said.

He gestured wearily to the town in the south. A few lights still twinkled, despite the fact it must have been the early hours of the night. "In a minute it will just be you, as I am afraid I will be passing out of consciousness very soon. Come. Let us find accommodation for the night. We are cold and tired and in need of a bath. We can discuss what we're going to do in the morning."

"What are you going to do with the Hall, Teddy?"

He sighed. "I am not sure. I have seen many strange and wonderous things today, and while I would love to for them to find their homes in a museum… well, in this case, as you say, the question is whose?"

With that he began to trudge down the sandy slope beneath the pale gaze of the ghostly moon, leaving Sam alone to stare darkly in the direction of the tracks, following them as far as she could make out.

The temptation to follow Jess was strong. Stronger than anything she had felt in quite some time.

But, in the end, she could not.

She took a breath.

And let her sister go.

EPILOGUE

Harry Moxley sat in his wheelchair, watching his daughter pack her suitcase.

Sam made no attempt to hide the revolver she threw in there. Nor the other weapons she had called in a few favours to find. The kind of favours she had been holding onto with old friends for just such an occasion.

She glanced up to see a look of disgust cloud her father's face. He swallowed hard and his trembling fingers tapped against his arm rests. But he said nothing.

After all, what could he say?

They both knew what had to come to pass.

She slammed the case closed as a car horn sounded outside.

"Got to go, Dad." She stopped to kiss his forehead as she passed, then continued to the front door.

He wheeled around. "She made a mistake, Sammy. We all do from time to time."

"I know."

Her father tried to smile. "Even you, sometimes."

Sam nodded, but didn't respond. She unlatched the front door and swung it open.

"Just remember, she's your sister. I don't care who she's

in with or what this Agent Taylor once meant to you. I can see the anger in you now as I always saw it when you were growing up. You always had to have your way. But for both your sakes, Sammy, just let it go. Before it's too late."

Sam stood balanced on the edge of the overcast Parisian morning and looked over her shoulder at her father one last time. He didn't need to worry. After all she had been through, all she'd done for Jess, her sister had made her choice.

Now Sam had made hers.

She stood straighter, as if a weight had been lifted. Then nodded towards Teddy at the end of the hallway, where he stood with his wife Aya bathed in the glow of the sideboard lamp. Their hands clasped together, fingers intertwined, as though they couldn't bear to let go of each other.

"When I find my contact, I'll be in touch. We'll meet at the rendezvous?"

"On Thera," Teddy confirmed, squeezing Aya's hand tighter. "Just like you said."

Sam smiled. "Don't keep me waiting, Teddy. You know how I hate that."

The barest hint of a chuckle followed her out of the door, as she walked to the waiting taxi.

Then they pulled away from the townhouse, slipping over the rough, cobbled street and through the subdued city, heading for the airport.

This is bigger than family now, she thought, as thunder crackled overhead and rain started to lash viciously against the windows.

The race to Atlantis had begun.

ACKNOWLEDGMENTS

I'm typing this in May 2020. For those who like dramatic context, that's week ten of lockdown in a global pandemic. And while the heroes in this book are all made up, the brave souls out there right now, getting essential jobs done that nobody else can (or will), are very real indeed. To them: a special thank you. We all owe you so much.

There's an interesting story behind this book, but that's for another day. The fact remains it is a book and draws on a lot of memories, experiences, friends, enemies and luck. Indiana Jones obviously played his part. I saw *Raiders* at Butlins in Pwllheli aged seven and *Temple of Doom* at the Rex in Wilmslow aged eight, and both changed me forever (not least because of those John Williams scores). Then there was *Tales of the Gold Monkey* (seaplane Indy), *The Rocketeer* (flying Indy), the good *Mummy* movies (horror Indy) and so many other adventures since. (Feel free to play spot the Easter Egg!)

However, the non-fictional characters I know are the ones who really helped this happen. A supportive family of any kind is a wonderful thing. Mine has been the best.

So Mum, Dad, Charlie, Beth, Lottie, Josh, Finn and baby bump – and my Australian family Paul, Jenny, Rosie, Glenn, Emma, and Abby – thanks for being both my foundation and safety net.

Andrew Patrick and Demetris Kyriacou, thanks for championing the 'other' versions of this story (and special thanks to Demetris for Sam's surname!).

Simon, Katherine, Fran, Katie, Patrick, Amy, Sean, Meg, Leo, Jules, and Chris, thanks for all your ideas and encouragement over the years.

Hanging with writers wasn't always as easy as logging onto Twitter and dicking about when you should be writing, so hugs to Tony Elliott and Matt Smith for being my first offline writing community. And thanks to the other super-supportive authors and editors I've known online since: Nina D'Aleo, Michael J. Martinez, Kristi Helvig, Andrea Hannah, Karina Halle, and Abigail Nathan (and SO many others, you know who you are). Jennie Ivins and the team at Fantasy Faction have been wonderful to me, both as a staff writer and an author. And the amazing Kathryn Alton and Anna Melander (Team OcTBR Challenge!), Audra Atoche, Rebecca Halifax, Beverley Jandziol, and Gemma Amor are the best virtual support group buddies.

Cover artist Dan Strange is an actual magician. Greatest. Cover. Ever. Thanks, man.

HUGE love to the Angry Robot family. My excellent editor Eleanor Teasdale, thank you so much for believing in this story, then helping to make it better. Same to Gemma Creffield and Sam McQueen, so patient and helpful throughout. And to my fellow Robot authors, Rob Greene, Chris Panatier, Ginger Smith and Reese Hogan; I raise a beer in salute across the Transpatial Tavern air waves.

Sara Megibow. You are the rock star-iest of rock-star literary agents. Thank you for doing what you do in this ridiculous world – even those times when you fire me on Twitter for being terrible at board games. (I promise to get better.)

To Elliott and Noah, if you're reading this it's because I've forced you off *Fortnite* to look at it and I'm not even sorry. Love you and thanks for all the high fives we did when I got the deal.

And to Fiona, you taught me about writing when I was all enthusiasm and no real talent, and unflinchingly supported me every joyful and soul-destroying step of the way. Thank you for everything.

Finally…

Thank you for picking this book up! I hope you enjoyed it.

1

Dear Rom

New Year's Eve, 1919
Manhattan, New York City

Sand.

For someone who has spent the better part of the last four decades digging, burrowing like a scarab, day and night it seemed, into mountains of dry, golden trickling, windswept tombs, I have never gotten comfortable with the stuff. Indeed, the sight of dunes often causes me a great explosion of nervous trembling. I must force my mind elsewhere. An excess of thought, my wife would say, as she often does. *You think too much, Rom.*

I am certain she is correct.

After an unfortunate childhood incident with a top-heavy traveling trunk, I will admit to more than a touch of claustrophobia, but the idea of being buried alive – in sand particularly – has haunted my dreams these last few weeks. Strangely, I wake some mornings, gasping, and taste crystalline grit on my lips. Haunted my dreams *once more* would be closer to the facts. I have suffered nightmares of smothering sands in the past, triggered by the actual experience of nearly drowning and witnessing others drown in waterless seas, the whirlpools and crushing waves of granular yellow death all around. I cannot help but think those long-ago events in the Sonoran Desert are at the core.

I received a letter at the beginning of last week.

The envelope.

Fine, creamy paper. Signs of travel evident on the creased packet. Rain had fallen upon it, but my hazy name and address remained readable. It could have been from anyone, anywhere. But somehow, I knew who wrote it. And with equal certitude I apprehended what news the pages inside would convey. I put off reading the letter as long as I could – two nights (*You think too much…*) – and then I swept it from the nightstand.

Dear Rom,

I regret to be the one who must tell you…

I stopped reading.

To my students, colleagues, and acquaintances I am Dr Romulus Hugo Hardy, Egyptologist, employed by the Montague P Waterston Institute for Singular Antiquities of New York City. The institute is a private research library and ancient history museum. Finest of its kind in the world, despite the unsavory rumors of its origins… all true by the way and then some, oh, the stories I could add…

Only my oldest friends call me Rom.

Dear Rom,

I regret to be the one who must tell you the great man is among us no more. He has gone to the stars. That was his wish, he confided, as I sat him up on his horse only two evenings ago, and we walked around the corral. Our world is more desolate for his having left it. I remind myself the bottomless grief I feel at this moment too shall pass. At least he did not suffer. I happily took away his pain during these final twilit days. My medical training proved worthy of the years I spent in study if only to accomplish this task. The opium tinctures made him sleepy yet inclined to conversation. We talked about old times! About Mexico, and the "bandaged bastards" as he still called them. To the end he slept with loaded pistols hanging from the bedpost, saying he saw the raggedy, gauze-bound corpses lurching forward in his dreams. Going through his night chest, I discovered a newspaper cutting of Miss Evangeline I had never seen before. Does an art song recital in San Francisco ring any bells? It was sweet of him to keep it for so long. Would you not agree? I hope this subject is not too tender to broach. I am aware your last parting was not on the best of terms, and in recent years no communication passed between you, the great rift only widening. Yet history – beginning with our dangerous ride south and the ill-fated Mexico expedition! – will always bind you together. So, I was wondering if…

I could not read another word.

The onrush of emotions was too strong. They trampled me, left me dazed. With them came memories like a parade of spirits marching before my eyes. I decided to go for a walk. The street life of Manhattan wields the power to distract even my most troubled state of mind. Not so this day. Through a flurry of snow, I gazed vacantly into shop windows. I saw every person on the street, including myself, doubled in ghostly reflections.

We are all transient.

This life is but a dream we dream together.

Some dreams are better left undreamt. I speak of living terrors that most people would never believe. But I believe. Though I am a scholar, a man of science, and a skeptic by nature, I cannot entertain doubts on this subject.

For I have witnessed them with my own eyes.

When I looked up I saw I was at the Institute. Bodies follow habits. My legs took me where they did six mornings a week. Dark hallways greeted me on this holiday afternoon. I locked the front door behind me and climbed three flights of stairs to my office and its adjoining state-of-the-art laboratory. I have come to prefer the lab over the field, choosing to toil in the stuffiness of classrooms rather than the dank and ruinous graveyard of ancient civilizations.

But this predilection was not always the case.

In my youth, I yearned for exotic travel.

One place called to me above all others: Egypt. Land

of the pharaohs. The Great Sphinx of Giza. Khufu's Pyramid. And the *Book of the Dead*.

If I had been a farmer like my father, and loved the land the way he did, then I would have missed out on many wondrous adventures, and the curses that have accompanied them, and were, some might speculate, their price.

I have no regrets.

A clot of shadows inhabited the lab, and I did nothing to banish them. Work was far from my intention during this unplanned visit. I opened the shutters beside my desk; in dull steel daylight, I crouched and built a small fire in the fireplace. I felt old and cold and I wanted a whisky. These Prohibition advocates hope to make Methodists of us all. Soon they will have their law. Thank heavens I live in New York City. I keep a bottle hidden in the cabinet behind my personal collection of ushabti. Mummiform figurines – my favorites are those made from chiseled stone or faience whose aquamarine glazes are splendid to contemplate while sipping Kentucky bourbon. I set four of the funerary statuettes on my desk top. They were the size of tin soldiers I played with as a child. I uncorked the bottle and filled a cut-crystal glass.

My desk remains barren when I am not working at it.

I balanced the glass in my lap.

The four figures stood alone on a mahogany plateau. I could almost imagine they were the four of us lost in the Sonoran – or the Gila Desert, if you prefer. Death advanced from every direction.

Four seekers in deep over our heads…

We knew nothing. The tip of the tip of the iceberg was all we saw. (Mixing talk of deserts and icebergs – I could blame the snow. Or the cursed sand still in my blood.)

I drained the glass. Then went to the cabinet and poured another, bringing the bottle along. I set it beside the leg of the chair.

The electric winds of memory lifted the hairs off my collar. These stirrings of the past were strong enough to make me feel physical sensations. The blazing Mexican heat slapped my face red (*though it might have been the whisky*). I breathed alkaline dust. My eyes squinted at the forge of a molten sun. I could swear I was traveling back in time, merging with my younger self. How did we get there? How did I survive? What catalyst, what driver, took hold and propelled me as if I had no free will, not then, and not now?

Egypt.

Egypt was how I got to Mexico.

2
The Waterston Expedition

Summer, 1886
University Hall Library, Northwestern University, Chicago

The word is like magic itself. *Egypt.* The letters look scrambled, a puzzle waiting to be solved. Who doesn't like a puzzle? What young man isn't convinced he's the one to crack it? I was no different. Ripe for an adventure, I wanted life to start. Nothing had ever happened to me and I was slowly becoming convinced that nothing ever would.

"Hardy, your mail."

A letter came flying over the top of my study carrel, landing in my lap.

"Thank you, Carlson. You deliver with speed if not precision."

"Speed's better." And Carlson was gone around the corner.

An Egyptologist without a wealthy sponsor is a lonely man indeed. I had been such a man until that day. I tore into the letter. I didn't know it yet, but I had received my first correspondence from Montague Pythagoras Waterston of Los Angeles, California.

He wrote that he had heard "promising things" about me from one of my old University of Chicago professors (he did not mention any names) and had read a scholarly paper I penned entitled *Magic and Mummified Kings*. He quite liked it. I liked it too, and the praise made me glow. He offered to pay for my very first expedition – near the Valley of Kings, no less – for the purpose of unearthing yet undiscovered tombs. I could not believe it. The man had never even met me and here he was opening his bag of gold for my expenses. I found later that he had much gold at his disposal (he owned several copper, silver, and gold mines in California and the western territories); also, unknown to me, he had made such offers to other young Egyptologists, and their excursions had ended in catastrophic failure and even death. All I knew at the time was he would pay my way. He only required that I keep him informed about every step of my project, and that any antiquities I might recover would become his sole property, to which I must surrender any claim, legal or otherwise. I also had to promise extreme discretion.

I had big dreams for my future, but my future had lagged in its arrival. Who can fault a person for chasing their dreams, even recklessly, when at first they seem to appear?

Without a second thought I wrote back and accepted the terms of his offer.

A shadow flickered above me.

"Carlson? Is that you?"

"Who else passes through the dullest aisle of the known universe?"

"Not me, not any more. I'm going to Egypt on an expedition. I leave this dreary little cubbyhole to you and the library mice. I am on my way to becoming a legend. Make a note of it in your journal. Someday you'll tell your children you delivered Rom Hardy's mail."

"Crack a window, man. You're delirious."

"If I am, then that's fine with me. See you in a year or so. I have to start packing."

"Beware the hyenas and malaria," Carlson said. I saw a hand waving.

Again, I was alone.

Summer, 1886
Cairo, Egypt (and environs)

Shall I say how I felt?

Like a boy transported to the land of his fantasies.

From the moment of my arrival I had to keep reminding myself I was really in Egypt and not dreaming. To see for the first time with my own eyes the silt shores of the Nile lined with spiky-leafed palm trees and dhows, sailing up and down the river, their lateens spread like the pectoral fins of giant flying fish. Over the water, I smelled fresh animal dung and smoldering cook fires. The low mud walls and squat buildings huddled under a sky of powder blue enormity dusted gold at the horizon. The sun above the delta blazed unlike the sun in my homeland; its piercing whiteness seared like the eye of eternity. Ashore, I sought shade among the sycamores. For a while that was how I moved, tree to tree, in my dark suit and derby. The streets of Cairo boiled with a cacophony of alien noise. Coffeehouses crowded with shisha-smoking men and their smoking stares. Everything appeared to me too big, too loud. Too much. My senses overloaded. I could not take it all in. Yet more and more came at me. Like a sleepwalker, I floated between worlds. But I was too excited to sleep. Too excited even to think! I wandered, outwardly blank and numbed but feeling very, very alive. I loved it so dearly, in fact, that I feared if I closed my eyes it might all disappear. The jet black night offered a bit of relief from my mania. I retired to my lodging and waited, prone but awake, restless for first light. The next days were going to be no less stimulating.

How much more did I love the sights from the Pyramid road!

And to know I was not there as a mere traveler. My life's work was truly beginning. I absorbed more in a week than I had in years of study. Though I might yearn to, I could not indulge my leisure like a tourist. I was a scientist on a timetable.

Inside Egypt, I sailed south to visit the megaliths at Karnak and ultimately to Luxor, where I set to work. I attempted to make contact with local guides, unfortunately with little success for my efforts and much discouragement. Yes, I found men willing to guide me into the burying desert, but none struck me as capable and trustworthy.

It was while I rested my feet at an outdoor café table that I met my future foreman, Hakim. I was bent over at the task of loosening my shoelaces, and when I sat up, there he was standing across from me and smiling warmly, a steaming pot of mint tea and two cups in his hands.

"May I join you, sir?"

"Certainly, you may. What I mean is, *please do*."

I glanced around and noticed several empty tables.

He filled the cups, sat down, and pushed one cup toward me. His brow furrowed for a moment as I hesitated. "Do men not drink tea in America?"

"No, we do."

"Enjoy then, sir. This café makes the second best tea in Luxor."

"Who makes the best?"

"I do, sir, and my wife agrees it is the finest she has ever tasted."

I sipped the tea. Indeed, it was delicious as he claimed, and it struck me that drinking a hot beverage in the heat did not make one hotter but rather equalized with the environment.

"How did you know I am American? Is it my accent?"

"No, sir, and although we have only just met I must

confess that it is not by accident. I have heard that an American in a derby hat has been asking for guides in the cafés. So, I came here to drink tea and wait. My name is Hakim, and I am the finest guide in Luxor."

Clearly a man of admirable bearing, he proceeded to tell me a long list of desert excavations which he had taken a part in or led. I did not doubt him, nor could I check his references, given my lack of contacts. We talked more over a second pot of tea. I was going to have to make a leap of faith based on what my father the farmer called "gut feelings." I wasn't exactly buying pigs here. But I hoped I had inherited my father's good intuition. My life was going to depend on it.

Hakim possessed a round jovial face and unusually large eyes, almond-hued, sympathetic and feminine in their cast: a gift from his mother, he said.

"Have you led many expeditions?" Hakim asked me.

"This will be my first in Egypt," I said, beaming.

"Ah, so where else have you dirtied your hands in the sands of time?"

I looked squarely into his almond eyes as I drained the dregs of my cup.

"Nowhere," I said.

Hakim was nodding and smiling as if I had told him a joke. Then the smile faded.

"I have read a great deal about your country and its history," I added quickly. "I know it as well as if I had been born on the shores of the Nile. My scholarly background is impeccable."

"Reading is good," he said.

He picked up the teapot to refill our cups but found it empty.

"I only need a chance to prove myself." My fists clenched under the table. I leaned forward as the words raced out of my mouth. "I know what to do. My sponsor, Mr Waterston, has confidence in my potential to achieve astounding things."

"A wise fellow, no doubt. His name circulates among certain men of my acquaintance. He has a lot of cash to spread around. I hope that is not impolite to say. You know him well?"

"Reasonably well, I'd say." In the heat of the café, I stretched the truth and found it to be awfully elastic. "The two of us have grown closer recently... much closer than ever before."

Hakim considered my exaggerations. His infectious smile returned.

"You will hire me then?" he asked.

"Absolutely," I said. "I believe you have the job. You earned it. We both did!"

Hakim drummed the table with his big calloused hands and let out a hearty laugh to accompany the racket. Men in the café looked over in alarm.

"Bless you, sir. My wife blesses you. My children, all of them, they bless you."

That was how I made my first Egyptian friend.

Like what you read?

Good news.

There's a sequel too!

The Beast of Nightfall Lodge

by S. A. Sidor